PRAISE FOR
THE AWAKENING

"Incredible"

"Amazing"

"Gripping"

"Exciting"

"Out of this world"

"Unputdownable"

"Loved it, loved it, loved it!"

"A new author to rival Koontz and King"

"If this book catches on, it's going to be huge.
Brilliant."

"Hands down one of the best fantasy books I've ever read."

"I laughed, I cried, I raced through the scenes in suspense. What more can you ask for?"

Also available by Stuart Meczes

The Corruption *(Hasea Chronicles Book II)*

The Veil *(Hasea Chronicles Book III)*

The Rising *(Hasea Chronicles Book IV)*

The Convergence *(Hasea Chronicles Book V)*

Misfortune Market *(A Hasea Chronicles Novella)*

Without A Heartbeat *(A Hasea Chronicles Prequel Novel)*

Tommy and the Simbots: *The Golden Wing*

Coming Soon:

London Burning *(The Grit Saga Book I)*

THE AWAKENING

DILECTI SURGEMUS ~ SOCII POLLEMUS

STUART MECZES

THE AWAKENING (HASEA CHRONICLES BOOK I)

Copyright © 2011 by Stuart Meczes
Cover art by Claudia Mckinney
Photography by Teresa Yeh

ISBN 978 1520 54943 9

Third Edition, published in 2020 by Amazon Digital Services. Originally published in 2012 by FeedARead Publishing.

British Library C.I.P. A CIP catalogue record of this title is available from the British Library.

To my fantastic parents.
No matter how lost I got, you were always there to show me the way back.

"What lies behind us and what lies before us are tiny matters compared to what lies within us."
- Ralph Waldo Emerson

0

The Depraved appear in the distance - hundreds of them, scuttling, jumping and crawling their way through the pouring rain. A sea of evil, surging towards me. It had all ended so fast. I look down at my twisted, broken body and a bitter laugh escapes my lips.

Some hero I turned out to be.

I was meant to protect the world; I couldn't even protect her. It dawns on me that I'll never hold her again; never smell her sweet hair.

I can taste blood in my mouth. I try to spit it out, but have no energy left. It just dribbles pathetically down my chin. More comes up to take its place. Not a good sign. I know I should get up, should fight to my last breath. I'm just so worn out, and without her, what's the point anyway?

The stench of smoke and scorched metal fills my nose. An intense throbbing in my side draws my attention and I discover with a flash of nausea that a scaffolding pole has speared through my ribs, pinning me to the ground. I'm not healing anymore; I can't even summon the will to try.

This is it then, the end of the road.

I'm going to die here.

I close my eyes, trying to let the images of her face occupy my mind. I want my last thoughts to be of her. For some reason I can't make them stay shut. The curiosity in me needs to see how it all ends.

The creatures surround me. There is a crescendo of baying and twittering laughter as they study me. Standing in the centre is The Sorrow. Even though the iron mask covers its face, I know it's wearing a sick, triumphant smile. It crouches down and presses a metal knee against my chest. The weight crushes all of the air from my lungs. I have to use all of my remaining strength to gasp the next breath.

The Sorrow lifts an armour-clad arm up to its artificial face, the screech of the metal joints like rusty door hinges. There is a click as it unlocks the straps. The mask dislodges with a wet pop.

So this is how it's going to be.

The excited chattering rises into an ear-splitting roar. There's no escape. It starts to pull the iron face away, wanting to show me what lies underneath. I let out a long, final sigh.

Now comes the end of everything.

PART I

AWAKENING
EDEN

I

Terry Burton's fist exploded into my stomach like a piston.

I grunted as the wind rushed from my lungs. He let go of my jacket and I crumpled to the ground of the school parking lot, chest wheezing and mouth flapping as I struggled for air. White-hot pain blazed through my abdomen and it took all of my strength not to vomit.

"Haha, the little bitch looks like a fish!" Terry smiled over his shoulder and I glanced up through watering eyes at the rest of his entourage. They were all laughing at my baffled expression. I didn't know what I'd done wrong – I never did. Not that it mattered anyway. Every day was the same, I would get a shoeing by Terry – my own fulltime, personal bully – and his mates would hover around him like flies on turd, egging him on.

He reached out and seized a handful of my hair. I winced, still gasping as he dragged me back to my feet. Terry was half a foot taller than me and well built, he had to hunch over to bring his face close to mine. There were only a few centimetres between us and I could smell his hot, reeking breath on my face. I gagged; he stank of alcohol and stale cigarettes.

"I don't 'member you askin' for permission to park in my spot, Eden!" He unclenched a fist from my jacket and stabbed an accusatory finger at my clapped out Peugeot. I tried to respond, even though it was pointless. We all knew what was coming. "B-but it's free parking and you don't own a c-"

Terry cuffed me across the face, making spots appear in my eyes.

"Don't you dare interrupt me when I'm speakin'," he barked in his thick, South London accent. A fresh wave of laughter rang from his gang behind him. My face went red hot from a mixture of pain and humiliation.

"Listen up. That is *my* parkin' spot and I'd already decided to loan it out to TJ's girl." He jerked his thumb in the direction of the wiry black guy, who stood at the right of the crew, arms folded. TJ nodded in agreement, a large smirk on his nasty face. "But like a selfish arsehole, you've been in that spot *all day*," he continued, stabbing a finger into my chest, "and she had to pay for parkin.' That ain't no way to treat a lady is it?"

He didn't wait for an answer, just wrenched my head from side to side. The pain made my eyes water. "Glad you agree, mate. Now why don't you be a good little girl and run along home." He let go of my hair and gave my shoulder a hard shove. "Have a good night sweetheart."

The gang pushed me about as I collected my schoolbag from the ground and shakily pulled out my keys. They gave my car a few half-hearted kicks as I reversed out of the space and headed back the way I'd come. I waited until I was out of eyesight and pulled over. With a scream, I started punching the steering wheel over and over as tears brimmed in my eyes.

Why? Why does this keep happening?

Something tapped against the window and I turned to see an old man peering in at me, clutching a walking stick in one hand.

"You okay, sonny?" he asked in a concerned tone.

"Uh, yeah, fine. Um thanks." I fumbled at the gearstick and revved away, leaving the old man staring after me.

By the time I had reached home, I'd managed to calm myself down enough to be back in control. I swung the car onto the driveway, its rusted blue paint job and missing passenger handle making it stand out against my stepfather's gleaming black Lexus. Once parked, I repositioned the rear-view mirror to check my face for damages.

Only a small bruise, I can probably get away with that.

I took a deep breath and stepped out of the car, fumbling through my keyring and letting myself in the front door.

"Alexander, we're in here!" called my mum from the kitchen. "You want something to eat?"

"Later," I mumbled and trudged up the stairs. Barging open the door to my room, I threw my bag next to the wardrobe and slumped down on my bed. Leaning over, I lifted the corner of the mattress and retrieved the photo from its usual spot. My father stared back at me, brown hair swept back over one side of his head, and face brimming with youth and intelligence. Sadness tugged at the walls of my stomach.

"Hey, Dad."

I'd never quite understood the emotion I felt. The man in the picture had died before I was old enough to even remember him, yet every single time I saw his picture the pain was immediate and raw. I lay back on the bed and stared up at the photograph as I always did, imagining what it would be like to still have him in my life – how different things might be.

"Alex, dinner!"

The barking tone of my stepfather John thundered up the stairs. My eyes snapped open and I wiped sleep from my eyes. The photograph was lying next to me on the bed. *I must have fallen asleep.*

Tucking the picture back into its place, I climbed out of bed. Outside, the heavy pattering of rain had started up. It was only early evening, but the darkness through the window was so thick; it could just have easily been the middle of the night.

Yet another miserable day in London.

I trudged downstairs and into the kitchen. It was one of those open plan affairs - the blue and white tiled kitchen blending into a carpeted area filled by a large oak table. The rest of my family were already assembled. Mikey - my half-brother - sat at the table, shovelling tomato soup into his mouth. John was leaning over one of the worktops, studying the evening newspaper spread out on its surface. He thumbed through the pages, tutting at the headlines and shaking his head. He paused occasionally to take sips of under-milked tea from the mug clutched in his gorilla-like fist.

"More murders," he grumbled, talking to no one in particular. "These poor bastards were found without any blood or organs left in 'em. Probably black market stuff. I'm beginnin' to wonder why we ever moved here. It's supposed to be a good area!"

Mum, who was as usual darting around the kitchen like an agitated wasp, murmured an agreement. Her famous – or rather infamous – chilli con carne was burning away on the hob. Thick steam curled up in rolling loops before getting sucked away by the extractor hood. She glanced over.

"How was Sixth Form today, sweetheart?"

Amazing. I got punched in the stomach and slapped in the face for stealing a free parking spot from a bully's girlfriend who doesn't exist.

"Uneventful," I said with a shrug. "How was everyone else's?"

"Good thanks, honey," said Mum. John grunted without looking up and Mikey mumbled something indecipherable through his mouthful.

"Dinner will be ready in two, soup is on the table if you want some," Mum added and went back to tend to the pan. "Oh no, I think I've burned the rice."

Taking my spot at the table, I poured a glass of cola, deciding not to risk the soup. A few minutes later a dinner that looked like it had been cooked by nuclear blast was set down in front of me. Mum was never going to win any culinary awards, but she did her best.

"Thanks," I said, trying out a smile.

John closed his paper, and limped over, tea in hand. Once seated, he absently rubbed his knee with one hand whilst using the other to drown his food in ketchup. For a while there was no sound but the clatter and scrape of cutlery. Then John looked at me. He held the gaze for a second before clearing his throat. I sighed.

Here we go.

"Alexander," he began in *that* tone. "I was chatting to Pete down at the pub the other night…you know, Andrew Pearson's dad?"

Yep, his son is one of the guys who enjoys making my life a living hell. "Yeah I know him."

"Well he said that the school is doing footie trials. Why don't you have a crack?"

Mikey descended into a fit of laughter, dribbling soup down his chin. He cut it short when Mum shot him a reproachful look. John kept his gaze fixed on me while he waited for my response. He might as well have asked me to pole vault Everest. There was no way I could ever join a football team. Not because I didn't want to. I'd often fantasised about being the guy who scored goals and girls. But I'd been born with an allergy to sports. I was liable to trip, drop, miss, fumble and foul my way through any game. Plus my fitness levels were worthy of any nursing home. Ninety minutes on a football pitch? No chance.

The problem was that my family revolved around sports. John had been a pretty talented striker in his better years and even managed to get scouted for Chelsea's youth team. That all ended when he'd beaten up a guy outside a pub after a drunken argument. The same guy had come back later with a crowbar and tested John's reflexes for him. After months of surgery he'd left the hospital with a fake kneecap and no future. He now worked as a sports physiotherapist, determined to make sure other people achieved what he couldn't. I had respect for that and would probably have told him as much, if he weren't such a condescending dickhead.

Mum coached children's tennis part-time at the local leisure centre. She loved her job and always came home armed with stories about how little Jimmy had done this, or Katie had said that. Everyone tended to switch off, appeasing her with nods and smiles.

Then there was Mikey.

Brilliant at every conceivable sport known to mankind, the prodigy had chosen to focus his efforts on football. Already playing for the county youth team, it was simply a matter of time before a sharp-eyed scout scooped him up. So it seemed only natural that I should follow suit. Instead I was the odd one out – the runt of John's alpha pack.

I tried to think of how best to proceed without igniting a row. "Don't think I'll bother. You know football isn't really my thing."

John took a long slurp of his tea and smacked his lips. "Alexander, you never know what your potential is unless you *try.*"

As if a button had been pushed, I felt my face flush as the familiar anger boiled in my stomach. "I'm sorry if being an A star isn't good enough for you John. How I must disappoint," I fumed.

"Actually, I was thinking it might help you make some *friends.*"

That defused me. I dropped my eyes down to my plate and stabbed at the overcooked food with my fork. Social status was a sore spot. I wasn't good looking enough to make instant friends and the awkwardness I felt within my own skin made it hard for me to hold a decent conversation. Most people never persevered long enough to see if I had a personality hidden somewhere.

I had manage to secure a single friend, Tim, who'd had the bad luck to choose a seat next to me in a lunchtime study club. Over time I'd managed to wear him down with bad jokes and proximity until we fell into the 'mates' classification. However, unlike me, Tim had plenty of other friends, so I spent a lot of time alone.

Not quite finished with his scrutinising of my existence, John looked to my mother for support. "Don't you agree, Elaine?" he questioned, gesturing towards me.

Mum gave a weary sigh. "Just let him be who he wants, John. He's not Michael."

Ain't that the truth.

Mikey was two years younger than me at 15, but looked older. His constant football and gym training had given him a pretty good physique. In comparison I was thin and gawky - skin stretched over twigs. He sported a healthy olive complexion, whereas my skin glowed with the anaemic pallor of a computer hacker. His hair looked like it had been lifted from a shampoo ad, whereas mine was as brittle as straw and took about half a tub of wax to smash into submission. The singular trait that we both shared was our bright green eyes. Apart from that, we looked so different; most people simply didn't believe we were related. Others liked to suggest that my real dad must have been an inbred.

Which was always nice to hear.

Not wanting to partake in any more judgemental conversation, I kept my gaze on my plate and ate my dinner in absolute silence. Switching off was the best way I knew how to deal with things. The rest of my family were used to it - they carried on talking to each other, as if I wasn't there.

No one noticed my bruise.

I shrugged into my black parka jacket and grabbed my bag from the sideboard in the hallway.

"Hey bro, can I grab a lift to school today?" asked Mikey, appearing from the kitchen. "I've got no football training this morning."

"Uh yeah sure," I said, wiping my eyes and trying not to yawn. I'd had a really bad night's sleep, full of strange dreams that kept making me wake up.

"I'm going in with Alex," Mikey shouted back into the kitchen, where Mum and John were still eating their breakfast.

"Okay, drive safe," came Mum's standard reply.

The air was bitter outside, winter creeping in from every angle. Mikey jiggled up and down on the spot to keep warm as I leaned across and opened the passenger door from inside. The wing mirror on his side hung loose like a droopy dog-ear. It clattered against the side as Mikey climbed in next to me.

"You need to get that fixed."

"That requires money."

"Maybe ask my dad to lend you some?"

I glanced at Mikey and he stifled a laugh. "Yeah, fair enough." He ejected my Soulfire album and tossed it in the glove compartment, replacing it with one of his own.

"Hey!" I protested.

"Come on mate, you listen to them *every* day."

"I like them!"

"Yeah, so do I, but I think listening to something that much is like an OCD or something."

I couldn't help but laugh. Mikey grinned and pointed ahead. "To school, Pele!"

Rolling my eyes, I pulled out of the drive.

After travelling bumper to bumper at the speed of a stoned snail, we passed through the front gates of Chapter Hill School. I pulled the car into a tight arc by the main steps and stopped so Mikey could jump out.

"Laters mate."

He gifted me with a swift punch to the arm and slid out of the car. A few seconds after slamming the door too hard, he was

13

locked in the arms of Lisa Harwood, an attractive blonde from my year.

I give it two weeks before he gets bored and moves onto his next victim, the jealous part of me predicted.

The five-minute warning bell clanged, stirring the crowds.

Damn!

I cranked the car back into first and charged around the main building towards student parking. I pulled into the last available space, between a silver Fiesta and a badly modified Clio. I switched off the engine and sat still for a moment, staring at nothing.

A second later there was a knock on the window. I turned around to see the familiar skinhead and unkind black eyes, and a knot tightened in my stomach. Terry waved his finger back and forth.

"Sorry Eden, no spaces for you today. Try somewhere else."

I stared up at him, trying to find some kind of mercy in his face, but there was none to be found. Gritting my teeth, I restarted the engine with trembling fingers and reversed back out of the space. Terry and the rest of his crew leaned against the car next to mine and watched, laughing as I pulled away. As I drove back through the parking lot, another car passed me. I glanced in my rear-view mirror and watched it swing into the space I'd just left. The car door opened and Elliot - one of the football guys from my Physics class - climbed out. He walked right past Terry and his crew - they didn't even give him a second glance. I bit my lip hard as the tears welled up.

Once back out of the main gate, I drove a few hundred yards to Tailor Street. I parked up and chinked a few pound coins into the pay and display. After slapping the ticket on the dashboard and slamming the door, I shuffled back to school.

Trying to cheer myself up, I re-imagined the scenario.

I vault out of the car and catapult forward, driving my forehead into his nose. There's a satisfying crunch as it crumples. I laugh as he staggers about screaming, as a waterfall of his own blood spills down his front. Then I glare at his idiotic friends. They all run away, terrified.

The blast of a car horn from somewhere down the road snapped me back to reality.

14

I wondered for the umpteenth time if I should tell the school. And for the umpteenth time I argued that it would only get worse. Mr Burton senior was chairman of the school governors. This fact had allowed Terry to do A-levels in the first place and pretty much gave him a free reign to do what he wanted.

Got to love politics.

As I reached the main gates for the second time that morning, the final bell rang. Picking up the pace, one hand holding my aching arm I ran through the empty grounds and up the stone steps of the main entrance. *At least he didn't push me down these again,* I thought bitterly.

The school itself was one of the largest in Chapter Hill, mainly because it accommodated for Sixth Form students like me as well as years seven to eleven. It was easy to get lost in the spider web of corridors and rooms if you didn't know where you were going.

I tore down the empty hallways, my footsteps echoing around me. By the time I reached my English class, the door was already closed.

Thanks Terry, you made me late as well.

I put a clammy hand onto the door handle, oblivious to the fact that everything was about to change.

2

Twenty-three faces glanced up as I stood panting in the doorway. Mr Hanley stopped writing on the whiteboard and turned his podgy, red face towards me, peering over the top of his spectacles.

"Ah Alexander, how nice of you to join us! Better late than never I suppose, please take your seat."

I muttered an apology and sat down at my desk.

At the start of the term it had been determined that I wasn't cool enough to be allowed on the back row and the rest of the desks were full. So, I'd been left with the spot right in front of the teacher's desk. This meant I was an open target to any onslaught from behind. A regular occurrence as Andrew Pearson shared the class with me.

Mr Hanley continued writing on the board until he was interrupted a second time by a light tap at the door. Miss Cleveland - the leather-faced school secretary - peered through the glass. Our teacher excused himself and waddled out of the room.

Instant disorder ensued. People shouted to each other from stools and others got up to go and talk to friends. No one spoke to me. Instead, an empty soda can smacked against the back of my head. I spun around to the sound of laughter as a bit of the cold liquid dribbled down my neck. Andrew stared at me from the back row, a satisfied grin on his face.

"Sorry Eden, I was aiming for the bin!"

"Leave me alone!" I hissed, which earned a collective "oooooohhhh" from the rest of the class. I turned back around and fumbled through my bag, producing a dog-eared copy of *Rebecca*. I pretended to look through, my face burning.

The door opened and Mr Hanley padded back in. "Okay everyone, playtime's over, back to your seats please," he said. Lots of shuffling and then order was restored. "I have just received some news. It would appear we have a new pupil joining us." He frowned down at a piece of paper in his hand. "A Miss Gabriella De Luca from *Italy*." A murmur waved across the classroom as the information was processed. "She should be here shortly. In the meantime, I want to turn your attention to '*Rebecca*'. Now I trust you've all managed to read pages one hundred to one hundred and fifty over the weekend. If you haven't, now is the time to panic, because," he drummed his fingers on the desk, "there will be a test for last part of the lesson!"

The revelation was met with groans and nervous glances. It appeared the majority hadn't even opened the book, let alone read fifty pages of it. A satisfied smile spread across my face. I'd read it from cover to cover twice already. Then I thought a little more morosely, *it's not like I have a social life to get in the way.*

Mr Hanley raised a hand to silence the class. "I'm in a generous mood, so for the next twenty minutes I'll let you... refresh your memories," he said with a chuckle. The class relaxed and silence descended on the room as everyone scanned through the chapters. I thumbed the relevant pages, looking for key scenes. Mr Hanley used the time to finish writing the questions on the board. After a few minutes there was a soft knock at the door.

"Come in."

The door opened and all the air left the room.

Standing in the doorway was the embodiment of perfection. Thick hair - iron straight and the shade of dark ink, spilled down to slender shoulders. Eyes like sapphires on ice, contrasted full red lips. Skin the colour of fresh honey. A slim biker jacket and figure hugging jeans emphasised a body most girls would kill their best friend for.

Flawless.

The class fell into a stunned silence. Even Mr Hanley seemed a little taken aback by the new girl's undeniable beauty. After a few seconds he composed himself and addressed her directly, peering over the top of his glasses as he spoke.

"Ah, Miss De Luca I presume. Welcome dear, I'm Mister Hanley," he fawned.

17

Gabriella De Luca dazzled the room with a smile. "Thank you, sir." I could hear a faint hint of an accent in her voice, wrapping her words in silk.

"Everyone is re-reading pages one hundred to one hundred and fifty of '*Rebecca*'. Do you have a copy with you by any chance?"

Gabriella responded by deftly pulling a pristine copy of the book from her leather bag and holding it in the air.

"Ah fantastic. Well now, there will be a test on those pages later, but you're excused of course. Just start the book and catch up in your free time."

"Actually Mister Hanley, I read the book on the journey over, so I'm happy to take the test too," the new girl replied in her subtle tone.

Mr Hanley beamed; his round face appearing worryingly close to bursting. "Oh that's wonderful! Take note people, this is what we call a *dedicated* student! Well now Gabriella, take a seat, I believe there's a free one next to Andrew there at the back." He pointed towards my tormentor. The new girl smiled again and made her way over to the back of the room.

Then something weird happened.

As Gabriella neared me, time crawled into slow motion. Something ignited in the depths of my chest and an immense heat ripped through my body, racing through my veins until it reached my fingers and toes. It was followed by a thousand miniature electric shocks, which crackled along every follicle of hair on my skin. Then I felt myself being unwillingly drawn towards her, as if she were a human magnet. I gripped the side of the desk to stop myself falling off the chair, but not before it tipped onto two legs. The new girl shot me a confused glance and hurried past.

As she moved away, the sensations stopped and my seat clattered back to its correct position. My mouth dropped open.

What the hell just happened?

Behind me I heard several loud sniggers and realised glumly that my bizarre behaviour hadn't gone unnoticed. I was clueless when it came to girls, but even I knew that it had not been a normal reaction.

I heard shuffling behind me and hushed words of greetings being exchanged as the new girl took her seat. I could hear people from other desks turning to speak to her. I kept my head fixed forward.

"Okay, okay everyone, let the poor girl get settled!" Mr Hanley said. He tapped the whiteboard with his marker. "You have a test to fail."

All eyes shifted from Gabriella to '*Rebecca*'.

Revision didn't last long. Out of the corner of my eye, I could see several classmates craning their necks to catch a sly glimpse. I had a worrying impulse to do the same thing. A stupid idea - it wasn't like she would notice me anyway. But as much as I tried to ignore the urge, it got the better of me. I inched my head around to catch a quick look at Gabriella.

She was staring at me.

My stomach lurched as if someone had applied the brakes. There was no question about it. Her eyes were locked with mine. She didn't look away or turn her nose up. Just kept calmly staring at me and I even saw the corners of her mouth inch up into a smile. A low squeak escaped my throat and I felt flames rising to my cheeks. I wanted to turn back, but couldn't bring myself to look away. I felt powerless.

I could sense people focusing on me, wondering what the weirdo was doing no doubt. Andrew leaned over and mouthed the word 'Loser' into the new girl's ear. At that point she mercifully detached her glance from me and flashed a smile at Andrew instead. I whirled my head back around. My face burned with embarrassment. I could actually hear my pulse hammering away in my ears. *Oh my god! Why did I just stare at her like an idiot? After almost falling on her? Jesus!* The new girl had probably just been looking around when I had optically attacked her. *Nice work Alex, the girl's only been here two minutes and I'll bet she already thinks you're a complete psychopath! That's got to be a new record.*

I tried to drown out the disapproving internal voice by filling my head with Daphne Du Maurier's words, but I couldn't concentrate. I kept reading the same sentence over and over, unable to make sense of it. After an eternity, Mr Hanley plodded over to each desk in turn and placed down some blank sheets of lined A4 paper. When we all had one, he made us put our copies of the book away and begin the test.

I stared at the first question on the whiteboard.

Q1. Why do you feel that the narrator of the story struggles to fit into her newly appointed position of power?

I frowned. I could understand the individual words, but my brain refused to comprehend the question. Looking away and looking back again made no difference.

My mind had gone blank.

The bell rang, signalling the end of the lesson. On my desk lay a piece of paper with my name on and nothing else. Mr Hanley walked around and gathered the answers. He raised his eyebrows when he picked up mine but didn't say anything. I was one of his best students; I guess that entitled me to a bad day or two. I watched as people gathered around Gabriella like moths to a flame. I made sure I didn't catch her gaze again, busying myself with packing my folder into my bag, while Mr Hanley spoke.

"Okay people, I want you to make sure you've read the next fifty pages by the end of the week. And actually make sure you do this time! You know, it's only your education at stake."

I battled my way through the crowded corridors, trying to shut out the roar of noise that came from hundreds of over energised students. I made my way through the main building towards my locker. A poster pinned to the noticeboard in the hub caught my attention. I stopped to look. It was black with little white snowflakes dotted all over. In the middle, an exterior photo of the school had been photo-shopped to look as if it were covered in snow. I scanned the white print running underneath, my heart sinking.

TICKETS NOW ON SALE!
SIXTH FORM WINTER WONDERLAND BALL
FRIDAY 14TH DEC, 7.30PM - 11.30PM
THE EXTREMELY POPULAR XMAS BALL IS BACK!
WITH GREAT MUSIC & GREAT PEOPLE, IT'S BOUND TO BE A NIGHT TO REMEMBER!

TICKETS £10. £2 REFUND ON THE DOOR FOR THOSE IN FANCY DRESS. ALL PROCEEDS GO TO CHARITY. USE IT AS AN EXCUSE TO FINALLY ASK OUT THAT SPECIAL SOMEONE. WHO KNOWS, THEY MAY SAY YES!

I shuddered and hurried away from the notice board. There was no one in this entire place who would ever consider saying **YES!** to me. So like the year 11 Christmas ball at my last school, I would spend the night with a book or gaming on the PC. Better that than the mortification of arriving on my own and spending the night alone.

I reached my locker, a thin grey affair that some kind soul had scratched 'dickhead' on. I battled with the padlock for a few seconds, before the door released. I traded my English folder for my science and maths textbooks. Swinging the door shut, I almost jumped out of my skin.

Leaning gracefully against the locker next to mine was Gabriella. Her arms were folded and she was regarding me with the same faint suggestion of a smile. She used her shoulders to push herself upright and moved closer to me. Instantly, I felt the charges popping under my skin again. I didn't react, not wanting to look like even more of an idiot in front of her. My heart smashed against my ribcage as she surveyed me with her brilliant blue eyes.

"Hi," she beamed, "I didn't get a chance to meet you earlier. I'm Gabriella De Luca." She extended a perfectly manicured hand and I paused for a beat, before offering my own, clammy version. As our skin connected, the sensations went off the chart. A sound similar to someone pouring popping candy into a glass of water filled my ears. If Gabriella had the same reaction, she made no comment, just held the greeting and I realised that she was waiting for a response.

"Uh h-hi there, I'm Alexander Eden," I stammered.

"Nice to meet you, Alexander."

Gabriella released my hand and the sensations dulled. Pausing for a second, she added, "Listen, I wonder if I could ask you a favour. It's my first day here and this place is pretty big. I could really use someone to show me around and help me find my classes." She fanned a slender hand through her hair as she spoke. "The problem is that a lot of the people I've met so far seem a bit...immature." The new girl gestured over her shoulder. I followed the direction and noticed for the first time a small gathering of people watching us talk, sharing a look of bemused interest.

I hurriedly glanced back as Gabriella continued. "You seem...different. So could I ask you to be my guide until I get settled?"

She's asking if it's okay to spend time with me. It took a while to process the illogical request. My throat dried up and I had to swallow a few times before I was able to speak. "I-I uh yeah, that's not a problem," I croaked. "Um, what class do you have now?"

Gabriella retrieved a fold of paper from her jacket pocket and scanned her eyes along its content for a few seconds. "This says that I have Art now." She looked up and smiled. "So I guess Art."

"Okay, well...that's this way," I gestured, my heart still thumping a rapid bassline in my chest. I motioned for her to follow me and we wound our way down the corridors, much to the confusion of everyone we passed. We walked in silence for a while. I kept my mouth shut as I struggled to calm myself, convinced that anything I said would be absolutely the wrong thing. But Gabriella didn't give me much of a chance to stay silent.

"So, how long have you lived in Chapter Hill?" she asked.

"Not long," I replied.

My companion gave me a sideways glance. "Is that it?"

I swallowed hard, and mentally made sure my answer was embarrassment free before replying.

"Well, I grew up in Wimbledon but moved to Birmingham when I was about eleven. We stayed for about five years. Then my stepdad got offered a better job in Chapter Hill." I swung my bag to the other shoulder. "We moved back down about a year ago. My half-brother Mikey and I joined the school. He's finishing his GCSE's and I'm doing A-levels in the Sixth Form. Uh, which I guess you already know, since you're in my class."

Gabriella nodded. "It seems really nice here. You must enjoy it."

I gave a strained laugh. "Ha...yeah." In an effort to shift the attention away from me I asked, "Uh, so what's your story then?"

The new girl drew a deep breath. "A very good question, but not one for right now."

Her odd response caught me off guard. I slowed my step, eyebrows arched. Gabriella hung back and placed a hand on my arm for a fleeting moment, sending the charges spiking again.

"Sorry, that must have made me sound a bit strange," she laughed. "What I mean is that it's a long story and I can explain when we have more time."

I decided not to press the point, if she wanted to tell me she would. Besides, it was rare that anyone other than Tim even spoke to me, never mind someone this insanely beautiful, I wasn't about to make it uncomfortable for her. Not to mention that her answer had implied we'd be spending more time together. I liked the sound of that.

Silence descended as we continued through the maze of hallways. We passed through the year seven Geography section. The walls were lined with colourful flow charts relating to world trade and drawings of the planet, scrawled with bright pens. We pushed through a set of side doors that led to the school grounds. The fierce wind rushed in to greet us. Invisible tendrils of ice scratched at my face. I pulled my scarf from my bag and wrapped it around my neck, deflecting some of the cold. Gabriella's clothes were pretty inappropriate for the weather, but she didn't seem to be bothered much by the cold.

To our left was the packed lunch area - a large grassy recess, set between two protruding sections of the school. Worn picnic benches, warped and bleached from years of facing the elements lay scattered around in no particular order. On the opposite side, a small bank of grass sloped up onto the school football pitch. I pointed towards it.

"If we cut across there, it'll be quicker than walking around," I explained. "The art block is across the road."

"Sounds good."

23

We climbed onto the pitch and made our way across, aiming for the gated exit in the northeast corner. As we neared the opening, I realised the shortcut had been a huge mistake. Coming through from the other direction - followed by his gang - was Terry Burton.

Adrenaline surged through my body. *What do I do?* Half of me wanted to turn back, but the other half didn't want to look like a coward in front of Gabriella. My legs kept walking even though my mind screamed at me to leave. Time ran out. TJ nudged Terry and pointed in our direction. A dark smile spread across my tormentor's face. Gabriella seemed to sense my unease and stopped to look at me, concern etched on her face. "Alexander, are you okay?"

I nodded and kept my head down as we started moving again. *Maybe he'll leave me alone because I'm with a girl.* I was kidding myself. Terry was no gentleman. It would just be twice as humiliating this time.

The gang's crude banter died down as they reached us. They stopped short in a curve, barring our way forward. Once again there was the stunned silence and the exchanges of glances as most the gang took in Gabriella for the first time. Terry, ever the classy guy, stared directly at her chest. After a few seconds he managed to prise his attention away. He took a final blast on the joint he was smoking and then crushed it under his boot heel. He stared at me through bloodshot eyes.

"Eden! What a lovely surprise! And there I was thinkin' you'd 'ad enough for one day." My body stiffened. "And who's this stunner?" he added, leering towards Gabriella. Instinctively I grabbed the new girl's wrist and pulled her behind me. I had no idea where my courage was coming from.

Terry leaned back again and narrowed his eyes. "No, wait...don't tell me that this hot piece of ass is actually wiv you?' He started snorting with laughter and his gang joined in, baying like a bunch of demented hyenas. I could feel the rage growing inside my stomach, like someone had lit a fire. I tried to relax, knowing that if I lost control and hit him, I would get destroyed. So I tried to keep my response calm, but my words came out shaky and flecked with anger. "Gabriella and I are not together. She just asked me to show her around. Is that okay with you?"

Terry's mouth shrunk into a thin line. When he spoke, it was through clenched teeth. "A little bit feisty today ain't we Eden?" he hissed. "Trying to impress the bird? Might want to watch your mouth though mate, else it's liable to get smacked."

I felt Gabriella tense behind me. Her hand squeezed mine, probably a comforting gesture, but it was far stronger than expected and I almost cried out in pain.

Terry's expression relaxed and his tone lightened. "What you said does make sense though," he mused, "there is no way a fine thing like this would be seen dead with a tit like you." He moved to the side so he could see Gabriella clearer and regarded her with a flick of the chin. "So babe, since you and this loser ain't hittin' it, how 'bout you come with me and find out what a real man can do?" On cue his gang started whooping and making crude gestures.

Gabriella shook my hand off and paced towards Terry. She cut right through his personal space and stopped inches from him. Even in heels, she only reached his chest, but her bare faced confidence unnerved him and he took a step back. Gabriella crossed her arms and rested on her back leg.

"That's funny," she said, scrutinizing Terry first and then his friends, "I don't see any real men here, apart from the one behind me." She turned and winked. "I also know you immature *cacacazzi* wouldn't have a clue what to do with me if you got me alone. So if you'll excuse me *boys*, we have classes to get to, so move!" She pushed Terry out of her way and walked through the space where he'd stood. He made no effort to stop her. The others were silent and parted like the Red Sea, allowing her through. Turning, she gestured for me to follow. I gave a confused shake of my head, but followed, thankful.

I passed Terry just as he came to his senses. I made a strangled noise as I was dragged backwards by my jacket hood. He turned his back to Gabriella, all his attention focused on me. "You go on sweetness," he said, waving a hand in the air. "Eden and I have to have a chat about his attitude. Don't we mate?" He slapped a humiliating hand against my cheek a few times.

I didn't expect what happened next.

Gabriella whirled around; her face contorted with a rage the likes of which I had never seen. Her teeth clenched and eyes blazed.

"LET HIM GO NOW!" she screamed. Her voice sliced through the air like a razor. Goosebumps shot across my skin and a chill rolled down my spine.

I felt the material around my neck go slack. I chanced a glance up at Terry. His eyes had glazed over and he was staring across the pitch into space.

What the hell?

I looked at the rest of the gang. They were shuffling around looking sorry for themselves.

When Terry spoke his voice was distant and disjointed, as if he were about to fall asleep. "I'm...sorry...think...drank too much...we'll go now."

My mouth hung open as I watched the crew leave without another word. I stared after them, watching them disappear into the distance. Gabriella's voice brought me back down to earth.

"Well they were assholes." Her tone was light-hearted and when I turned to look, her expression had reverted to one of angelic tranquillity. She flashed her perfect teeth at me. "Sorry about that little outburst there. I don't like bullies. Oh and don't think I didn't notice you trying to protect me. You're a sweetheart, Alexander." She planted a quick kiss on my cheek. I was lost for words as it bloomed like a rose. Gabriella laughed. "Come on, let's go. I don't want you to be late for helping me." She gave my arm a gentle tug.

As we continued our trek across the field, my mind was working overtime. I struggled to process the enormity of what had just happened. This incredible girl had made Terry Burton leave me alone, *by telling him to*. It was like she had a weird control over him. I thought about the weird reactions I had when she was in close proximity to me. It was clear she had an effect on me too - very different, but an effect nevertheless.

There was definitely something going on with Gabriella De Luca.

We reached the Art block - a squat blue building situated between the canteen and gymnasium. It was always buzzing with life. Art students pushed in and out of the main doors, carrying models and large plastic folders heavy with coursework. I asked to see Gabriella's timetable.

"Uh okay, it says here you're in class A-Six," I said, reading the paper. "I think it's the second door on your left once you go inside. It's a double lesson so it lasts for two hours." I grimaced. *I'm pretty sure she knows what a double lesson is idiot!* "Um, it also looks like this is your last lesson today. A half-day. I uh, don't have any of those, although I start later on a Monday." I handed her back the timetable.

"Thanks Alexander. I'll see you tomorrow then. You okay to meet me at the main entrance in the morning?" she tapped her timetable with a white tipped fingernail. "I don't know where Performing Arts is."

The butterflies began fluttering around my stomach again. "Uh yeah, that would be amazing, I mean fine. Um yeah...no worries. Well...I-I better go to class and um-"

"I'll see you in the morning," Gabriella said, mercifully cutting off my stammering. "Shall we say eight forty?"

I drew in a deep breath, composing myself. "That sounds good."

"Oh and Alexander, don't let those guys bother you. People like that always get what's coming to them in the end."

"Uh...yeah I guess so. Bye Gabriella," I said with an awkward wave.

"See you tomorrow," she replied, a slight curve of a smile on her face.

As I walked away, I plucked up the courage to glance over my shoulder, hoping to catch a final glance of the incredible girl that had chosen to talk to me.

But she had already gone.

3

I glanced at my watch. *Five to nine.*

I was sitting on the main steps to the school, bag lodged between my legs. I'd arrived at half eight, not wanting to miss the chance to show Gabriella to her lesson. I'd watched the first drips of students arrive, the mass flow as time had swept on and finally the dregs. There had been no gorgeous brunette in the crowd.

The familiar ache of disappointment curled through my chest.

Of course she isn't here.

I stood up, scanning the area one final time. No sign of Gabriella. Throwing my bag onto my shoulder, I shuffled inside, getting barged from side to side as people overtook me.

A sudden stab of pain in my temples made me delve into my bag for some Paracetamol. Once again I'd slept badly, this time mainly due to the vicious headache I'd been sporting since the previous morning. I washed a couple of tablets down with a swig of water.

As I made my way towards maths class, I heard someone calling my name. I turned to see Tim weaving his way through the crowd.

Tim's full name was Timothy Clement Matheson. In my opinion that was far too many M's and T's for one person to handle. He stood over six feet tall, topped by a mound of wavy blonde hair. He was a bit geeky like me, but better looking so far more socially acceptable. As far as school life went, Tim had a pretty successful one. A fact I was very jealous of.

He waved, a foppish grin smearing its way across his face and fell into step beside me.

"Hey man, how's things?" he said, patting me on the back.

"Uh yeah, not bad I guess. How about you? Good weekend?" I asked, trying to sound interested, despite my aching disappointment.

"I'm good thanks mate. Had a wicked weekend! Saturday, went to Bakoo with Baz and Charlie and got smashed. Baz - the idiot, got so wasted he took a swing at a bouncer! Earned a trip down the front steps. So then Charlie tried to have a go! Pretty sure they're barred now." He gave a chuckle and I squeezed out a laugh. "Then on Sunday my sister guilt tripped me into taking her to see that new horror film with James Franco. Seriously mate, biggest waste of eight quid ever! I fell asleep after an hour. So what did you get up to?"

I struggled for a way to make my weekend sound interesting. My action packed Saturday had consisted of finishing '*Rebecca*' for the second time then helping Mum make lasagne. My equally riveting Sunday had involved History coursework. The day had culminated by playing Call of Duty on-line for five hours straight, whilst arguing the semantics of sniping with a prepubescent American kid.

"Uh, not too much, went out for a couple of drinks myself on Saturday. Was a bit worse for wear Sunday so just chilled really, had a big session on Call of Duty with some mates." My blatant lies seemed to satisfy him.

"Cool."

"Um, so what lesson you got now?"

Tim's smile spread. "None mate, got a free period for an hour. Thought I'd head to the library, work on that equation Mr Norman gave us in maths club last week. You done it yet?"

I nodded. *Yet another night sacrificed to the God of academia.*

"Nice one."

We kept walking in silence for a few moments, and then Tim piped up again. "Oh dude I meant to ask, who was that hottie you were with yesterday? Mate she was awesome!"

I felt a jolt in my stomach as I thought about the new girl. I gave a shrug, trying to appear nonchalant. "Oh, you mean Gabriella? She's just a transfer from Italy who asked me to show her around the school."

Tim raised his eyebrows. "She asked you?"

I glared at him.

"Ah nuts, that came out wrong. All I mean is with a girl like that, you would think she'd ask the most popular person she could find, that's what most new people do."

"Well maybe she isn't like most people," I snapped.

Tim raised his hands, his tone apologetic. "Yeah sorry, you're probably right."

"Besides," I continued, "she seems genuinely nice. She even gave Terry a hard time when Terry he picked a fight."

Tim was the only person that I'd ever properly told about Terry and even then I didn't tell him just how often he roughed me up. He slowed, eyes narrowing in concern. "Again? Screw who his dad is Alex, you need to speak to somebody. He's bad news."

I sighed. "Come on Tim, you know that if I get the school involved, It'll just get worse. Anyway I'm sure he'll get bored soon and move on. Then I only have Andrew and TJ to worry about." I laughed, trying to sound unbothered, but ended up sounding a little hysterical.

"Well it's your life dude," he sighed with a shrug.

Tim was never bleak for long. He ran in front and spun around so he was walking backwards. "Anyway, you gonna ask her out? I mean, she asked you to 'show her around!'" He used his fingers to invert the words. "Mate, if you got with her, she would be worth at least ten normal girls, easy!" As he gesticulated, his backpack collided with a first year coming in the other direction.

"Oww!"

"Sorry about the face buddy!" Tim shouted after the boy, cringing theatrically. This time my laugh was genuine. It was hard to be down around the guy. He was always so high on life.

"Look, don't get me wrong," I said, still laughing, "as much as I would love to ask her out, I'm pretty confident I'm not her type. I get the impression she just felt unthreatened by me." I paused and then tacked on, "have you seen her today by the way?"

Tim shook his head "Sorry mate, not at all. Trust me, I'd remember."

We reached the library and stopped by its sweeping glass doors. Tim shrugged his backpack onto his opposite shoulder and held out his knuckle. I went to shake it, but managed to curl my hand into a fist at the last second and bump it awkwardly against his.

"See you later."

"Peace broseph. Good luck with the hottie!" Tim turned and disappeared through the doors.

I continued to my lesson, keeping an eye out for Gabriella. There was no sign of her, before my maths class, or after it. I spent double History chewing my pen to the nub and wondering why she hadn't turned up.

When the bell rang for lunch, I took a slow walk down to the canteen. I avoided the shortcut across the football pitch, not wanting to chance another accidental meeting with Terry and Co.

As I headed up the path, an uneasy feeling swept over me – a sensation of being watched. I stopped walking and stared around. There were a lot of people about, but as usual none of them were paying me any attention. As I scanned, I saw a flash of black fur through the hedge across the road. The leaves rustled as whatever was behind them darted away. Intrigued, I headed over. Stretching on my tiptoes, I glanced over the top and looked from side to side. There was nothing there. I shrugged.

Probably a dog or something.

The canteen was a sizable room, with fading white walls that made it appear even larger. The linoleum floor was littered with circular tables surrounded by red plastic chairs. Many of them were filled by students, who chatted and laughed between mouthfuls. All the sounds blended into a roar of noise, which echoed around the room. Glass counters ran parallel to the wall nearest the entrance, behind them grumpy dinner ladies in hairnets dumped various types of mush onto people's plates. I joined the back of the queue and grabbed a tray from a pile sat on the side.

Wet as usual.

As the line inched forwards, I picked up a pre-packed tuna salad and bottle of water from inside the counter. I politely declined a grouchy offer for hot food. Whilst waiting to pay, through the incoherent babbling, I heard someone mention both Gabriella and my name. I strained to hear, without turning to avoid attention. I recognized Rita Sharma and Lucy Healy's voices - two well-known gossip queens from my year. I caught only scraps of the conversation as I struggled to tune in.

"Gabriella...so pretty...why...Eden?" said Lucy.

"Well...new...doesn't know...weirdo..." replied Rita.

"Did...hear? Apparently she's weird herself...Stacy...you?"

"No what..."

I pretended to fumble for change in my pocket and ushered a few people in front of me, so that I could hear better. It worked.

"So, Stacy told me that she came in about an hour before school started this morning to work on her Media assignment. Anyway, she gets to the main entrance and Gabriella's there, just standing on her own and staring into thin air, like she's in a trance."

"No way!"

"Seriously. And Stacy said she was talking to herself too!"

I drew a sharp breath and held it, wanting to make sure that I didn't miss anything.

"Then the weirdest part of all is that she starts shaking, like she's having a fit. Stacy ran over to help, but as soon as she did Gabriella stopped. Then she turned and ran right out of school like she was being chased!"

Rita gasped. "That's crazy! How random?"

"Yeah, I feel better about how pretty she is now; the new girl is a mental case!"

They both started cackling like two bitter witches. I turned around and shot them both a dirty look.

Bad move.

"Who the hell do you think you're death staring, loser?" Lucy demanded.

"Yeah piss off geek!" Rita barked. "Oh and don't think for one second that even a nutter like Gabriella would be interested in you. You're a nobody mate."

My mouth dropped open. I hadn't realised that my unpopularity had spread to pretty much every corner of the school. Now it seemed that even the plain, middle of the road gossip girls were subscribing to the Alex hate campaign. Other people in the queue started sniggering. I turned away, feeling worthless and angry with myself. *Why do I feel so protective of her? I brought that on myself.*

I resumed my waiting.

*

Later that evening, I lay in bed staring at the photograph absently, whilst the soft thud of TV bass floated up from downstairs. The rest of my family were watching some feel good Steve Martin film on Sky. They'd invited me to join, but after the misery of the day and the headache I still couldn't shake, all I wanted was to be alone. So I'd explained that I had coursework to finish and instead wasted a bit of time on the PC.

Dad's picture was worn from all the time it had spent in my hands. The edges were lined with creases, collected like wrinkles over time. I'd discovered the photograph about seven years ago in the attic of our first house, whilst rooting around for something or other. I'd spotted it wedged between a floorboard and the insulation in the far corner. As soon as I'd picked it up, I knew it was of my real father. Something in his eyes had seemed familiar to me - seemed warm. In the picture, Dad was sitting on a set of stone steps in a grand garden. His wavy brown hair hung around his strong face and his emerald eyes shone out at the camera. He was cradling a baby in his arms. Swaddled in blue, its tiny pink hand stretched up and cupped his chin. Dad looked happy. On the back, someone had written:

Peter and Alexander aged 1. August 1995.

Two months after the date on the photo, he'd popped out to get a newspaper. A speeding car had ensured that he never made it home again. They never caught the driver.

Mum was a closed book when it came to the subject of my real dad. She got misty eyed and left the room if I ever brought him up. Beyond the details of his death, all I knew for sure was that his full name had been Peter Eden. A surname Mum had insisted I keep even after she became Mrs Wilson.

I kept the picture a secret. Somehow I knew that Mum would throw it away if she found it - just like she must have done with all of the other memories. I mean, who gets married and has no mementos?

"Night, Dad," I said.

Tucking the picture back under the mattress, I switched off the bedside lamp. Eyes still wide, I watched the shadows dance in the pale moonlight that shone through a crack in the curtains. As time passed, my mind wandered to Gabriella. *So she had planned to meet me after all*, I thought and a wide smile crept across my face. Then I remembered what Lucy and Rita had said. Dull anger began to burn in my stomach over their comments. I had no idea why I was so protective over the new girl. After all, I'd only known her for one day. It just seemed clear that someone as incredible as her didn't deserve to be the subject of ridicule by people as mediocre as Lucy and Rita. I'd been right though; something was different about Gabriella. To me she seemed totally unlike everyone else...unique somehow. A divine jigsaw piece forced to fit into the wrong, worn out puzzle.

I was still imagining her and what it would be like to kiss those soft red lips, when my eyes began to grow heavy, and I felt the contented waves of sleep wash over me.

I was standing in a graveyard. The moon was full; its milky light cast an eerie glow on the area. A damp fog hung low and thick in the air. There was no sound at all. No animals or insects. Not even the rustlings of the nearby trees. Everything was deathly still. It felt wrong.

All around me were rows of tombstones. They looked to have been there centuries - their loving messages lost to the ravages of time. In the middle of it all stood a decaying crypt. Its aging stone walls were fronted by a large wooden door that hung on thick iron hinges. There was no handle. Above, the word MOONSTELLA had been carved deep into the stone.

I felt a cloying fear in my throat. The crypt didn't look like the resting place of a dearly departed. It looked like it was hiding something.

A deafening crack shattered the silence. My heart spasmed. Instincts took over and I dived behind a large black headstone.

The noise was coming from the crypt.

CRACK!

This time the noise was louder. I saw with horror that it was the door making the sounds. Something was pulling it fiercely from inside, creating deep splits on the wood.

CRACK!

The door shuddered and large splinters burst from its wounds. My breath snagged in my throat. I was too scared to exhale. Whatever was inside grew agitated and the shuddering became frenetic. The door rattled and twisted on its thick hinges as it strained against the tremendous force.

CRACK!!

Finally with a protesting groan, the door gave way and buckled, disappearing inside the crypt.

The unnatural silence returned for a few moments. In absolute horror, I watched as a colossal figure appeared in the doorway, shrouded in darkness. A metal clad foot emerged into the moonlight. The grass that it landed on instantly turned black and wilted to the ground - devoid of life. At that moment a thick cloud swept across the moon, plunging the graveyard into darkness. From within the black mire, the figure barged its way through the opening. I could hear the dull thuds of rubble dropping from the wrecked hole where the door had once stood. Then silence again. Nothing but my pulse jackhammering against my temples and my own ragged breath.

When the cloud passed and the pale moonlight returned, I strained to catch a glimpse of the creature.

Nothing.

I let my tense body relax. It hadn't seen me.

For a few more minutes, I stayed huddled behind the tombstone, creeping my head out every now and again to make sure it wasn't lurking anywhere.

It's gone.

I turned to stand...and screamed.

The creature was right next to me.

4

I woke up screaming. Sat bolt upright, eyes wide and staring. The bed-sheets stuck to my sweat-soaked skin and matted hair clung to the sides of my face. I stopped screaming and sat quaking, my breath coming out in short rasps. The bedroom door burst open, giving me another scare.

"Alex!"

Mum and John ran into the room - John clutching a cricket bat. "Alex what's wrong?" cried Mum, rushing over to me. Seeing her had the effect of calming me down a bit.

"I'm fine. I had a nightmare," I whispered as she sat down on the bed.

"Oh thank god, I thought something terrible had happened!"

John grunted and stormed out of the room, muttering under his breath, "at his age…"

I sank back into the mattress. Mum pushed the damp stands of hair from my face and kissed my forehead. When she spoke, her voice was full of sincerity. "I know how awful nightmares can be. But everything's okay now. Go back to sleep darling."

She stood up and walked to the door, but paused – fingers on the handle - as if lost in her own thoughts. A moment later she seemed to come back to her senses.

"Goodnight, Alex."

"Night, Mum."

Once the door had closed, I tried to remember what I'd dreamt about, but couldn't - I kept hitting a mental wall. *Perhaps it's better that way.* So I stopped trying to think and let my eyelids droop.

I didn't dream the second time.

*

First lesson the next day was Physics. As usual I walked to the science block on my own. The room itself was pretty much the same layout as English, except instead of desks there were rows of tall benches lined with stools. Between each bench sat a sink with curved taps descending into them. Instead of a whiteboard, the front wall sported an archaic blackboard. Various chunks of dusty chalk lay scattered on a tray fixed to the bottom.

A smell of sulphur lingered in the room. The pungent scent made my nose itch. There was no teacher yet, so people were chatting amongst themselves. Once again, my seat was at the front – making my back a target. In Physics, my tormentor came in the form of Thomas Jenkins. Or TJ as his friends called him.

I called him Thomas.

Not that I ever looked for opportunities to speak to him. He was the skinny black guy with the imaginary girlfriend from Terry's crew. He wasn't quite as bad as his leader. But then that was like saying Hitler wasn't quite as naughty as Stalin.

At only twelve students, the class was pretty small. The seat next to me was - and always had been - empty. On the far end of the desk sat Simon Proctor - geek incarnate. He was staring at me when I sat down, his eyes magnified to epic proportions through his thick lenses. I offered him a smile. He snapped his head away, looking down at his textbook instead. Sighing, I opened my bag.

Social poison.

I was retrieving my own textbook from my bag when I glanced up and saw Gabriella heading towards the room. My heart stuttered in my chest. Her dark hair was piled on top of her head, held in place with various pins. A long brown cardigan hugged her slim figure and matching boots beat against the floor as she walked. Three girls from the row behind me buzzed around her, chatting and laughing.

Gabriella's presence confused me. I'd seen her timetable and was pretty confident I hadn't seen Physics on there. *I'm sure I would have noticed if she shared more than one class with me.*

The girls separated simply because the doorway wouldn't allow four people simultaneous access. Once through, they swarmed around the new girl again, continuing to giggle and gossip. I felt a pang of unexpected jealousy and hastily locked it away. One of the girls pointed to the seats behind me, but their companion shook her head and whispered a reply. There were frowns, but nothing said aloud. They smiled and walked over to their places.

I almost had a heart attack when Gabriella settled her bag on the desk next to me. I wasn't the only one surprised, a wave of murmured confusion and disapproval rushed around the room. There were plenty of other seats around, most of them next to people several rungs higher up the social ladder. She looked at me, eyes gleaming like pools of sun-kissed water.

"Morning Alexander!" she breezed, "I'm not stealing anyone's seat am I?"

I swallowed audibly. "Uh...no that's fine. But wouldn't you rather sit with your friends?"

She raised an eyebrow. "Aren't we friends?"

My cheeks went hot. "Oh, yeah - I mean of course we are. Sorry, that came out wrong."

Gabriella waved a dismissive hand and smiled, taking her seat. Removing her science book from her bag, she placed it on the table, along with a folder and an expensive looking gold pen. She did everything with a hypnotic fluidity, as though all of her moves were pre-planned. As I watched her, I felt a dull hum of electricity build up under my skin. I squeezed my eyes shut and the sensation faded. After a few seconds, Gabriella half turned in her seat to face me.

"So, I owe you an apology," she began, leaning forward and resting her chin in her palm. "I know I was supposed to meet you yesterday," she paused, "something...came up."

"No worries, I didn't wait long," I lied. For a second I considered mentioning what I'd heard in the lunch queue, but discarded the idea. *No need to embarrass her.*

"Well anyway it was rude, since you were so sweet to me on my first day. Would you let me buy you lunch as an apology?" The corners of her mouth lifted up. "You can fill me in on where the rest of my lessons are then."

My eyes widened at the unexpected offer. *She wants to take me to lunch?* The jolt in my stomach reminded me that this was a very good thing. I must have taken a while to answer because she frowned and drew upright. "I mean unless you have other plans…" her voice trailed off and she stared past me at the rain slicked school grounds through the window.

"No!" I said a little too loud. Quieter I added, "That would be great."

She flashed her perfect teeth again. "Okay good." I watched as she swivelled back around to face the front and opened her writing pad. My mouth hung open. I still couldn't wrap my head around how hard this girl was trying to be my friend.

At that moment a petite woman glided into the room and stood by the blackboard. The chattering stopped, replaced by fresh silence normally reserved for Gabriella. I had never seen her before in my life, but she was undeniably glamorous. Shining blonde hair ran down to her shoulders and piercing jade eyes shone out from behind black designer glasses, which perched on a slim and pointed nose. Clothed in a grey skirt suit with black tights and matching heels, she looked like a film star shooting a school scene.

Brand new murmurs of confusion swept around the room.

The woman picked up a long piece of chalk from the tray and wrote 'Miss Steele' on the board in sweeping letters. Once finished, she whirled back around to face us. Her thin pink lips parted into a presenter smile. When she spoke, her voice was high - almost musical. Her words were pronounced perfectly in the Queen's English.

"Good morning everyone. As I am sure you have all noticed by now, I am not Doctor Potts."

That's for sure, I thought. Dr Potts was a moody, grey haired old woman who wore oversized jumpers she knitted herself. The old bat had one foot firmly in the grave and I guessed maybe she'd finally fallen in.

"My name is Miss Steele," the woman said, aiming a delicate thumb at the blackboard in confirmation. "Unfortunately Doctor Potts has been taken quite ill. As a result I will be taking her position as your Physics teacher until she's well enough to resume her duties."

Several guys made low whooping sounds and exchanged 'subtle' hi-fives. Miss Steele rolled her eyes.

"In case any of you are nervous about changing teachers this late in the game, please let me re-assure you. I may be a supply teacher, but I have taught at some of the most prestigious institutes, including Eton and Charterhouse. I've lectured Physics for about seven years after graduating with a Master's degree in the subject. My student pass rates are on average about ninety four per cent. So you are in safe hands with me." She finished with a wink, which got all of the boys grinning like idiots.

Miss Steele walked over to her bag and plucked an attendance sheet from inside. "Now you all know who I am, but I have no idea who any of you are," she gestured to the class, "so I'd like you each to tell me who you are and a little about yourselves."

My body stiffened. Public speaking was not my strongest attribute. I had enough trouble talking to one person.

"We can start with you at the back there." The teacher pointed towards TJ and took a seat at the desk. Fishing a pen out of her suit jacket, she held it poised over the sheet like a hawk waiting to attack.

Everyone spoke in turn, giving their names, chosen subjects and going on about their personal interests. As people reeled off the cool things they did, I racked my brains for something interesting to say about myself. I settled on pool. It was a lie, I'd played about twice in my entire life and sucked both times, but it was the only thing I knew I could get away with - you didn't need to be sporty to be good at pool.

Simon finished droning on about himself and Miss Steele's eyes shifted to me. My tongue turned to sawdust. I cleared my throat. "Um...my name is Alexander Eden. I study Physics, English, History and maths. Socially I enjoy-"

"-Being a complete loser!" interrupted TJ.

The class erupted into fits of laughter. I felt the heat rise to my face. Looking down at the desk, I mumbled, "playing pool."

"Wow, it must have taken all night to charge your two remaining brain cells so you could come up with that gem!"

Fresh laughter rang around the room. Even Miss Steele appeared to be struggling to keep a straight face. I turned to see Gabriella glaring daggers at TJ. He scowled and fumbled with his pencil case. Clearly he wasn't comfortable being on the receiving end of a joke. Gabriella winked at me. I felt a wave of warmth, mixed with shame. This was the second time she'd stood up for me, but the fact that someone else needed to bothered me. *I should be able to fight my own battles.*

I smiled as best I could.

"Okay now, settle down everyone, lets continue," said Miss Steele. "Oh and Thomas?" He looked up. "If I ever catch you insulting another student again, I will have you thrown out of my class like that!" She clicked her fingers and the sound echoed sharply around the room. "This is Sixth Form, not primary school. Are we clear?"

"Yes, Miss Steele," TJ mumbled.

I couldn't resist an indulgent smile. It felt good to see him put in his place.

"Good. Thank you very much Alexander. Now who do we have next?"

Gabriella and Miss Steel's eyes met and the two smiled at one another, as if sharing some private joke. Without so much as a nervous dip in her voice, the new girl filled in some of the blanks.

"My name is Gabriella De Luca. I was born in Roma, Italia. My family moved here after Papa transferred with work to London. I've chosen to study Art, Physics, Performing Arts and English. Outside of education, I practice martial arts. I'm a black belt in Taekwondo and Kyoshi rank in Kenjutsu." She knitted her hands together to symbolize she was finished. The rumble of approval swept around the class.

I shook my head. *This girl just gets better and better.*

"Well," said Miss Steele, placing a tick next to a handwritten name at the bottom of the register. "That was an impressive way to finish the introductions." She clapped her hands together. "Okay, now would be a perfect time to get the lesson underway. Today we are going to talk about electricity and its effects. Please turn your text books to page seventy-three."

The bell for the end of the lesson sounded and the usual rustle of bags and shuffling papers started up. "Right class," finished Miss Steele, "homework today is a summary of what we've learned. It doesn't have to be war and peace, but I expect to see the key topics in there somewhere."

I jotted the word 'summary' at the bottom of my notes and stuffed my folder back in my bag. Gabriella turned to me.

"So what lesson do you have now?" she asked.

I thought for a second. "Uh...double maths." Then put both my thumbs up. "Fun!"

She laughed – a soft sound, like a purr. "Okay then, meet me by the main entrance at lunch?"

The thought made my heartbeat race. I agreed. With that, Gabriella swept off the chair and joined back up with the girls. Their chatting and laughing resumed as if there had been no hour-long interruption.

Miss Steele was wiping her notes from the board, so didn't see TJ seize me by the back of the neck, digging his fingers into my skin. His mouth moved close to my ear and he spoke low and harsh, sending spittle spraying onto my cheek.

"Think you're cool now Eden, getting birds to stick up for you?" His eyes were wide with anger. "You better watch your back mate, because I'm coming for you." He released his grip and shoved me as he stomped away. I collided with the desk, whacking my ribs against the edge. Groaning, I rubbed my side. At that moment Miss Steele turned around from the board. She frowned at my pained expression. "Are you okay Alexander? You look hurt."

"Uh I'm fine thanks. I fell against the table...I'm a bit accident prone."

Miss Steele set the cloth down on the desk. "You know you can talk to me if you need to. That's what I'm here for."

Something about the way she asked seemed genuine. If I'd been in my normal state of mind, I may even have told her. But knowing I was going to spend some time with Gabriella had lifted my spirits. Not even TJ's threat could do much to bring them down. "Really, I'm fine," I assured her, heading for the door.

"Alright then, please close the door behind you." She shot me a dazzling smile then busied herself with the collection of papers on her desk. As I pulled the door shut behind me, she muttered something under her breath. It sounded like 'not long now.' I shrugged and headed for maths.

42

When lunchtime rolled around, I eagerly made my way to the main entrance. As promised, Gabriella sat waiting for me on the front steps.

Problem was she wasn't alone.

There was a hive of people hovering around her. *Most of them guys,* I noticed, with another stab of alarming jealousy. Even worse was that the gossip witches Lucy and Rita were in the group. It seemed that in just over a day, Gabriella had managed to climb higher up the social ladder than I had done in my entire school life.

My bag swung around my legs, as I stood frozen in the doorway unsure of what to do. By now there was no doubt Gabriella would've been told how uncool I was. It suddenly occurred to me that it could all be some kind of trick. Maybe if I went over, she would humiliate me in front of everyone, which would cement her social status - maybe that had been the plan all along. I just didn't know if I could take a confidence knock like that - *not from her.* After weighing my options, I decided the best course of action was to simply walk past the group and pretend I hadn't seen her.

I got three quarters of the way down, before a familiar angelic voice floated over to me. "Alexander, there you are!"

My stomach knotted at the words. I turned to the direction of the group and saw Gabriella looking at me, wearing that delicate smile and waving with excitement. The others regarded me in silence.

No choice now.

I returned the wave awkwardly and shambled over, praying to god that I didn't do something crap, like trip up the stairs.

Gabriella stood up and pulled me into a tight hug. There were no tingles this time, but her body felt soft and warm and she smelled great.

"Were you trying to ignore me Alexander Eden?" she questioned, holding me at arm's length, eyes suspicious.

"Uh...I...no I didn't see you," I stammered.

Gabriella nodded, appeased. She turned away, but left a hand on my lower back. Its presence sent a warm glow running up my spine.

"You all know Alexander right?" she said to the group.

Some nodded and a few even said hi, which wasn't expected. I gave a few stiff replies. I wasn't used to this much attention and could feel my cheeks turning red.

"Okay so I have to go," said Gabriella. "I promised to buy Alexander lunch."

I could see the surprise on the group's faces, but most tried to hide it. I understood then what she was doing. *She's trying to make me popular, by letting everyone know beyond doubt that we're friends.* It was singlehandedly the nicest thing anyone had ever done for me.

We walked away from the crowd, me travelling on jelly legs. I started in the direction of the canteen, but my companion shook her head.

"I was thinking we could walk up to town. One of the boys was telling me there is a really good fish and chips place. That okay?"

I breathed in deep to help calm my racing nerves. "You mean Cods Haven? Sure, sounds great."

We crossed the road and headed up towards the main town centre. As we walked, Gabriella fired a barrage of questions at me. She seemed really interested in my life. I told her about my favourite music and books and when my birthday was. She raised her eyebrows a little on the last one, but then carried on to inform me that my star sign was Leo, which meant I was caring and a born leader, but harboured intense anger which could be released when provoked. I smiled and nodded, just enjoying the sound of her voice. She was vibrant and used her hands a lot whilst she spoke. I felt little pangs in my stomach every time I looked at her smiling face. Occasionally I tried to dig up more about her personal life, but somehow the conversation always ended up back on me.

As we reached Chapter Hill town centre, the bright fascias of the various shops and restaurants sprang into view. The town itself was one of the biggest in South West London. It had countless supermarkets, a handful of schools, a top 20 University, two libraries and a theatre - which always attracted only the best D list celebrities for Christmas Pantomimes. Central London and all its souvenir flags and hats were only a District line tube or over-ground train ride away. However, the most unique thing about Chapter Hill was how green it was. The whole town was surrounded by thick woodland known as Susurrate forest. Plus there were numerous lakes and parks dotted around. It felt like a paradise hidden in London's urban jungle. I loved it. To me, Chapter Hill felt more like home than any other place I'd been.

It was just a shame about the people.

Cods Haven stood sandwiched between a phone shop shop and a bookstore. A little wooden sign shaped like a fish hung over the door, swaying gently in the icy breeze. It was a quaint place with pale blue walls and cream leather booths. A Greek couple owned it. They got under each other's feet, so would serve with a smile and then storm out the back to argue. When I'd first joined the Sixth Form, I'd gone to Cods Haven quite a bit. It was quiet - a good place to escape to. All the students seemed to favour the McDonalds further up the road, which meant I could make it through an entire lunch break without any hassle. That all changed when Terry and the gang spied me in there once.

I'd been too embarrassed to go back since.

As we neared the door it became apparent that the golden arches were no longer the venue of choice. The queue for Cod's Haven stretched out of the door. Most of the people standing in line were students. To my surprise the queue shortened faster than I expected. When we got inside, I saw this was because the owners had done a fair bit of hiring since I'd been a regular. Aproned teenagers - most likely students from the university - darted about behind the counter, serving and taking orders. In a booth tucked near the back, I noticed Mikey sitting with a couple of guys and girls, including Lisa. His friend nudged him and pointed at us. He looked up and raised his eyebrows, followed by a grin and an over the top thumbs up. I rolled my eyes and gave him a curt wave.

"Friend of yours?" Gabriella asked.

I sighed. "Kind of. That's Mikey."

"Your brother?

"Half-brother," I corrected.

"You don't look all that similar," she mused.

I felt the shame. "Don't I know it," I mumbled.

"Yeah, you're much cuter than him."

I couldn't help but laugh. "I'm sorry, *what*? You think I'm better looking than the popular 'can have anyone he wants' Mikey"?

She waved a hand. "Not my type."

Lightning hit my chest. *Hold on a second*, the voice in my head deduced, *if Gabriella doesn't fancy someone like Mikey, then maybe...* I was jolted back to reality by a nudge to my ribs. The attendant was staring at me.

"I said what can I get you pal?"

On Gabriella's suggestion we wandered over to Providence, the largest and most popular park in Chapter Hill. The grass was damp from the morning rain and gave off an intoxicating smell. We made our way into the kid's adventure playground area and settled on some swings, resting the food on our laps. The heat seeped through the carton, warming my legs. I rocked back and forth, scraping up woodchips with my foot whilst absently stabbing at my food with the little plastic fork.

"Can I ask you a question?" I said, skewering a chip.

"Of course."

"Why are you here?"

Gabriella shrugged. "I thought it would be nicer than the canteen."

I shook my head. "No, I mean why are you here with me? Surely you must know how much everyone hates me by now. Why are you bothering?"

She sighed. I could sense her turn, eyes scanning for mine. I kept staring down at my chips.

"Because I like you."

I snapped my head up. "But...you don't even *know* me."

The corners of her mouth lifted up. "Well I like to think I'm a good judge of character and I get a good feeling from you." She bumped her swing against mine playfully. "Can I ask you a question?" she added.

"Uh...sure."

"Why are you so unhappy?"

Her words hit me like a battering ram. I had no defence prepared. "I-I'm not," I blurted. "Why would you say that?"

"Because you wear it like a sign" she replied. "Come on, you can talk to me...we're friends."

Inside the feelings I'd pushed deep down so long ago were stirring, like a bag of snakes, twisting their way free.

"I-I don't want to talk about it," I said looking away.

"Alexander..." she placed a hand on my shoulder.

"Because I hate my life!" I yelled, hurling my chips across the playground. They smacked against a tree-trunk and slid to the ground in a heap. I pressed my hands against my forehead. "I hate my life," I repeated in a whisper. Gabriella tried to put her hand on me again, but I shrugged it off and stood up. Instead she placed her food down and used the chain to haul herself onto her feet.

"Why?"

I stared at her. "Would you want to be me?"

"I don't know. What's wrong with being you?"

"Are you kidding? I'm an absolute loser."

"Don't say that."

"Why not? Everyone else does! So I guess it must be true. Even my dickhead of a stepdad thinks I'm a stain on his perfect family."

Gabriella placed a soothing hand on my arm. "Screw him. What does your real dad think?"

I stared over her shoulder into the park. "I don't know. He isn't around anymore."

"Did he leave?"

"He's dead."

Gabriella's expression softened. "I'm so sorry. To lose a parent is...awful."

I shook my head. "You don't understand. He died when I was a baby. I didn't even know him! Plus my mum refuses to talk about him, which means he must have been a special kind of arsehole. But for some reason when I think about him I feel pain, like...I miss him. How messed up is that?"

Gabriella moved so she was standing next to me. "That isn't messed up at all Alexander. A child not having a dad around to support and guide them is tough. It makes sense that you'd want that void to be filled."

A strong wind picked up, rushing through the trees and rippling the grass beyond the playground. A gust lifted the collar of my jacket, pinning a portion of it against my cheek. I absently smoothed it back down.

"I don't even know if he cared about me."

She placed a hand on my back. "Of course he did."

Inside, the snakes were still slithering their way up. I could feel myself wanting to talk more.

"If losing one dad and being stuck with a replacement who hates you isn't bad enough, I have Mikey to compare myself to. Gabriella, he's better than me at *everything*. Oh and doesn't John let me know it!" I added bitterly. "If it wasn't for Mum I'd have left a long time ago."

I walked over to the metal fence that separated the playground from the rest of the park. Gabriella followed. To my horror, I could feel tears threatening to gather. *I can't cry in front of her!* I panicked inside. It wasn't my choice any more though; the words couldn't be stopped.

"I always thought I could gain acceptance at school. You know, make friends. But the harder I tried, the more I repelled people. It's as if there is something fundamentally wrong with me, like I'm *diseased* or something. It's been that way for as long as I can remember."

My eyes stung from the effort of holding back the tears. I wrapped my hands around the fence, twisting until my knuckles went white. Gabriella placed her hand on top of mine - it felt warm and comforting. She looked at me, her eyes urging me to continue.

"When we moved to Chapter Hill, I thought that maybe I could start again. That things could finally get better."

She squeezed my hand. "I'm guessing they didn't."

"They got worse. Not only did no one want to know me, but somehow I got on bloody Terry Burton's bad side. The bullying is worse than it's ever been." A tear spilled over and rolled down my cheek. I quickly wiped it with the back of my hand, hoping Gabriella didn't notice. "What you saw the other day was just a glimpse of what I get *all the time*." My voice was growing thick.

"I can't believe no one has done something about that *cazzo* yet."

48

I laughed humorously. "Why should anyone care? As long as it's me and not them on the radar." Another tear slipped down my cheek. I watched it drop and splash onto the fence. "You know, I have one friend and to be honest I think he just feels a bit sorry for me." On my last words my voice cracked. "Truth is, if I disappeared, I don't think anyone would care." My chin was trembling, but I couldn't stop. Willing myself not to look at Gabriella, I added, "So if all this is some kind of horrible joke, just don't okay? Leave now and I promise I won't ask why. I won't ever bother you again. You can tell everyone you humiliated me or something if that's what you want. I just...can't take any more."

I waited for Gabriella to leave. Instead her fingers slipped into mine and she pulled me around to face her. "How could you even think such a thing? Why would this be a joke?" she said, her tone more hurt than angry.

"Come on Gabriella, look at you...look at me!"

"Alexander, this isn't a joke, I promise. I would never do that to you."

Without another word, she wrapped her arms around me and pulled me close. As she held me there, my head buried in the crook of her neck, the last of the barriers crumbled and the tears came. I cried until there was nothing left. Then I opened my eyes and let Gabriella's blurry face swim back into focus. With surprise I saw that her eyes were damp with tears too. She blinked them away and took my hands in hers once more, giving them a gentle squeeze. Her skin was soft and there were no shocks, just a glowing feeling, which seemed to radiate through me. Somehow I didn't feel ashamed that I'd just cried in front of her. All I felt was lighter, like a weight had been lifted off my chest.

"Feel better?" she asked.

"Yeah I do." I scratched the back of my neck. "I'm sorry for dumping all that on you."

Gabriella shook her head. "You don't have to apologise to me. Never be ashamed of who you are or how you feel. Maybe you aren't the problem, maybe it's everyone else."

Her look intensified, as if she were dealing with something internal. She crossed her arms over her chest. "Alexander, when

I first saw you, I sensed something...different. I can't explain it, but I wanted to know you. That's why I asked you to show me around." She stared right into my eyes. Alexander, I believe - no," she pressed a hand against her chest, "I *know* that you have more courage and kindness within you than those..." she waved the hand in the air, "*testa di merdas* could ever dream of having! If they can't see what a sweet, kind, human being you are then it's their loss. But I can and *that's* why we're friends." Something seemed to flash in her eyes. "I'm here now and god help anyone who tries to hurt you." Her face relaxed into a warm smile. "Things are going to be different, I promise," she said. "You just need to have more faith in yourself. Okay?"

I nodded.

"Good."

She moved back over to the swing, picking up her food. I followed and sat back down. After popping a few chips in her mouth, Gabriella held the carton towards me.

"Since you clearly didn't like yours," she said through her mouthful. We both broke into a relieved laugh.

"Thank you, Gabriella," I said, taking a handful of chips.

She swallowed. "You're welcome and call me Ella if you like."

"Oh...okay. Is that what you like people to call you?"

She shook her head. "People, no. Only those I like the most."

The comment gave my stomach a little squeeze. "Okay, well you don't have to call me Alexander either. To be honest I prefer Alex."

She nodded, sending her raven hair spilling down her face. "Deal."

*

That evening, I was hot topic at the dinner table. Mikey - reverting to irritating twerp mode - had told Mum and John all about seeing Gabriella and me together.

"She is super-hot. I mean like on another level. Everyone at school is talking about her!" he enthused, animating his words with over the top hand gestures. John raised his eyebrows as he swirled spaghetti around his fork.

"And she was with Alexander?"

"Nice," I muttered under my breath.

Mum beamed, clasping her hands together and leaning forward. "So is she your girlfriend Alex?"

I groaned internally. I could feel the red fingers of embarrassment crawling up my face. "No, we're just friends." I replied in a firm tone. "I've been showing her around school, that's all."

John nodded as if an internal question had been answered. But he surprised me by adding, "Well, I think you should go for it. You never know, it could work out."

Mikey seemed a little confused too. "No Dad, she is like really hot."

"Shut up!" I yelled.

"Sorry," he shrugged looking at me, "I'm just saying."

At that moment I had to resist the urge to dive across the table and beat Mikey to a pulp. *Calm down, he's just being an idiot,* I reminded myself. Slowly, my anger ebbed away. The problem wasn't really him. It was more...me. My emotions had been up and down all day. After my heart to heart with Gabriella, I'd been in a euphoric state for hours. Then like a switch had been flipped, I was so angry I'd almost punched a first year in the face for bumping into me.

Mum smiled, "Well I agree with John. If you like her, then ask her out on a date."

Desperate to get the attention away from me, I agreed that if the situation arose I would ask her out. I knew I'd never have the confidence to actually do it, but it got them off of my back.

*

After dinner I started to feel ill.

To my family's surprise, I'd accepted an offer to watch a film. It was a pretty good one about a kid whose next-door neighbour is a Vampire.

The movie was about an hour in when I started to sweat. Thick beads crawled into my eyes and made them sting. I blinked, trying to focus on the film, but I was getting too hot. I started to fidget on the sofa, trying to find a comfortable position. A stuffy sickness began to rise in my stomach. My mouth filled with spit.

"Can you open a window?" I asked John, whose chair was closest to the outside wall.

He looked at me like I was mad. "Are you kidding? It's bloody freezing in this house as it is!" He made a tutting noise and turned back to the screen.

Mum gave me a concerned glance. "Are you feeling okay honey?"

"Uh, yeah. I'm just going to grab a drink."

My legs could barely support my weight as I stood up. I stumbled my way to the kitchen, gripping the walls to keep myself upright. I grabbed a glass off the draining board and filled it with water. Finished the whole lot in three gulps and repeated the process.

Then I threw up.

I stood over the sink, heaving until there was nothing left. With shaking fingers, I clawed for the kitchen roll and used it to wipe my mouth. *Something I ate?* But even thinking was hard. It felt like my brain was shutting down.

Tiredness seized my body. Every joint became lead, every muscle a bag of stones. My vision wavered as my eyelids started to grow heavy. I knew I should feel scared, but I couldn't raise the energy to feel anything. I dragged my body into the hallway and slumped to my knees, crawling up the stairs.

"Are you okay, Alex?" called Mum from the living room.

"Bed," was all I could muster, as I heaved my way on all fours up the steps.

I was drenched in sweat. My clothes looked like they'd been retrieved from a swimming pool. The carpet chafed against my wet skin, leaving fierce red marks on my arms and stomach as I dragged myself upwards. I reached my room in what seemed like hours. I barged my shoulder against the door. It swung open, knocking against the wall with a low thud.

I pulled myself onto the bed without even stopping to remove my sodden clothes. A wave of sickness rushed through my stomach. I leaned over the far side and vomited into the bin.

Whimpering, I rolled onto my back. The ceiling spun around like a car wheel. A pitiful moan escaped my lips and with no strength left, my body sank into the mattress and my eyelids closed.

I was still in my room but I sensed that I wasn't alone. People were moving about in the shadows, their voices barely a whisper.

The bed shifted as someone leaned over me. I could feel them near my skin, could hear their low, steady breathing. I tried to open my eyes, but they wouldn't respond. Panic exploded in my stomach. I wanted to scream for help, but my mouth wouldn't work. It felt like it had been glued shut. Terror replaced the panic. Inside I was writhing around like a wounded animal, screaming and fighting, but on the outside I would have appeared as still as the dead. More closed in around me, their breath warm on my face. I could smell something familiar, but couldn't place it. They spoke in small hushed bursts.

"It's definitely happening."

"We should take him now."

"I'll carry him."

Someone scooped me up from under the covers as if I were a baby and flopped me over their shoulder. I fought with all my strength to get some part of me to respond - to fend off my kidnappers and escape - but nothing happened. I was a rag doll.

I felt the slight rise and fall as my kidnapper walked across the bedroom. My stomach lurched as the ground dropped away.

A second later a jarring sensation shook my body and I heard a loud crunch like a hammer on gravel. I realised with pure shock that whoever was carrying me had jumped out of my bedroom window. If I could have screamed I would have. No human could do that without serious damage to us both.

There were a few more heavy thumps on the gravel as the other intruders followed. Then the rhythmic walking started again - the steady rise and fall.

With everything I had, I strained once more against my paralyzed muscles. I felt the fingers on my left hand flicker. A wave of hope replaced the fear.

"Wait!" I heard one of them hiss. My heart stalled. We shuddered to a stop and warm set of fingers felt for something in my neck.

"God, he isn't out properly! Quick, give it to me!"

There was a rustling sound followed by a sharp sting on the back of my hand. A cool sensation washed all the way up my arm. The last thing I remembered was tasting the sharp tang of metal in the back of my mouth, before the darkness rushed in and took me.

.

5

M y fingers stretched out, reaching for the pillow, but I couldn't find it. Instead I felt something soft and damp. I tried to lift my head up, but it was filled with lead. It pounded relentlessly.

Then the rest of me began to follow suit, starting with a low ache, which escalated into an intense throbbing. I tried to open my eyes, but they were slow and unresponsive.

The strange material was all around me. It rubbed gently against my stomach, face, arms and feet. After an age, my sluggish eyes rolled open and through my blurry vision I saw that I was not in bed at all.

I was face down in grass.

Using all of my strength I managed to force my jelly arms to push my aching body upright. After three tries, I was able to stand up onto spaghetti legs.

Only the briefest glance made it clear that I'd woken up in Providence Park.

My head thrummed and I clasped at it, rubbing furiously in a desperate attempt to blot out the pain. Eventually it subsided enough for me to focus.

The sky was a blend of orange and grey - the rising sun locked in battle with the winter clouds. An icy breeze traced the contours of my skin. The park was empty apart from a pair of joggers on the far side, dressed in matching blue tracksuits.

How the hell did I get here?

I tried to remember what happened the night before, but my brain wouldn't play ball. It only made my head pound worse. I stopped trying to think too much. Instead I concluded I must have sleepwalked. It was the only possible explanation for my makeshift bed. Looking down at my trembling body, the theory faltered.

I was wearing someone else's clothes. A simple pair of grey jogging bottoms and white vest, but definitely not mine.

All I cared about now was getting home.

I staggered forward, only managing a few steps before collapsing.

Gritting my teeth, I stood up again. Wobbling like a drunk on my bare feet, I took baby steps to ensure I remained upright. The aching grew worse, aggravated by my stubborn movements.

I felt broken. Every part of me smashed beyond repair. But I carried on, step by step, until after an eternity, I'd made it through the gated exit and onto the pavement that followed the main road through town. I noticed a phone box across the road. It stood proud, offering its salvation to those who could reach its graffitied glass doors.

I dug for change in the jogging bottoms. No luck. *Reverse the charges*, managed to squeeze through the dagger stabs in my brain. My head lolled from side to side as I vaguely checked for traffic. Meanwhile the throbbing in my body grew into a roaring crescendo of agony. With each boom in my temples, bright flashes of yellow burst into my eyesight. It felt like I could pass out at any moment. So focusing my squinting eyes on the telephone box, I stumbled into the road, arms outstretched like a toddler reaching for its mother.

Straight into the path of a speeding car.

I heard the sound of tyres locking, mixed with a bloodcurdling scream that sliced through my ears like a blade. My head turned in time to see a silver hatchback trying to veer around me just a little too late. Its back end skidded out and swung at me like a sledgehammer. There was no time to move. I closed my eyes and waited for the impact.

The morning calm was pierced by the inhuman smash and screech of twisting metal, followed by the tinkle of thousands of cubes of glass pattering onto the road like hailstones. Then the angry hiss of a dying engine. The kind of sounds you only hear when something very bad has just happened. All I could feel was something cold wrapped around my lower body.

Am I dead? I wondered, eyes still squeezed shut. If I was, this wasn't how I had expected it to be. There were no snapshots of my life, no white light to enter into.

My skin goose bumped from the frosty embrace of the unknown object. Whatever it was, it was holding on for dear life. I inched my eyelids apart. What I saw defied all logic.

The car was a steaming wreck, wrapped around my body.

At the impact point just behind the driver's door, it had caved around me in a rough V shape. Steam billowed in dark clouds from the exposed engine. The rear wheels had buckled and folded in on themselves, causing the car to sink down at the back and all the windows were smashed from the force of the impact.

It was the sort of result you would expect from a head on collision with a lamppost, not a seventeen-year-old kid. I looked down at my body, fearing the worst.

I didn't have a scratch on me.

Straining, I prised myself free from the car's steely grip. The metal groaned in protest.

I turned and stared at the wreckage, my mouth a wide O. My shocked expression was mirrored by the young, fair-haired woman who crawled across the driver's seat and flopped out of the passenger side. She staggered around the car and slumped against the twisted chassis next to me.

"Oh my god!' she breathed. "Are-are you okay?" She glanced at me and then back at her destroyed vehicle. "How...how did you...how are you...? I was going fast. Oh no...maybe too fast... I didn't see you in time, you..." Her words dissolved into a hysterical panic attack and she slid down onto the ground, sinking her head into her knees. I watched her frame expand and shrink again and again as she hyperventilated.

As I gazed around in a shock, a crowd gathered. People on their way to work stopped and drivers - not content with rubber necking - pulled over their cars and got out. I saw one man retrieve a phone from his pocket and make a call, presumably 999.

Everyone had the same look on their face, a combination of confusion and disbelief. They knew that I should be lying in a crumpled heap twenty feet away.

They knew I should be dead.

All I knew for certain was that I didn't want to be there. I took a step forward, my legs feeling much more solid than they had a minute before. The girl looked up at me, realising my intentions.

"N-no..." she wheezed and flailed out an arm to stop me. I ignored her and stumbled away from the crash in the direction of home.

"Hey son, come sit down," suggested an overweight man in jogging bottoms.

"You might be hurt," said an elderly lady with purple rinse hair.

They were all closing in on me, offering their own opinions on post collision aftercare. I saw the man with the phone weave towards me, his hand stretched out in my direction. He signalled for me to stop, all the while talking in rushed bursts to the person on the other end.

I turned and ran.

I ran as fast and as hard as I could, snaking through the gathering crowd. They called out and made weak efforts to stop me as I darted past. The strangest thing was, even though I was confused, all of my aches had gone and my head felt crystal clear.

My bare feet slapped hard against the pavement as I raced down the street. All I could think about was escaping the madness and getting home. The shop fronts whipped past, changing to houses and rows of bushes as the area became more residential. I pushed harder and the scenery became lines, blurs of colours that ran parallel to me, shifting in size and shape. A moment later I skidded to a stop when I recognised where I was. For the second time my mouth dropped open.

I was home.

I stared, refusing to believe my own eyes. There was no way that I could have arrived so fast. It took me fifteen minutes to drive and that was at full speed. I'd just run the distance in less than five. But no matter how many times I blinked, the red-bricked semi with the white window frames and leaking drainpipe was still there.

I didn't know what to think. *First waking up in the park wearing someone else's clothes. Then the car wreck. Now this.* It was too much. I felt like I was going insane.

I needed to see my family, needed to see something normal.

Rushing up the driveway, I noticed that both Mum and John's cars were gone. I prayed that someone was in. As I neared the door, my strength began to fade again. The dull throb started back up and the ache swept through my body. It felt like I was wading through water.

"*What is going on?*" I screamed. No one answered. A dog barked from somewhere down the road.

I slapped my hand against the wall, and then used it to steady myself as I stretched up to the hidden ledge above the front door and felt around for the spare key. My fingers were shaking as I jiggled the lock open and half fell through the door.

"Hello?" I croaked. "Anyone?"

Silence.

I swiped the door closed too hard, jumping at the sound. I called out again as I shuffled to the living room, using my hands to keep me upright as my legs dissolved into water. The couch in front of me looked soft and inviting. I was confused and terrified, but nothing could have stopped me from resting on it. I fell into it and sighed as its welcoming, overstuffed cushions wrapped around me.

After a few seconds I was sound asleep.

*

The sound of the front door closing woke me. My eyes snapped open, alert and clear. The light from the window had been replaced by the unnatural glow of streetlamps.

I swung myself upright and rubbed the sleep from my eyes.

A few seconds later Mikey walked into the room. He caught sight of me and swore loudly.

"Alex is that you?" He moved over to me and peered close, like I was a caged animal.

I swatted him away, not in the mood for games. "Of course it's me idiot. Who did you think it would be?"

He drew back and raised his eyebrows. "But you look...different."

Fear rocketed through me. *What does he mean different? Has the accident done more damage than I realised?* I swallowed and pointed a shaking finger towards the portable mirror that stood on top of a side table.

"Pass me that," I said.

Mikey grabbed the mirror and handed it to me. I breathed in deep, expecting the worst, and looked. I gasped. Staring back from the glass was a superior version of me.

My spots had gone. Instead my skin was smooth and no longer anaemic white. My jawline looked stronger and my eyes gleamed as if they had been polished. Even my hair had lost its coarseness, looking more like Mikey's than my own. As I opened my mouth in shock, I noticed that my teeth were whiter and less uneven than they had been before. As I prodded and poked at my face, Mikey asked a question that sent a shiver down my spine.

"Alex, where the hell have you been?"

I lowered the mirror to my lap and stared up at him, eyebrows knitting together. "What do you mean?"

He put a hand on my shoulder and crouched down so he was level with me. "You've been missing for three days."

"No," I breathed, suddenly feeling very dizzy. I shook my head. "No. That can't be right."

He stood up again and picked up the television remote. "What day do you think it is today?"

I thought about the night before. It hurt my head to try and remember, but I managed to catch fleeting images of us all watching a horror film together. That had been the day that I'd confided in Gabriella. I thought about the lessons I'd had before lunch. That had been a Wednesday. *Which means today must be...*

"Thursday," I said with confidence.

Mikey looked concerned. He flicked the television onto Satellite. The blue bar popped up below the program and my eyes went wide as I read the date.

Sunday November 18th

"No..." I whispered.

Mikey switched the television off and threw the remote onto the couch next to me, before sinking down into the adjacent chair. He was wearing tracksuit bottoms; they crinkled against the seat as he settled in.

"So where have you been?" he repeated.

I buried my head in my hands. "I don't know."

Mikey leaned forward, raising his voice. "What do you mean you don't know? How in god's name can you not know? Do you think this is a joke? Mum and Dad have been going out of their minds. Especially Mum, she has been acting mental. Calling up anyone she could think of who may've had a clue where you were. She even called the police. She was convinced something terrible had happened to you! Dad thinks you ran away. You didn't even take your phone! You - argghh!" He threw up his hands in exasperation.

Tears of frustration spilled onto my hands. I wiped them away and looked up at my half-brother. When I spoke, my voice sounded thick and throaty.

"I really don't know, Mikey. You need to listen to me. Something weird is going on."

"Explain."

I told him everything I knew. About waking up in Providence Park in strange clothes, about the accident and running home way too fast.

When I had finished, he folded his arms across his chest.

"Bollocks."

"Mikey, I'm telling you the truth. I mean look at me. How do you explain my extreme makeover?"

He gave a slow nod. "Okay, prove it."

"How?"

He jumped up and headed for the door. "Put something on your feet and meet me outside."

I ran upstairs into my room. Everything was as I remembered it. Nothing had changed, except that my normally neat bedcovers were screwed in a heap at the end of the mattress. Also someone had cleaned out the bin.

Stopping at the mirror, I had another look at myself. My full-length reflection showed that the subtle changes hadn't been limited to my face. For one, I seemed taller, even though I was sure I hadn't grown. It was like I carried myself better. Taking off the top showed the rest. I was still slim, but underneath my skin were the faint definitions of muscles. I tensed a bicep and was shocked to see a respectable sized lump appear. Overall, the changes weren't drastic, but still noticeable. Like I'd become an alternate version of myself, who'd spent his life dedicated to health and fitness. Not knowing what to think, all I could do was shake my head in amazement.

I threw the grass-stained vest into the wash basket and changed into an old hoodie and a pair of trainers. As I headed for the door, I noticed my phone lying on the desk.

I'll check it later.

A few minutes later we were standing on the street, illuminated by the overhead glow of a streetlamp. They continued all the way down the road at even distances, casting little pools of orange onto the shadowy pavement.

Mikey pointed into the distance. "Run down to the fifth light and back and I'll see how fast you are." I couldn't see any reason to object, so I turned and faced the gloom, waiting for his signal. "Go!" he shouted and I sprang forward as he was still finishing the word.

My trainers pounded mercilessly against the concrete as I sprinted forward. For some reason, it didn't feel fast enough; I was still travelling at a normal pace. "Come on!" I shouted at myself.

Then something inside me changed. A mental switch flicked inside my brain and everything went into overdrive. I could hear the steady thumping of my heart and the pounding of the blood swimming around my temples. The thuds of my soles hitting the ground sounded like echoing booms. The streetlights flashed past and I had to remind myself to stop as I rocketed past the fifth. Hopping around on one foot, I turned and charged back. Mikey was just a little blob in the distance, but as I rushed forward, slipping in and out of the light, he grew until he was full size. I could see his face, frozen in shock. Then I was past him, skidding to a halt about twenty yards further up the road. The strange sensation stopped as fast as it had started. I was barely out of breath as I reached my half-brother.

He stared at me and blinked.

"So how did I do?" I asked, anxiously rubbing the back of my neck.

He made a spluttering noise and backed away from me. "I-I don't know what to say. That was impossible! No one can run that fast!" He pointed to the spot next to him. "When you passed me you were a blur. I mean seriously, you were a *blur* Alex!"

"Okay not so loud!" I hissed and tried to pull him towards me. Instead, he went sailing past and flew to the ground, sliding along the pavement.

"Mikey"! I gasped, running towards him. He groaned and rolled over. "Oh crap! Are you okay?"

He nodded. I was afraid of what might happen if I tried to help him up, so I let him stand by himself. Apart from a graze on his left hand he appeared unharmed.

"I'm so sorry. I didn't mean to do that. Oh god, what's happening to me?"

"Relax, I'm fine," he assured me, dusting himself down. Then he smiled. "I guess we can put a tick next to super-strength. Guess that would explain the car crash."

A thought came to me. "The car crash! I bet it's on TV!"

We both ran back into the house and piled into the living room. I switched on the local news and waited.

The headlines and even filler news came and went. Nothing about a crash.

Mikey looked at me as I powered off the set.

"Internet," I said.

He pulled out his phone and was silent for a moment as he typed things into the search engine. After a while he gave a shrug. "Nothing at all. Maybe they didn't report it."

I rolled my eyes. "Mikey, I was hit by a car doing at least fifty. It folded in half and I walked away without a scratch. In what world would that not be news?" I sat down on the couch and rubbed a hand against my head. "None of this makes any sense."

The sound of a car pulling into the drive caught my attention.

"Mum and Dad," said Mikey, stating the obvious.

Somehow telling them seemed like a mistake. I stood up and walked close to my half-brother. I whispered, as if afraid I would be heard through the outside wall. "Mikey, I don't want you to tell them anything okay? Let's keep this between me and you."

He arched his eyebrows. "Where the hell are you going to say you've been?"

I wasn't sure. "I'll think of something, just back me up okay?"

He stared at me.

"Please?"

He sighed. "Fine."

I clapped him on the shoulder, making sure to be gentle. "Thanks."

The engine rumbled to a stop and I heard the *thunk* of doors slamming, followed by a clatter of keys in the lock.

"Hello?" Mum called as the front door clicked shut.

"Mum, Dad, in here! Guess who's back?" called out Mikey.

Mum and John came rushing into the lounge.

"Hi," I said awkwardly as they appeared, actually waving at them.

"Alex! Oh my boy!" sobbed Mum and ran over, wrapping her arms around me. "Don't ever scare me like that again!" As she held me close, I rested my head into the crook of her neck. There was nothing quite like a mother's comforting to make all of your troubles disappear.

Looking up brought me back to reality with a bump. John had held back, his thick arms folded across his even thicker chest. He was eyeing me suspiciously. "Where in the bloody hell have you been? Your mother has been going out of her mind with worry!" he growled. "And what's with the makeover?" He gestured his hand towards me.

Until he had said the last part, I'd had no clue what I was going to say. Now I knew.

Mum unravelled herself and stood away from me, wiping her eyes.

I raised my hands in a defensive pose. "I'm really sorry I worried everyone. I've been feeling pretty down lately, so I decided to go to this new alternative health place down the coast." My words sounded confident to my ears. I hoped it was the same for them. "They were advertising it for sixth formers. A winter retreat. I had to get the train really early in the morning and because I was so tired, I forgot to take my phone." I breathed in deep. "I was going to call you from the place, but you weren't allowed to use phones unless it was an absolute emergency. Part of the treatment they said." I felt the last few words hang in the air, like vapour.

64

John was staring at me, trying to see if I was lying. Before he could call me out on it, Mikey came to the rescue. "He's telling the truth Dad. I've seen it advertised in the hub. This is actually my fault a bit. Alex mentioned he was thinking of going the other week, but I completely forgot."

That seemed to work. There was no way that perfect Mikey would lie to his Dad.

John nodded and flicked his eyes back to me. "Why didn't you tell us you were going?" he demanded.

I looked down at the floor, trying my best to look ashamed. "Because I didn't think you would let me."

He shook his head and sighed. "Well you're a bloody idiot for leaving your phone behind." He turned to Mum who was staring out of the window. She looked lost in thought. "I'm going to call the police and let them know. You coming babe?"

Mum snapped out of her reverie. "Yes, two seconds honey."

John headed for the door and stopped. He seemed to be dealing with some kind of internal struggle. When he spoke and the words were a little strained. "Whatever they did at that health place, it's done the trick. You look...better." He gave a follow-up grunt and then disappeared from the room.

A smile crept across my face at yet another unexpected compliment courtesy of my stepdad. It soon switched to confusion when Mum hugged me again and whispered something so low into my ear I could barely hear. I drew back at her words, confused. She squeezed my arm and turned, heading out of the door.

What on earth did she mean by that?

I shook my head and let her odd words fade away for the moment. It had worked - they believed me. To be honest, what choice did they have? There was no other rational explanation. I would have believed it.

I turned to Mikey and smiled. "Thanks for backing me up there."

Shrugging, he scooped his bag up off the carpet. "That's what brothers are for right?"

He squeezed my shoulder and followed the others out of the room, leaving me standing on my own.

Later, after the buzz of me not being face down in a ditch had subsided, I snuck away into my room. Flopping onto my bed, I tried to get a handle on my thoughts. I knew I had super strength and speed, but what else? Were these effects permanent? Could I have been involved in some kind of radioactive accident, like in the comic books? Is that why I couldn't remember where I'd been? I also couldn't get what Mum had said out of my mind. Did she know something I didn't? Or was I reading too much into it? There were so many questions swimming about in my head, they made me feel dizzy. So I shut my eyes and let my thoughts drift. Instead, more questions squeezed into my crowded brain: *Is this real? Have I gone mad? Why me? Is there a reason?* I couldn't cope; it felt like my head was going to explode.

"Stop it!" I hissed, pounding my fists against my temples. "Just stop!"

Silence.

I sighed and sat up on the edge of my bed, my head in my hands. *Get a grip Alex.*

Suddenly I remembered my phone. Leaning over, I scooped it off the desk. It had run out of battery, so I had to rummage through my desk drawer for the charger before I could switch it on.

When the logo had faded away and the information had loaded, I saw that I had five missed calls and voicemail. A personal record.

The first missed call was from my parents. I figured they must have called me and heard it ringing upstairs. The next was from Tim and the last three were all blocked.

I tapped the voicemail button and waited as it connected. The woman's disjointed voice informed me I had **four new messages**.

The first was from Tim, left Friday evening. He explained that my mum had called him in a panic. He asked if it had anything to do with Terry. He offered to go to the school principal for me if I didn't want to. Asked me to call him and rang off.

The next was from a telemarketer. Apparently I could consolidate my existing debts into one easy monthly repayment. I sighed and deleted the message.

The third made my stomach jolt. It was Gabriella. Her angelic voice floated through the speaker into my ear. "Hi Alex its Ella. I hope you don't mind but I got your number from your friend Tim. After our chat the other day, I was a little worried when I didn't see you at school. Has something happened? Anyway, please call me back as soon as you get this." She read out her number then clicked off. I repeated it over and over in my head as I scrambled about for a pen and paper. After jotting it down, I made a mental note to call her the first chance I got.

I saved the message and waited for the final one. It had come through this afternoon. As soon as it started, the hairs on the back of my neck stood up.

At first, there was nothing apart from what sounded like fierce wind. It crackled loudly in the receiver, forcing me to hold the phone away from my ear. Then a robotic voice cut through the noise, like the ones they used in hostage films. It was slow and deep and the mobile reacted to it, buzzing electronically like it was getting interference.

"Alexander, we are the ones who took you. Please understand it was to help you. To try and keep you safe. Your escape was...unexpected. There is no point trying to remember where you have been, or what happened, because it will be impossible. You will know only when the time is right. We are aware that you have discovered that you possess abilities that defy logical explanation. Our advice is experimentation. But be careful. Your body is still adjusting and therefore will be quite unpredictable. You may end up hurting yourself or others."

The voice stopped for a long beat and there was nothing but the crackle of wind again. My ear was glued to the phone and I had stopped breathing, not daring to miss a thing.

"Alexander, you always wanted to be special and now you are. Go and be the person you always wanted to be. Remember though, we are keeping an eye on you. We will be in touch."

The message ended, followed instantly by the recorded operator informing me that the message had been successfully deleted. I pulled the phone away and stared at it. I hadn't pressed anything.

The message had deleted itself.

Freaked out, I threw the phone away from me like it was a giant insect. My heartbeat was a hummingbird fluttering its frantic wings inside my chest. *Someone took me? To keep me safe – but from what? I escaped - how? And from where? Where have I been?* Millions of questions began to pour into my brain again. I felt so confused that I wanted to scream and rip my hair out. The rational part of my mind was yelling things like this simply did not happen in real life. But I couldn't deny it, I had been taken, and these things were really happening to me. I felt torn. On the one hand, these people had kidnapped me and done god knows what. On the other hand – as crazy as it seemed - I owed these people a lot. I looked and felt incredible.

The caller's words echoed in my mind.

Our advice is experimentation.

I leaned over the edge of the bed and fumbled in the abyss between frame and floor. Eventually my hand closed around what I was looking for and I dragged it out. It was one of a twin set of dumbbells John had given me for my 16th birthday. Looking at it now, I rolled my eyes. He might as well have written 'man up' on the gift tag.

I stripped the weights off and pushed them back under the bed with the heel of my foot. I was left with the metal bar. I weighed it in my hands. It certainly felt solid enough. I curled my hands into fists and took a deep breath. Then I twisted them against the bar, pushing upwards and towards the middle. The bar didn't want to bend. I grit my teeth together as I used all of my strength, my biceps threatening to split through my skin. I could feel the tendons in my neck straining from the effort. A growl of effort came from deep within.

Eventually, something gave way. When I looked back down, the bar resembled a U shape.

"No way!" I breathed. I pushed the metal further with the palm of my hands. It crossed over itself. I grabbed one end and with much less effort pulled it through the loop, tugging both ends like a shoelace. Now the bar was a giant knot. I stared at the lump of metal in utter disbelief.

This is insane.

The phone ringing almost made me scream. I crawled over the bed and looked at the screen. The number was unknown. A cold chill ran through my body. *Is it them?*

My throat was sandpaper as I picked up the handset and pressed the answer button.

"Hello?" I croaked.

"Alex, that you?"

I sighed with a mixture of relief and disappointment.

"Yeah it is, hi Tim. Your number came up unknown."

"House phone mate. Ex-direct. Anyway, just checking you're okay."

I looked at the pretzel shaped dumbbell.

"Yeah I'm fine...great actually."

Tim made an approving noise then stopped to shout at someone. "Sorry, my sister's doing my head in. Anyway, glad to hear you're alight. Oh before I forget, I wasn't the only one worried about you." His voice had changed and I imagined him wearing his trademark dopey grin.

"What do you mean?"

"That ten…Gabriella? She was asking about for your number. I gave it to her, did she get in touch?"

"Yeah she left a message," I said.

Tim whistled. "Mate, I am so jealous, that girl has a soft spot for you. And she is so hot! I mean like...wow. Things are looking up hey Alex?"

I gave a little chuckle. "You know what? I think you may be right."

"So where were you anyway?"

I paused. I hadn't thought about whether I was going to tell him or not yet. I needed time to think.

"Sorry mate, I've got to go. My mum's calling me for dinner."

"Err...okay, cool. So does this mean you'll be back tomorrow?"

I glanced over at the wrap of metal on the bed and then to my upgraded reflection.

Go be the person you always wanted to be.

"I'll be there."

6

As I wolfed down my breakfast the next day, I heard the post drop. John walked out to collect it.

I'd woken up an hour earlier than usual, almost jumping out of bed with energy. My hair had taken seconds to style. Clothes fit, rather than hanging off me like sacks. I'd bounded downstairs and helped Mum prepare breakfast and tidy the kitchen. She made no reference to the strange comment she'd made the night before. Instead she was back to normal - all smiles and laughs.

"Well, you seem different today," she'd laughed as I danced about, putting plates away, and humming a Soulfire song.

"I feel different."

As I sat eating team effort pancakes, John returned to the kitchen and dropped a letter next to my plate. I frowned and picked it up. The envelope was high quality, its surface thick and the colour of fresh cream. The writing on the front was elaborate, dark ink scrawled across the paper like spider legs. No stamp. My fingers pressed against something hard inside.

Mikey glanced up at me and I shrugged. I knew this wasn't a letter to open in front of an audience. So I waited until after breakfast and locked myself into the downstairs toilet.

"Bro, we going or what?" Mikey called through the door.

"I'll see you in the car," I replied. "Keys are in the bag."

Slipping my thumb into the corner of the flap, I tore the envelope open. My heart was beating double speed. I tipped the contents into my hand and stared. It was a black key fob. Confused, I peered into the envelope and noticed a small folded note. I opened it up. The message was written in the same spidery handwriting.

Parked on Mason Avenue. This should help you with your new life.

That was all. I crammed the note and key into my pocket and flushed the toilet for effect. Grabbing my bag from the hall, I shouted goodbye and rushed out the door.

Mikey leaned back in his seat, lost in thought. I'd filled him in on everything I knew so far. The only thing I hadn't mentioned was the letter and key. I wasn't even sure what they meant yet. He looked over when I took a left instead of a right.

"Hey, just how badly did your memory get affected? You're going the wrong way!"

"I need to make a quick detour," I replied.

Mason Avenue was a little street not too far from town. Devoid of streetlights, it was dark and gloomy in the winter morning. Cars were parked nose to bumper on either side. Given the road's closeness to the high street, it was doubtful that many of them actually belonged to the owners of the houses.

I parked up on the corner and climbed out the car.

"What's going on?" asked Mikey, winding down the window.

I ignored him and pulled the key out of my pocket. Holding the fob in front of me, I clicked the button as I walked. About a hundred yards away something flashed and beeped. I ran over and my jaw dropped.

Sitting unassumingly between a Skoda and a Toyota was a brand new Audi sports car.

Its sleek silver body gleamed in the emerging sunlight. I pressed the fob a few more times just to make sure I was seeing things right. The lights blinked and the car beeped in response.

"Oh my god," I breathed. I didn't know a huge amount about cars, but I knew this was a bloody expensive one. Excitement swept through me as I opened the door and the intoxicating smell of new leather rushed out to greet me. On the driver's seat was another small note.

Check the boot.

I fumbled about and found the button that opened it. Once popped, I headed around and lifted it. Bags filled the space. Names like Selfridges, Boss and Versace stamped on them like awards. They contained what must have been thousands of pounds worth of designer clothes: t-shirts, jackets, jeans and shoes. I even found a brand new pair of Ray Ban's.

Picking up a knitted beige jumper, I checked the price tag and let out a disbelieving laugh. *These people must really like me.*

I looked around to see who was about. The street seemed empty. Even Mikey was blocked from view, so I shrugged off my clothes and slipped into the jumper and a pair of jeans I'd found in another bag. I finished with a black leather jacket and matching shoes. Everything fitted perfectly. I shut the boot and walked back to my old car.

"What's going on...where did you get those clothes?" Mikey quizzed, a deep frown etched in his face.

I leaned against the door and grinned.

"How do you feel about sports cars?"

The engine roared as I gunned down the road. The car was so fast I wouldn't normally have been able to handle it - I'd had my licence less than a month. But something was different now. I seemed to know exactly what to do at every possible point - when to drop a gear, accelerate, when to brake. Out of the corner of my eye I could see Mikey staring at me wearing a look of disbelief.

"Listen," I said, taking a corner a little too fast, "before you ask, I still don't know what's going on. A letter arrived today with the key and this note inside." I handed him the fold of paper. "That's all I can say. But if someone gave you all this stuff, would you say no?"

He scanned the words and shrugged. "Depends on what they wanted in return. I mean, why else would they do all this?"

I paused. With everything going on, the thought that there may be a catch hadn't even occurred to me.

What could they possibly want from me?

"Do you think it could be some kind of government experiment?" Mikey asked, fiddling with the CD player. "It would explain the reason you were taken and why you suddenly have all these sick abilities."

I lifted a hand off the wheel and pinched at the bridge of my nose. "Maybe. I mean it's possible, I guess. Argghh I don't know!" I hit the wheel with the palm of my hand. "Screw it; I'm going to enjoy this while I can."

Mikey gave an approving nod. "That's what I'd do."

The CD activated and the soft rock intro of 'Rise' by Soulfire filled the plush interior.

Mikey raised an eyebrow. "Yours?"

"Nope."

He settled back into his seat as we gunned past another car. "Well they certainly know you."

Eyes bulged and jaws dropped as the car rolled through the gates of Chapter Hill School. I parked near the main steps, buzzing from all the gawping stares. As Mikey pushed open the door, he turned and looked at me.

"Quick one, how do you plan to keep *this* from Mum and Dad?"

I shrugged. "I'll swap it for the Peugeot whenever I drive home."

"And what do we tell everyone else?"

"Tell them a rich uncle on my dad's side died and left me money."

Mikey smiled. "Got all the answers these days huh?"

He patted me on the shoulder and climbed out.

Not all of them.

People stared even harder when I slipped out of the sleek sports car and flicked the alarm. With a large smile etched on my face, I weaved past them and up the main steps. As I made my way through the school, people glanced up and social circles stopped talking to stare. It was an odd sensation, being the focus so many people, but minus the suffocating feeling of awkwardness. *This must be what actual confidence feels like.*

As I turned the corner, I saw a familiar blonde topped shape ahead of me.

"Tim!" I shouted and caught up with him.

"Yeah?" he said, turning and regarding me with a momentary blank expression. His eyes widened. "Alex?"

"The one and only," I smiled. "Miss me?"

He shook his head in disbelief. "Mate what happened, you look so different!"

I'd been confused and in need of support when I'd confided in Mikey. Now I had a better handle on things, it seemed better to keep the circle of trust tight - at least until I knew more. So I decided not to tell Tim, yet. Instead, I fed him the exact same

73

story I'd used on Mum and John, with the rich uncle bit tacked on the end. Explained how I'd used some of the money to pay for the expensive, private retreat. I must have spoken with conviction, because he didn't even frown.

"Well rest assured mate, it was money well spent."

*

I killed a free period in the Sixth Form common room, sitting on a worn sofa, flicking through an old GQ magazine someone had left on the side. Out of the corner of my eye I spied a group of girls staring at me and giggling. One of them - Grace Evans, shared my History class. She was pretty. Not Gabriella pretty, but very attractive by mere human standards. I'd never so much as exchanged a single vowel with her before, but she was certainly paying me attention now. She ran a hand through her wavy auburn hair and flicked her eyes between her group and me. After a while she made her way over to me. Normally that would have been the exact point in which I started sweating and said something mortally embarrassing. None of that happened. My heart rate didn't even increase. I lowered the magazine and looked up. She stood in front of me, clutching at her bag strap and dug the heel of a boot into the carpet.

"You're Alex Eden right?" she said, with what sounded incredibly like nerves in her voice.

"I am. And you're Grace Evans."

She giggled. "Yeah, that's me. We have History together."

I nodded.

"You um...you look different," she said awkwardly, twisting the strap of her bag between her fingers. "Like in a really good way - I mean you look really good."

It was the first time a girl had ever referred to my looks in a positive way. The unexpected compliment raised my already good mood up a few notches.

I grinned. "Thanks, Grace."

"Ha, um, you're welcome." She glanced over at the group and someone signed something to her. "Oh, I heard you have a sports car. Is that true?"

Wow, that was fast.

"Uh yeah, I do."

She suppressed another giggle. "Wow that's so cool. Um, sorry for asking, but how can you afford that?"

"Oh, a rich uncle died and left me some money," I lied with complete confidence.

"Wow, amazing! I mean - no, wait...that's not amazing him dying and that. But leaving you money, *that's* amazing."

I smiled again.

"So anyway...I mean we don't really know each other, but I was wondering if...well if you wanted to go for a drink some time?"

First I'd been complimented and now the same girl was asking me out. I was deep in unexplored territory - a surreal experience. I stared at her, unable to produce an answer.

"Um look, don't worry about it," Grace said, her cheeks flushing. "Sorry for bothering you."

She swung on her heel and started to walk away.

"Okay," I blurted.

Grace spun back round, a smile forming. "Great! Um well, do you want my number or something?"

"Sure."

I slid my phone out of my pocket and we exchanged numbers.

"Cool, well, text me or something. I'll see you soon," she said and hurried back to the safety of the herd. They were all giggling and she went more and more red, trying to shush them.

I paused for a moment, struggling to believe what had just happened. I'd been asked out within an hour of attempting to re-invent myself. It was unbelievable. The notion that it was all very superficial was not lost on me, my improved look and car clearly playing a large part, but I was an seventeen-year-old brimming with hormones, I wasn't about to get all resentful about it.

Without warning, my heart began to hammer against my chest and a sheen of sweat appeared on my palms. Tossing the magazine aside, I unsteadily left the common room before my body could give me away.

I headed to the bathrooms and splashed cold water on my face, to calm myself down. *It's like a delayed response. Maybe this is what they mean about my body adjusting* I thought, through the dizziness. I stayed there, clutching the sink for a few minutes until the sensations passed. I wiped my face with paper towels from the dispenser and stared at my reflection in the mirror.

"Keep it together, Alex."

After weaving my way through the crowds, I reached the science department. My heart thumped louder with each step I made towards the classroom. In my mind I tried to imagine what she would be wearing, how her hair would be done. My heart sank as I reached the door. Full class - no Gabriella.

The gossip machine had been running at full speed. Half a dozen people came over to my seat and I had to repeat what I'd told Tim half a dozen times. Everyone seemed to believe the lie as easily as Tim had. I guessed it was just a matter of confidence. Only one person didn't utter a word, but sat hunched over his desk with a deep scowl etched on his face.

Silence descended as a slightly harassed looking Miss Steele paced through the door. Her eyes scanned the room and seemed to settle on me. Her posture relaxed and she gave a smile. Pulling her specs from her bag, she slid them over her petite nose. Her hair was unfastened today. It swept over one shoulder and hung just below her breast line. The thing I noticed the most however, was the perfume she was wearing. It was both intoxicating and overpowering, like she'd used half the bottle. It surged up my nose and flooded my brain with images of majestic flowers, which stretched up towards the sky, glossy black petals open like outstretched fingers. I blinked a few times and the images faded, followed shortly by the scent.

Super smell, I assumed without much thought. It seemed that nothing could surprise me anymore.

I was wrong.

Halfway through the lesson, Miss Steele asked for a volunteer. As expected, every single male in the class put up their hand. She chose TJ.

I decided it was time for a little revenge.

I waited until he was almost at my desk and pretended to drop my pen. As I hopped off my seat to pick it up, I used my heel to slide the stool into his path. His foot caught against it and he let out a cry of surprise as he fell, bringing it clattering down with him. The room erupted into laughter. He clambered back up, with a face like a storm. I feigned innocence. "I'm sorry, I dropped my pen." I waggled the offending object to emphasise my point.

"You dick!" he shouted and shoved me as hard as he could. I didn't move.

I stepped towards him until my face was inches from his. Powerful waves of sizzling anger rolled through my body.

"Bring it arsehole!" I spat.

Miss Steele was quick to intervene, wedging herself between us. "Stop it this instant!" she hissed. "This is not a playground. I will not tolerate this type of behaviour. Do you understand me?"

Neither of us said a word, our bodies still squared up to one another. I was clenching and unclenching my fists, trying to resist the urge to throw Miss Steele out of the way and break the prick's jaw.

He glared daggers back at me, probably thinking the exact same thing.

"I SAID DO YOU UNDERSTAND ME?"

I sighed, letting the anger ebb away. I nodded as TJ mumbled "yeah."

"Good," she said. "Now both of you sit down so we can continue the lesson. I think I'll do the demonstration myself...honestly I have never seen such immaturity." She shook her head and marched back to the front. As she passed me, I could have sworn I saw the faintest hint of a wink.

The lesson continued without further incident, although I could feel TJ boring holes into my back. If looks could have killed, I would've been six feet under.

At the end of the lesson, Richard Lawrence and Elliot Shaw - two guys from a few rows back I'd barely ever spoken to - came over to my desk as I was packing my things away. Elliot clapped a chubby hand on my shoulder. I tensed up, anticipating the worst. But when I turned, I saw he was smiling.

"I had no idea you were such a nutter pal. Fair play, TJ is a knob." He spoke in a low voice, making sure the subject didn't hear as he disappeared through the door, giving me a final glare.

Richard nodded, his curly blonde hair bobbing with it. "I really hate Terry's lot. I mean this isn't school anymore, I can't even believe they get away with this crap."

I raised my eyebrows, surprised that one: they were even talking to me, and two: they were being *sympathetic.*

Elliot patted my back and gestured for me to walk with them. "So how does this car of yours handle?"

It wasn't until I'd reached the hub that I realised I'd left my bag in class.

Elliot and Richard were still chatting to me about something or other. Being honest I'd stopped listening, but somehow managed to keep the conversation flowing. It was as if one part of my mind switched to autopilot, whilst the other went exploring. My focus was on Gabriella. *Where is she?* I wondered. *Why does she keep missing lessons?*

It was then that I remembered we hadn't spoken since she'd left me the message. I'd tried to call her the night before but her phone had cut straight to voicemail and I'd been too nervous to leave a message. I decided to try again.

Except I couldn't find my phone.

Where is it? I panicked, pawing at my empty jean pockets. Then I remembered I'd put it in my bag before science...which was still in the classroom. *Crap!*

"Sorry guys I got to go." I left them standing in the hub, sharing a confused expression. I threaded back through the hallways, making sure I kept my speed below superhuman levels. When I reached the room, the door was closed and the window blind down. *Great, I bet it's locked and I'm going to have to hunt Miss Steele down.* But when I twisted the handle, the latch clicked and the door inched open.

Miss Steele was facing the outside window. And her whole body was shaking like someone had electrocuted her.

"Oh god!" I gasped, clamping a hand over my mouth.

As if someone had cut the power, Miss Steele stopped pulsing. She whirled around and glared at me. As she did, a gold signet ring she'd been clutching in her fist clattered to the floor.

"I... I forgot my bag," I said in a strained voice, pointing a trembling finger at the offending item under the table.

The teacher bent to pick up the ring. When she stood up again it was like a cloud had passed. Miss Steele presented me her award-winning smile. "Of course," she said slipping the ring back into her pocket. "I hope I didn't frighten you." She cleared her throat. "This is actually quite embarrassing. The thing is, I suffer from epilepsy. I could feel a seizure coming on, so I shut the door and closed the blind." She leaned forward and used a slender hand to sweep a wisp of hair from her face. "I don't like people knowing you see, I worry they'll think it may affect my ability to teach...silly really." Moving the hand to her chest, Miss Steele gave an exaggerated sigh. "I'm sorry you had to see that Alex."

"Uh, it's fine. Don't worry." I smiled and edged over to my bag. I wasn't convinced – it didn't look like a normal seizure to me. Pulling the bag from under the desk, I asked if she needed me to fetch the school nurse. She assured me that it had passed and she would be fine.

"Oh and Alexander?" she added as I went to close the door behind me.

"Yes Miss Steele?"

"Let's make this our little secret."

7

That evening, the first one came for me.

It was dark by the time I climbed into the Audi. I took a relaxed drive back to Mason Avenue, enjoying the roar of the engine and the tight handling, not relishing the swap back to my juddering heap. When I reached the Peugeot, I swore loudly.

It had been trashed.

The windows were smashed in and the car was up on bricks, wheels stolen. The CD player had been ripped out. Wires poked out of the backing like curious worms. The worst part was that whoever had broken in had felt the need to urinate on the front seats. The acrid smell hit my sensitive nostrils like miniature daggers, making me gag.

I stood still for a moment, thinking. This was a problem. I mean, I didn't know how long I was going to have the Audi for and I certainly couldn't drive it home. There was no way I could explain it away to Mum and John - the rich uncle lie wouldn't exactly work. Plus there were far nicer cars lining the street, why choose mine?

The only option I could think of was to drive my new car closer to home, walk the rest of the way and explain that I was trying to keep fit. I'd have to get my car fixed at some point...once I had some money. I guessed I could always eBay some of the clothes.

Still seething, I ground the car to a halt on Trinity Road - a quiet street not too far from my house, but still far enough for me to have calmed down by the time I got home.

Grey terrace houses ran the length of the road on one side. Lining the other was Susurrate forest. The dense trees created a canopy of leaves and thin slices of pale moonlight cut through the darkness.

I pressed the fob and as the car winked goodbye, I prayed it would stay intact. The bitter chill of the evening hit me. I pulled the collar of my jacket up around my neck and headed in the direction of home. In the stillness of the evening, the only sounds I could hear were the faint rustling of the trees and the click of my shoes on the pavement.

Crack!

The sharp sound echoed through the woods. I snapped my head around, staring into the gloomy depths. Every fibre of my body stood on end. My muscles became taught like overstretched chords. The noise stopped abruptly. I stayed frozen in position, scanning the darkness for a source.

A logical thought occurred to me. *It's a forest Alex, probably home to hundreds of harmless animals that could have made that sound.* That relaxed me. I continued walking, opening my bag and rummaging about for my iPod. I'd just finished detangling the earphones from around my textbooks, when I happened to glance back into the forest.

And saw the eyes.

Red eyes. Unnaturally long and angled, burning like coals in the darkness. They shimmered with an intense hatred. Staring at me.

I ran.

My feet pounded against the ground in a frantic drumbeat. The rustling from within the woods grew louder and more forceful as something followed. I could hear the thumps as whatever it was battered past trees. They shook violently, dusting off leaves like flakes of skin. Out of the corner of my eye I saw a thick, black mass darting through the forest and heard the sound of heavy, harsh panting. The ember eyes were always there, flicking in and out of my view, locked on me. The creature was matching my speed.

My heart smashed against my chest, my senses in overdrive. The harsh wind whipped at my face as I sprinted forward. Still it was there, watching, enjoying the chase.

What is it? My mind screamed. *A wolf? Panther? But...red eyes?!* My skin crawled as if someone had walked across my grave.

I threw off my bag and vaguely saw it clatter to the ground, spilling its contents like road kill. The weight change made no difference; I couldn't go any faster. I wasn't fast enough. The road I sprinted down seemed never ending, as if some cruel spell had been cast which meant I would be chased for eternity. Eventually though, I *did* see the end. The road split into a T-junction. The forest had been cut back and ended there. In a manner of seconds, whatever was chasing me would come into full view.

The thought made me want to throw up.

As I shot forward, a deep growl came from the close to my right and I stifled a scream. In that moment a dawning realisation filled me with dread. *Where am I running to? I can't go home. My family!*

So I made a decision. One I would never had considered before. I chose to stand my ground. After all, I had these new abilities. I could handle anything...couldn't I?

At the junction, I split off to the right and spun around so that I was staring into the wall of trees. I clenched my fists into tight balls and tensed my muscles, preparing to fight. Beads of fearful sweat rolled down my neck. The glowing eyes grew larger as the creature neared. Its throaty growl rose in pitch and it let out a demented howl. It was like a cross between a scream and a bark. The sound sliced straight through me and my knees went weak. My heart was in my mouth as the last of the trees twisted out of the way.

The creature pounced out of the darkness.

At the same time something flashed across my line of sight and dived at the black mass. A deep thud echoed around the street and I only caught a glimpse of fur before the creature was shoved back into the forest. It let out an indignant squeal and I heard its teeth chomping together as it tried to bite its attacker.

The two shapes rolled around in the darkness. Trees split and crashed to the ground as the fight intensified. Frozen to the spot, I stared, not sure what was happening or what to do. I got my answer when a voice shot out of the woods.

"Alexander, *run!*"

I didn't need to be told twice. Spinning on my heel, I charged away. Behind me the epic battle continued. The cries of human and animal pain mixed together into a cacophony of agony.

Tears streamed down my face as I ran. I felt tainted, as if the creature's eyes had stared into my very soul.

When I reached home, my hands were shaking so badly I could hardly get a hand into my pocket. The keys jangled together as I rattled them into the lock.

Once again no one was in. Running upstairs, I burst into the bathroom. I jumped into the shower and switched it on, not even stopping to remove any clothes. I slumped down to the tray and as the warm water rushed over my head, wrapped my arms around my legs and cried.

The shower made me feel human again. My sodden clothes were balled up in the washing basket and I was sitting on my bed, trying to get a handle on what had just happened. Something *very* nasty and *very* powerful had come after me. That much was clear. It had managed to keep up with me, which meant it had to have been something with serious speed. A large, feral cat seemed the most logical explanation. I'd heard stories of wild panthers living in England. But the fur I'd glimpsed had been thick and shaggy, more like that of a dog than a cat. And those eyes – a nightmare straight out of a Stephen King novel. Even thinking about them made me shudder.

Then there was the second fact. Something - someone had saved me. They'd called out to me, called out my *name*. So this person knew me…did that mean I knew them too? Everything had happened so fast; I hadn't been able to tell if they were a man or woman. They had run even faster than I could, and the strength they'd attacked the beast with had been incredible. *Is it possible there are others like me?* The thought was both comforting and concerning.

I needed to talk to someone. Confide. Grabbing my phone, I dialled Mikey. It directed straight to voicemail. I swore and dropped the phone onto the bed. I looked down at it again and sucked in a deep breath. My finger had tapped Gabriella's name before I had a chance to talk myself out of it. As the ringing tone filled my ear, I walked around my room, agitatedly picking up random objects and setting them down again.

After several rings, it connected and a slightly breathless voice floated from the speaker.

"Hello?"

"Uh hi Ella, it's Alex."

"Alex! Hi, sorry I was training."

"Oh, if this is a bad time..."

"Not at all. I'm glad you called." She sounded genuinely pleased to hear from me. "How are you?"

"I'm...well actually I'm not too good. It's uh..." I rubbed a hand across my eyes. *What do I say?* "I need to speak to someone – to a friend about something. Are you free later?"

She didn't even pause for a second. "Where do you live?"

I gave her the address.

"I'll be there in half an hour."

The phone disconnected.

*

The doorbell rang and I stopped pacing.

Running downstairs, I swung open the front door. My stomach clenched as Gabriella was revealed. She looked great, even in a baggy Lacoste jumper and jogging bottoms. Her dark hair was pulled into a ponytail, which rested on one shoulder.

Her eyebrows rose as she took in my appearance. "Wow Alex, you look...different!"

"So everyone keeps saying."

We headed upstairs and I told her everything. I demonstrated by straightening the knotted dumbbell out of its pretzel shape. I ended with what had happened on my walk home. When I had finished, I held my breath waiting for her response.

"That's quite a lot to process," was all she said.

"Tell me about it. I'm still trying to get a handle on everything myself."

"So this thing chased you? Are you okay?" She gave my arm a comforting squeeze. The charges were still there.

I nodded. "I think so, just a little shaken up. It could have been worse if that person hadn't saved me."

Gabriella looked thoughtful. "So do you think what happened this evening and what's happening to you in general is connected?"

84

"I think it has to be. I don't see what else could be going on. I mean, that thing was *after* me." I gave a heavy sigh. "I don't know, what do you think?"

"I think you must have been chosen for a reason."

I frowned. "What do you mean?"

Gabriella shifted into a cross-legged position on the bed. "Well, it's like I said to you that day in the park, there's something about you. I noticed it the day we met. It sounds stupid, but I felt sort of drawn to you. Maybe these people - whoever they are, maybe they noticed it to. It could be that these abilities were always inside you, they have just been...unlocked somehow." She gestured a slender hand towards me. "And maybe this animal thing noticed it too. That could be why it singled you out. Or maybe you were just in the wrong place at the wrong time," she added with a smile.

I considered what she was saying and gave a slow nod. "I guess it's possible about the ability thing. But I don't understand why these people don't just come out and talk to me, instead of being super cryptic. I just want to know what's going on. It's driving me crazy!"

It was her turn to nod. "I can imagine. But I guess all you can do is wait until they do; I mean, it's not like you have a choice."

I idly spun my phone between my fingers. "Would you trust them?"

Gabriella sighed. "That's a tough one. It's all very surreal. All I could say is that from what you've told me it seems these people are trying to help you. If they'd wanted to hurt you, they could have done it when they took you. But here you are, better than ever. So I would at least give them the benefit of the doubt."

What Gabriella was saying made sense. Her objective way of looking at the situation somehow made me feel better.

"Maybe I'll give them a chance once they drop the smoke and mirror act," I said with a grin.

Gabriella laughed and swept a strand of stray hair over her ear. All it took was that simple movement and I became very aware that I was a teenager sitting on my bed in an empty house with a beautiful girl. In an instant, I became old Alex again.

Clasping my hands together, I tried to look anywhere other than in her eyes. I could sense her looking at me, the faint lift of a smile tugging at the corners of her lips. *Those soft, perfect lips, which you could lose hours kissing.* The waves of electricity started to buzz underneath my skin.

"Are you okay"? Gabriella asked, clearly sensing the shift in atmosphere.

"I um...yeah I'm cool," I croaked. *I need to change the subject.* "Listen since you're here, do you want to watch a film downstairs or something?"

Her face brightened. "Do you have popcorn?"

"Um, I think so."

She leapt off the bed like an excited child and curtseyed.

"Then I accept your invitation, kind sir."

We were watching a comedy on Satellite, when my family came back. In truth Gabriella was watching the film and I was secretly watching her. The way her eyes crinkled at the corners and tiny dimples appeared on her cheeks when she laughed; it made it hard to breathe. After a while she leaned her head against my shoulder. It made the charges inside me spike, but I wouldn't have moved for the world.

The jingling of keys followed by the familiar sound of three shoes on the hardwood signalled the return of the family. Gabriella's head flicked up, much to my disappointment. A second later, the lounge light clicked on and three sets of surprised eyes stared at us from the doorway.

Mum composed herself first. "Hello there! Now *you* must be the Gabriella Alexander talked about," she gushed, setting a new time record for mortally embarrassing me.

Gabriella didn't seem at all fazed. "That's me," she replied sweetly, standing up and shook her hand. "You must be Elaine. It's really nice to meet you."

Mum beamed. "Well it's a pleasure to meet you too. This is John and Alex's brother, Michael."

"Half-brother," I muttered under my breath.

They all greeted each other. John's eyebrows were lost in his hairline throughout the exchange. Mikey tried to give me a sly wink - which Gabriella noticed and smiled. Then to my complete mortification, they all sat down around us.

What could easily have been a social train wreck ended up actually not being too bad. As I prayed for the ground to swallow me up, my family only asked Gabriella a few questions about herself - which she answered, I noticed, without actually giving much away. My guest certainly knew how to hold a crowd, cracking jokes and making everyone laugh. She also complimented me, explaining how I was the friendliest person she'd met at the Sixth Form and how I'd been looking after her. I went very red in response.

Finally Gabriella announced that she had to leave, and I jumped at the offer to see her out. Out of the corner of my eye, I saw my family nodding their approval.

"Sorry about them," I apologised once we were outside.

"Don't be silly, they're lovely."

"So where are you parked?" I asked, scanning the road for a likely match.

"There," she pointed. I had to stop my jaw from unhinging.

She was gesturing towards a sleek, black motorbike resting at an angle behind a car. An equally black helmet hung on the handlebars, the throttle poking through the open visor.

"That's your bike?"

She laughed. "Well I'm pretty sure I didn't steal it!"

I shook my head. "You are a very interesting person Ella."

"Right back at you Superman," she smiled, patting my chest.

We walked over to the bike and she picked up the helmet, resting it against her hip like a basketball. She started the engine and the pulse of it filled the quiet night.

"Just remember I'm here for you whenever you need me." She leaned in and kissed me on the cheek, causing it to catch fire.

"Thanks."

"I'll see you tomorrow."

She slid the helmet down over her head and jumped onto the bike. I watched as she raced down the road and disappeared around the bend.

I shook my head. *Wow.*

87

Running. I was running for my life. Tearing through the blinding fog, an indescribable terror clawing at my chest.

I turned down endless, identical streets, trying to find somewhere to hide. Grand houses stood protected behind towering metal gates, denying me solace. Behind me, I could sense something approaching. My back prickled as if death's cold hands were inches away. I didn't dare turn my head. I kept going, pressing forward in the desperate hope that I would find a place to hide.

A wooden fence solidified out of the spiralling mist. With a glimmer of hope, I clambered over the top and fell into an overgrown front garden. A house stood ahead, one that once would have outmatched the beauty of those around it, but had long since fallen into disrepair. The numerous windows were boarded up and several ceiling tiles had fallen away, exposing yawning holes. The whole house seemed to sag in on itself, as if it were dying from loneliness. I noticed a crumbling family crest etched into the stone above the front door. It depicted a crescent moon with a pyramid of 3 stars in the centre.

Trembling, I turned back to the fence and pressed an eye to a hole in one of its panels. The fog blanketed the area, swallowing the horizon in all directions. Streetlamps lined the road, their glow turning everything an eerie orange. The long grass where I crouched was wet and the damp spread through my jeans, numbing my knee. I didn't move. I knew that doing so would be suicide. So I kept myself hunched down...waiting and watching, not daring to breathe.

From somewhere in the distance I heard a sound that froze the blood in my veins. Some unfathomable baying from a creature that had no place in this world. It was followed by a thunderous pounding on the pavement. The vibrations swept along the ground, shooting up my body like waves of electricity. The noise was deafening; it sounded like an army of ten thousand approaching, charging in perfect unison. The rough wood scraped against my cheek as I pressed closer to the fence. I was shaking uncontrollably, but I needed to see.

The armour clad creature appeared through the fog like an apparition from Hell. This time it was riding atop the most deformed and horrific beast I had ever seen. It resembled a horse, but was at least twice the size and misshapen. A large, twisted horn protruded from its forehead, contorting downwards at an unnatural angle. Its eyes were two shining red orbs.

Pulsing welts covered its decaying black skin and fleshy tendrils protruded from multiple deep wounds. They flailed around wildly, whipping the air with sharp slashes. Its tangled mane was coated in congealed green slime and thick chains wrapped around the beast's muzzle, cutting raw grooves into its flesh.

As I stared, a sharp pain in my chest reminded me I wasn't breathing. I had no choice but to take a gulp of air. As I did, a sickly sweet smell – like honey coated decay, invaded my nose. It was too much. I twisted and vomited by my feet.

Please god, don't let it have heard me.

My body was a shuddering wreck as I peered back through the gap. Mercifully the creature galloped past my hiding place, the rider never even turning its head in my direction. It was focused on something in the distance, body leaning forward, the rusting metal reins clutched tight in its gauntlets. Rider and steed were enveloped by the fog and vanished from sight as fast as they had appeared.

I stayed as still as a rock, listening as the sound of the beast's booming hooves faded. I breathed a sigh of relief and slumped with my back against the fence. It was only then that I felt the dampness on my cheeks and discovered I was crying. I wiped my hands across my face and screamed.

They were covered in blood.

I woke up. My breath ripped through my lungs in harsh bursts. I detangled myself from the damp sheets and half fell to the floor. The fading remnants of the dream still clung to my mind like cobwebs - images of blood and fear flashed in the darkness. I clawed for the light switch in the gloom, squinting as the room flared up. When my eyes had adjusted, I turned to face the mirror and a second scream caught in my throat.

My eyes were bleeding.

8

I sat on the edge of the bed, feeling unrested and irritable. I lightly slapped my cheeks, trying to liven myself up. After the blood incident, I'd woken up Mikey. He'd sworn a few times and then tried to explain it away. *Maybe some kind of bug? A side effect of my change? Or stress?* His answers had been both random and inane, but simply talking to someone else had made me feel a little better. I'd tried to recount my dream to him, but all I could recall was blood and the awful, suffocating fear. After an hour or so, exhausted from talking, I'd crawled back to my room and sank into bed for an uncomfortable, dreamless sleep.

As I trudged downstairs, the sight of the hallway filled with suitcases made me raise my eyebrows.

Have Mum and John had an argument?

In the kitchen, Mum was standing over the sink. Dishes were caught in a torrent of sloshing water, scourers and soapsuds, before being slammed down on the draining board. John stood to the side, rolling his eyes and drying the abused crockery with a haggard looking tea towel.

Looks like I was spot on.

"Going somewhere?" I asked, pointing a thumb in the direction of the hallway.

John looked up. "Are you taking the piss?"

I stared at him blankly.

He frowned. "Ireland. Connie and Edgar...remember?"

The cogs turned and my brain engaged. My grandparents on Mum's side had moved to Killarney about ten years ago. It was a tradition for us to visit them once a year, just before Christmas. But this year, the only time John could get off work came before Mikey and I broke up from school. Rather than cancel the trip, we'd insisted they go anyway. Secretly I'd been a bit gutted. I liked Connie and Edgar. They were the type of couple that had been together so long, they lived their lives through a series of combined routines. Connie made the bed, Edgar prepared breakfast. Connie poured afternoon tea, Edgar put out the biscuits. Connie fixed dinner, Edgar laid the table. The list went on. Plus, without fail, every morning, they got up at seven and went for a twenty-minute stroll along the beachfront - hand in hand. They relied on each other to make their world revolve. It was heart-warming to see.

I frowned. *Is it really that time already?* I'd been so wrapped up in myself that I hadn't noticed anything else going on around me.

Mum smacked another plate down onto the draining board. A piece chipped off and clattered onto the tiled floor.

"Bloody hell, stop it now Elaine!" John cried out, retrieving the rogue shard.

"What's going on with you two?"

Mum turned to face me. She'd been crying. Her mascara ran down her face in two thick lines. The image reminded me of the night before and I shuddered involuntarily.

John sighed and flopped his tea towel down on the worktop. "As you know we've had this trip planned for some time. But at the last minute, your mother has decided that she no longer wants to go." He glared at his wife. "Isn't that right, Elaine?"

I leaned a hand against the worktop. "Mum, why don't you want to go?"

John folded his arms across his chest. "Because of you Alexander...because of you," he said, chewing on his irritation.

"Me?" I said with genuine surprise.

"Your mother has got it into her head that you need her right now."

"Mum?"

She walked over to me and placed her hands on my arms, leaving a topping of soapsuds. "You've seemed so troubled lately sweetie. Up and down all the time. I just don't think leaving you right now would be the best idea."

I stared at her swimming eyes, trying to work out what she was thinking. *Does this have something to do with what she said the other day?* I couldn't be sure, but I knew for certain that with all these crazy things happening, it would be better to have them both out of harm's way.

91

I shook my head slowly. "Mum you don't need to look after me. I'm fine - better than fine, I'm great! Go enjoy yourselves. Mikey and I are more than capable of surviving on our own." I tried my best to look as serene as Buddha.

"I don't think that-"

"Mum, honestly, nothing's going to happen!" I interrupted.

"But-"

"I'm *fine*. Go!"

"If you're sure..."

"I'm positive. Nan and Granddad will be disappointed if you don't go."

"He's right, Mum," yawned Mikey appearing in the doorway. "Besides, they'll have rota'd you into their day-to-day by now."

"Rostered, sweetie," corrected Mum, as she pulled me into a hug. I glanced over at John, who winked and gave a thumbs up. No doubt thinking of the two weeks of dog tracks and local pubs that were now back on.

The rest of the morning was devoted to the torrent of information, which served as a precursor to any of Mum's trips away: a list of food in the fridge and cupboards, where the emergency money could be found - for food, not alcohol, how to successfully operate the oven, washing machine and dryer, and finally how the neighbours would be watching and would duly report any parties. The latter seemed to be aimed at Mikey, who mumbled a response, rubbing the sleep from his eyes. Mum made me promise that if I needed her at all, I would call immediately and they would cut their trip short. After the fifth round of promises, she seemed convinced. They loaded their bags into John's Lexus, beeped the horn and backed out of the drive. Mum's eyes stayed fixed on me the entire time. Her guilty expression stayed in my memory long after they'd disappeared.

Rubbing my arms against the cold, I turned to go back inside.

And saw my schoolbag.

It sat innocently in the space between the doorstep and hedge like a patient visitor. With a shaking hand, I opened the zip to be greeted by the sight of all my things, which had previously lain scattered over Mason Avenue. I snatched up the bag, clutching it between my arms like a baby and scanned the street for signs of elusive Samaritans.

Nothing.

The next few days were crazy free. Mikey and I got to and from school without being attacked by any demented creatures. The new car remained in one piece. I had no disturbing nightmares...that I remembered anyway. I certainly didn't weep any more blood. Mikey and I developed a kind of camaraderie over the whole situation and he always looked a little disappointed when I had no new news for him.

Lunchtimes were shared with Gabriella and Tim. Once he'd got over her looks and could string words beyond my phone number together in her presence, we got on well as a trio. Meanwhile I'd become a bit of a talking point. Other students were intrigued by the new and confident, Audi-driving Alex. I went from being a nobody to a blip on their radars. When I walked down the corridors, those coming in the other direction moved out of my way, instead of ploughing through as if I didn't exist. Others gave the slightest nod in the hallways. I moved from the reject seats in History to the middle. In English and science, there were suddenly more people on my row. I had received a social promotion. No longer a bottom feeder, I'd evolved into a respectable sized fish. There were no delusions on my part. I knew everything could be attributed to superficial improvements and a certain girl I hung around with. But I'd have been lying if I said I didn't enjoy it. I'd spent so much of my life living on the outside; it felt good to walk on the other side of the fence.

My only remaining problem had a skinhead and drank too much. I hadn't bumped into Terry for several days. This meant I was overdue a run in. No doubt TJ would have informed him of my unacceptable behaviour in Physics class, and no doubt Terry was itching to beat an apology out of me. But this time, if he tried, things were going to end differently. I was tired of playing the victim.

Friday morning, the school had an air of the approaching weekend to it and everyone seemed to carry a relaxed vibe around with them. Students leaned against lockers and chatted away, bright looks filling their faces. First years sat around, wired into iPods and handheld gaming consoles, until stern looking teachers came and collected them up. Girls gossiped in small circles, giggling in unison. As I made my way in, people I barely recognised smiled at me. I returned the gestures, submitting to the good atmosphere. I lounged through my History lecture, doodling on my folder as Mrs Carter droned on. I could feel Grace glance at me every now and then. I slipped out my phone and text her a smiley face, just for the hell of it. She sent me one back with a tongue poking out and an x. A landmark - the first electronic kiss I'd ever received from anyone other than Mum. I smiled and put the phone back in my pocket.

A surprise test dumped me back into reality. Taking the sheet, I groaned. I hadn't been listening to a word Mrs Carter had been going on about. But to my surprise, when I flipped over the sheet I found I could answer all the questions without so much as the briefest second to ponder what the answer could be. It was as though my brain had automatically soaked in all the information and could retrieve it as easily as my own name. I left the class with my high spirits still firmly intact.

At my locker, as I changed my History textbook for '*Rebecca*', I turned my head to see Richard and Elliot walking in my direction.

"Hey, Alex!" Richard said, shaking my hand. Elliot clapped me on the shoulder.

"Hey guys, what's up?" I said, unzipping my bag and dropping the novel inside.

"The usual, full day and then footie training," said Elliot.

"Kill me now," groaned Richard as he opened a locker near mine. The inside was adorned with pictures of sporting legends and supermodels. He pulled out a Geography textbook, before turning back to face me. "Anyway, glad we caught you. What are you doing tonight?'

My social calendar was a shameful block of white.

"Um, nothing really, was going to chill. How come?" I asked.

Elliot leaned in close, like he was about to share a secret. "Some of the footie lads are heading to Bakoo tonight. Gonna be sweet mate, loads of fit birds. What you sayin'?"

I paused, processing the invitation. I literally couldn't remember the last time someone other than Tim had asked me to do something outside of school. Now I was being invited to a social interaction, with the *football guys*. This was a big deal.

"Sounds good," I said.

"Cool, so we're meeting at the Pheasant at nine for a couple of pints then heading down after. Make sure you wear shoes and a shirt or you won't get in yeah?"

The bell rang for class. Richard slammed his locker shut and spun the combination.

"Can I bring some people?" I asked as they were leaving.

"Sure mate, the more the merrier," said Elliot "See you tonight."

We parted ways and I headed for English with my spirits climbing even higher. I knew exactly who I was going to ask.

"I can't, I'm sorry," Gabriella said as she took her seat next to me. "I've got a family thing I can't get out of."

My emotions crashed like the Hindenburg. It was amazing how much of an effect she could have on me. "No worries," I mumbled, trying to act like it didn't matter. I flipped open my folder and scribbled the date.

"How about Saturday?" she asked.

My heart tripped up. "Sorry?"

"Why don't we do something together on Saturday instead? Like go into Central London maybe?" She gave a mischievous grin and nudged me. "If you're not too hungover that is."

It took me all of about 3 milliseconds to agree that it sounded like a brilliant idea.

"Great, I'll pick you up from yours about twelveish."

My hand instinctively pressed against the car keys nestled in my jacket pocket. Maybe this was an opportunity to impress her. "Let me pick you up instead. Where do you live?"

Gabriella went silent for a second. "I've got some errands to run in the morning, so you can grab me from outside that chip shop at twelve. That's okay right?" She gave me a look that suggested this was as good a compromise as she was willing to make.

"Sure," I replied, just as Mr Hanley wheezed his large frame into the classroom and deposited his gelatinous mass onto the chair.

"Okay, settle down people. Let's get this story underway."

*

As if my thoughts of a run in with Terry had tempted fate, he appeared at the end of the school day. Mikey and I were chatting away as we descended the main steps. I'd just finished telling him about my social invitations for the weekend. He congratulated me and confessed that he could now go to a friend's house party guilt free.

"Watch out for the neighbours," I warned with a smile. "If they're anything like ours, the police will be there within ten minutes."

"Bloody curtain twitchers," he said, and we both laughed.

It was then that I heard my name being bellowed in the fading light. I turned towards the main gates, to the source of the noise. Other people milling about stopped to look too.

I saw a thundering mass of fury marching its way towards me.

As soon as I realised who it was, I felt the rage bubble in my stomach like someone had turned up the heat. Mikey gripped my arm and stared at me. "Leave it Alex, he's scum."

I shook his hand off, speaking through gritted teeth. "This bastard has been making my life hell for too long."

"Oi Eden I want a word wiv you!" Terry growled as he neared. The electric crackle of an impending fight gathered the observers into a crowd.

"I've got your back," Mikey whispered.

Warmed for a second by his allegiance, I shook my head regardless and nudged him behind me. "This is a problem I need to deal with by myself."

"EDEN!"

"What do you want, Terry?" I said as calmly as I could manage when he finally reached me. The air was invaded with the foul stench of stale cigarettes. Terry was clearly very angry. His eyebrows were dipped into a dark V. Lips pulled into a

96

cracked little line. Hands coiled into tight fists. He was working himself up into a rage. Unfortunately for him, I was fuelling a rage of my own.

He pointed a finger at me, which I had to resist snapping off right then and there. "You tried to act all hard man with TJ. Big mistake." He grinned, exposing his nicotine stained teeth. "You think that having a little pansy makeover and some new friends is gonna stop me from kicking the crap out of you?"

There were at least forty people watching now. None dared to move for fear of affecting the outcome of the confrontation.

"Oh just do one Terry!" barked Mikey, folding his arms across his chest.

"Shut it bitch, or I'll batter you too!"

Mikey moved forward. "Come on then! I'm not scared of you!"

I gently pushed him back for the second time.

Looking at Terry, my hatred overflowed into every pore of my body. My skin bristled with it. In front of me stood the bully who'd made me scared to come to school. The man who'd humiliated me and made it unacceptable to be my friend. For no reason, he had singled me out above all others and made my life a living hell. And to top it off, he had the audacity to threaten Mikey, my half...no my *brother*.

Enough was enough.

But unlike Terry, I was reasonable. Trying to control the anger in my voice, I spoke loud enough for everyone to hear. "I think Mikey has a good point. If you walk away, that's the end of it all. You leave me alone and I'll leave you alone. Otherwise what happens next is on you."

Terry laughed. A dark, dirty noise, which rumbled from his chest then exploded into the air. He tilted his head back and I watched as his body shook from it. When he finished he wiped a pretend tear from his eye. "I'm sorry but that was too funny." His eyes narrowed. "You're going to wish you were dead mate."

I cast one last look at Mikey, who gave a shrug, which clearly meant, 'Screw it, kick his head in.'

And with that Terry exploded a fist towards me. Without thinking, I put my hand out, palm first. The two connected with a fleshy slap and his hand jerked to a stop like a dart in a wall.

Terry's eyes bulged as he realised what had happened. He tried to yank his fist back, but I held on - my grip as tight as a lion's jaw on a gazelle's neck.

"This is the hand you like to hit people with, isn't it?" I said through gritted teeth. I stared right into his eyes as I squeezed against his fist as hard as I could. The air was filled with a sound similar to dry twigs snapping, followed by an inhuman scream. Terry's bones crumbled like old biscuits.

The crowd gasped.

He dropped to his knees, frantically clawing at my closed fist in a futile attempt to prise my steel fingers from his shattered hand. I yanked him up and kneed him in the stomach just hard enough to wind him, like he'd done to me so many times before. Grunting, he folded over and I switched my grip from his crushed hand and seized him by the collar, wrapping the other around the base of his jacket.

"Not so fun being on the receiving end is it?" I spat into his ear.

With a tug, I lifted him right off his feet and spun around. Nearby were rows of bikes padlocked to a low rail. I ran forward and ground to a halt, launching Terry at the bikes. He sailed through the air and clattered headfirst against them. Bully and bikes collapsed into a pile of spokes and gears. Terry made pitiful moans as he rolled about on the heap, cupping his broken hand.

My breath was ragged as I stared unbelieving at the scene in front of me.

I just beat up Terry.

All eyes were on me. I breathed out hard and when I spoke, my voice was shaking. "You all saw right? He started this."

There were murmurs of agreement from the crowd as people woke up from their roles as observing statues. Someone shouted "He deserved it!" from within the masses. With a shaking finger, I pointed at a young kid with a Mohawk and un-tucked shirt.

"You got a mobile phone?"

He nodded.

"Okay, call an ambulance. I'm going home."

9

That evening, after the hype of my fight with Terry had died down; I focused on getting myself ready for the night out. My stomach buzzed with excitement. Soulfire pounded from my computer speakers at full volume and several different shirts lay strewn across my bed.

My phone vibrated on the desk. It was Tim replying to a text I'd sent earlier, inviting him out.

Well up for it mate! I'll be at urs in bout an hour.

Tim arrived armed with a shopping bag full of lager cans. He bounded up to my room and sank down on the desk chair. Mikey came in to say hi and Tim pulled some beers out of the bag. He threw one to each of us, then cracked a third open himself. He took a long pull from the beer and set it on the side. I opened mine; the beer was warm but tasted pretty good.

"So, any gossip?" he asked, resting his arms over the back of the chair. Mikey and I exchanged a look.

"You could say that," laughed my brother.

Tim straightened up. "Serious? Like what?"

"Rocky here beat Terry to a pulp."

Tim's jaw dropped. "Shut up, no way!"

Mikey gestured towards me and I nodded, trying not to smile. Maybe I should have felt more remorse for what I'd done, but I simply didn't. Terry was a truly vile human being who revelled in my misery. Now he wouldn't be bothering anyone else in a hurry. There were of course potential backlashes due to his dad being who he was, but I'd decided I would cross that bridge when I came to it.

"It's true," I smiled.

Tim took a second to shake the confusion from his head. Then he stood up and gave me a hi-five. "Yes! Alex, you legend! I am so happy right now. That guy is *such* a dick. I want a full breakdown - spare nothing!"

So I told him what had happened. He gasped and winced at the right time in his usual theatrical way. Afterwards he held out his can towards me. I tapped mine against it.

"Here's to standing up to dickheads all over the world!"

Downstairs, I put a couple of pizzas in the oven and slipped thirty pounds out of the emergency money jar, giving Mikey the remaining half.

"Looks like someone has finally grown a set of balls," he said with a smile.

*

The taxi dropped us all off on the road leading to the house party. I could hear the steady boom of music as soon as I opened the car door. The party was only a few minutes from town, so we said goodbye to Mikey and started walking in the opposite direction.

"So, Gabriella out tonight?" asked Tim pulling the collar of his jacket up around his neck.

I felt the familiar stab of emotions at the mention of her name. "No, she has some family thing going on."

He made a disapproving noise. "You would have been the centre of attention with her on your arm."

"Tim, she wouldn't have been anywhere near my arm. It's not like that."

He made a sarcastic sound. "Sure mate, whatever."

Ahead of us, I could see the bustling life of Friday night Chapter Hill. In the evenings, the place shed its casual town vibe and pulled on a seedy big city coat of bright lights and thumping music. Groups of underage teenagers hung out near off licences, drinking from cider bottles wrapped in paper bags and dragging on badly rolled cigarettes. Drunk patrons talked loudly outside pubs and bars, and yelled at women who wobbled past in miniskirts and tall heels.

We headed for the Pheasant, stopping shy of the old style door. Tim pulled a cigarette out of a pack in his shirt pocket and sparked it up. Thick trails of smoke climbed into the air. He offered me one, but I raised a hand. He shrugged and took a deep drag before continuing his argument.

"Regardless of what you say, I think Gabriella has a soft spot for you."

The idea made me smile, even if it was one that I didn't truly believe. I got the impression it was more of a wounded puppy scenario; she felt that I needed looking after. Still it was an amazing thought. Just thinking about the possibility made my stomach do somersaults.

"Maybe," I shrugged in an effort to appease him.

After Tim had smoked his cigarette, he dropped it to the ground and crushed it under his boot heel. As we headed inside, I noticed with a sigh of relief that there were no bouncers to deny me entry.

The interior looked like any other English pub. A long wooden bar lined one side, manned by bar staff in black shirts. The opposite was home to tables and chairs as well as cracked leather sofas. Gambling machines stood huddled in the far corner, winking and whistling like shady con artists hoping to dazzle patrons into giving away their money. The pub had no music, instead dozens of voices mixed together, producing a hum of friendly sound. Richard, Elliot and a good chunk of the football team were already drinking at the bar. Richard saw us enter and walked over. He draped his beer-arm around my shoulders.

"Lads, can I have your attention please!" he shouted.

The rest of the crowd turned to face us. Confused, I turned to Tim, who gave an 'I don't know either' expression.

"Let's hear it for Alex Eden, Chapter Hill's very own Chuck Norris!"

There was a roar of cheering from the football guys and beers were held skyward. I felt my face flush. *Guess they heard then.*

Richard ushered me towards the bar. "Two of your finest lagers please mate," he said to the barman, who rolled his eyes in response and poured two Fosters.

The conversation flowed as freely as the alcohol. Word had spread like an epidemic about my fight with Terry. Everyone wanted the inside scoop. The guys crowded around as I recounted the story, making sure to downplay the part where I had crushed his hand with mine. They made approving noises and cheered at each key point. It appeared that no one actually *liked* Terry. Instead it seemed most people had been too scared to stand up to him. My actions had burst the fear bubble.

My encounter was a cue for others to recount stories of idiotic things Terry and his gang had done. I laughed so hard I had to grip the bar to stop myself falling over. The beers kept pouring and the good atmosphere carried on.

On my way to the toilet, I noticed the one person not enjoying himself. Andrew Pearson glowered at me from a table near the back corner. His girlfriend, Leila Riches was busy talking to him, but he didn't alter his focus. When I emerged from the bathroom a few minutes later, he still hadn't changed position. He simply rolled his half-empty pint on its axis and glared.

Looks like he heard about Terry too, I thought as I made my way back to the group. I couldn't have cared less.

After four more beers and a couple of shots - none of which I paid for - we left the Pheasant and headed for Bakoo. Richard suggested we stagger our arrival. Apparently bouncers often turned away large groups of guys. I had no clue about nightclub etiquette.

Tim and I joined the back of the queue first. I leaned against the wall. My head was starting to feel woolly; all my thoughts had to wade through water.

A group of girls tottered past us. One of them leaned towards me. "Wake up darlin' I'll be expecting a snog later!" Her words were followed by a cackle of drunken laughter as the group moved on.

"You okay?" asked Tim, inspecting me with a squinted eye as he drained another cigarette.

I sighed. "Yeah I'm fine. I'm a bit of a lightweight if I'm honest."

Understatement of the decade.

I'd only ever been drunk once before in my life. At a barbeque Mum and John had hosted in Birmingham. I'd sat in a corner of the garden alone all night, nursing my contemporary woes with several bottles of cider. Nowadays the very smell of the stuff made me want to chuck.

"Total lightweight," laughed Tim. "Well you better suck it up or we won't be getting in."

102

I waved a heavy hand. "I'll be fine, don't worry."

We moved up the steps to the front of the queue and I scanned the doormen. One, a stocky black guy looked like he won UFC championships in his spare time. The other, a fat bald man, had a bright orange beard and a metal rod speared through the middle of his nose. To top off the look, he had the word hate tattooed across both knuckles. If these were the guys Tim's friends Baz and Kel had picked a fight with, then they were two very stupid people indeed.

We reached the front and the biker bouncer frowned at me. I waited for him to turn me away, the typical result of every attempt I'd ever made to enter any drinking establishment before tonight. I sucked in a mouthful of air and stared back. For a moment, we were two predatory animals, sizing each other up in the wild, deciding which one was the alpha. Then he gave a slight nod, lifted the rope barrier and ushered Tim and me inside.

"It's a fiver," he grunted. "Pay on the left."

I let my breath out with a whoosh as we paid. A pretty Asian girl in the cloakroom stamped my hand, letting her fingers linger on mine for a beat too long. She smiled as I turned to move into the club.

Tim gave me a nudge. "Looks like you're going to be on it tonight mate!"

I wasn't really sure exactly what 'on it' meant, but I got the gist.

"I hope so."

As we opened the door into the main club, the bassline hit me like a punch to the stomach. Lasers shone a kaleidoscope of colours in a dozen directions. Ahead, a walkway led to a sunken dance floor where a DJ stood in a suspended box, like a musical judge. Granite topped bars ran either side of us. On the far right, giant glass doors opened into a smoking area, where circular wooden tables glowed red underneath suspended electrical heaters. Tall umbrellas protected the huddled smokers from the elements.

The club was busy, but not packed. Everywhere I looked girls were laughing and dancing. Their sequined dresses and bright jewellery winked in the lasers like shards of sunlight. In

103

every direction I turned, people had smiles on their faces. Girls screamed as their friends arrived. Guys did manly hugs or hi-fived and navigated towards the bar.

So this is what I've been missing.

To me it seemed both incredible and ridiculous at the same time. Either way, I was going to embrace for the night at the very least.

I turned to Tim. "Bar?"

"You read my mind."

The rest of the football lads trickled into the club. One by one they marched to the bar.

Then the real drinking began.

I was introduced to the disastrous combination of Vodka and Red Bull, which hit my head like a brick. It was followed by shots of Jäger and beers.

I was just starting my third Vodka and discussing with Tim why my History teacher got on my nerves, when a girl sidled up to me. Tim nodded behind me and I spun around, almost knocking my drink into her. It was Grace. She'd curled her hair; it hung in cute ringlets around her pretty, heart shaped face. She gave me a hug and planted a gloss-coated kiss on the cheek.

"Alex, how are you babe?" she said in my ear.

I nodded and yelled over the music. "Good thanks. Well a bit drunk actually."

She smiled. "I think that's the idea!"

With a pink and white tipped finger, she pointed towards the dance floor. I turned to see her friends - the ones who'd giggled when she'd spoken to me for the first time. They were all grinding their bodies in time to the music and sneaking occasional glances in our direction.

"Want to come dance with us?" she asked.

I felt a sudden wave of panic.

"I um...I'm not a very good dancer," I confessed.

"So?" she laughed, "It's not a very good song. Come on!"

Before I could protest, she took my hand in hers and dragged me towards the dance floor. I shot Tim a pleading look. He gave an understanding nod and rounded up the others. Drinks in hand, they abandoned the bar like a flock of birds, heading to the dance floor. Grace led me to the middle and her friends closed in around us. My heart hammered at the thought of making an idiot of myself - that or the Red Bull. I couldn't tell.

"Let's see your stuff, Alex," she laughed, as she moved easily and fluidly to the deep thump of a dubstep song. I tried to watch how other guys were doing it.

Then I shut my eyes and went for it.

Trying to feel the music, I waited until each drop of base. When it hit, I moved a body part in a particular direction. I kept my movements jerky at the start and then rolled them into a smoother action as the base lifted.

I opened my eyes. No one was laughing at me. In fact, I noticed that I was a bit better than a lot of the other guys.

"Not bad," Grace chuckled in my ear.

The two groups mixed together and we all made a large circle, moving to the music. And then something I didn't expect at all happened.

Grace kissed me.

She grabbed my waist as I was dancing and pulled me towards her. Our lips connected and she raked her fingers through my hair. Her tongue pushed gently into my mouth and wrapped around mine. It was a strange sensation, but one I could happily get used to. Around me, I could hear the lads cheering. After a minute she pulled away and gave me a foxy smile.

"That wasn't bad either," she whispered. Running a finger along my lip she nodded towards the bar. "I need a drink. I'll be back in a minute okay?"

I stared dumbly at her.

"Okay," she laughed and squeezed my waist. Then Grace and her entourage tottered off the dance floor, leaving me with my mouth open, having received my first real kiss. The lads slapped my back and Tim held out his drink. Coming around, I laughed and chinked my glass with his, then carried on dancing. With Grace gone, other girls closed in. All of a sudden I was a trophy to be won at any cost. Girls I had never met passed me around like a toy, draping their feminine arms around my shoulders and pressing their made up faces against my cheeks, as the bright flashes of cameras made spots appear in my eyes.

Drunk. Very drunk. *Head pounding.*

When I shut my eyes everything spun around very fast. I'd been sick in the toilet three times. Grace had gone home after I'd made a special promise to text her. I was propped up against the bar, drinking water from a big glass. Tim was with me. I liked Tim. Tim was a good friend. He'd given me a cigarette, when I asked. *Strange, I don't normally smoke.*

I gave Tim a hug to show him how much I liked him. He patted my back.

"I think it's time you went home now mate. You need to sleep it off."

What a silly thing to say! I'm having fun! Silly Tim.

I tried to tell him he was wrong, but my legs flopped and I fell over. My friend Tim caught me and propped me back up.

What a good friend! Tim is such a good friend! Maybe I should go home.

"I'm hungry!" I announced.

Tim nodded. "That's cool, let's grab your coat. We'll go eat then find you a taxi."

"Chicken?" I asked, hoping for chicken.

Tim laughed. "Yes Alex, we can get chicken. Let's go."

"What about the people?" I asked, thinking of the people.

"It's fine. I told them you'd be going home."

"I like them. But - you - are - my - best - friend," I said poking his chest, "I love you mate." I hugged him again to show him that I loved him and he patted my back again.

"That's why I want you to stay," I added.

I stared at my watch, which was nice and chunky. The hands were blurry. I held it under Tim's nose.

"It's half twelve, Alex."

"Half twelve! See, I'm not letting you leave. No. You stay. Have fun. I'll grab a chicken after some taxi. No wait…"

"Honestly, I don't mind-"

"No," I interrupted. I will be fine Timothy Clement Matheson. That is a lot of M's and T's. I will get a chicken and taxi. I'm not ten, I'll be fine." I patted his chest and pointed over there. "Go, fun!"

He narrowed his eyes. "Are you sure you'll go straight home after eating?"

I nodded, which made me feel sick. "Yeeeesss, I am giving you my widest promise."

I gave Tim one more hug and left him. I staggered through the door. I got my coat from the Asian coat lady who was pretty and smelled of soap. She gave me her number, even though I didn't ask, which was fun. It took me a long time to get my arms in the holes of my jacket. I kept hitting the wall.

I wandered up the street and saw people I wanted to talk to. They told me to go away because I was drunk. So I fell over.

I saw a place that sold kebabs. Lots of people were outside, eating food from paper bags.

"Chicken?" I asked a girl who looked as if a clown had put on her makeup with his elbow. She stared at me blankly. I pointed towards the door and repeated the question louder.

"Yeah sure," she shrugged.

I told her she looked as if a clown had put on her makeup with his elbow. She slapped me. It didn't hurt. I was strong now.

I bought chicken wings, which tasted nice. Then not so nice. I threw up against a post box. Afterwards, I staggered to an alleyway and gulped down two bottles of water whilst leaning against the wall. Shutting my eyes, I prayed for the drunkenness to go away.

It's not fun anymore.

For a long while I stayed in that position. Gradually things began to grow clearer. Like an island appearing in the foggy sea, sobriety appeared on the horizon. I drained the remnants of my water into my parched mouth.

"EDEN!"

I opened my eyes and saw TJ blur into focus. He was blocking the entrance to the alleyway.

Holding a wooden baseball bat.

I snapped to attention in an instant.

"I thought so!" he sneered and stalked into the opening. "I've been looking for you."

"What do you want, Thomas?" I asked, trying to remain calm, but already the familiar rage was rising, overtaking the surprise of seeing him. It boiled under the surface.

Not twice in one day...it's too much. I'd only wanted to have fun with my new friends. *This isn't fair.*

"Andrew told me what you did to Terry. How you've been boasting about it. You must hav' got lucky." He slapped the bat against his palm menacingly. "You ain't gonna get lucky twice."

I looked behind me. The alleyway ran behind the shops that lined the high street. The far wall was fronted by a dozen dustbins and broken wooden pallets. The top coated in razor wire.

A dead end. Nowhere to run.

I put up my hand trying to appease TJ, but he swatted it away.

"Listen," I continued regardless, "I don't want to fight you. I don't deserve any of this. Just leave me alone..." I paused, "...Please."

A jeering smirk slid across his sour face. "Haha look at you, you're brickin' it! It's so pathetic! I can't wait to break your ribs." He stepped backwards and raised the bat over his shoulder like a baseball player. My drunkenness had vanished, replaced by keen alertness and the rage. It grew inside me like before, but fuelled by alcohol it felt darker. Primal. So much so, it frightened me. With Terry I'd known what was happening, but this time it felt like it was taking me over.

"Listen to me," I warned, my voice shaking from the fury brimming just below the surface. "You have to leave now. I can't control myself. You're going to get really hurt!"

Confusion clouded TJ's face. This was not the pleading he'd clearly expected. "Control yourself? What are you going on about? God you're such a freak!"

The fury spewed to the surface like a raging volcano.

"I AM NOT A FREAK!"

I shot out my fist as TJ swung the bat. The two collided and there was a tremendous crack as the wood splintered over my knuckles. The jagged pieces clattered to the floor. TJ cried out in shock and recoiled. I paced forward and exploded my fist again. It smashed against the side of his face and I felt his cheekbone shatter. He screamed and clutched his damaged face. But I wasn't done. I grabbed his shirt and spun him around, shoving him further into the alleyway. He flew back at least six feet, sprawling over a dustbin and landing awkwardly on his back. He scrambled to his feet and tried to dart past me to escape, but he might as well have been crawling. I seized him by the neck and hurled him into the wall. His nose burst in an explosion of claret. He was sobbing now, the tears mixing with blood. He doubled over and raised his hands, begging for me to stop. It was no use, I couldn't. All I could think about were all the times I'd been humiliated. All the times I'd been used as a punching bag by Terry and his gang - including this blubbering wretch. I drove a fist into his ribs. He spiralled to the floor and I started to kick him. He wailed in response. I kicked him again and again. His bones cracked from the hammering of my foot. I was screaming, a demented sound of fury and anguish, which filled my ears and drowned out his cries of mercy. I kicked him in the face, stomach, legs, back, anywhere I could connect. He had rolled into a ball and made thick distraught sounds with every impact. Again and again and again. Eventually, the fury started to drain away, like a receding wave. I stopped kicking and bent over, sucking in mouthfuls of air. Everything was silent. Only the dull thud of the nightclub could be heard in the distance.

The rage disappeared; retreating into whatever pit it had sprung from. Then I was left with the utter horror of what I had done. TJ was a crumpled mass, lying in a pool of his own blood. My eyes went wide with fear as I looked at his broken, abused body.

"Oh my god, what have I done?" I gasped and leaned over him, pressing my fingers against his neck. It was slick with blood. They kept slipping off the skin. Eventually I managed to keep them in position long enough to check for a pulse.

I couldn't find one.

I withdrew my shaking, blood-drenched hand and covered my mouth.

"Oh no. Please no!"

I backed away from TJ's body, stumbling over trash bags and fled from the backstreet. I almost collided with a couple who were kissing passionately and heading into the alleyway. I staggered past them and sped towards home, keeping my head down in case someone recognised me. A few seconds later I heard the girl's piercing scream.

I ran as fast and as hard as I could. My mind was blurry, my temples pounding. The voice in my head just kept repeating *He's dead! He's dead! Oh god, I killed him!* Tears flowed down my face, I could feel them edging down my cheeks, warm compared to the whipping wind that clawed my skin as I shot forwards.

When I reached the house, I raised a trembling hand to the lock and fell through the door. The house was quiet. My legs felt like jelly as I mounted the stairs. *Why did I hit him so hard? Why didn't I stop?* I knew how strong I was. What did I think would have happened? *Oh no, what have I done?*

I kept waiting for the wail of police sirens. In my mind I saw dozens of squad cars weaving their way towards my house, blue lights blazing. I hesitated on the landing, not sure whether to go to my room or call Mikey and tell him what I'd done. I was so scared.

Sweat clung to my hand as I opened the door to my room.

The lights were out and the curtains drawn. The room was shrouded in darkness. I was completely blind, but I could sense something. My breath caught in my throat as I realised that someone was in the room with me.

"Who's there?" I whispered into the abyss.

No answer.

My hand fumbled for the light switch. After a few seconds I found it and pressed. The result was blinding and it took a few seconds for my eyes to adjust. When they did I gasped. Sitting on my desk, arms folded, was Gabriella.

"Hello Alexander," she said. Her voice was eerily devoid of emotion.

"Ella, what's going on? How did you get in here?"

"Not important," she retorted.

"I don't know what you want, but I can't handle this right now. Something really bad has happened."

She slammed her hand down onto the desk, making me jump.

"Why the hell do you think I'm here damn it?" she hissed through clenched teeth.

Vaulting off the desk, she marched towards me, finishing a few centimetres from where I stood. Sweet Ella was gone and the powerful force I'd witnessed on the football pitch was back. I recoiled instinctively, pressing my back against the wall.

"You stupid *idiot*!" she spat, her eyes brimming with fire. "You know how strong you are. Hell, you showed off to me about it. What were you thinking, beating TJ within an inch of his life?"

My jaw fell open. "H-how could you know about that, I literally just came from-"

"I know everything!" Gabriella blazed, cutting me off. She stormed over to the other side of the room and threw up her hands in exasperation. Turning back to me her tone was softer but still flecked with anger. "All I can say is you're lucky he didn't die."

Her words sank in.

"He...he isn't dead?"

Gabriella sighed. "No he isn't dead, thank god. We got to him in time. If you'd killed him we'd have much bigger problems. As it stands, he's going to be okay. Luckily, we managed to keep it contained. Everything would be so much more difficult if we had unconnected police crawling around us."

My eyes went wide and my throat dried up. "Keep it contained? We...unconnected? What are you talking about?"

Her eyes flashed up at mine. "Are you really that stupid? The car accident? Beating up Terry in front of two-dozen witnesses and now this? Aren't you a little surprised there have been no repercussions to any of it?"

Finally it dawned on me. "Gabriella, are you a part of all of this?" I croaked. "Do you know what's happening to me?"

She nodded, her face solemn. "Yes."

The room started to spin. I couldn't take any more. I felt like I was going to pass out. The words slipped out of my mouth, barely a whisper.

"Gabriella... please...tell me what's going on."

Concern flashed across her face and she sighed.

"Okay, Alex. It's time you knew everything. But I'm not going to tell you...I'm going to show you."

PART II

CHOSEN

10

W hat time is it?" Gabriella barked.

I looked at my watch. "It's almost one," I said quietly. I was still pressed against the wall, beads of sweat trickling down my forehead. I couldn't think straight. It felt as if the thread that held my world together was coming loose.

"Good, there shouldn't be any trains then."

"Trains?" I managed to ask.

Gabriella shot me a glance that suggested I be quiet. Grabbing my arm, she pulled me into the bathroom and pointed to the sink. "Clean yourself up. You look a complete state," she ordered.

I turned to the mirror and heaved. My mouth and chin were smeared with TJ's blood. My knuckles were coated in it. I froze, staring at the fallout of my actions.

"Alex!" hissed Gabriella.

Her voice snapped me back into action. I washed the evidence off my mouth and hands, watching as the blood diluted into a pale pink under the flowing tap. Shaking, I shut off the water and dried myself with a towel.

"Come on," commanded the girl with the answers.

Together we slipped quietly down the stairs and out the front door.

"We need to head for the tube station," she said.

I followed her down the road a little way, where her bike stood parked.

"Get on the back."

I obeyed without a single argument. I felt numb. Gabriella was the key to it all. *Why didn't I see it before?* I'd known from the start that something was up with this girl, how had I failed to connect the dots? The answer was glaringly obvious. I'd been blinded by her beauty.

As I put my arms around her waist, I laughed humourlessly to myself. I would have killed for the chance to ride together on

116

her bike. Now I nearly had and felt nothing but sick to my stomach.

Gabriella kicked the bike into life and we surged down the road. Parked cars blurred into trees and shops as we sped into town. The bike slowed as we neared the alleyway where I'd... I didn't want to think about it.

I noticed with shock that the alleyway was completely empty. There was no evidence that anything had happened at all. The bins had been tidied and the bloodstained concrete had been cleaned. TJ was gone. Those around acted as if nothing had happened. They ate food from kebab shops, chatted and smoked in drunken bliss.

There were no police in sight. No crime scene tape. No crying witnesses.

Nothing.

Gabriella twisted the accelerator and we sped up again, climbing the hill towards the north part of town, where the tube station was situated. We arrived at the station and I clambered off the bike. My guide stepped off afterwards, killing the ignition and pocketing the keys.

"Do you think it'll be safe here?" I asked, nodding to the bike.

She gave me a glowering stare. "Who the hell cares?"

The tube station was closed - a black gate pulled barring the entrance. Gabriella gestured towards it. "Would you like to do the honours?" she said humourlessly.

"Ella, I don't think we should be breaking in here. It's illegal."

She shot me a cold glance. "Yeah maybe we should just stick to GBH."

I winced.

"Fine, I'll do it then."

Gabriella glanced around to make sure no one was looking. This part of town mainly consisted of supermarkets and car showrooms, so was pretty dead at this time of night. Just a handful of drunks stumbled past, cans of beer clutched in their hands. When they'd vanished from sight, she positioned herself in front of the barrier. Stretching her arms wide for greater coverage, she yanked hard against the gate. With a scream it snapped off its hinges and into her hands. She placed the entire thing against the adjacent wall. My expression must have been one complete shock, because she laughed.

"Oh come on Alexander, did you *really* think you were the only one?"

We went inside and hopped over deactivated barriers.

Leading the way, Gabriella headed in the direction of the platform. We descended a few flights of concrete steps and jumped more barriers. When we reached the platform, I took her arm.

"What now?" I asked.

"We keep going," she stated in a matter of fact tone and jumped down onto the track. My heart lurched in response.

"Are you insane?" I hissed. "You're going to get yourself killed!"

Gabriella glared at me. "Alexander, for the love of god get down here!"

I stayed perfectly still, wondering if she had actually lost her mind. She put her hands on her hips impatiently.

"You want to know what's going on, right?"

I stayed on the spot for a few more moments, thinking. *I need to know.*

I nodded.

"Then stop being such a baby and get down here."

So against my better judgment, I lowered myself onto the tracks and followed Gabriella. We ran between the rails for what seemed like forever. Eventually the tube went underground. I could feel the track sloping under my feet as we entered the yawning black mouth. We were plunged into complete darkness, but that didn't seem to bother my guide.

"Take my hand," she said without breaking her stride. I closed my palm around hers and felt the familiar crackle along with a harsh tug as she surged forward, pulling me along.

Incredibly, not long after, my eyesight seemed to adjust to the dense darkness and things grew clearer. Not a huge amount, but enough that I could make out the track and tunnel walls.

Ahead I saw the dim light of a station platform. As we reached it, Gabriella slowed. "We need to get out here and change to another platform," she informed me. I followed her, leaping up onto the platform with surprising ease. The platform sign read **Earls Court**.

Not stopping, Gabriella paced along the tiled corridors of the station, leading us to another platform and back onto the tracks. There was a strong smell of diesel and a flash image of thundering tubular trains shot into my mind. I shook it away.

Once again we sank into darkness, and once again I became blind. We ran in silence for a few more minutes and just as my eyes were beginning to adjust, Gabriella stopped. I barged into her, and felt her body tense up. "Alex, be careful," she hissed.

"Oh I'm sorry if sprinting through pitch black tunnels makes me a little clumsy," I bit back.

I heard her stifle a laugh. "Fair enough." Then she became serious again. "Okay, it's around here somewhere."

"What are we looking for?" I quizzed.

"You'll know soon enough," was the reply.

My guide busied herself with whatever she was looking for. I could vaguely see her rapping her knuckles against the dank concrete walls. The thuds sounded hollow and echoed around us. Gabriella shuffled further along the track, repeating the process. As the minutes wore on, I could sense her getting more and more frustrated. She swore under her breath.

Something caught my attention. I turned around, staring into the gloomy distance. I squinted my eyes, forcing them to focus. After several seconds I deduced that it was a glowing yellow orb. I continued to watch it, trying to get my head around what it could be. It grew steadily and then broke into two. Two pulsing yellow orbs. I craned my neck forward trying to make sense of what I was seeing. The cogs finally turned and a cold sweat washed over me.

Headlights...train headlights.

My heart jumped into my mouth. I reached out, aiming for Gabriella's shoulder. She tried to shake off my hand when I found it.

"Stop it! I'm trying to concentrate!"

"Ella," I squawked frantically, "There's a train coming!"

"What? Oh, just my luck!"

119

The headlights grew larger. They shone in the gloom like two menacing eyes hovering above the hidden jaws of some hideous beast, racing towards us, hungry and terrifying.

I could hear the sound then. The rhythmic clacking and screeching as the train rattled along its rails. The vibrations raced along the tunnel and up my feet. Small stones and hidden debris started to tremor on the ground, like the tap of a thousand impatient fingers. Adrenaline started to flow through my body as my fight or flight reactions kicked in. The train was coming too fast and we were too far down the track, I didn't think there was time to escape before it reached us. But we had to try.

"We have to go *now!*" I yelled over the increasing noise.

"No, wait a second…I know it's around here somewhere."

"Ella!" I pleaded.

The lights were huge. The ground a few hundred yards in front of us was suddenly illuminated. The light swept towards us as the hulking train thundered forward.

"Ella for god's sake, *we are going to die!*"

The sound became deafening.

"Hold on…it's here. I know it!"

The train was so close I could see Gabriella as clear as day. Then I discovered what she was looking for. A metal door was set into the wall a few feet away from us. It was curved to fit the arch of the tunnel and had it not been for the tiny cracks of space around the edges and the strange symbol etched on its front, you wouldn't know it existed at all. Gabriella noticed it as I did.

But it was too late, the train was too close.

Then came the blast of a horn and the screech of brakes as the driver desperately tried to stop. I shut my eyes and waited for death.

Something yanked me hard to the right and I heard a deep slamming sound. The horn continued to blare, distant and muffled.

It took me several moments to understand that we were still alive. I opened my eyes and gasped. We were sprawled on the plush carpet of what looked like an extravagant waiting room. Golden wallpaper lined the walls, with a silver border that ran the entire length of the room. Large pictures of important

120

looking men and women hung in various positions. A coffee table stood to one side. It sat in-between two salary destroying executive sofas. On top were several leather bound books, presumably to pass the time for those waiting. The room smelled like a mixture of varnished wood and freshly cut grass. I noticed a large ornate vase beside me. It held beautiful flowers with vivid green stems and oil black petals. It looked like no plant I'd ever seen. *Or have I?* Lastly I looked straight ahead at a large desk carved from rich mahogany. Behind it sat an attractive woman in her late forties. She had short brown hair chopped over...*purple eyes?* They were wide with surprise as she stared at the tangled mound of arms and legs.

My guide stood up, pulling me with her.

"Heavens, Gabriella, are you okay?" asked the woman.

"We're fine thank you Iralia. Sorry about the entrance." Flicking her head in my direction she added, "New recruit."

"Ah so that's what all the fuss was about upstairs." The woman smiled warmly at me. "Welcome, dear."

"Uh, thanks," I replied, not sure of a correct response to the situation.

"Okay, now all potential recruits must be signed in regardless of creed. It's procedure. So let's get you booked in shall we?" Her tone was soft and comforting, like the way a nurse would speak to a terminally ill patient. "What's your full name then, dear?"

I stood like an idiot, my mouth opening and closing like a fish out of water. Iralia put up her hand. "No matter. In fact Gabriella, if you don't mind I'd prefer to do it the old fashioned way. I'm a little out of practice."

Gabriella shrugged. "Be my guest."

The woman smiled, leaned back in her chair and breathed in deeply. The papers on her desk lifted up and the leaves on the exotic flowers trembled. Then I felt something invisible tugging gently at my skin, like a million tiny hooks. Shivers swept down my spine. After a few seconds she stopped and clicked a pen.

"Right. Alexander Eden, Human. Born Seventh of August, nineteen ninety-four, aged seventeen. Thanks lovely." She wrote the information on a form attached to a clipboard.

"What the fu-"

"If you could just sign at the bottom for me," Iralia interrupted, gesturing the form out towards me, before setting it down on the desk.

I stared at Gabriella, mouth wide open. She nodded towards the desk, and I shuffled over. As I got close my blood turned to ice in my veins.

The woman had wings.

From the angle I'd been at I hadn't been able to see the leathery appendages protruding from her back. They were folded, the ends spilling over either side of the chair and grazing the carpet.

The woman looked up at me and cocked her head sideways. "What's wrong dearie? Never seen a set of wings before?"

There was a rush of wind as they opened up. They were colossal, spanning at least eight feet. I heard a high-pitched scream and realised it was coming from me.

"IRALIA!" shouted Gabriella. The woman instantly re-folded her wings. I fell to the floor and scrambled away on my backside, trying to put as much distance as possible between the creature and me.

I felt a warm hand squeeze my shoulder and the waves rolled through me like morphine, calming. Gabriella squatted down and smiled. "Don't mind Iralia, she's harmless. She just likes to mess around with the new guys."

As my heart smashed against my chest, I looked up at the thing behind the desk. She gave a butter wouldn't melt smile.

"I'm sorry Alexander. I just get so bored whenever I'm stuck down here. I promise I won't scare you again. But I do actually need you to sign this form." She waved it at me.

I refused point blank to go back over to the desk, so Gabriella had to bring the clipboard to where I was cowering. I had to hold my wrist with the other hand to stop it shaking. My signature resembled a series of lines and splodges.

Gabriella returned the form to the creature. Then she came back to me and offered her hand. I took it and stood up.

"It's okay, we're moving on now," she soothed.

I followed her through a set of double doors at the far end. As we passed Iralia, I made sure I was as far away as the room would allow.

When the doors had shut and we were safely on the other side in a long white corridor, I turned and yelled, "What in the hell was that thing!?"

Gabriella motioned for me to lower my voice. "Have you ever heard of a Succubus?" she whispered.

"What, you mean as in the life-force stealing demon?"

"That's a fairly accurate description."

I pointed at the door. "A-are you saying that the monster in there is one of them?"

Gabriella's eyes narrowed. "Iralia is not a monster, but she is a Succubus."

I backed away from her, hands up. "That's it, craziness levels just hit unacceptable. I want to go home. Let me out please."

She walked towards me. "Alex, surely you must have suspected something out of the ordinary was happening by now."

"Of course I did," I snapped. "But I didn't expect something off the X-files!"

"I never said the truth would be easy."

"Easy?" I had to force myself not to scream. "How about not even in the realm of sane?" I clamped my hands against my head. "I can't handle this, it's too much."

I paced down the sterile looking corridor with no idea of where I was heading. There were many doors, with god only knows what hiding behind them.

"Wait!" cried Gabriella running after me. She put hand on my arm. "Alex, we need you." She paused. "I need you. Please allow us to explain. Then if you still want to go, I'll take you myself." Her eyes bored into mine, searching for some common ground.

"Explain then," I said, folding my arms.

My guide shook her head. "I'm not the right person to do that. But if you come with me, I promise you'll get the answers you want." She held out a hand, which I pushed away.

"Fine, but no more surprises." I could still feel my pulse jackhammering away in my ears. "I'd prefer not to have a heart attack."

"I'll do my best," Gabriella agreed with a sober expression. Pointing towards a set of metallic double doors at the end of the

123

corridor, she added, "But you have to understand, once we get where we're going, you will see and learn things you never believed possible. I need you to keep an open mind."

"It's wide open. Trust me. Batwoman back there made sure of that."

"Okay then," Gabriella said with a faint hint of a smile.

We walked the length of the corridor, me lagging behind. I couldn't help it. I didn't know what to expect, all rationality had been thrown out of the window. Gabriella pressed a circular pad by the double doors, which glowed at her touch. They doors rolled open after a few moments and we walked into an elevator. The sides were all mirrored and the floor was the same plush red carpet as the waiting room. The panel only contained one button, which looked like a triangle with a circle inside. Gabriella pressed it. A voice from somewhere said:

Temple of the Divine Elements.

Temple?

The corridor disappeared from view as the doors slid shut. I waited for the typical lurch of vertical movement, so was shocked when the lift jerked backwards. It went slowly at first and then gathered speed at an alarming rate. It became so fast that I shrank back to one of the sides, gripping the rail for fear of falling down. The metal felt cold and damp in my nervous hands. Gabriella kept her head down and didn't say anything for the entire ride, which took an uncomfortable minute or so.

After what felt like an eternity, the elevator slowed and then even more unnervingly, rotated 180 degrees. There was a loud ding and the doors opened. Gabriella walked out with the confidence of those in the loop. I edged out, still wary of what I might find, my hands leaving clammy prints on the rail.

We were in some kind of tunnel. The walls around us were carved from uneven rock, and our footsteps echoed on the slabs of granite that formed the ground. At regular intervals we passed between rows of what looked like golden birdbaths. Odd green flames curled and flickered from their centres. The scent they released was smoky but not unpleasant. It reminded me of roasted chestnuts.

After we'd been walking in silence for some time, we reached a set of stone steps leading up to a gigantic oak door. The tops of the arch were so high I had to tilt my head back as far as I could to see them. Thick iron handles were attached to the middle and above them a Latin phrase had been etched into the wood. Curious, I moved closer to study the words.

DILECTI SURGEMUS - SOCII POLLEMUS

"Chosen we rise - allied we prevail," I translated. "Wait...how did I know that?"

"All in good time," Gabriella said from behind me. I wiped a line of sweat from my forehead with the back of my hand. The preternatural flames made the area very hot.

"So, what is this place?" I asked.

"This," she replied, "Is the entrance to the Temple of the Divine Elements.

"Please tell me this isn't a cult."

Gabriella gave me a sarcastic look and climbed the steps. With a feeling of great apprehension, I followed. There was a moment of hesitation and she took a deep breath. Then with a shaking hand, she knocked in a complicated sequence and drew back, regarding me with her vivid eyes. She looked nervous.

"Here we go."

There was a cranking sound and the doors yawned open.

11

The room was monumental in size. Thick, golden pillars stretched up and disappeared into the darkness above. The floor beneath our feet was literally paved in gold; my reflection stared back at me from the shining surface. Lush tapestries hung from the expansive walls around us. One depicted a colossal bird covered in flames, soaring up into the sky; comets of fire rained down from its tail, igniting the ground below. Another showed a gigantic face in the woods, formed out of trees and other foliage - even its beard was made from thick leaves. It smiled down with benevolence at various woodland creatures below.

Ahead, more flame baths lined a purple carpet that ran along the room towards a shallow set of stairs. A golden chair sat at the top, with two bizarre looking men dressed in white robes standing either side of it. They were completely bald and their pale skin was as smooth as wax. Roman numerals had been tattooed in the centre of their foreheads. The one on the left read XII, the right XIII. They stared at us through blood red pupils, powdery hands clutching silver staffs that curved into spirals at the top – they reminded me of the crosiers catholic priests carried. Except these were clearly weapons.

Must be guards of some kind, I thought. *To protect...him.*

Him was the old man who occupied the chair. Dressed in long black robes rimmed with gold, most of his face lay hidden underneath a deep cowl. I could just make out cotton wool eyebrows and a long beard that tapered to a point below his waist. In one hand he clutched a walking stick with a bright green orb attached to the top. His other hand rested in his lap. He raised it and beckoned.

"You may approach."

The acoustics of the room made his voice boom like a megaphone.

"Ella," I whispered.

126

"It's okay," she reassured, nudging me forward.

The old man pushed back his cowl. I swallowed hard, taking in the rest of his face. His skin was wrinkled and thin, like worn parchment. In contrast to his full white beard, his head was a smooth dome of baldness. A glistening black, tattooed eye stared out from the centre of his forehead. His actual eyes were just as odd as his two protectors', but instead of being red, they were totally white. Not like he had cataracts, but more like he'd been born without pupils.

He smiled, exposing a set of bright teeth. "Welcome Alexander, I am so pleased you are finally here." His voice seemed to echo around the room, coming from nowhere and everywhere all at once. "I was beginning to think our time and resources had been squandered," he added in a more disapproving tone. The statement appeared to be aimed at Gabriella, who shifted uncomfortably on the spot like a chastised child.

"I apologise Sage Faru. Alexander's infiltration was badly handled. But he is ready and willing to listen."

I shot Gabriella a confused glance, but she remained facing the old man.

He nodded. "That is good news."

I couldn't handle the riddles any more, my head felt ready to implode. The frustration boiled up and before I could stop myself, I stormed towards the stairs.

"This is ridiculous!" I barked, stabbing an accusatory finger at the old man. "I need you to tell me-"

I didn't get near to finishing my sentence. The guards reacted instantly, smashing their staffs against the ground causing the coils to burst into blue flames. I heard Gabriella scream "No!" before one of the guards vaulted into the air. Before anyone could react, I was lying on my back with the sizzling neon flame inches from my cheek. The heat seared my skin. Bloodlust blazed in the guard's crimson eyes. I had offended his master; he wanted to hurt me.

"Enough Thirteen!" shouted Sage Faru, clapping his hands together. Without a word, the guard released me. I crawled away with a whimper, holding my tender cheek. The guard returned to his position next to Faru. Both kept their unnatural eyes locked on mine, staffs flaming. From the corner of my eye I saw Gabriella staring at me in disbelief. As I climbed to my feet, she bowed onto one knee.

"Sage Faru, please forgive him. He is confused and scared."

The old man waved a dismissive hand and began to chuckle.

"No harm done. I like this one, he reminds me of an old friend." He turned his head in my direction and stared with his blanched eyes. "Young man, you have passion in your heart, which is an admirable trait. However, I believe that you have held your frustrations inwardly for too long. This mixed with your recent..." he paused and waved a hand, "...transformation, makes for a dangerous cocktail. As this evening's earlier events confirm."

An image of TJ curled in a silent, bloody heap entered my head. Horror and shame at my actions rushed through me.

Sage Faru pointed a finger. "You must learn to control that anger of yours..." The same finger tapped his temple, "...And rely on this instead." Smiling, he passed his ornamental staff to XII. Then he gestured his papery hands towards me. "Alexander, it is time for you to shake off the bliss of ignorance. Please come here."

I didn't want to, but after what had just happened there was no way I could refuse. So I shuffled forward and climbed the steps until I was a few feet away from the old man. The guards glared at me, hands wrapped tightly around their crosiers.

"Please kneel."

I lowered myself onto one knee and stared at Sage Faru. It felt like I was waiting to be knighted. The old man pushed himself out of the seat. His guards motioned to help him, but he swatted them away like an agitated animal. Lifting his beard, he swept it over his shoulder like a scarf. Then he took a few steps towards me and leaned over, placing his hands on my shoulders to steady himself. Being so close made me nervous. His blank eyes unnerved me.

"Please try to relax. This is going to be quite intense."

Before I could reply, the old man's icy claws grabbed my face with a vice-like grip. Pulses of electricity coursed into my body. It felt like I'd touched a live wire, my teeth chattered and my tongue slammed to the roof of my mouth. I tried to scream but the sound died before it escaped. Bile shot up into my throat and burned. Bright flashes splashed across my vision. My mind screamed at me that I'd been tricked, that these people were evil and I should run, but I was paralyzed. It felt as if I'd been coated in cement, my traitor feet sealing me to the floor. The electricity continued to rack my body until the pain became excruciating.

I'm going to die!

I tried to move my hands to prise the human mantrap from my face. No use, my arms were pinned to my side. Then as suddenly as it had started, the shaking stopped. The pain faded away.

My eyes snapped open.

Faru had gone. So had the temple. Instead I was standing on the most beautiful beach imaginable. Sand the colour of cream and as fine and soft as dust covered the ground like a magnificent blanket, collecting between my toes and warming my bare feet. In front of me, a crystal clear sea lapped gently onto the shore. The cool water felt its way onto dry land before gliding back home with a soft, swishing sigh. Palm trees arched over me, their giant leaves hovering above my head. Just offshore, a tiny wooden boat bobbed up and down on the waves, fixed to an old wooden jetty by a fraying piece of old rope. The place seemed strangely familiar, although I knew beyond doubt that I'd never been there before. *There's no way you forget a place like this.*

The whole gorgeous setting was illuminated by a bursting sun, which hung between cotton clouds. Beams of light reflected off the sea, making the surface twinkle like a bed of jewels. For a while I forgot everything and shut my eyes, sighing with contentment as the sun's warm fingers caressed my skin, and a cool, refreshing breeze ruffled my hair. For what could have been hours, I stayed that way, allowing all my confusion and frustration to wash away. Finally with a reluctant sigh, I called out.

"Where am I?"

"Hello, Alexander."

I jumped. Sage Faru was standing next to me. He looked fifty years younger and far less intimidating. He had hair. It fell past his shoulders, sparkling silver in the sunlight. His beard was in its infancy, only reaching the top of his chest. The cold, unseeing eyes that had unnerved me before now seemed to glow with life and intelligence. The only things that really appeared to have remained the same was the tattoo and his decorative robes - which hung better around his fuller, healthier frame.

Faru placed a comforting hand on my shoulder. "I apologise if I startled you," he smiled. "In answer to your question, you are exactly where you were before. It is your mind I have taken on a journey." He chuckled and smoothed out his robes. "Ah to be young again. Shame it's only in the mind hey!" He nudged me as if I had a clue what he was going on about.

When I didn't respond, he gestured towards the view in front of us. "Wonderful isn't it?"

I nodded in complete agreement. "Stunning. But...why do I recognise it?"

"The process of mind merging can be somewhat invasive. Therefore, I try to take the person to a place that makes them feel safe afterwards. I found this little paradise whilst rooting about inside your head. It's not actually a destination you have visited in reality, but rather somewhere you've dreamt about." He bent down and picked up a handful of sand, letting the fine grains slip through his fingers. "You come here when you are unhappy," he said. With a sympathetic edge added, "Which I'm sad to say seems quite often."

I felt a slight unease at the idea of someone rifling through my thoughts. Knowing all my heartaches and fears. *Does that mean he knows about my thoughts of Gabriella, how I imagined kissing her?*

Faru wiped his sand covered hand on his robes and stood back up. "Anyway, I hope you aren't offended by this. I just wanted you to be relaxed before I explained everything to you."

I shook my head. "No it's fine. I-I love it here."

He nodded then looked at me, in as much as he could look at anyone. "I'm afraid we cannot stay much longer. Are you ready to continue?"

I took one more look at the scene in front of me, breathing in the salty aroma of the sea air and trying to capture the sounds of the waves in my mind.

"Yes."

"Good, then please take my hand."

As soon as I did, there was a furious lurch. I cried out in surprise as my feet left the ground. The beach shrank until it became nothing more than a crescent shaped patch of land in a mass of blue. I saw ships; large cruise liners and oil tankers dotted over the sea, shrink to tiny specks and then vanish from sight. We burst through clouds, which left my clothes and skin damp with moisture. My heart thundered against my chest as the wind slapped against my face - it felt like falling, but in reverse. I craned my head up against the wind resistance and saw the blue sky dissolve into black as we left Earth's atmosphere. Too shocked to react, I clung onto Faru's hand for dear life. With a mixture of horror and wonder, I watched as he pulled me higher and higher, like some human rocket. We left Earth's orbit and entered space. Faru slowed and twisted, so that we both faced the direction we'd come from. My mouth dropped open as I witnessed the full beauty of my planet from the outside. It was breathtaking, almost too wonderful to be real. A palette of vivid blue mixed with rich greens and sandy browns, topped with swirls of white. If anything could make me believe in divinity, it was this incredible piece of universal artwork. Regardless of whether I was actually here or imagining it due to the mind merge, it was enough to bring a lump to my throat. Faru released my hand and I floated in slow motion, jaw still somewhere in the region of my chest.

He looked over at me and smiled. "Unbelievable isn't it? This is exactly how Earth appears from Space. Obviously some sensations cannot be as realistic as the genuine experience. I dare say you would be a little short of breath and somewhat compressed otherwise." He gave a little chuckle at his own joke. When I didn't respond, Faru gestured towards the planet. "This is Earth as you know it, but there are elements which are hidden from your eyes. Observe."

As he finished speaking, the world began to change in front of my eyes. Islands shifted and altered shape. Pieces joined together, like magnetic puzzle pieces drawn to one another, and when they had settled, the world looked much younger. There were no manmade landmarks - no Great Wall of China, no

Egyptian pyramids - just a single giant mass of green and brown which floated inside a vast moat of blue.

I remembered a Geography lesson as a kid where I'd learned that the entire world's land mass had once existed as a single supercontinent known as Pangaea, before erosion and shifting of tectonic plates split it apart. This rewind of millions of years seemed to agree with the theory. But something my Geography teacher definitely hadn't mentioned was the shimmering line that ran as far as the eye could see down the centre of it.

"What's that?" I asked.

"That Alexander..." Faru answered, "...is the Veil."

I frowned at the bizarre line. "What's the Veil?"

Faru pulled his legs underneath him, so he was floating cross-legged. He steepled his fingers and fell silent for a moment, as if trying to recall a forgotten speech. Finally he spoke, pointing his joined fingers at me.

"The Veil is like an ancient, natural doorway. Back when Earth was far younger, it was divided in half by this doorway. However, if one were to pass through, they would not end up on the other side you see here, but rather another world entirely."

"Like a parallel dimension?" I gasped.

"Exactly," smiled Faru. He smoothed out his robes before continuing. "Earth is a twin to another world. Whilst in some ways the two are very alike, such as sharing similar laws of physics and gravity, in others they are remarkably different. In fact to a human, some differences would seem unbelievable and could probably be best described as magic."

I couldn't believe what I was hearing. *A parallel world, full of magic?* I shook my head in disbelief.

"Alexander, are you alright?" Faru asked.

I made a squeaking noise, which he took as a cue to continue.

"Well as I'm sure you are aware, the world is in a perpetual state of evolution. It is forever changing."

I nodded.

"The same applies to the Veil. What was once an entire ring that encompassed the world has eroded away over millennia. Parts dissolved, or broke off and sunk to the depths of the ocean. Now only a few sections of the doorway remain, all of which are well hidden and well guarded. Though before that, many of the life forms existing on the other side escaped through into the human world."

My mouth dried up. *Life forms?*

"In the parallel world, creatures exist that you couldn't imagine in your wildest dreams." He paused and took a deep breath. "And others you will be all too aware of, although would never have believed could possibly be real." Faru looked up at me with his blazing white eyes.

"Like what?" I asked, not sure if I actually wanted to know.

"Take my hand," he replied.

I extended my arm towards Faru. It glided in slow motion through the black nothingness and my palm connected with his. My arm was yanked so hard that for a moment I was convinced my shoulder had been wrenched from its socket. We plunged back towards the Earth. My stomach lurched and cheeks flapped from the sheer speed.

Then silence.

All I could hear was the frantic beat of blood pulsing in my ears. We continued to blaze downwards into the planet's atmosphere.

BOOM!

We broke through the sound barrier. The explosion echoed behind me and noise returned as a torrent of wind and my own yells. The ground below spun around like a broken carousel, rushing up to greet us. We weren't showing any signs of slowing down. Fear began to rise in my chest. If Faru didn't do something, we'd smash right into it. For a fleeting moment I considered letting go of his hand, but what good would that have done - I'd fall anyway. *But it's not real! I can't die...can I?*

Either reading my thoughts or sensing my distress, Faru slowed and changed the angle of our descent. The landscape was now parallel and about twenty feet below us. We rocketed over a carpet of treetops; flocks of birds fluttered out of the dense leaves in fright.

I'd finally managed to calm down enough to stop screaming, when I forced my chin up to see ahead and started all over again.

We were heading straight for the Veil.

Up close it appeared to be a shimmering pool of thick, silver water. Rising vertically, like a giant liquid wall. We plunged in headfirst and the chord to my scream was cut. A sensation like slimy, ice-cold fingers pressed hard against my skin, starting at my head and rushing down my body. I shuddered. As I slid deeper at incredible speed, the pain began. At first it felt like someone pressing down on me, but the further I was drawn into the Veil, the stronger and more forceful it became. Soon it was an unbearable crushing pressure, like being squashed under a rock. The air compressed from my lungs and my eyes were forced shut. I tried to gasp for oxygen, but couldn't even part my lips a millimetre to draw anything in.

I can't breathe!

The thought was loud and clear. An alarm bell, which shrieked into every corner of my mind. *I'm trapped in this thing until it spits me back out...alive or dead!*

The pressure rolled upwards and collected at my skull. The pain amped up to a level I didn't think possible. It felt as if someone had clamped my skull in a vice and was happily twisting the lever. Bursts of white-hot pain seared through my temples and bloomed in yellow patches behind my scrunched eyelids. Just when I thought I would pop, drown, implode and suffocate all at the same time, I felt a new, unexpected sensation - similar to breaking through the surface of water, but denser. The slimy fingers raked my skin once more and then the pressure vanished. We shot out of the Veil like a bullet. Faru landed on the ground, sliding gracefully along the dirt. I followed, tripping over my own feet and toppling forward. His iron grip snapped me back like a seatbelt, keeping me upright.

I spent the next few minutes doubled over, greedily gulping oxygen back into my aching lungs. I vowed that from then on, I would never take the beautiful gas for granted again. Faru walked over and placed a hand on my shoulder. Blind with anger, I shoved it away and swung my fists at him. He dodged every punch and caught my wrists, holding them tight. He was surprisingly strong.

"Please calm down."

"What the hell was that?" I screamed in pure fury. "I almost died!"

134

Faru's voice remained placid. "Alexander, please believe me. You were never in any real danger. The sensations of travelling through the Veil are unpleasant but rarely fatal."

"*Unpleasant?*" I shrieked. "Stubbing your toe is unpleasant! That was horrific!"

Faru nodded. "I apologise. I merely wished to show you the other side first hand. I felt it beneficial for you to experience the whole process as completely as possible to help you understand better." He paused. "Perhaps it was a little too soon."

"Yeah perhaps! Or perhaps you could've given me some warning before you fed me to a celestial grinder," I seethed. "Give me my hands back please."

I tugged against Faru's shackling grip. He seemed to weigh up the options for a second before releasing my wrists. I glowered at him as I rubbed the sore spots.

"I am sorry, Alexander. I promise that you will come to no more harm whilst you are on this mind journey." He attempted a friendly smile.

For a moment I said nothing. Then I softened. It was difficult to stay angry with someone who kept apologising. Plus I was starting to feel more comfortable around my guide. Something about him I hadn't noticed before, maybe because I'd been so initially shocked by his appearance. He seemed noble - kind even. Even his white eyes appeared to give off a soothing glow.

I sighed. "It's okay. I'm sorry too. It's just that all this...it's a lot to take in you know?" I turned away from Sage Faru and froze. I'd been so busy being angry; I hadn't noticed the place we'd travelled to...until now.

It was terrifying.

There was no other word that could describe what my eyes could see and even that failed to truly capture the horror. Menacing clouds the colour of fresh bruises dominated the sky, making the scene as dark as a moonless night. The only source of illumination came from the constant stream of jagged lightning bolts, which forked down on the horizon. They were followed by thunderous booms that sounded like battle cries from a war god. The ground was as black as midnight, with pale, jagged rocks jutting out of it like broken bones. To the right, an

135

angry sea heaved waves onto a blood red beach. In the distance, I could just make out the twisting spire of a towering fortress. It resembled a gnarled finger, accusing the skyline.

A fierce wind picked up and whipped around us, yanking at my trousers and seizing my hair. Faru's robes billowed around him as if they had come alive.

"W-what is this place?" I shouted above the roaring of the wind.

Faru clicked his fingers and the tempest died down in an instant. He became a statue, staring into nothingness with his dead eyes. After a few moments he spoke.

"This is my world."

12

Y our world?" I choked, recoiling in horror.

"Yes Alexander, I am not from Earth." He gestured towards the grim landscape. "This is Pandemonia, the realm I call home."

The name sounded like pandemonium, which seemed fitting for the chaotic world that surrounded us.

Faru looked sad for a moment. "I have not visited it physically for many years." Sighing, he added, "Please stop backing away from me, I mean you no harm and it's quite distracting."

I pointed a shaking finger at him. "So that's the reason you can do all this crazy mind stuff, because you're not...human."

He made an agreeing noise. "I am indeed what you would consider to be a supernatural creature." He inverted the last two words with his fingers. "In fact most of the creatures from your legends and folklore are actually Pandemonians who passed through the Veil."

"You mean like that woman in the waiting room - Iralia?" I said. "She's a Succubus right?"

Faru frowned. "I see Gabriella has been revealing more than her role permitted." He waved a hand. "No matter, you are correct. Like myself, Iralia's true home lies on this side of the Veil. However, unlike me, she is Umbra."

In the same way I knew what the description on the Temple doors meant, I knew the word meant shadow. I repeated it aloud.

Faru folded his arms behind his back. "Yes. The 'Liberi Umbra' or 'Children of the Shadow' are the darker creatures of our world. You see, Pandemonia has countless different species and sub species just like your world. Except, instead of mammals, invertebrates or reptiles etcetera, ours have been categorised into three main types or classes. The first is the Umbra, as I already mentioned. The second are 'Liberi Luminar'

– 'Children of the Light'. They are the Umbra's natural enemies. Finally, the third...neutral type if you will, are the 'Liberi Fera' – 'Children of the Wild'.

I folded my arms across my chest. "Okay, so if Iralia's a Succubus, then what legendary creature are you?" I said, not really sure if I making a joke or not.

Faru smiled and turned towards me. He opened his arms wide, as if waiting for a hug. "I am a Seelian."

I blinked. "I have no idea what that is."

Faru looked a little deflated. "Hmmm...well no of course you don't, Seelians have always been very careful to keep human exposure to a minimum. Allow me to explain. Seelians are the nobility of the Luminar. More specifically the Seelian are a species of Fae." He scanned my face for a reaction. "Or Faerie," he offered finally.

"You...you're a Fairy? "As in Tinkerbell?"

"I do not know what a tinky bell is."

I decided not to elaborate on the potential insult. "But you don't have any wings," I pointed out instead. "So I assume fairies can't fly then, for real."

"Actually you are incorrect. Several species of Fae do indeed have wings. I myself once possessed a magnificent set. Unfortunately Seelians shed them after their prime years, when they are no longer of any use to us. I lost mine many cycles ago." He smiled at me. "That is one element of your legends which is actually based on fact. However, much is inaccurate."

"How so?"

"You see Alexander; Pandemonians usually prefer to remain anonymous to the human race. It's easier that way. Nonetheless, over the centuries inevitable sightings have been made, or humans have fallen foul to rogue predators. As nothing was known about their true nature, guesses were made. These rumours warped over the ages - akin to Chinese whispers I dare say - and became legends. Some have factual elements to them...others are simply nonsense. Most of what fills your books and television screens are based in pure fiction and are the result of nothing more than wild imaginations. Others are based on misinformation. Take Werewolves for example."

"Werewolves exist?" I choked.

138

"Not really no. The Lycanthrope myth is based on what we refer to as Skinshifters."

I let the word roll about in my head as Faru continued. It sounded creepy.

"Skinshifters are a species of Fera similar in appearance to Earth's canines, although far larger. They have the ability to metamorphosise into other animals, via a method known as imprinting. That is, they can alter their appearance and actions to perfectly impersonate another animal. This includes humans. But whereas a Skinshifter can emulate another animal indefinitely, they run into difficulties when acting as humans."

"Difficulties?"

"A full moon. You may be aware that lunar activity has the ability to affect humans in various ways. Hence the term lunatic."

I nodded.

"In this case, it somehow displaces the Skinshifter, forcing it to shed its new skin and resume its old shape."

A light bulb flicked on in my brain. "And at some point someone mistook it for a human changing into a beast."

"Exactly and thus the legend of the Werewolf was born." Faru laughed as if the stupidity of how such a mistake could be made was beyond ludicrous. I stayed quiet, arms folded, heart thumping against my chest.

"So what other creatures are real?" I asked finally, not sure if I was ready to hear the answer.

"There are far too many to go through. Although, I suppose the most well-known would be the Vampire."

"Vampires exist?" I gasped.

Faru rubbed at his forehead in a weary manner. "Yes Alexander, Vampires do indeed exist and most originate from my world."

Most? I thought. *What does that mean?*

"Hivemind Vampires are the most common," he continued, "but by contradiction are the least known in your folklore. This is presumably because it is very unlikely that any human would ever survive an encounter with them. They are lethal creatures who travel and hunt in packs. Hiveminds are indigenous to the Darklands, an area of Pandemonia completely devoid of natural light. As a result, they evolved to be effective night hunters and developed intolerance to sunlight."

Faru turned and placed an arm around my shoulder. He began to walk as he talked, gesturing me forward. I moved like a robot, scanning the ground to make sure I didn't cut my bare feet on the sharp stones. I needn't have bothered though, when I did manage to stand on one, it crumbled into dust. *I guess Faru wasn't lying about me coming to no more harm.* I had a sneaking suspicion that it would be a very different story if I were in Pandemonia for real.

"In every Hivemind litter, one Vampire will always evolve further than its siblings," the Seelian explained. "They become another type of Vampire known as a Bloodseeker. Fully formed Bloodseekers are intelligent, humanoid creatures that look and act very similarly to humans. Typical to most evolved species from our world, they have an average lifespan five times that of a human, but are *not* immortal. They too are susceptible to sunlight, but nowhere near as much as their feral counterparts.

"Whereas Hiveminds are carnivorous and will consume their prey until nothing is left, Bloodseekers only require blood to survive. Therefore, a normal Vampire attack would consist of the leader draining the prey's blood then leaving the carcass for their pack to devour. Furthermore, male and female Bloodseekers can mate with one another. Their offspring become Hiveminds and thus the cycle continues."

We walked closer to the shoreline. The roar of the sea grew louder as we drew nearer. In each burst of lightning, I watched as the waves smashed against rocks in the distance, sending dark spray spitting high into the air.

I frowned. "So something I don't quite follow. You said *most* Vampires come from Pandemonia."

"Indeed I did. But I fear we are getting off track. Rest assured you will learn everything in time, but for now we must concentrate on what is most important."

"Okay. But can I just ask, are all Vampires evil?"

Faru shook his head. "Alexander, I fear you misunderstand me. Vampires are not evil. They simply do what is in their nature, like all predators. However, just like humans, all the sentient creatures of Pandemonia have free will. When presented with a

140

choice, some chose to be benevolent, whilst others choose malevolence. Only then are they evil, not before. Do you understand?"

I nodded. "Morality exists in Pandemonia, just like Earth."

Faru looked impressed. "Exactly. Now to continue."

The Seelian stepped forward and gestured out towards the grim view in front of us. "Despite its macabre appearance, Pandemonia was not always like this Alexander. Long before my time, it was a peaceful place of immense beauty."

Looking at the fierce landscape, it was hard to imagine it ever being anything other than terrifying.

"Like your world, Pandemonia was once split into two halves by the Veil," he continued. "The Umbra populated one side and Luminar the other. The Veil ensured that the two sides never met or interacted with one another. In addition, it acted to protect your world from ours and vice versa."

"How did it do that?"

"It gave off a vibration which could imbue a sense of chronic fear and danger. This meant that instinctually no creature would ever venture too close."

I nodded. "So what went wrong?"

"Over time - as it did in your world - the Veil broke apart. For the first time, the separate halves of Pandemonia met. By this time several life forms had evolved to a sentient state. You see, in your world humans are considered to be the only fully sentient creatures. In mine there are many." Around us, the thunderous booms grew louder and more frequent, adding a sense of tense drama to everything that Faru said. "It all went well to begin with. The two halves of our world traded and lived in a peaceful truce for what would be centuries in your world. In this time several smaller creatures mixed and bred and produced new species of Fera."

As I listened to Faru, I noticed my palms had started to sweat profusely. I wiped them on my trousers and shoved them in my pockets. "So I'm guessing that that truce fell apart. What happened?"

The Seelian gave a long sigh. "Greed. The darker side of nature began to show itself. Some species weren't content with

141

their lot and on both sides there were murmurs of war. The Umbra have their own nobility known as Demons."

Demons. Now there's a word I've heard before.

"Demons are renowned for being particularly fierce and bloodthirsty, but equally intelligent and cunning. One in particular shared the desire for war. He sought to control the whole of Pandemonia and for Umbra to become the dominant class." Faru gave a shake of his head. "Unfortunately he was also in a position to achieve that desire. His name was Azraiel, King of Demons."

As if to add menace to the name, another loud crack of thunder burst overhead, making me jolt.

"Azraiel roused a colossal army and unleashed them against the Luminar. He expected it to be a walkover owing to the Umbra's natural predatory nature, but the Luminar were more powerful than he anticipated. We all have a fierce lust for life and will not go down without a fight." A glimmer of a smile appear on Faru's face. "Nevertheless, the Luminar were pushed back into smaller pockets of land, losing most to the Umbra. We never gave up and fought back under the leadership of Kishen the Wise." He stopped for a moment and put two fingers to his forehead before placing them over his heart.

A salute of some kind? I wondered.

"So began the Ageless War."

Faru lowered his hands and folded them behind his back before continuing. "Like its name suggests, the war itself has been raging for as long as anyone can remember. Today, the original leaders are long gone and their descendants have inherited the war. The Umbra are now ruled by the Demon King, Hades. He is as thoroughly evil as his forebears - the absolute epitome of all things unjust. He rules his domains with an iron fist, and destroys anyone who displeases him or even questions his decisions. His opposition comes in the form of the Seelian Prince Ashan." Faru repeated the action of pressing his fingers to his forehead and then holding them over his heart.

Okay he's definitely saluting these guys. I guessed they meant a lot to him.

"Prince Ashan is a benevolent leader who cares for each and every one of his subjects. The cities and lands of Pandemonia he still rules over are fertile and more beautiful than you could imagine. Furthermore, he is a noble warrior who fights alongside his people, unlike Hades who commands from behind the walls of his impenetrable fortress, allowing his followers to suffer and die for his cause." Faru gestured towards the foreboding structure in the distance, an unmistakable look of contempt on his face. Lightning crackled around the spire, framing the shape in the gloom. He swept his hand around to indicate the rest of the cursed land. "What you see before you is an area of Pandemonia touched by the corruption of this mindless war."

I stared out at the scene in front of me again. It didn't matter how many times I looked, it still filled me with terror. A fork of lightning slammed into the ground only fifty yards or so ahead, blinding me. I instinctively covered my eyes. As I did, I felt something rush past me, close enough to touch my skin. It made the hairs on my neck shoot up. I jerked my eyes open and stared until I could just about make out a dark shape moving at an incredible speed towards the beach.

In the bursts of illumination that the torrent of lightning provided, I watched the running creature launch itself with a feral scream at another dark shape standing on the blood red sand. It slashed out with clawed hands and a black jet of liquid sprayed out of its victim's throat. The wounded thing let out a piercing howl of agony, which faded into gurgles as it collapsed onto the sand. Other silhouettes appeared from nowhere, running onto the beach, tearing and biting at each other. The bursts of lightning exposed the carnage like macabre photographs. Every time the battle was lit up, more horrifying details seared themselves into my brain. Bodies slumping to the ground, flaps of skin being shredded off bodies, blood pooling around the dead. Each crack of thunder was accompanied by screams of anger and agony.

I couldn't take any more. I turned away and covered my eyes. "Stop please!" I begged.

The sounds faded. Once again there were only the fitful waves and the angry crack of the thunder, which was rolling away. I peeked through my trembling fingers; the creatures were gone. Letting out a deep breath, I composed myself.

Before I could say a word, Faru put up a hand. "I apologise, but that was something you needed to see to understand the dire turmoil Pandemonia is in. Thousands die every day." He sighed and shook his head slowly, dealing with some kind of inner anguish. "After all of this mindless fighting, the Ageless War is coming to a close. Unfortunately it is Hades who is winning.

"Because they Umbra are stronger?"

"No. Because of the arrival of another."

I frowned at Faru. "Who?"

"Not who Alexander...*what*. An unstoppable force. No one knows where it came from. It simply appeared over a hundred years ago and joined the Umbra. A soul eater known only as The Sorrow."

The words sent a fierce shudder running through me, as if they were unmentionable. It took a few seconds before I was able to speak. "By soul eater, you mean..."

Faru looked grim. "Exactly that. The Sorrow feeds on the life force of others to feed its own twisted soul. The poor victims become deformed husks with no recollection of their former selves. The Depraved as they are known, have no purpose other than to serve The Sorrow without question." The Seelian cast his blind gaze downwards. "The Sorrow is worse than anything you could possibly imagine." For the first time I saw something different in his eyes as he spoke. Something that made my skin go cold.

Fear. Faru was scared of The Sorrow.

"So...is it some kind of Umbra?"

Faru shook his head. "No one knows. Some think it's a primordial Demon. One of the first, somehow awoken by the everlasting battle. Others think it is evil incarnate, created by all the misery and death of the war. There are many theories, none of which can be proven. The truth is that no one knows. All we do know for certain is that it serves Hades. Although, that may only be because it somehow furthers its own evil agenda, which as yet is not clear."

The Seelian stopped speaking and stared out towards the black sea, which swelled and bucked with angry waves, lost in thought. His hands were coiled into tight fists and his body rigid with the strain of what could only be countless horrific memories.

I didn't know what to say. For some reason the mention of The Sorrow had filled me with a sense of dread that was gnawing away at my insides. I squeezed my eyes shut; trying to replace thoughts of an unstoppable soul eater and the grizzly show I'd just witnessed with the calming images of Earth and the beach. It didn't really work. I re-opened my eyes. The Seelian was still in the same position, staring across the angry sea.

"Sage Faru?" I said gingerly, walking forward and placing a hand on his arm. He snapped out of his reverie and turned towards me, giving a smile that convinced no one.

"I apologise Alexander. I have seen many atrocious things in my time in Pandemonia. Please speak your mind."

I swallowed, my throat dry. It felt like years since I had eaten or drunk anything. "Well I err...it's bad about The Sorrow and the war and everything, but well...I just don't see what any of this has to do with me."

Faru placed a hand on my shoulder. "You will Alexander. What comes next will make it all easier to understand. I think it's time to move on."

They were the words I'd been hoping for. I couldn't wait to get out of this hellish place - vision or not. Faru clapped both hands together and the world began to tear off from itself. Little pieces flaked away and dissolved into nothing as though the whole setting was wallpaper being stripped by the hand of an invisible deity. In the spaces left by the flakes, there was nothing but a bright glow.

Soon we were surrounded by nothing but pure, brilliant white. To me it seemed like nonexistence; the blank canvass between life. There was no horizon, no background, no sky, no floor, nothing but endless white. As far as I could tell I was upright, but there was no way to know if I was standing or floating - I couldn't feel anything beneath my feet. The brightness took a while to adjust to, like switching on a lamp in the middle of the night. For a few disturbing seconds it appeared as though Faru had two holes in his head, due to his glowing eyes blending in with the background. Thankfully the effect passed. I waited, but the Seelian didn't say a word. He simply folded his arms across his chest as if he expected something to happen.

Then something did.

A point a few feet away began to shimmer. Frowning, I stared at the patch of nothingness, which continued to waver like heat in the desert. Then out of nowhere a blue ball of energy formed. It started out the size of a marble and grew until it was roughly the size of a tennis ball. Then it hung motionless, releasing an electric blue glow.

A small gasp of wonder escaped my throat as I gazed at the orb. I had never witnessed anything so glorious in all my life. It was better than the beach, better than the view of Earth from space. Better than *everything*. Tears spilled down my cheeks. I wiped with the back of my hand, unable to stop staring at the divine orb. When I managed to locate my voice and use it, the words were soft and dreamlike.

"It's...so...beautiful. What...is...it?" I whispered.

"This is a human soul Alexander.

"Soul," I repeated slowly, mouthing the words.

I reached out to touch the shining orb, but was dismayed when my fingers glided right through as if it were a mirage. The soul shimmered for a second, then solidified again and drifted away from me. I cried out and tried to snatch at it, but Faru placed a hand on my shoulder and shook his head. I dropped my eyes to my fingers in disappointment and drew in a sharp breath; the tips were glowing blue like oversized matchsticks.

I breathed a sigh of awe and looked back up. All around, more souls appeared, unfurling and growing in the emptiness of the non-world. Soon there were hundreds of them gliding around us like atoms under a microscope. They seemed to radiate peace and happiness. I felt calmer than I could ever remember being in my life. Nothing else mattered, just these precious little souls.

Faru glided around so that he was facing me. "Souls are the life force of all species," he said. "A miraculous, eternal energy that cannot be destroyed. In humans, a soul unites with a newborn child and stays with them until death, before moving on to another. They do this for millennia and then simply disappear, as if they have moved on to somewhere else."

He scooped a hand through the air and caught a soul, much to my jealousy. It lay sheltered in his closed palms, shining rays of neon light from the cracks between his fingers. Faru widened the space between his two thumbs and gestured for me to look. I discovered that I could move forward without actually walking - a sort of glide. Once in front of the Seelian, I peered into his cupped hands. Inside, amongst the glowing blue, I could see flashes of cycling images, like short videos on a slideshow. A young boy clothed in rags running from a bakers - a loaf of bread clutched in his grubby hands; a middle aged man with curly hair driving an American convertible, holding hands with the smiling brunette sitting next to him; an elderly lady lying in a hospital bed, surrounded by family. A young woman standing by a-

The images were cut short as Faru dropped his hands away. He gently released the soul and it floated off to re-join the others.

"Snapshots of past lives," he answered before I could ask. "The existence of souls is nothing short of a miracle and impossible to explain. Because they cannot be seen by the human eye, it has often been debated that they do not really exist. But I can assure you they do and if you could see them, they would look like these here."

"Wait, you can see them?" I asked.

"I can. Although I am blind by conventional standards, my unique style of vision allows me to see things that do not exist on the physical plane. I can also manipulate them."

"So you could touch a real soul?"

"I could yes. Not that I have had much reason to ever do so. But I digress." He raised a long index finger and tapped it once in the air. "Now, to explain how all this fits together. As I already explained, the Veil had broken down and with this, its repelling effects diminished. As the Ageless War raged on, countless died on both sides. Many grew weary of the battle, of the constant fear. They wanted to escape the bloodshed. They hid anywhere they could to avoid fighting - in caves, ruins, underground, and those that could, underwater. Desperate to escape and confronted with a greater threat to life than the diminishing Veil could present, it was only a matter of time before someone stumbled into your world. Before long, word had spread of a solace away from the war, a safe haven where one could seek refuge."

"That doesn't seem too bad," I mused, wiping a bead of sweat from my neck. "A kind of inter-dimensional asylum seeker."

Faru gave a chuckle. "Yes, I like that. And indeed that would have been fine had all those coming through been peaceful. Alas this was not the case. As I mentioned, the sentient creatures of my world are subject to character flaws, just like humans. Not every visitor to Earth was friendly."

"Oh."

"Oh indeed my dear boy. Many realised they could exploit the weaker life forms of this world, namely humans. Your kind went from being the dominant species to a low link in the food chain for some very dark and powerful entities." He furrowed his brow over his white eyes. "As much as I am dismayed to admit, it was not only Umbra who did this. Luminar were just as much to blame." His unhappy face brightened and he clasped his hands together. "However, this unbalancing of the equilibrium was not without its consequences. The act of Pandemonians coming through triggered a truly miraculous reaction in certain human souls. A process referred to as an Awakening."

Faru turned and gestured to the sea of souls. Many of them started to vibrate. They shook so hard they became a blur. I watched as the light they emitted grew brighter until it became difficult to even look at them. When they settled, their mass had expanded by at least half. Small tendrils formed in their centres and stretched out like little feelers, searching the air. More and more appeared. I tried to count them, but there were too many. I guessed around fifty or so. As their appendages snaked around, the tips crackled with bursts of electric energy.

Faru attempted to pick up one of the newly transformed souls. It darted away and snapped its tendrils at him like miniature whips. He snatched his hand back and chuckled. "As a kind of natural defence against these strange intruders, some souls evolved to a higher state with incredible results. Such an immediate and miraculous leap forward in evolution is

148

unexplainable, but not entirely unexpected. A dominant species will always endeavour to save itself from extinction."

I leaned forward, hanging off every word.

"Now because the soul controls the mind, which in turn controls the body, this sudden evolution allowed the people who possessed these evolved souls to become in effect...superhuman. These chosen humans were those favoured by natural selection to become Earth's defence against the darker creatures from my world. You see, the Chosen possess abilities that no other human could hope for. They have superhuman strength and speed, can withstand attacks that would kill a normal man and heal faster than is naturally possible." He waved his hand, "Plus a few extra abilities which vary from individual to individual. To all intents and purposes the Chosen are walking biological weapons."

He stopped speaking and stared at me.

As his words sank in, all the pieces fell into place. My heart did a backflip. I shook my head from side to side. "No...you don't mean? It can't...I can't!"

Faru glided towards me and gripped my shoulders. "Yes Alexander *that* is why you are here."

His next words seemed to slip out in slow motion, each one hitting me with the force of a cannonball.

"You are a Chosen."

13

No, you've got it wrong," I insisted. "I can't be a Chosen. I'm not special. God, I'm not even average!" But I knew that the words spilling from my mouth carried no weight. After all, Faru had simply put a label on all the things I could already do.

"Alexander, you know what I am telling you is the truth. You are capable of feats that most humans can only dream of; and that is at this early stage - as you grow in confidence, so too will your abilities. You have been chosen by natural selection to be the defence against those who seek to do your species harm."

I ran my hands agitatedly through my hair, no longer feeling at peace with the souls that floated around me. My heart raced and I felt dizzy. "But I don't even like people most of the time!" I said. "And they definitely don't like me! Most of the people in my school only started speaking to me a few days ago!"

Faru pressed his fingers together. "Alexander, the reason you have always struggled to connect with humans is because you are not like them. You never really were."

I let the Seelian's words sink in. *Is this why I could never make friends? Why everything I tried made people dislike me more? Because I'm different?* "But what if I don't want to be one of these...Chosen?" I asked.

Faru gave a slow shake of his head, as I feared he would. "It makes no difference I'm afraid. Whether or not you join us, you still had your Awakening. It is not something you have any control over."

I wiped a fresh layer of sweat from my hands and let out a long sigh. "Fine, then tell me who this *us* you keep referring to is."

Faru gave a nod. "As I mentioned, when the creatures of Pandemonia first came through the Veil, they dominated. Umbra massacred, Vampires fed without consequence, Luminar took humans as pets and treated them like slaves. The list goes on. It was a dark time for humanity. Those who were Chosen did not understand what was happening to them, or why they were suddenly bestowed with these fantastic abilities. They were confused and alone, unaware that others such as themselves existed all over the world. All they knew was that they could sense these foreign creatures and they had an overwhelming urge to fight against them. So they fought...and died alone."

The souls around us lifted into the air and ghostly forms materialised around them. The glowing orbs lodged into the centres of what became hundreds of men and women. I could just about make out the armour they wore. The various designs and styles alluded to countless countries and time periods. They all seemed to be locked in their own personal battles. Some swung weapons at invisible enemies or defended themselves from attacks that weren't happening. Others fired shimmering arrows at non-existent targets. They roared silent cries of victory and whimpers of defeat. They circled around, trapped in their looping conflicts. At one point, a ghostly sword swept right through my arm. I didn't even feel a chill. As I watched the epic scene with awe, Faru continued to speak.

"However, their heroic bravery was spoken of for decades to come. New Chosen learned of the stories and realised that those who had come before were the same as themselves. They began to seek out each other. With all of them searching, they located each other swiftly. An alliance was set up between them. United, they stood against the darker creatures of Pandemonia and prevailed."

The figures around us for the first time acknowledged each other. As they formed a line, their uniforms shifted into black suits of armour with swirling capes that depicted a grand sword, dividing a horned skull in two.

"The scale tipped the other way. In a time known as the Great Purge, the Chosen hunted down and killed every single Pandemonian they could find without mercy. Entire families of peaceful Luminar were dragged into the streets and murdered. Kind Succubi and Incubi who lived good lives, and only ever took just enough life force to stay alive were chained up and starved of energy until they turned to dust. Witches and Shamans - the offspring of unions between humans and Umbra,

151

were burned at the stake, even though they were half human and completely innocent. Even non-carnivorous Fera were hunted down. If it wasn't from Earth it was killed."

"That's awful," I breathed, shuddering at the thought of all the mindless violence.

Faru made an agreeing sound. "It was only about two hundred years ago that the Chosen accepted that not all Pandemonians were evil. It took a lot of convincing, but eventually certain species were permitted to aid them in their quest to rid Earth of evil. This allowed for mediation in determining if a Pandemonian was malevolent or not. Over time that assistance became an alliance. As with everything, the alliance evolved and has now become the powerful organisation known as the HASEA."

"What's that?" I asked.

"It stands for the Human and Supernatural Entity Alliance. The HASEA is essentially a supernatural police force made from a mixture of Chosen and Pandemonians, known as Guardians. We govern all supernatural activity and are committed to ensuring the safety of both humans and peaceful Pandemonians. Furthermore, it is the Alliance's responsibility to protect the Veil. When the HASEA's ancestors first took control of each remaining segment, they hid them from view and destroyed all written records of the Veil's existence, to keep it a secret. It was and still is guarded around the clock by Guardians.

"In the distant past, any new travellers into your world had to join the HASEA, or were sent back through the Veil. Nowadays the Alliance has adopted a slightly different view. Pandemonians do not have to join us; they can live their lives freely in the human world. However, there are two strict overarching rules. One: they must never intentionally reveal their true identities to a human unless that person is connected to the Alliance, and two: they must never harm a human or Chosen, except in an act of self-defence. If either of these two rules are broken, depending on the severity of the crime, the offender will be hunted down and killed, or permanently deported back to Pandemonia."

"Seems fair."

"It is. Of course, there are benefits to joining the Alliance. The Pandemonian receives accommodation, employment, and by extension an income, as well as support for any of their...desires."

I raised my eyebrows. "Desires?"

"Blood for Vampires, life force energy donors for Incubi and Succubi, Imprint loans for shifters-"

I put up a hand. "Okay I get the gist."

"They can even progress through the ranks." Faru gestured towards himself. "Of which I myself am living proof."

"So what does the HASEA get in return?"

"More manpower for one. In addition, the benefit of Pandemonians' unique abilities. For example, Fae are required to regularly donate blood, which is put to good use. In addition, our single most important alliance is between ourselves and the various Arcane Covens. Witches are able to tap into the ether and receive premonitions of attacks *before* they happen. That way we can have a hunter team there before anyone gets hurt." Faru stopped speaking and stared at me with his glowing eyes. "Have you understood everything so far?"

I ran over everything he'd told me. "Yes."

"Good. Then let's move on to our final stop." Faru clicked his fingers and the world around us began to change once again. The knights disappeared one by one in quick succession, like bubbles bursting. The white space around us began to fill itself in. It started with lines, which grew denser with shape and then filled with colour, coming to life as real objects. The same was true with people, who were sketched into life and then started walking around and speaking with one another.

Once the scene was finished, I saw that we were in the entrance hall of a vast mansion. A huge staircase with plush red carpet swept up to a gigantic painting of Sage Faru, before splitting off to the left and right - the twin stairs led to parallel balconies with countless doors and archways. Around us, dozens of people moved in all directions like frenzied ants. Some went up the stairs, others filtered through various openings and doors. None of them were paying us the slightest bit of attention. In this reality - or whatever it was - we were invisible.

153

"This is a HASEA base I'm guessing." I said.

"It is. In fact, it's the very one you came to earlier and the one which your body is still in right now."

Body?

The Seelian chuckled at my expression. "Don't worry you will be going back to it shortly." He gestured towards the bustling scene. "The Warren is the main headquarters for the Alliance in the United Kingdom. I'm proud to say it's one of the most powerful in the world. It was built - as most Alliance headquarters are - around a remaining section of the Veil."

"It's so...nice looking," I remarked.

"Indeed. The beauty of the HASEA in this day and age is that it receives full support from the government - off the record of course. We keep the planet safe, they aid with financing and support. Plus many Pandemonians have forged very successful careers in the human world. We receive regular financial donations." He stopped talking and pointed towards the floor. My stomach clenched when I realised the marble had vanished. Instead we were hovering in mid-air. Far below us, a maze of metal tubes twisted around one another. Some led to boxed in areas deep underground. Others stretched out in countless directions as far as the eye could see. I tracked one of them back up and saw that it led to a set of elevator doors nearby.

"Below you is the Nexus," Faru explained. "A subterranean network of elevators, which travel at speeds in excess of three hundred miles per hour. It allows us to reach most areas of London in less than a minute."

A few of the tubes shuddered slightly, probably caused by elevators racing through them. Staring at the web of metal tunnels, I had to admit it was pretty impressive. Although my earlier experience of riding inside one had been nausea mixed with terror, rather than wonder.

Faru's voice snatched me out of my daydream. "So then, to finish the explanation." He straightened upright and drew in a large breath. "Everything was going perfectly on this side. The HASEA was flourishing and we were keeping most of the Rogues in check. The ones that fought against us, well..." he gave a slow shrug and opened out both hands. "Then it all started to go wrong."

154

I placed a hand against a wall near me, my brain still struggling to accept that it was okay to be standing several hundred metres in the air. "I'm listening."

"As I said, the Ageless War is coming to an end. Many Pandemonians we thought were with us have been re-claiming allegiance to Hades, most likely in fear as to what will happen after he prevails."

"What will he do?"

"Isn't it obvious? Hades craves domination. With The Sorrow serving him, he is unstoppable. Where do you think he will go once he has claimed Pandemonia?"

I breathed in sharply. It *was* obvious.

"Can't you send Guardians through to help fight the war?" I suggested.

Faru sighed. "If only it were that simple. The reason we cannot is actually part of a bigger problem. One that involves the Awakenings, and one which has made you very important Alexander."

"And that is?"

"They haven't been happening."

My eyebrows knitted together. "Huh?"

Faru pointed a long slender finger at me. "Alexander, you are the first new Chosen in over three years."

I didn't know what to say. It was a bit difficult to gauge how important that was. Or what it meant.

"There used to be about six hundred new Awakenings every year across the world. Now there are none...apart from you."

"What? I mean why?"

"We don't know, but it is something the other Sages and I have been trying to understand for some time."

Gathering my thoughts I said, "So I presume it's a problem for the Alliance."

Faru gave a long sigh and rubbed at his neck absently. "A very large problem. We are being stretched thin, trying to deal with all the troublesome Pandemonians. It's the same all over the world. To make matters worse, since reclaiming allegiance to Hades, many traitorous Pandemonians have formed their own alliance, calling themselves the Soldiers of Sorrow. They act on the will of Hades. Over the last two decades, hundreds of

Chosen were sought out and killed by the SOS before we had a chance to reach them. It appears that they attempted to do the same to you."

I remembered the creature that had chased me from the woods. Recalled the hatred I had seen in those blood red eyes. I shuddered when I thought of what would have happened if that shadowy figure hadn't intervened.

"But you managed to protect me," I said in a small voice.

Faru nodded. "The Coven experience premonitions of Awakenings from time to time. They predicted yours. We have members of the Alliance called Infiltrators. It's their job to work themselves into your life so that you turn to them when your Awakening comes. Normally we have much more time between detection and Awakening. In this instance it happened far sooner than we expected, so the infiltration became more to keep you alive and ultimately bring you here.

A cold wave washed over me. *He's talking about Gabriella. She was forced to become my friend. She didn't want to know me.*

I couldn't bring myself to say anything. I felt sick to my stomach. Sage Faru's face clouded with concern, clearly not sure what he had said to upset me.

"Alexander, is something wrong?"

I shook my head, trying not to let tears that had formed in my eyes spill over and give me away. "I'm fine," I managed to croak. I guessed Faru couldn't read my mind right now, or he would know how utterly betrayed I felt.

Without warning, a sharp pain hit my temples. I yelled out and tried to hold onto something. The nearby wall passed right through my outstretched fingers. I fell to my knees and sank down towards the Nexus. I felt hot and sick. I wiped a shaking hand at the rolls of sweat, which were appearing all over my skin.

"What's happening to me?" I managed to gasp through the pain.

"We have held the mind connection for too long. I have to release you or it could cause us both damage."

Faru sank through the floor with me, as we drifted down through the air. He stretched out his hand and placed it onto the crown of my head. My back arched as once again, electricity surged through my body. The world around me grew blurry. The people above us became less defined. Their bodies melted away into shapeless blobs. The house interior broke down, pieces of wood and bricks falling into piles around the unidentifiable mass of people. As my thoughts diminished and the world dissolved around me, I heard Faru's voice, a megaphone blaring in my head.

"Alexander Eden," he boomed. "It is time for you to become what you were always destined to be." My head was swimming, his words darting in and out of my brain. I flailed a hand around trying to reach for something. Clutched at nothing.

"A hero, chosen from billions. The evolution of souls." His voice grew faint.

My vision grew darker. Yellow spots flashed like paint specks in my eyes.

"You have a choice to make. You can either deny your true path, or you can join us."

The words became whispers as the last circle of light faded and the darkness seeped in with its midnight cloak. I could sense the sharp grip of the old man once more, his fingernails digging into my skull. I was too far-gone to feel the pain. My knees buckled and I fell forward, tumbling into the abyss below.

"Alexander Eden, will you join us?"

Even though the swirling feeling of misery still gnawed at my insides, threatening to consume me from the inside out; I knew there was only one real answer. I parted my lips and breathed out a single word.

"Yes."

Faru clicked his fingers and everything went dark.

*

My head throbbed and my tongue felt like a damp sock. Unsticking my eyes, I looked around. I was lying on a four-poster bed; the room around me was a blend of dark wood flooring and cream walls. Thick crimson curtains had been pulled together, a solitary shard of light sneaking through a crack in the middle. A dim glow came from a bedside lamp beside me. On the other side stood a grandfather clock; its pendulum swung lethargically from side to side, filling the room with its soft ticking.

Then I noticed the large chair on the far side of the room. Gabriella lay curled up on it, covered by a small blanket. A sense of longing tugged at my stomach. It felt like years since I'd seen her. She sighed softly in her sleep and nestled into the chair. The more I looked at her, the more the hurt and betrayal overtook the desire. I'd stupidly believed that this girl actually cared about me.

All lies.

It had been her job to get me here. I was an assignment.

Forcing myself to look away, I stared up at the beamed ceiling. My mind replayed everything Faru had told me. Lying in the soft bed, it would be easy to pass everything off as a crazy dream. But the very fact that I was there at all meant the exact opposite. My headache grew worse, so I let my eyes drift together.

I must have dozed off, because I woke to the sensation of being watched. Gabriella was sitting upright in the chair, gaze focused intently on me. Seeing that I was awake, she bolted out of the chair, sending the blanket sliding along the floorboards.

"Alex!" she exclaimed. "How are you feeling?"

I let out a thick groan.

"That good huh?" she smiled and sat on the bed.

"What happened?" I croaked. "Why do I feel so rough?"

"It's a side effect of mind merging. You should feel better soon."

"How long have I been out?"

Gabriella looked up at the grandfather clock, which ticked in response. "About fourteen hours."

"Wow, that's one hell of a power nap." I lifted a cement hand and rubbed at my blurry eyes. "Where am I?"

"Still at the Warren, in my room actually."

"You live here?"

She nodded, sending raven hair spilling down her face. Absently she swept at the strands with the back of a hand.

A sudden wave of sickness rushed through me. I leaned over for a glass of water that had been placed on the table. My shaking fingers knocked it off the edge. Before the tumbler could hit the

158

ground, Gabriella shot out a hand and caught it without spilling a drop.

"Here, let me," she offered, motioning towards my lips.

"I can do it myself!" I barked, snatching it from her.

She looked taken aback. "Alex, is everything okay?"

Without drinking, I lowered the glass. "Is that supposed to be a joke? Gabriella, I thought you were my friend. But it was all an act wasn't it? You don't care about me at all. You just wanted to get me here!"

Her eyes went wide. "No, that's not true!" She tried to take my hand, but I snatched it away. The look in her eyes suggested she was about to cry. The thought of her upset knotted my stomach. But I was hurt.

"Then after everything I've been through," I persisted, "kidnapping, car accident, almost rage killing someone and getting dragged halfway through London's underground system - oh and nearly flattened by a train - I find out that monsters exist! For all I know *Dracula* is a frigging biography! But hey, that's okay because it's my job to fight the *really* bad ones. Because I was chosen. I don't get a say. Apparently my soul decided this before we'd been formally introduced. So no, for your information everything is not okay!" My anger added handfuls of spite into the last few words. Gabriella recoiled as if struck.

Drained, I flopped back onto the mattress. My head buzzed angrily.

I felt a hand take mine. I tried to move, but Gabriella held on tight. The charges were soon replaced by the warm sensation, which flowed through my body. Almost instantly I felt calmer. Gabriella's face moved into view. Her eyes were damp with tears. She cupped a free hand against my cheek, which felt soft against my skin. I wanted to be angry but it was getting harder to manage. Her voice was calm and soothing when she spoke.

"Alex, please believe me when I say I *do* care about you. Look, I can't deny that my mission was to become part of your life. But I'm not sorry, because it meant that I got to meet you and find out what a kind, good person you are."

I stared, trying to work out if she was being genuine. Her face seemed to suggest so.

"Really?"

"Really."

"How can I believe you?"

"Because you know I mean it," she said staring into my eyes.

I felt something release in my chest. As if a valve had been opened and I could breathe again. *She does care.*

"And being a Chosen may seem like a curse," she continued. "Trust me I know that better than anyone. But it's also a privilege to be able to protect those who can't protect themselves."

Her sincere words made me feel a bit guilty about my petulant outburst.

"So how many others like me have you brought in?" I asked in an effort to change the subject.

"None. You were my first infiltration. I requested the assignment after the Coven made us aware you were out there. I don't even know why." Smiling she added, "Given the way I handled it, I doubt Faru will ever let me do it again."

I raised my eyebrows. "What did you do wrong?"

"You got away from us...from me. When we were returning you home after your Awakening. You were heavily sedated, but somehow, you managed to jump from the car and escape. It took five hours before you turned up back home. I was frantic!"

I snapped to attention. "Wait, that's the reason I woke up in the park! But how is that possible?"

"Your soul acting on autopilot I guess. Survival instinct. It must have felt we were a threat."

I ran a hand along the nape of my neck. It felt sore - like the rest of my body. "I don't understand. If the Awakening is such a big deal, why try and take me home, why not keep me here and explain, instead of being so secretive?" Gabriella drew her legs up onto the bed. "We wanted to make sure nothing went wrong. That's why we took you the moment your change started happening. It would have been impossible to keep you sedated the whole time. Then we would have two options; tell you everything, or keep you captive until we felt we *could* tell you. Both options were equally dangerous." She leaned forward. "The time just before and after an Awakening is critical. It's your body's adjustment period. Too much stress could have caused

160

your soul to eject your body prematurely. Then you would be...lost. So I came up with a third option. Wipe your memory. Take you back home and keep you under constant protection - without your knowledge. Sage Faru was against the idea at first, but I managed to convince him eventually." She playfully slapped my leg. "That's when you decided to perform your disappearing trick."

I frowned. "How exactly did you wipe my memory?"

Gabriella looked slightly uncomfortable. "Neural manipulation or Charm as we call it is an ability some Chosen possess. I'm one of them."

"You mean mind control?"

"Yes."

"Have you charmed me since then?"

"Only that one time, I promise. Plus I couldn't now even if I wanted to. Your Awakening is almost complete. I can't manipulate another Chosen."

Once again her expression looked genuine. I nodded. At that moment, I caught the flowery scent of her hair. It stirred a memory.

"You were there on the night of my Awakening."

"I was. How did you know?"

I cleared my throat. "I erm, I recognise the way you smell…"

Gabriella's face broke into a half smile. "Interesting. Not in a bad way I hope."

"No you smell…um, good."

She laughed. "Well that's a relief."

Didn't think that one through did you Alex, my internal voice chastised.

"So what was the cryptic phone call all about?" I said, in a desperate attempt to change the subject again.

"That was the second part of my idea. To drip feed you information until we felt you were ready for the truth. But after our conversation in the park, I wanted to do more than just that."

"The car and clothes," I said.

"Exactly. You get those sorts of perks once you join anyway, but I wanted to give them to you early so you could feel special. I convinced Sage Faru it would be a benefit to your state of

161

mind. Thinking about it now, it was all a bit childish, but I wanted to do it."

Warmth bloomed in my stomach. *She took risks to make me feel better.*

Nothing more was said for a moment. The mellow ticking of the clock filled the silence.

"You have an interesting phone voice," I said after a while.

"Sorry?"

"The voicemail you left me."

Gabriella gave a chuckle. "Sadly I can't take credit for that. Delagio, a teammate of mine did it. He loves that kind of thing. But I was there when the Skinshifter attacked you."

I swallowed, once again reminded of the horrific creature with the evil red eyes that had hunted me down. "That thing in the woods? You saved me?"

Gabriella shifted her gaze from mine. "Yes. Plus several other times you didn't know about. I always made sure you were safe Alex."

"Thank you." I squeezed her hand.

She squeezed back. "My pleasure."

I stared down at my hand, still clasped in hers. Without looking up I said, "I'm sorry...you know for snapping at you."

Her smile brightened the dim room. "Don't even mention it. What you're going through is quite intense. I should know." Gabriella released my hand, and the skin tingled from the ghost of her touch. "I have a gift for you," she said.

I pulled myself into a sitting position as she opened a drawer in the bedside table. She carefully removed a book and handed it to me. It looked old and worn, and about the size of a pocket journal, but much thicker. The jacket was made from mottled brown leather. It reminded me of the books I'd seen in the underground waiting room. A worn string held the book closed. I pulled at it and was greeted with the aroma of old paper. The wafer thin pages fell open to show an artist sketch of a grim looking creature called a Redcap. Lots of notes had been handwritten underneath it.

"What is this?" I asked, flicking through.

"The HASEA Handbook. It contains all sorts of information about the Alliance and Pandemonians. It explains how to defend

162

yourself against an attack, or what various weaknesses and strengths a specific lifeform has – that kind of thing. Basically everything you need to know to stay alive. All new Guardians get one."

I turned the weighty book in my hands and ran my thumb over the bumpy leather. "This is really cool. I'm surprised it's handwritten though, you'd think it would be easier to just mass print them or something," I said.

"They do. This is my personal copy. It's was handed down to me from another Chosen. It's yours now. Think of it as an early Christmas present."

The warm feeling returned. "Are you sure?"

The little half smile appeared again. "Of course. Just make sure you look after it. It's...very dear to me."

"Thank you Gabriella, it's great."

I flicked through a few more pages, stopping to read a passage about how to defeat a Redcap with household items. Apparently lemon juice was like acid to these little Goblin things.

"Are you understanding it okay?" Gabriella asked.

"Yeah. I mean it's a bit weird and I'm still trying to get my head around the fact that these sorts of things exist, but I get what it's saying."

"How good is your Italian by the way?"

"Non parlo Italiano," I replied with a grin.

Gabriella tapped a finger on the section I was reading. "Alex, this whole guide is written in Italian."

I stared at her. "What? No it isn't."

"Of course it is. I come from Italy, why would my guide be written in English?"

"But that doesn't make any sense. I don't know any foreign languages!"

"You do now. And just so you know, I've been speaking to you in French for the last few minutes."

I lowered the guide into my lap and stared at her. "Ella, have you lost it? You're speaking English! I can even hear your accent!"

Gabriella leaned forward, eyes bright. "My accent will be inherent in any language I speak that isn't my mother tongue. A

Chosen understands every language current or dead from both sides of the Veil. Remember earlier, you wanted to know why you could read the motto written on the Temple door? It's because your mind translated it. Now that your Awakening has progressed, that translation is automatic. Unless you think about it, it always will be. You've been speaking French with me without even realising."

I thought of when Faru had been explaining the Latin terms for the various species and how I'd known what they meant before he'd explained. *How else could I know that?*

"I can speak and read any language I want."

"And write," Gabriella added.

"Wow that's..."

"Amazing?"

"Handy. Like if this whole Guardian thing doesn't work out, I can always get a job as a translator," I said with a cheeky smile.

We both burst out laughing. It felt good, like when we had just hung out together at school, back when everything had been simple. It seemed crazy to think it had only been a week ago. It felt like I'd known Gabriella for years.

When we had both stopped laughing, she held out a hand. "I'll hold onto the guide for you until later."

"So what happens now?" I asked, passing her the book.

She pointed to a barely noticeable door in the far wall. "The en suite's through there. Freshen up. I left some clean clothes that will fit you." Standing up, she headed for another door by the chair. "I'll wait for you outside. Take as long as you need."

I took a sip of water, already feeling much better. "Okay," I answered. "Then what?"

She turned back to face me.

"Then you meet the rest of the team."

14

After a soothing shower, I changed into the comfortable pair of jeans, jumper and white trainers that Gabriella had laid out for me. Stepping out of the bedroom, I emerged into a luxurious living area. A dining table and chairs stood underneath impressive bay windows to my left. The far wall was home to a large stone fireplace. Flames danced on wooden logs, their smoky scent filling the room. To the right an archway led off to what must have been the hallway, and in the middle of the room carpeted stairs lead down into a sunken seating area. The space was home to a large red corner sofa and glass coffee table. At the end of the space sat a television, playing an old episode of Family Guy.

But by far the most interesting part of the room was the people who occupied it. Gabriella was perched on the arm of the sofa. Sprawled over the rest of it was a lithe man who looked in his mid-twenties. Wavy black hair ran all the way to his neck; another tuft sprouted from his chin, expertly tapered into a point. He wore a grey waistcoat and a pair of long brown boots, which he rested on the coffee table, and a brown Stetson hat lay on his chest. He was playing idly with a wooden marble, rolling it between his fingers, whilst chuckling at the show on TV.

A behemoth of a man stood next to the window. He must have been close to seven foot tall and was as stacked as Arnie in his prime. A tribal tattoo ran from his bald head all the way down one side of his face to the jaw, covering some kind of scar. His eyes were as dark as shadows, topped by scythe eyebrows. The only contradiction to his intimidating appearance came in the form of a delicate silver locket, threaded through a leather string and hanging from his tree-trunk neck.

Sitting between Gabriella's legs on a thick shag-pile rug was a sweet looking girl of around ten or eleven. She hummed to herself, tapping at a portable Nintendo whilst Gabriella braided a section of her long, blonde hair.

They all looked up as the door clicked shut behind me.

"Hi Alex," Gabriella said, motioning me over. "Come and meet everyone."

Swallowing a lump of nervousness, I walked over.

"This is the rest of our team, or Orion as we're more officially known." She pointed a slender finger at the Spanish looking man. "This is Delagio."

He gave a salute.

"The midget by the window is Midnight."

The hulk grunted then fell silent.

"And this is Sophia."

I was given a quick grin and then attention returned to the game, tongue poking out with concentration.

"Sophia's actually half Witch, but decided to join us instead of the Coven."

"They smell weird," Sophia said screwing up her nose. The group laughed and I nervously joined in.

"Uh, nice to meet you all," I said, feeling my face flush.

Gabriella glanced at her watch. "There is actually one more member of Orion, but they're running a little late. It's someone you already know."

My stomach knotted up. *Someone I know? Oh god, please don't be Tim. I don't think I could handle that.*

A door in the hallway opened. Gabriella peered behind me. "Speak of the devil."

I turned to see Miss Steele pass under the archway. She surveyed the scene with squinted eyes, then leaned against the wall and crossed her legs. The toe of her thick black heels made a muffled clomping sound on the carpet. "Pixie actually," she corrected sarcastically. Then she turned her attention to me. "Hello, Alexander."

My throat had dried up. I didn't think I could manage any more surprises. "H-hi Miss Steele," I croaked.

"I think Rachel will be okay from now on. But don't think this means you are getting out of your homework." She gave a shrill laugh, which bounced off the walls and hurt my ears. I forced out a chuckle.

"Right, Alex." Gabriella's words cut mercifully through the awkward silence that followed. "You're probably hungry by now."

My stomach rumbled in agreement. "Starving."

"Let's find you something to eat. Then we can begin your training."

"Training?"

Rachel raised an eyebrow. "Well you didn't think we were going to send you straight out into the big bad world without making sure you were ready did you? We have a lot of work to do before your test."

"Uh, test?"

Gabriella shot my teacher a frown before turning to me. "Before you can be considered fit to become a Guardian, you have to undergo an initiation of sorts. A trial to ensure that you're mentally and physically prepared. It varies from person to person and species to species." Seeing my expression she added, "Don't worry, you'll do fine when the time comes."

I didn't share her confidence.

"Okay guys let's get things moving." Gabriella snapped her head around to Delagio. "Del, I need you on speed." To the giant, "Midnight you are on strength...obviously. And Rachel can I have you on combat?"

The Pixie nodded her head. "Not a problem."

"I'll take abilities. Let's do this. Right *mia bambina*," Gabriella said ruffling Sophia's hair, "you can go with Midnight if you want."

"Yay!" shouted the girl and snapped the machine closed. She ran up the stairs to Midnight, who smiled and knelt down. Sophia clambered up his back and wrapped her legs around his neck. He stood up and locked a securing arm around her shins.

As the team stirred under Gabriella's orders, a simple fact became clear. *She's the leader.* The notion that I'd expected anything less surprised me more than her impressive position.

I followed the team out of the apartment. Midnight had to duck so Sophia could pass under the doorway successfully. We emerged into an extravagant hallway. The marble floor had been polished to a shine and television monitors flush with the

167

smooth white walls displayed rotating 3D maps of tunnels and rooms, which I figured were schematics of the base.

Gabriella motioned for me to follow her to the left. Everyone else headed right. "Tell Midnight I'll send Alex down in about twenty minutes," she said to Delagio, who was last out the door.

"Sure thing boss."

I was surprised to hear a Southern American twang in his accent. It sounded nothing like the voice that had left the message on my phone. He tipped the rim of his hat and turned to follow the others. In the distance, Sophia and Midnight were playing about. She would cover his eyes, and he'd bump into the walls on purpose. Or he'd spin on the spot until she fell into fits of giggles. The sounds of their laughing echoed back up the hallway towards me. Midnight seemed utterly natural with the girl and she didn't seem at all nervous of him. I wondered if he had children of his own.

Gabriella touched my arm. "Let's go."

We passed dozens of doors on our way down the hallway. Each one had a metallic plate with a name embossed on it. I read names like Ivy Affron, Sam Clarke and Jessica Black.

"Each apartment belongs to a resident Chosen," Gabriella explained. "Alliance Pandemonians have apartments too, but they're all underground."

I stifled a laugh as I imagined Vampires unwinding on sofas - sipping blood from chalices - or giant wolves sitting around a table playing poker against fairies who buzzed about on silvery wings. It was stupid, but who knew what they did in their spare time?

"Your apartment is a work in progress. It should be finished by the time you join officially."

I snapped my head around. "I get a place like yours?"

Gabriella laughed. "Of course. Permanently if you decide to serve at the Warren. Although you can choose to relocate to any base you want."

"Is that what you did?"

My companion's gaze dropped to the floor. "I transferred from Castello in *Roma* a few years ago. I couldn't even tell you why to be honest. It just felt like something I needed to do."

So she didn't transfer a few weeks ago with her family then. I aired the thought.

"No."

Her direct response implied that nothing more would be said on the subject, so I left it alone.

"I can't see any reason why I'd want to transfer. I'll serve here."

Gabriella smiled.

We emerged onto the right-hand balcony high above the grand entrance I'd seen in the vision. As we moved along the carpeted walkway, Gabriella pointed to the large portrait hanging above the stairs.

"Sage Faru's quarters are through there. So is the section of the Veil the Warren is built around. Fae magic seals the entrance. It's impossible to get in or out without his permission."

I looked up at the towering picture. Faru's unique eyes seemed to stare down, keeping dutiful watch on all the people who bustled about below.

We reached the ground level. In contrast to the mind merge vision, several of the doors were now blocked by more of the hulking guards I'd seen in the Temple. They were like statues, heads bowed against staffs as if in prayer. That was until someone moved towards a door. Then they lifted up their heads and scanned the individual with pinprick eyes. Like mechanised robots, they stepped aside to allow access, before moving back and falling silent once more. It was creepy.

"What's behind all these doors?" I asked as we walked through the hallway.

"Offices mainly. Normal humans we call Agents work here. They do most of our clerical work for us. You'd be surprised how much paperwork has to be filled out when we deport or kill a Rogue."

I couldn't help but smile. *Even the supernatural has red tape.*

"Others lead to normal places like reception rooms, the library and the kitchens," she continued. The final word made my stomach growl. "Guarded doors tend to lead to the Nexus." Gabriella gave me a playful nudge. "Most of the cool stuff happens underground."

My eyes were drawn towards a vast set of golden double doors near the staircase. An impressive jewelled display depicted a knight crossing blades with what appeared to be an upright wolf with bat's wings. The same motif was written underneath in Latin.

Chosen we rise - Allied we prevail.

"I'm guessing something important is behind there," I said, pointing.

Gabriella nodded. "That's the Feasting Hall of Unity. It's where all joining ceremonies take place. You'll see inside when it's time for yours."

She peeled away from me, heading towards a guarded door. A gorgeous aroma teased me from the other side. My mouth began to water. Gabriella stopped at the entrance, hands placed impatiently on her hips.

"So you're guarding the kitchen today. The kitchen...really? What am I going to do, leak recipes to the SOS?"

The guard simply raised its head in response and stared with its blood filled eyes.

"Move!"

The hulking giant stepped to one side. I eyed it warily as we passed.

Inside the grand, steam-filled kitchen I saw the reason for the added security. Numerous miniature creatures flew about on dainty wings, tending to an array of bubbling pots and pans that sat on large hobs. They stirred wooden spoons bigger than they were and shook condiments into the various pots with both hands. They were pretty little things, sporting silvery hair and wide eyes with baby pink pupils.

"Asrai," whispered Gabriella. "They're preparing for the joining feast."

I stared at the cute creatures as my mind attempted to rationalise the fact that I was casually watching a group of fairies cook. At the same time I felt an odd sense of acceptance. *All this hard work is for me.*

One of the Asrai noticed us enter. She swooped over to a plate of sandwiches sitting on a metal sideboard. Leaning over, she grabbed the edge with both hands and floated back up, plate wobbling between knees and wrists.

170

"Faru told us to prepare this for Alexander," she breathed as she drew near. Her voice sounded like tinkling glass.

I stared at her.

"It's quite heavy," she added.

"Oh, right!" I plucked the plate from her grip. "Uh, thank you."

"Fresh Quinberry juice is in the fridge." The fairy gave a little mid-air bow, then without another word, floated off and resumed cooking.

Gabriella grabbed a glass of pinkish liquid from a fridge next to us and handed it to me.

I ate ravenously, tearing off thick chunks of the soft bread with my teeth. The food was delicious. Thick rolls of ham coated in some kind of sweet and sour marmalade, topped with crunchy lettuce. The juice was even more incredible. It tasted like sharp apple mixed with strawberries, and fizzed on my tongue. Afterwards I felt like my insides had been spring-cleaned.

"Wow," I said after draining the last few drops from the glass. "That was good."

Gabriella nodded. "It's made from a rare berry that grows in Pandemonia. Should help clear the last remnants of your brain fog."

I set the plate and glass down on a storage unit behind me. A sudden rush of air forced me to cover my mouth with my sleeve and deliver a sly burp.

"It'll do that too," Gabriella winked. "Ready to go?"

"Absolutely."

"Okay, time to toughen you up."

*

"Don't worry, I'll see you soon" said Gabriella as the elevator doors rolled shut.

Searching the multitude of buttons on the panel, I found the one she'd told me to press - a coiled fist. I pushed my finger on the symbol and it glowed blue.

GYMNASIUM, said the hidden voice.

My breakfast almost made a reappearance as the elevator dropped into free fall. Bending my knees against the force, I

171

pressed into the corner and lowered myself down, hands gripping the railing above me. Bowing my head into my knees, I tried to settle myself as the elevator plummeted through the Nexus. After an eternity it stopped descending and rushed forward, every now and then lifting up and sinking down as if navigating speed bumps. Mercifully after a few more seconds, it rolled to a stop. The elevator beeped and the doors cranked open to reveal an amused Midnight and Sophia staring down at me. A bear like hand was extended and I was yanked to my feet.

"You get used to it", Midnight grunted in a thick cockney accent.

"I certainly hope so," I said, exiting the steel death trap.

A cavernous gymnasium stretched out in front of us. All manner of equipment ran along the vast walls; treadmills, weight benches, rowing machines and punching bags. The roar of whirring and clanking equipment hit from every angle. Several boxing rings were scattered about too. At first glance, it seemed like any other gym. But on closer inspection, it was anything but normal. A pale looking man on a treadmill ran so fast, his lower legs were blurred - the type of thing you'd see in a cartoon. A dainty looking woman bench-pressed what seemed to be solid stone weights. The bar sagged like an unhappy face as it struggled with the incredible loads stacked on either side. I had to stifle a cry when I saw the two fighters sparring in the closest ring. The towering beasts made Midnight look vertically challenged. Their skin was a mixture of shining black and red scales. Skull-like heads topped with a cluster of arching horns. Eyes like dying embers and parted mouths, which revealed teeth like hypodermic needles. They ducked and parried, grunting and striking each other with sledgehammer fists.

"Oni," whispered Sophia. "They're strong but usually pretty dumb." I noticed now that we were closer that she suffered from Heterochromia. One of her eyes was a vivid blue, the other the velvet green of a tree leaf. If anything, it made her even more adorable.

I didn't know how to respond to the information, so nodded quietly. We weaved through the room, passing all manner of creatures. Sophia acted as visual translator, listing off the species as we walked.

172

"Pixie, Incubus, Goblin, Bloodlings, oh - that group over there are all Chosen like us." She pointed to a cluster of guys and girls who looked a few years older than me. They raised their heads in curiosity as we passed. Then they placed both hands across their chests in an X shape before extending them to us. It took a few confused seconds to understand it was a greeting. Midnight and Sophia returned the gesture and I tried my best to emulate it before we moved on.

A colossal thump echoed around the room. I turned just in time to see one of the Oni fighters slam to the mat, eyes rolling up in its head. The other pumped both fists in the air and let out a roar that would have any lion running for cover. Shuddering, I turned away.

Eventually we reached the end of the sizable room and passed through a looming archway. The room on the other side was completely white and about the size of a tennis court. A bench sat at the far end, next to a complicated looking machine. Buttons blinked and screens flashed all over it. In another corner stood what appeared to be a large, metallic fridge. The wall straight ahead was in serious need of repair. Thick chunks of plaster were missing and large cracks scattered out in all directions, some even reaching the ceiling. Sophia plonked herself down on the bench, folding her skinny legs under herself. Her big, multi-coloured eyes were fixed on me and she wore a look of fervent interest.

Midnight pointed to a red spot on the floor I hadn't noticed. "Stand there," he grunted.

I shuffled over. He walked to the large fridge and returned a second later carrying some kind of injector. It looked like an insulin dispenser, more pen than needle, except this one was see-though and full of dark blue liquid.

"Hold out your hand," he ordered.

I didn't respond.

He stared at me. I sighed and offered out my trembling arm. He jabbed the needle into it and liquid fire seared up my wrist. I yelled and shook the wounded appendage, but the pain kept sweeping up regardless, through my bicep and into my shoulder. My entire arm ballooned and the veins swelled into thick blue worms.

173

"Damn that hurts!" I yelled, clutching my infected arm.

Midnight rolled his eyes. "Give it time."

"I've had them before. They don't hurt *that* much," giggled Sophia.

Great, I'm more of a wimp than a little girl, I thought in between the swear words.

After a few more seconds the pain dissipated and my arm shrank back to normal.

"I think I'm okay now," I admitted.

"What do ya want, a prize?" snorted the hulk.

I stared at the red welt left by the injection. It grew smaller until it had completely gone. "What was that?"

"Something to help if you get hurt."

I don't like the sound of that.

"Face the entrance."

I rotated so that Sophia and the equipment were to my left and the cracks on the wall were behind me. Midnight lumbered over to the computer and tapped at the main screen. I couldn't see properly past his large frame, but I did notice the words 'begin training' appear in flashing green letters. He glanced over his shoulder and a wide smile spread across his face.

"Get ready."

"For w-" I began to ask, but saw the answer swing towards me from the ceiling.

A battering ram.

It dipped towards me at an immense speed. I dived out of the way just in time. I felt the wind as it rushed past me followed by the deafening crack of stone connecting with brick. The fractures in the wall increased and small fragments of plaster dropped to the floor.

"Are you trying to kill me?" I shouted at the giant madman, who looked even bigger from my position on the ground.

"No," he said simply. "If I was trying to kill ya, you'd be dead." Then he turned back to the screen and started tapping away again. "Reaction speeds are good," he muttered to himself.

The ram winched itself back up on its supports.

Midnight tapped the screen one last time with an over the top motion. "Right," he said without turning. "Let's do that again, but don't move this time, k?"

"Don't move?" I spluttered, picking myself up off the ground.

Sophia shouted encouragement from the bench. "Come on Alex, you'll do great! If I can do it so can you!"

I was shocked that they had let a little girl take part in something like this. Then I remembered that she wasn't a normal little girl at all, just like I wasn't a normal teenager. *Nothing around here is normal.*

"Okay," I said positioning myself back on the spot. My heart punched against my chest. I clenched my fists and gritted my teeth, ignoring the rational part of my brain, which screamed that I would die in the next few seconds.

The ram came down harder this time. It carved through the air, heading right for my midsection. I shut my eyes and forced myself to stay put.

Smack!!

It felt like a nuclear bomb had hit my stomach. My feet left the ground and I flew backwards, arms flailing wildly. Then there was a second impact as my back smashed into the wall. The air rushed from my lungs and I slipped to the ground, wheezing as I struggled for precious oxygen.

"Calm down," said Midnight. "Your body can handle this."

"Glurrgh," I replied.

Eventually my lungs reflated. I ran a hand through my hair, sweeping away the flecks of plaster that covered it like bad dandruff.

I waited to see how I felt. Apart from the initial blow, there was no longer any tangible pain. Only a dull ache, which soon faded. I looked over at Midnight who gave a noncommittal shrug.

"Not bad for a first try I guess," he grunted. "Let's do it again."

Three more times we tried and three more times my body was sent careering into the wall, which began to look as if it were in danger of collapsing altogether.

Midnight shook his head in disappointment. "Come on, you're not trying!" he growled.

His response sounded like something John would say. I felt the anger rise in my stomach. "It would help if I knew what the

175

hell I'm supposed to be doing!" I barked before I could stop myself.

Midnight's eyebrows descended over his dark eyes. He looked like he was brewing an anger of his own - one that could rip mine into pieces.

"Stop the ram with your body," Sophia whispered. Midnight gave the girl a sideways glance and she went red. "Sorry."

The behemoth composed himself. "You ain't supposed to know what to do in this trainin'. We like ya to use intuition to work it out. But we'll pretend pint size didn't say anythin' yeah?"

I nodded and stood up. The battering ram cranked up on its chain supports.

"Come on, Alex!" encouraged Sophia.

Placing my feet on the red target, I tried to mentally prepare myself. My mind flashed back to when the car had hit me. I remembered how without trying, I'd stayed rooted to the spot, whilst the car folded itself around me. *Sophia's right, I can do this.*

"Okay I'm ready." I clapped my hands together and jumped a little on the spot. Midnight seemed to approve my change of attitude. He nodded and almost threatened to break a smile.

I was prepared when the ram swung down this time, but my reaction still surprised me. Instead of just letting it hit me, I sprang forward, driving both fists into the stone. There was a thunderous crack and for a second I thought I'd shattered my knuckles. But then several deep, jagged lines appeared on the ram's surface. A second later it crumbled into a shower of concrete rain. I rotated my wrists and was relieved to see that they were fine. There was a light dusting of powder on my knuckles, which I brushed off.

Midnight's expression was one of pure shock. Sophia copied it like a ventriloquist's dummy, staring at the pile of rubble at my feet.

"That, I have never seen."

"Whoa..." breathed pint size.

"Better?" I asked trying to keep the smugness from my voice. Midnight nodded and rubbed a large finger on his chin, surveying the destruction. Sophia started clapping like an overexcited seal.

176

The sound of footsteps approaching made me glance over at the doorway. Delagio entered the room, his Stetson hat emerging before he did.

"Just in time," said Midnight. "Alexander just smashed strength trainin'...literally."

The American raised his eyebrows at the pile of rubble on the floor. "Not bad man. Let's see if ya'll can bring that energy to part two." His southern drawl combined with waist jacket and hat reminded me of a bad guy from a cheesy western. I couldn't resist a smile.

He gestured for me to follow. We were almost out of the room, when a loud siren started blaring from a speaker near the ceiling. It sounded like something from a World War II film.

"Well I'll be damned," cursed Delagio. "Looks like trainin' is gonna have to wait. Come on."

All three charged out of the room and I followed. We ran through the gym, which was quickly emptying of people - they were all squeezing into various elevators. There was a sense of absolute urgency.

What is going on?

"Let's take the stairs," called Delagio over his shoulder.

We headed through a set of double doors and into stairwell. We were at level B18. Thundering up the steps, we twisted up and up, until we reached B2. We exited into a long white corridor and rocketed along. Doors whipped past us as we ran. If anyone were to have come out, they would've been mowed down, no question. At the end of the corridor, Delagio burst through a set of double doors and we piled into the room beyond.

It looked like a control centre of some kind. Rows of desks were covered with dozens of computers. They were occupied by a myriad of people who were tapping frantically at keyboards. On the wall at the front was a staggeringly large screen. It showed a map of the UK on a grid system; currently one section of it was flashing red.

I noticed Sage Faru at the front of the room, staring up at the monitor, his staff pressed firmly into the tiled floor. Two of the odd bodyguards stood just behind him, hands clutched around their precious crosiers. There were several people standing around in white lab coats, but no other Chosen appeared to be here yet. I wondered where they'd all gone.

"What we got?" Midnight grunted.

"Vampire pack," said a female voice.

Gabriella moved past us into full view. My breath snagged in my lungs when I saw her. She was wearing some kind of black leather uniform. A miniature silver version of the emblem on the Feasting Hall doors was emblazoned on the breast of her jacket, reminding me of a police badge. Her raven hair was tied back into a long ponytail. Guns, knives and other strange weapons I couldn't identify hung from a thick metallic belt wrapped around her waist. A samurai sword ran diagonally down her back, secured by a scabbard. She looked like she meant business - she looked like a soldier.

Gabriella paced over to one of the computer screens. The assistant - a squirmy looking man with round glasses - scrambled out of the way so she could use it. Her gloved hands muffled the sounds of the keystrokes. "Quite a large pack," she informed the room. "At least fifteen. They tripped the perimeter sensors at the five mile marker."

Faru's voice boomed across the room. "Do you think it could be Rahuman?"

Gabriella tapped a few more keys and the large screen changed to show a blue line originating from a point roughly in the middle of the country. It wasn't entirely straight, sometimes shooting off in random directions, but mainly heading down towards London. At certain points, the line had thick blue pulsing circles marked on it.

"Judging from the direction of the attacks and where we've encountered him before, I'd say yes."

There were nervous murmurings from the people in the room.

Faru nodded. "He is coming for us then. Let's save him some time." The old Seelian looked in my direction, then back at Gabriella. "I want you to take Alexander with you."

Her head shot up. "But sir, with respect, he hasn't even finished his training yet. He isn't ready!"

"I am aware of that, which is why he will be observing only. Take Twelve and Thirteen with you as an extra precaution." He gestured towards the silent guards.

Gabriella's face looked conflicted. Sighing, she conceded. "As you wish Sage Faru."

"All remaining teams are in their assigned defence positions around the base. Atlas will be here shortly to handle coms and I'll place Echo on standby for support. Be safe." He crossed his arms in the same salute the Guardians in the gym had used. Everyone returned the gesture. I tried and failed.

Midnight smacked a fist into his palm. "Alright let's go finish this arsehole once and for all."

I stood motionless looking and feeling like a lost child.

"Five minutes everyone. Get ready and meet me in the garage." Gabriella pushed away from the computer and took my arm. "You come with me."

"What's happening?"

"It's Showtime."

15

Gabriella led me to an underground parking lot somewhere in the cavernous depths of the base. Shining black tiles covered the walls and arching wall lights provided a purple glow to the area. Around us were dozens of parking spaces. Most of them were filled with enough beautiful cars and bikes to make even Bruce Wayne jealous. I followed her over to a sleek black Ferrari. She rested against the bonnet and stared at me with her captivating blue eyes.

"Alexander, I need you to listen to me."

When Gabriella looked at me like that, there wasn't anything else I could do *but* listen.

"Okay."

"This could be a very dangerous hunt. If it's the Vampire pack we think it is, they're extremely powerful. We've lost several Guardians to Rahuman, including Chosen. So I want you to stay behind us the whole time. I don't want you to get involved *at all*. No matter what happens. If anything goes wrong, I want you to take a car and drive away as fast and as far as you can. Do you understand me?" Her voice carried a no mess authority tone.

"I understand. I won't do anything," I promised. *What can I do anyway?*

Gabriella's face broke into the reassuring half smile that I loved. Looking behind me she rolled her eyes. "Here comes your protection."

I spun around to see Faru's guards walking towards me. Instead of robes, they now wore long white trench coats, with matching boots. As well as the menacing electric crosiers, they carried an array of impressive looking pistols and knives on their belts. Up close I discovered that the numbers on their foreheads weren't tattooed after all, they were *carved*.

They reached us and stopped. Gabriella pointed toward a silver Range Rover sitting opposite the Ferrari. "You two travel with the rest of the team." She tapped the metal of the bonnet. "We're in here."

The guards shook their heads like twins. One moved forward to grab me, but Gabriella jumped up and swept me behind her.

"Listen to me you moronic clay dolls. I'm the leader of Orion and what I say goes. When we get there, you protect Alex with your lives - if that's what you call them. Until then, he is not leaving my sight. Clear?"

I felt a rush of warmth at how protective she was being over me.

The guards paused before nodding in eerie unison. They both turned and walked over to the jeep. I frowned, watching the odd figures fall silent as if their batteries had run out.

"Why did you call them clay dolls? Is that like an in joke or something?" I asked.

"Not at all. Have you ever heard of a Golem?"

"Never."

"They're literally made from clay. Sage Faru creates them and brings them to life using Fae magic. They help serve and protect us, but they can't speak and have no compassion whatsoever. They just do what they are told like mindless dogs. I hate the things."

It suddenly made sense why their skin had been so devoid of lines. To all intents and purposes they were living statues.

"I'm getting the impression Faru is pretty powerful," I said.

Gabriella glanced over the driver door. "You have no idea."

I sank into the bucket seat just as the rest of Orion ran in. They were all dressed in the same black leather uniforms - Delagio still wearing his cowboy hat. They paced over to the Range Rover and jumped in. Sophia climbed into the boot space so there was enough room for the Golems to crank themselves in.

A second later the window buzzed down. Delagio leaned out and yelled, "You got a lock on em right?"

"Yeah, follow me," Gabriella called back.

"Sure thing, boss." He tipped his hat and the window glided back up.

Gabriella turned the key and the engine roared to life. I hardly had time to put my seatbelt on before we lurched forward, tyres squealing. We raced towards the coiling exit ramp. Behind, the jeep rumbled into existence and followed. We spiralled up and up like a helter skelter stuck in reverse.

The slope straightened and ahead, a large garage style door cranked open. We shot out into the daylight - car soaring off the ground. It slammed back down and Gabriella spun the wheel sharply to the right, power sliding around a decorative circular fountain. Gravel sprayed up from underneath the tyres. I craned my neck back and saw that we were on the front drive of the grand mansion. From the outside, the exit we burst through was designed to look like the rest of the building. As the jeep roared through, it closed automatically and all trace of it vanished.

The Ferrari raced down a long, winding driveway. The G-force pinned me against the seat as the speedometer slipped past the 100 mark. I squinted my eyes and gripped the sides of the seat as Gabriella jammed her foot to the floor. A looming brick wall appeared ahead, stretching as far as the eye could see in both directions. An iron gate stood in the centre. Four Golems stood guarding it - two on either side. One pressed a button on the wall and the gate swung open just in time for the car to blitz through. On the other side, we roared down a long road. A few expensive looking houses flashed past in between the hedges and trees.

"Who lives here?" I asked over the thundering engine.

"Humans in key positions to aid the Alliance," Gabriella answered. "Like police chiefs, judges and MP's. We look after them and their families. In return they help us maintain the cover of normalcy. As far as anyone knows, Faru is Mr Farris, a retired oil billionaire."

The speedometer now hovered over the 150 mark. The scenery whipped past in a blur of colours. *Still, it's better than being underground in one of those elevators. Wait...*

"Why aren't we using the Nexus?" I asked.

"Hold on a second."

Gabriella gunned the sports car out of the private road, onto a slip road and then onto a duel carriageway without breaking speed. The screeching of the wheels matched the sound of my fearful yell as we slewed sideways, narrowly missing a Ford estate. The driver blasted the horn and raised a middle finger. Gabriella eased up on the accelerator before stamping her foot down again once we were straight.

"Ella!" I shouted.

"Calm down you big baby! I won't crash, trust me. And in answer to your question, the Nexus is for travelling around London quickly." Her lips thinned. "Problem being that the pack is already in Chapter Hill."

I shuddered when I thought of the danger being so close to my school...to Mikey. All of those people oblivious to the horrific creatures hiding in the shadows. *Until it's too late.*

"Faru said something earlier about *most* Vampires being from Pandemonia. What did he mean by that?" I asked.

Gabriella jerked the car down a gear and overtook a Porsche. The young businessman inside scowled with defeat.

"He's talking about Bloodlings. Human Vampires." She tapped a gloved finger against her tooth. "Bloodseeker teeth are coated in a poison which paralyses their victims. But it has a far worse effect on humans. If one gets bitten and doesn't die from their injuries or the change, they'll be reborn as a Bloodling."

In my mind I imagined being the victim of a Vampire attack. The despair of helplessness, mixed with the dawning horror that there *were* creatures that went bump in the night. The thought made my stomach twist with dread.

"So what happens if a Bloodling bites another human?" I asked.

"Same thing. Only difference is that Bloodlings have a bizarre affection for their maker if they're a Bloodseeker. If they're a Bloodling, well..." She shrugged. "Let's just say we've had to clean up some big messes before."

I gave a silent nod.

Gabriella gave me a sideways glance. "It's not all bad. I mean apart from the whole living forever and needing to feed or you decompose aspects." She gave a wry smile.

"Like?"

"Well, the sun doesn't affect them for one. Plus they are far stronger than any normal human. Also most of them tend to join the HASEA, which as mercenary as it sounds, we need."

Something Gabriella said stuck in my brain. *Sun doesn't affect them.*

"Hold on a second, it's daytime. Faru said that Pandemonian Vampires are allergic to sunlight."

My companion pointed through the windshield at the thick grey clouds. "Direct sunlight yes. Unfortunately it's overcast, which means they'll be weaker, but far from a pushover."

We fell silent. Gabriella wove in and out of the traffic with expert precision. In fairness, there wasn't a moment where she looked as if she would lose control.

"Open up the glove compartment," she instructed suddenly.

I did as she asked and saw a silver gun lying in the narrow recess. I curled my hand around the base and slid it out. The metal was cool to the touch.

"This what you wanted?"

She glanced over and nodded. "That's for you. Just in case. It's all you need to take out any Vampire. Keep it hidden though; you aren't supposed to carry weapons yet."

I smiled. "Most girls keep CD's and eyeliner in their glove compartments. Trust you to have a gun."

"I have eyeliner in there too. A real girl's ready for any situation." She winked. Then her expression sobered. She pointed a finger towards a switch on the side of the gun. "To load it, push that all the way down. Then pull the trigger. Simple as that. It only holds six rounds though, so be careful."

I looked up. "If I'm not allowed to carry a gun yet, why are you giving me this?"

For a split second, I could have sworn her cheeks flushed. But on second glance it could've been a trick of the light. "Because I don't want you to get hurt Alex," she answered plainly.

We drove on in silence for a while. I rolled the weapon over in my hand, testing the weight. It felt solid and powerful. It was easy to see why people became obsessed with carrying them. The gun itself looked different to those I'd seen in films. The barrel was long and wide and the grip looked as if it was coated in wet black paint, but felt rubberised to touch. I'd never felt anything like it and had a sneaking suspicion that some of the materials weren't from my side of the Veil. I tucked the gun in the waistband of my jeans and pulled my top over it. I sat back and glanced in the wing mirror to check that the Range Rover was still following. It was right behind us.

"It doesn't look like a revolver, so why only six bullets?" I asked.

"Because it doesn't fire bullets. It fires compact wooden stakes. If you need to use it - god forbid - aim at the chest or throat."

I swallowed audibly. "I don't know if I can. I've never fired a gun before."

Gabriella shot me a look. "If you're about to be Vampire food, I'm confident you'll learn fast."

Something beeped next to the handbrake. Gabriella picked up a silver device, which resembled a curved phone. I strained to see. Above numerous buttons, an LCD screen displayed a sweeping radar. A red square flashed in the top left corner. Without warning, Gabriella veered across the lanes. Cars mashed their horns and skidded out of the way. My stomach knotted as we mounted the verge and ploughed into Susurrate forest. I gasped, grabbing hold of the seat as the foliage swallowed us. Trees scraped along the side of the car as it rocketed forward, slipping and sliding on the damp grass as if it were ice. Gabriella had to frantically pull the wheel from side to side to keep the vehicle from spinning out. I wished she'd chosen the Range Rover. If we were going to crash, it would be now.

Mercifully, after a few minutes of vehicular slalom, Gabriella slammed her foot on the brakes, bringing the Ferrari to a grinding halt. I breathed a sigh of relief. She checked the device and nodded, apparently satisfied. As we climbed out - me trembling with adrenaline - the Range Rover pulled up a few yards away and settled. With a deft movement, Gabriella slipped the car keys into my back pocket. Then she squeezed my side and walked over to the idling off roader.

The rest of the team climbed out and instantly I was wedged between the two Golems. I re-adjusted my jumper over the waist of my jeans and prayed they wouldn't notice the slight angle of the gun butt.

Gabriella slid a powerful looking gun out of its holster and pushed a lever on the side. The gun clicked, ready for action. She walked a few feet ahead and turned around to face us.

"Listen up. They're close. I don't need to tell you how dangerous this could get if it's Rahuman. However, we have the element of surprise on our side. They'll be expecting us to hold at the Warren and wait for them to come to us. They won't be prepared for a small hunter squad. I want eyes sharp and backs covered. We offer HASEA terms as usual. Let's hope they refuse them. That bastard doesn't deserve mercy."

There were murmurs of agreement. Midnight cracked his knuckles in an exaggerated manner.

Gabriella looked over at Sophia. "Honey, you're up.

"Okay," grinned pint size and walked to the front of the group. Crouching down, she placed her fingertips to her temples. Her lips barely moved as she breathed out some kind of incantation. After a few seconds a blue haze appeared around her body. Her frame began to tremor slightly, then she stood up and pointed to our left.

"It's Rahuman. Plus about twenty Hiveminds. They're down there, about quarter of a mile." She ran over to Midnight who gave her a hi-five.

"Brilliant. Okay, so does everyone have at least one booster?"

The team nodded - all except for Rachel. I looked around blankly. Midnight gestured towards me. "New kid got dosed about twenty minutes ago. It'll cover him for now."

Gabriella frowned. "Well I don't want Alex getting involved." She slid an injection pen out of a pouch at the back of her belt and held it towards me. "But...take this anyway."

I warily deposited the booster into my free back pocket, careful to avoid any unwanted injections. One of the Golems swung around to face Gabriella and cocked its head, questioning her with its glowing red eyes.

"As I said doughboy, I want my team sharp...whether they're fighting or not," she said flatly.

"What are boosters exactly?" I asked.

Everyone apart from Rachel and the Golems pulled the medical pens out of their pouches and injected themselves with the blue liquid, their faces showing the faintest signs of discomfort. I noticed their arms didn't swell. *Must be a first time thing.* Gabriella put the empty injector back in her pouch before answering.

"We heal about five times faster than a normal human. Boosters will help you heal twice as fast as that. It's a liquid compound refined from Luminar blood."

I remembered what Faru had told me about the Fae being required to donate blood if they joined the HASEA. Now I knew why Rachel didn't need one.

We made our way through the forest. Everyone was as silent as shadows. The only sound I could hear as we crept over tree roots and moss patches was the nervous beating of my own heart. The air was thick and oppressive. Small particles floated in what remained of the daylight. Gabriella led the group and I was part of the Golem sandwich at the back. One inched forward ahead of me whist the other edged backwards. Their humming crosiers swished from side to side as they surveyed the area.

After a few minutes, the trees began to thin. Ahead many had fallen over, creating a clearing. As we heaved ourselves over the carcass of a fir tree and into the opening, a rustling sound from the trees beyond made us all freeze. It was met with another from further to our right. A twig snapped. The Golems shoved me behind them and stamped their staffs on the ground, igniting the tips. I had to peek through the narrow space between their arms to see what was happening.

The most horrifying scream I'd ever heard ripped through the trees. My blood crystallised. The sound echoed all the way around the forest, repeating itself over and over. Birds took off in fright.

Then came the steady snap of twigs in the near distance. It grew louder and my skin crawled as a pack of Vampires stalked their way into the opening. Unprepared for how they looked, I struggled not to let fear overwhelm me.

Their skin was dark grey and scaled. They walked on all fours, sharp claws digging into the ground. Black marble eyes stared at us, shimmering with hatred, and when they blinked, grey lids twitched sideways across the slick surfaces. Their noses were singular horizontal slits, which flared wide like a gaping wound. Slick black hair protruded from their heads, some spilling over their hunched shoulders, the rest tapering into a mane that ran the length of their backs. They growled in unison, exposing yellowing fangs. These weren't lords of darkness and seduction…these were *creatures*.

More dropped out of the trees, their feet padding softly on the ground as they landed. I felt the fear rise from my stomach all the way into my throat, thick and burning.

"Stay back," whispered Gabriella.

She didn't need to ask twice.

I counted ten in total. They all stood in a line, as still as death. Watching us.

What are they waiting for?

As if answering my question, their bat like ears began to twitch as they heard something before we did. A moment later the trees parted and a man stepped into the opening. He wore a long cape, which he clutched around his body with a clawed hand. His skin was sallow, cheekbones protruding from his face at sharp angles. His ears were only slightly pointed and his eyes looked far more human than the feral beasts in front of him, except for the fact that they were yellow. His greasy hair had been combed backwards, the excess flowing down the sides of the cape.

He stepped forward and stroked the faces of two Hiveminds. They pushed their heads into his hands like adoring pets, making guttural sounds of happiness. He continued forward until he was between the pack and us. His lips peeled back across yellowing dagger teeth. The canines were curved like viper fangs. He wrapped a tongue around them as he took in each member of the team, one by one.

There was no doubt this was the Bloodseeker.

"Ah, the Alliance," he spoke at last. His voice sounded like stone scraping against gravel. "It seems you've located us before we had an opportunity to reach you." He clapped his sinewy hands together in a drawn out dramatic way. "Bravo."

"Rahuman," breathed Gabriella. She clenched her hands into fists. The sound of crunching leather filled the tense silence.

188

"Nevertheless, the location of our meeting is irrelevant, for the same result will occur...lots of dead Alliance." The Vampire lifted his hands up and the creatures behind him coiled back onto their hind legs, ready to pounce.

Metal clicked. In a split second, half a dozen guns were pointed at Rahuman. All except Delagio, who dug into his pouch and retrieved a selection of wooden marbles like the one I'd seen him playing with earlier. He held them out in his palm and they lifted into the air - about six inches from his hand, spiralling around each other like atoms. Despite our situation, my mouth dropped open in awe.

"You even brought the kinesist with you. Oh I am honoured," Rahuman mocked. The Golems drew in even tighter to me. I had to put my hand on one to stop it pushing me over. The skin underneath its coat was cold and hard. Just like a statue.

"Rahuman," said Gabriella, her voice thick with tension, "you are a traitor to the HASEA. As a valued member of the Alliance you were treated with trust and respect. In return you betrayed that trust by leaking vital information to the SOS. In addition, since escaping, your pack has spilled both human and Chosen blood. However, as stated in the HASEA treaty, because of previous service to the Alliance, surrender now and we will allow you to bypass the death penalty in favour of life imprisonment at White Mercy Prison in Pandemonia." She stopped speaking and a heavy silence hung in the air.

Under his breath, I could hear Midnight chanting over and over. "Don't surrender, don't surrender..."

The Bloodseeker laughed and the entire Hivemind pack cackled with him. My insides crawled; the sound was so far removed from human it was indescribable.

"As kind as your offer is, I think I would rather let my brothers and sisters suck the meat from your bones if it's all the same to you," Rahuman taunted with a poisonous glare. He raked a long fingernail across his chin. "Do you remember the previous Huntmaster of your unit?" He waved his hand in a dismissive manner. "Forgive me, I forget his name. Chopper or something."

"Cooper," corrected Gabriella in a biting tone.

"Ah yes that was it. Now I don't know if I ever told you this, but did you know that before I snapped his spine in half he pissed his pants? Pissed his pants like a little girl." He sniggered like he'd been told a dirty joke. I felt close to losing my lunch.

"You disgusting creature!" snarled Rachel, her gun trained on his forehead. "I should end you right now."

Rahuman seemed amused at her outburst. "Me...disgusting? At least I know what I am." Quick as a flash he drew back a sleeve, exposing a tattoo of what looked like a primitive eye on his forearm. "A true Pandemonian and proud Soldier of Sorrow! What are *you*, some kind of tamed pet to these mutant bloodsacks? Where's your dignity?" As his tone grew more aggressive, the pack started snarling and baying. Yet still they didn't attack. It was as if they were tethered to the spot by their leader. My heart smashed against my chest. A thousand snakes writhed inside my guts. We were vastly outnumbered and they looked raged.

"And you!" he hissed, thrusting a spiked finger at Gabriella, "you are an abomination!" He spat the words, flicking yellow spittle onto his pale chin. He wiped it with the back of his sleeve.

I shot my head up to look at Gabriella. *Abomination? What's he talking about?*

The only reaction she made was to unsheathe the sword from its scabbard. It had an ornate silver handle, with red grips spiralling to the top. The blade was carved entirely from wood. Rotating her hand, she rested the tip on the grass, her left hand still aiming the gun at the Bloodseeker's head.

Rahuman gestured towards us. "Don't you see? The HASEA is finished. Hades is on the brink of winning the Ageless War. Pandemonia will be at his mercy. Earth will fall soon after. You cannot hope to stop him. So I will make you a counter offer."

"Oh and what would that be?" asked Delagio, the marbles picking up speed around his hand.

"Surrender now and I promise that your deaths will be swift and merciful."

"It's you who's gonna die leech!" growled Midnight.

Rahuman started to laugh and then stopped abruptly. I froze...his eyes were fixed on mine. He cocked his head, staring through the gap between the two Golems and a dark smile slid

190

across his face like a shadow. The rest of the pack emulated his action, thin lips slipping back over their bared teeth. A gravelly noise escaped their throats, providing an eerie bassline to Rahuman's words.

"Now then, what do we have here? Could it be...I think, yes! I believe you have been so kind as to deliver me the very person I was sent to find! I must remember to send the Alliance a thank you card after we tear him apart."

A shiver ran through my body, so deep it rattled my bones.

"Leave him out of this, Rahuman; he has nothing to do with it," warned Gabriella. "This is between us and you."

The Vampire tutted and waved a bony finger in the air. "Silly little girl. He has *everything* to do with it." Gabriella turned to look at me, confusion and concern filling her face. The Bloodseeker's eyes remained fixed on me, no longer blinking. "This is turning out to be a simply fantastic day. Hades will be *very* pleased with me. After we kill you all, I can take my time with the boy." He tapped a daggered fingernail against his chin like he was deep in thought. "I think I'll let my siblings eat the eyes first."

I balked.

"You aren't going to get anywhere near him," snarled Gabriella. "I'm going to rip your head off, you bloodsucking parasite!"

"Then let us not waste any more time!"

And with that, the battle began. Rahuman raised his hands and the pack sprang forwards - gnashing and snarling. The rattle of automatic gunfire shattered the silence of the forest. Something shoved me backwards...hard. I tripped over a root and sprawled into the shrubs. The two Golems stood in front of me, creating an X shape with their staffs. Blocking anything from getting to me - I hoped.

From my position, I watched with a mixture of horror and amazement as the two groups clashed. Several Hiveminds lay dead already, their bodies reduced to twitching heaps on the grass. Delagio thrust his hand out and the marbles shot out like bullets. They tore into a Vampire's face, bursting out the back of its skull in an explosion of claret. He flexed his fingers and they circled back to his open palm, stained red. Immediately he fired them again.

Meanwhile, Gabriella dispatched another Hivemind with a well-placed shot to the chest. It joined its fallen brethren on the ground, smoke billowing around the edges of its twisted carcass. With horror I watched as two more leapt at her. Holstering her gun, she rolled underneath one, pulling a wooden stake from her belt and rammed it into the beast's chest. It screamed and collapsed, writhing in torment as it dissolved into ash. The second landed on her back. Salivating fangs repeatedly snapped at her exposed neck. Only her wrenching fingers, tangled in its lank mane stopped them from connecting. She wrestled, trying to throw it from her back, but couldn't get a good enough purchase.

I have to help!

Within seconds of making it to my feet, one of the Golems sent me spiralling back down again. Helpless, all I could do was watch. So I did the only thing I could.

"Someone help Gabriella!" I screamed as loud as possible.

Midnight glanced at me and then to his struggling leader. As he moved to help, a hidden Hivemind vaulted at him from the trees. He dodged to the left and unleashed an almighty kick. His boot tore all the way through the creature's chest as if it were paper. The tip crashed out the back, severing its spine. He shook off the carcass, marched over to Gabriella and wrenched the Vampire's head off with one colossal tug.

"Thanks, Midnight," Gabriella breathed.

My eyes switched to Sophia and Rachel. They were back to back, surrounded by three Vampires. There was a ripping sound and a large set of silvery, insect style wings burst out of my science teacher's back. She furled them backwards around Sophia, giving her extra protection. The baby Witch pushed her arms through the gaps. The Vampire she fought looked enraged, perhaps aware of how many of its pack had already died. Snarling, it arched up onto its hind legs and slashed at her with razor claws. With incredible skill Sophia parried each blow, then smashed her fist into its face. With a hideous squeal it shrank back. Sophia stretched her arms out towards the creature. A jet of flames shot out of both palms, igniting the Hivemind in a searing ball of fire. The beast thrashed about, screaming in agony as it burned. One final gurgle escaped its throat and then it became a heap of dust.

Now I finally understood why they let a child on the team.

More Vampires flocked out of the trees to take the place of the ones that had died. Gabriella sprinted forward and ran up the chest of the nearest, driving her sword downwards into its skull. She wrenched it back out and vaulted off as it burst into a cloud of ash. Still in mid-air, she lifted the sword above her head and brought it down on another. It sliced clean in half, before dissolving into two symmetrical piles of ash. Landing in a crouch, she jerked the blade through a third creeping up behind.

Rachel was making good use of protecting Sophia whilst dispatching her fair share of feral Vampires. Several lay dying at her feet, riddled with long wooden stakes. Her gun oozed smoke. Still, everywhere I looked, more Vampires appeared. Sophia had underestimated the amount by at least half. Even the Guards were busy fending off a few which had managed to get through. Then like a light switched on in my brain, a wave of panic washed over me.

Where's Rahuman?

I scanned around, but only saw the feral Vampires locked in battle with Orion. That was when I felt a rough arm lock around my neck and yank me backwards.

Now I knew exactly where he was.

Rahuman sank backwards into the forest, one hand clamped over my mouth to stop me yelling. It was ice cold and smelled foul - like rancid meat. I watched helplessly as the Golems continued to fight Vampires, unaware of my kidnapping. My heels raked lines in the dirt while my fingers clawed at the Bloodseeker's arm, trying to break free. No use. His grip was too tight and my angle was wrong. Bright spots splashed across my vision and my head started to feel light as the crook of his elbow cut off my airwaves. He was strangling me to death and there was nothing I could do about it.

"That was far too easy," he snarled, his hot reeking breath pouring over my face. "Just like stealing a baby. It pains me to lose my precious siblings in the process, but your death will make up for their sacrifice. I shall take great pleasure in snapping every bone in your body as I drain your blood." He drew his arm in tighter and my neck muscles strained against the pressure. As the darkness began to seep in from the edges like a puddle of dark ink, a single word flashed into my head.

Gun.

I had to let the word marinate for a moment before my oxygen-starved brain could decipher it.

I have a gun.

Acting fast, I let my hands go slack, which made the iron grip across my neck double. Spittle flew from between my clenched teeth onto my lips and chin. I grabbed for the gun, but it snagged on my waistband. I tugged again with no success – I was becoming too weak. The grip coiled tighter still and the darkness spread. I knew I only had seconds before I was out, and then it was game over.

The Bloodseeker smiled. I could hear the wet slide of lips parting over teeth. "Ah...you are so close to the edge Alexander. I can feel it." He sounded almost aroused.

With a final desperate tug, I yanked at the gun. It broke free into my hand. After thumbing the switch into the fire position I jammed the barrel into Rahuman's arm, right underneath the elbow. I knew there was a chance I could hit my own face, but I didn't care, I had to get this repulsive thing off me.

I squeezed the trigger.

There was a loud boom followed by a sickening scream. The grip around my neck went slack. I whirled around and collapsed to the ground, choking and gasping for air, as a high-pitched whine filled my ears.

Rahuman was doubled over, clutching at his arm, which had been reduced to a stump. White smoke billowed out of the wound and the edges glowed red with embers. Thick lumps of congealed black blood spilled onto the grass with muted, plopping sounds. The severed part of his arm lay twitching on the ground like a wounded animal.

"Gaaaaahhhh!" he screamed in fury. "You little bastard! What have you done?"

That was my cue to escape. As I staggered past, he swung desperately at me, his clawed nails missing by inches.

The forest seemed to be against me as I fled. Every thick branch seemed to be trying to grab me, every root tugging at my feet, attempting to trip me up. I stumbled forward to the sounds of anger and hatred from somewhere close behind. Every few seconds I descended into a coughing fit - my throat felt like I'd been gargling acid.

My heart leapt when I saw the two cars in the distance. I prayed that the keys hadn't fallen out in the struggle. I fumbled in my back pocket and felt the unmistakable jagged metal of car keys.

Yes!

Unlocking the Ferrari, I flung the door open and dived in, slamming and locking it. My hands were trembling as I tried to jam the keys into the ignition. They slipped out of my grip and fell down the side of the seat. I swore loudly. As I bent down to retrieve them, there was a massive thud from above and the car roof sagged. Fear seized me. I couldn't move. Couldn't breathe. Silence reigned for a few moments. Then I whimpered as I heard the high-pitched squeal of clawed nails scraping against the metal roof.

"I still have one good arm Alexander," came a calm voice from above. "More than enough to flay every inch of skin from your flesh."

There were two more thuds on the roof and I saw a couple of Hiveminds drop to the ground around the car. As they glared at me with their slick marble eyes, I felt despair spread its way through every part of my body.

From deeper in the forest, Gabriella was shouting my name frantically.

"She won't get here in time I'm afraid," Rahuman snorted.

With a flash he'd jumped down onto the bonnet. I looked directly into the cold eyes of the Bloodseeker as he loomed over me. A true predator.

My heart sank. I knew he was right.

There was a loud crash as he plunged his remaining hand into the windshield and tore it right out of its frame. He cast it deep into the forest. Now the last bit of protection I had from the monster had gone.

195

"I really can't see why everyone is making such a fuss about you. You're nothing but an annoying insect I shall take great pleasure in squashing."

I snatched the gun, but Rahuman swatted it out of my hand before I even had a chance to aim. It clattered down several yards away from the car.

"That trick only works once, boy. Time to die."

I shrank back into my seat as he leaned into the car and bared his teeth. Each one was shining with poisonous secretion, which dripped onto the dashboard. Desperately, I felt around for something...anything that I could use to defend myself. My hand curled around something long and cylindrical on the seat cushion.

The Booster! It must have fallen out of my pocket when I jumped into the car.

Rahuman pounced.

I shut my eyes and stabbed out the injector. It connected with something soft and once again Rahuman's screams filled the silence. Without even waiting to see what had happened, I dived across the seats and scrambled out of the passenger door. Hit the grass and rolled. Heading straight for the gun, I scooped it up into my hand, stood upright and breathed out hard.

As I stood there - sweat slicked hand curled around the handle of the gun - something inside me began to shift. Slowly the fear slipped away, replaced by the survival instinct I'd felt when I'd been attacked by TJ.

It's him or me.

For the first time I looked over to see what had happened. Rahuman was writhing around on the car bonnet, screaming in agony and clawing at his face. As I moved towards him, I was also vaguely aware of the two Hiveminds around me. They were rolling around on the ground and screaming, mimicking their leader with eerie precision.

As I got close, I saw the full extent of the damage. The booster had lodged into the Bloodseeker's left eye. It was bulging and the veins around it had turned a disturbing shade of blue. The left side of his face had swollen up like a balloon. The macabre horror of it only registered for a second before being replaced by the knowledge that I temporarily had the upper hand. It knew it wouldn't be long before he recovered.

Marching over, I seized Rahuman's oily hair, sliding him down the bonnet and onto the ground. He landed hard on his side. I drove my foot forward into the injector, forcing it even further into the wound. The noise he made was horrific, but it didn't stop me. This psychopath had killed countless already, and had now tried to kill me. *He has to be stopped.* I rolled him over onto his back and pressed the gun into his chest over his blackened heart.

I pulled the trigger.

The recoil launched me backwards. Rahuman's chest crumbled from the impact, rippling from the centre outwards like a shockwave. Thick white smoke curled from the wound and the area around it caught on fire. The flames spread, until his whole body became a raging inferno. As his flesh burned, the Bloodseeker stared at me with his remaining good eye. I could tell he was confused - not quite sure how he'd come to be the one dying. He stretched his mouth into a demented smile before choking out his final words. They were barely audible over the roar of the flames.

"It's coming for you."

Then his eye rolled up into his head and he became still. From around me, there was a crescendo of noise. I turned to see the Hiveminds jerking and thrashing about on the ground, as they too burst into flames. Sweat dripped from my forehead as the heat from the burning Umbra reached me. From behind I heard Gabriella crying out for me.

The next few minutes were vague, like a dream. I barely felt Gabriella's arms wrap around my waist and pull me away from the increasing flames. The rest of the team arrived minus the Golems. Most of them were covered in blood...I couldn't tell whose. Rachel's wings were shredded; the bottom section of one had been completely torn off. Midnight was limping, one arm wrapped around Delagio. The right arm of his suit was ripped. Blood seeped out, dripping to the grass and staining it red. Sophia hurried behind, retrieving a booster from her belt pack. When they spoke, their words were distant and slow, like they were travelling through glue.

197

"Alex took out Rahuman. I can't believe it," uttered Rachel.

"Unbelievable," breathed Delagio.

Midnight gave a slow thoughtful nod.

Arms still locked around me, Gabriella looked into my eyes. Hers were wide and damp. "Alex, I'm so sorry, I didn't realise it was a trap. I-I should have known. Please forgive me."

"It's okay," I said, my words booming in my head like I had earplugs in. "I'm alive. I'm fine. Everything's fine."

Then I passed out.

16

My eyes opened and I clutched onto the fading whispers of my dream. Flashing images of an iron mask and the thundering of hooves. A derelict mansion. A graveyard. Gabriella's angelic face. As the fog of sleep parted, her face remained. I blinked and understood that she wasn't part of the dream. The raven beauty was holding me in her arms and staring into the distance, a sweet smile on her face. Then I heard the steady hum of a car motor and felt the small bumps of a road.

I was in the Range Rover. Delagio had the wheel and Rachel was in the passenger seat, talking on a mobile phone. I was lying on the backseat, head resting in Gabriella's lap. Her fingers stroked my hair as she stared out of the window. Small waves of the mysterious sensation buzzed from where her fingers touched me. It felt good this time. So good I was about to close my eyes and pretend to be asleep when Gabriella looked down and noticed I was awake. Her rose lips blossomed into a smile.

"Hi, honey," she said in a soothing voice. "How are you feeling?"

"Tired," I confessed.

She tapped a hand on my chest. "I should think so too. Taking out a sociopathic Vampire leader will do that."

Delagio swung around in his seat - which was probably a bad idea, but I was too tired to care. "Man, you nailed Rahuman back there!"

"Err thanks."

"Road, Delagio," ordered Gabriella.

He swung back around and shook his head. "Wow, usin' Luminar blood on an Umbra. Genius idea!" He drummed his hands on the wheel.

"Are we going back to the base?" I questioned, focusing back on Gabriella.

"No, we're taking you home."

"What about my training?"

"Another day. Right now you need to rest."

Everyone fell silent, and I settled down, watching the tops of trees sweep past from the window. "So what was that tattoo about, on Rahuman's arm?" I asked after a while.

"The Eye of the Abyss," answered Gabriella. It's a marking that Rogues use to identify each other. All of them have one somewhere."

"Oh right. It sort of reminded me of Faru's tattoo."

Gabriella laughed. "That isn't a tattoo, it's a ritual marking given at birth to the few Seelian that possess Farsight." Her expression changed to one of consideration. "I guess the two do look mildly similar. But Sage Faru's marking is of the third eye. It symbolises peace and higher consciousness. The Eye of the Abyss represents fear and death. Symbolically they couldn't be any more different."

I was about to respond when it dawned on me that we were minus some of Orion. I remembered how Midnight had been limping.

"Wait, where are Midnight and Sophia - are they okay?" I fretted, trying to sit up. Gabriella eased me back down. It was Rachel who answered my question. She hung up her phone and rotated to face the back.

"They're fine. That was Midnight on the line. He's with Sophia back at the Warren. Apparently your dispatching of Rahuman has caused a bit of a stir." She raised an eyebrow. "You appear to be somewhat of a celebrity, Alexander." And with that she turned back and fell silent.

Celebrity? The word bounced about in my mind. It seemed like a word that didn't fit when applied to me. Just like another word that until now had always been something other people had. *Popularity.*

Gabriella squeezed my arm. "See, everyone is okay. Well, everyone apart from the Golems, but they don't count." She shrugged, "Faru will just make more anyway."

Silence descended in the car and I let my mind wander. Rahuman's grizzly death kept replaying in my head. Now that I'd left survival mode and become me again, the thought of the fire singeing his flesh and his swollen eye made me feel sick. I thought about the last words he'd said. *They had to mean something…but what?*

"It's coming for you."

"Sorry?" said Gabriella.

"That's the last thing Rahuman said to me, right before he died. Does that mean anything to you?"

Gabriella's smile slipped from her face. She seemed to shudder internally for a second. "No. I don't know what that means."

"He probably meant the SOS," Rachel suggested.

I pulled myself off of Gabriella's lap. "Rahuman did say he'd been sent to find me. But why am I so important to the SOS? You're a far greater threat to them than I am."

"An example would be mah guess," interjected Delagio. "They want to destroy ah hope. The idea that we could grow strong again."

"Exactly," agreed Rachel.

"So, what do we do?" I asked, watching the greys and greens of Chapter Hill slip past the window.

Gabriella placed a hand on mine. "We kill every single SOS who comes anywhere near you."

Her fierce expression told me that she meant every word.

*

It was gone midday when we pulled up at my house. Gabriella came around to help me out. I noticed for the first time that she had changed back into normal clothes - probably so that it wouldn't arouse suspicion. As we headed up the driveway, I was surprised to see the Audi parked by the house. Gabriella noticed me staring.

"We got an agent to drop it off. All of your things are by the back door."

I nodded and pressed the doorbell. As we waited, Gabriella unzipped her jacket and pulled out the handbook. She pressed it against my chest.

"Read it. All of it."

"Okay," I promised. I took the book and clutched it tightly in my hand.

201

After a minute or two there was the sound of movement in the hallway and the door swung open. Mikey stood in the doorway, hair dishevelled, wearing a tatty t-shirt and shorts.

"Bro you could have dropped a text, I haven't heard from you all da-" he stopped when he noticed Gabriella standing next to me. A boyish grin appeared on his face. "Say no more. Hey, Gabriella."

"Hello, Mikey," she replied with a pleasant smile.

"Sorry for ringing the bell, I forgot my keys last night," I said.

"Not a problem. Anyway, what you both still standing there like a couple of Jehovah's for? Get in here!"

"I can't" said Gabriella, flicking her head towards the Range Rover. "I've got to get back home. Have a good evening you two." She gave me a hug, letting her lips linger near my ear. "Don't worry, the house is protected," she whispered. Then she kissed my cheek and walked to the car. Soon it had disappeared from sight.

I stepped through the door. The television in the living room was blaring out a scene from *Mean Girls*. Mikey only put that particular film on when he had female company – he called it his secret weapon. He grinned and I raised a hand before he had a chance to speak. "Not right now, Mikey. I'm shattered. We can exchange details later."

He laughed and padded into the lounge, closing the door behind him. I heard him talking with someone in excited whispers.

As promised, my things were in a waterproof bag outside the back door. Grabbing them, I dragged myself upstairs, collapsed onto my bed and was asleep in seconds.

*

I was in the garden again, peering through the fence. Drifting tendrils of fog breezed around me, their ghostly touch leaving cold, damp patches on my exposed skin. My pulse was hammering in my ears. I stared into the swirling fog.

One by one, disgusting creatures started to materialise in the gloom. They looked like human experiments gone wrong. Their skin was the colour of mottled flesh and as smooth as pebbles. Lipless mouths filled their faces and exposed gums housed hundreds of needle teeth. They had no noses and their eyes were slick, pink orbs. They crawled forward on all fours, or leapt over each other like abhorrent frogs. Loud, cricket style clicks escaped their throats as they jerked around each other. The sound grew louder and more intense as they neared. I was so busy watching the sickening creatures that I didn't notice the armoured hand reach over the fence until it grabbed me by the hair.

I screamed as the creature hoisted me up. It pressed me close to its iron-grey mask. Where its eyes should have been, there was nothing but blackness – an abyss that stared into my soul.

The creatures were so loud now, the noise was deafening. Then all of a sudden they stopped. There was nothing but silence.

The creature threw me away like a broken toy. I smashed through the wall of the house. It let out a pitiful groan and collapsed around me, smothering me in darkness.

In among the crushing, suffocating blackness, three words formed in my head. They weren't thoughts, but words that had been placed in my mind by something else.

You are found.

I woke up gasping for air and fell out of bed, landing in a heap on the floor. Once again, the dream was already fading from my memory, leaving me only with a terrible feeling of dread and panic. I ran for the bathroom and splashed cold water on my face, trying to wash away the feelings. *It's just a dream Alex,* I told myself. But somewhere deep inside I knew it was more than that.

After a while, I started to feel better. A dull rumbling in my stomach reminded me that it had been a while since I'd eaten. I slipped downstairs and returned armed with a ham and cheese sandwich and a glass of orange juice. On the landing, I stopped for a brief second until I heard Mikey's snoring. It was followed by the sound of a girl's soft sigh. With a satisfied nod, I returned to bed. As I ravenously munched my way through my food, I noticed the handbook sitting on the computer desk. Knowing there was no hope of me sleeping again, I flicked open its worn pages and thumbed through them as I ate, letting the wrinkled bible paper slide across my fingers, being careful not to get any crumbs on it. I was aware that the last person to touch the book had been the girl I couldn't get out of my head.

I read each page in great detail, letting the information sink in. There didn't appear to be any particular order to the entries, but rather that the writer had added information as they found it out themselves. Still it was all beautifully and painstakingly written. Numerous updates and side notes had been added in the margins. I doubted that the new guides would have this kind of care.

I switched to geek mode and studied.

I learned about the different Alliance bases, the various Nexus tunnels and their relevant maps. I read about the Guild of the Arcane - the overseeing body that governed the various Covens. I discovered that Heterochromia was fairly common among Witches. I learned about Apotropes - natural resources that could subdue or kill a Pandemonian. Oak wood or naked flame to kill a Vampire – which had already been put to the test. Iron or diamond to take out most Luminar. Silver for Skinshifters. I discovered the five different types of gifts that a Chosen could have. I paused over those pages, wondering what mine could be with a flush of excitement. *Telekinesis, Teleportation, Levitation, Charm, Pyromancy?* Each one seemed so incredibly cool - like something lifted from the pages of a comic book. I made a mental note to ask Gabriella about them when I next saw her.

I studied dozens of species, how they hunted and what their weaknesses were. I learned about Devils - terrifying looking beasts related to Demons that walked on cloven hooves. I found out that you could tell if a Bloodling had fed recently by the colour of their eyes. Silver meant full. Grey meant they were hungry. Dark grey meant it was time to leave.

I kept pouring through the pages, learning about creatures that a few weeks before, I would have only believed resided in the pages of pulp fiction and superstitious lore, not walking around ten odd miles from my house. My scan came to a stop at the heading 'Skinshifter.' I let the book fall open at the pages. An artist's sketch of a monstrous dog stood over the passage, as if guarding the words. Its huge eyes had been shaded red. I remembered the blood-filled orbs that had stared at me from the shadows of the forest and a shudder swept down my spine. I covered the picture with my palm and read on, slowing over the section on how to effectively kill one.

204

N.B. Only pure silver can be guaranteed to kill a Skinshifter. Even if decapitated by other means - such as a steel blade, in as little as an hour a new head will grow in place of the one removed.

The remaining half of my sandwich no longer looked appetising.

I kept reading the handbook, trying to soak in as much information as my brain could handle. By the time my alarm clock went off, I had less than a third left. I knew I'd taken in a lot of information and no longer felt totally clueless. After clicking off the alarm, I absently flicked through the rest of the book until I reached the final few pages.

Some had been torn out.

I ran my fingers down the rough remains of the edge of the pages. No doubt about it. Some had been removed. I counted the stumps - four. Scanning back through the pages, I figured that given the amount of detailed information per section, it was likely that a singular creature had been removed. I frowned, rifling through the entire book to make sure the pages hadn't been stuffed anywhere. They hadn't. *Gabriella?* I wondered. *No - why would she?* Maybe it was a misentry. The meticulous nature of the writer made the removal of any incorrect information entirely plausible. But the roughness suggested they had been ripped out, not carefully removed. I shrugged. *If it's been removed, it's probably not important.*

I lifted up the corner of my mattress and retrieved the worn picture of my father. I ran my thumb over his face and smiled down as he smiled back at me.

"Morning Dad. Sorry I'm a bit late; it's been an interesting day."

I opened the handbook and placed the picture in to mark the page I'd reached. It fit to the edges perfectly, as if it had been designed to go there. Still smiling, I leaned over and slipped the book into my schoolbag.

Heading for the shower, I was sidetracked by my phone ringing. I doubled back, hoping for Gabriella, but it was Mum, checking in. I spoke to her for a while, assuring her that yes, we were both alive and intact, and no, there hadn't been any house destroying parties in their absence. I found out that just as I'd predicted, John had spent most of his time in Killarney propping up the bar at the local pub. Mum didn't seem too bothered though, in fact she sounded quite relaxed.

It actually felt good to talk to someone who had no knowledge of what was going on. I could have been any normal kid talking to his mother. She told me of her time spent visiting the markets in the town centre. How they had all walked the local hills and taken a jaunting car tour around Killarney Castle. Then I spoke to Connie and Edgar on loudspeaker. They asked about school and if I had managed to get myself a girlfriend yet. They made me promise to come and see them next year in-between arguing about where the discount vouchers for the supermarket had been left. By the time they rang off, my smile reached both ears.

As soon as I reached the bathroom, the bizarre re-entered my world.

Without warning, images of Faru began to flicker in my brain. Then his voice entered into my head, as loud as if it were my own.

"Alexander, may I speak with you?"

I couldn't work out if this was a hallucination or not.

"Okay..."

Instantly an incredible force gripped me. My towel slipped from my waist, exposing my boxer shorts. Paralysed, I fell backwards, slamming into the shower cubicle as my body shook from head to toe. Flickers of light streaked across my vision and then I saw Sage Faru standing by the sink as clear as day. My body freed up again.

"Good afternoon Alexander, I trust you are well."

I tried to speak, but nothing came out. My mouth flapped open and closed like a fish. Finally I managed to get my voice box to respond. "Faru I was trying to have a shower!" Remembering my manners, I added "sir."

"So I can see...my apologies. However, a mind link is the best way to communicate with you."

"I have a *mobile phone*."

The Sage gave a short laugh. "I'm afraid I am somewhat of a traditionalist. Plus people lose their phones. Losing your mind is much more difficult." He tapped two wrinkled fingers against his temple. "You see, now we have merged minds, your brain wave frequency is stored in my head. We can now communicate with each other whenever we need to." He gestured towards me whilst attempting to suppress a smile. "Although, as you can see, there is an initial effect when linking in."

I retrieved my fallen towel and re-established my dignity.

"So I can call on you too?" I asked.

"Indeed. If ever you need to speak with me, simply concentrate your thoughts on me, and I should hear you. Now on to the matter in hand. I was incredibly impressed with your handling of the Rahuman...situation. His focus on you confirmed my suspicions that you are being targeted."

"Hold on...you mean you used me as bloody *bait*?"

"I can appreciate your anger Alexander and I am sincerely sorry for putting you in danger. Nevertheless, it was necessary to ensure Rahuman did not disappear as he has done on previous incidences. His pride would have made it impossible for him to leave without your death. Orion, albeit unconventional is the Warren's most successful hunter team. I never expected him to get anywhere close to you. It was a mistake on Gabriella's part."

I shook my head. "Do *not* blame Gabriella, Sage Faru, or the rest of the team for that matter. They were outnumbered five to one. They did the best they could. It's a miracle any of us survived."

The Seelian cast his blank eyes downwards and his shoulders seemed to sag slightly. "Yes, I suppose you are correct, the odds were certainly not in your favour. It never used to be this dangerous. A normal team used to consist of a Huntmaster and at least ten supporting Guardians. Unfortunately now it is too risky to have large groups, as the shortfall means another crucial area could be left exposed. I am just relieved none of you were hurt."

I thought of the hideous Hiveminds that had stalked their way through the trees. Each one salivating at the prospect of sinking their disgusting fangs into living flesh. A sudden and very disturbing thought occurred to me.

"If I'm being targeted, what's to stop them finding out where I live and coming here?"

"I am not going to deceive you Alexander. There is every possibility the SOS do know where you live by now."

I felt a rush of dread sweep through my body as the news sank in. I imagined legions of Hiveminds and Skinshifters pouring through the doors and windows.

"I have arranged for the house to be protected," he added.

"So Gabriella said. But by who?"

"Echo and Trojan. Beyond Orion, they are two of the best teams the Warren has to offer. They are alternating the duty of guarding your house around the clock. If anything happens, they will be here instantly."

"But for how long, Sage Faru? They can't watch this place forever. And what if the SOS get to my family? They can't protect themselves against something like that!"

Faru stepped forward and put his hands on my arms. It was bizarre - I could feel his cold touch as if he were actually there with me.

"Alexander, please try not worry. I would never leave you or your family defenceless. I am aware that your mother and stepfather are currently in Ireland. Until we understand exactly what is happening, I have taken steps to ensure that they stay there. As for your brother, special conditions relating to his safety have already been arranged."

Special conditions? I wasn't sure I liked the sound of that, or exactly how he was going to 'ensure' that Mum and John remained in Ireland. But it meant that everyone would be safe and right now that was enough.

"As for the reason I called on you," continued Faru. "As I said, I am very pleased with the way you handled yourself under the threat of Rahuman, but as yet you still are not an active member of the Alliance. So if you are up to the task, I would like you to return to the Warren and complete your training."

I blew air through my lips. "Okay. I can come today if you want."

The Seelian placed his pale hands together. "Perfect. I shall send an agent to collect you."

"Actually, if you don't mind Sage Faru, I would prefer to drive. I need to collect my thoughts."

He smiled. "Of course. I shall get Gabriella to send you a textual message with the address of a suitable entrance."

I suppressed a smile and agreed to leave as soon as possible. A sensation similar to a cold breeze rushed through my mind and Faru disappeared as fast as he appeared. There was no evidence of him ever having been there and it could have been put down to nothing more than a dream.

A minute later my phone bleeped with the address of an entrance.

I jumped into the shower and with the water beating down, broke into hysterical laughter at the madness of it all.

*

The Audi's navigation system informed me that I'd reached my destination.

Mikey had still been fast asleep by the time I left the house. I'd paused at his door, which had been left ajar. His 'friend' had gone and I figured she must have escaped pretty early, although I couldn't remember hearing anyone leave. I'd left a note on the kitchen table promising to tell him everything when I got home. *If I can get my own head around it all first*, I'd thought as I left the house.

I parked outside a shining column of an office block in the corporate area of Chapter Hill. The morning rain had dyed the pavements a darker shade of grey, leaving behind an intoxicating scent. Harried weekend commuters skirted around puddles, cups of coffee clutched in their gloved hands. As I slipped out of the car, a man in a black suit headed towards me. He rubbed his hand on his trouser leg before offering it. I stared at it for a second then closed my own around it. His was clammy.

"Good morning Mister Eden, I'm Agent Noble. I'll take care of the car for you." He gestured towards the office. "Please head inside and use the furthest elevator on your right. Hold the two, six and twelve buttons together for six seconds. Miss De Luca will be waiting for you in her apartment."

"Thanks," I said, passing him the keys and pushing my way through the revolving glass door.

The place was practically deserted. Just a few overachieving businessmen and women were gathered in a mini huddle to my right, laughing and slurping their coffee from Starbucks cups. My trainers thumped on the marble floor, the sound echoing around the vast lobby. A matching marble desk lay ahead, manned by an overweight security guard. Beyond were the elevators. The guard didn't say a word as I walked past, just lifted his hat and dabbed a worryingly sweaty brow with a wad of tissue paper.

The metal doors closed with a dull thud. I listened out for others, before holding down the buttons that the agent had mentioned.

Warren, said the hidden voice.

The light inside the elevator switched to neon purple. My teeth glowed white in the mirror. "Cool," I breathed then gasped as the cab plummeted diagonally downwards. For the next half minute, my stomach was a pancake, getting flipped in all directions as the metal rollercoaster surged down, forwards then diagonally upwards again. Then like a click of the fingers, the elevator shuddered to a halt. My hands groped the walls as I wobbled out of the opening doors.

I found myself in the grand entrance hall of the mansion once again. Guardians passed around me. Several paused to throw me a smile or a salute. As before, most of the doorways were guarded by the stony Golems.

I climbed the grand stairs and navigated along the balcony into the plush hallway where the Chosen's apartments were. I stopped at the redwood door marked with Gabriella's name on a gold plate. As I looked at it, my heart started to beat faster. A small doorbell sat next to the door. Swallowing hard, I pressed it and fiddled with the edges of the nameplate as I waited for her to answer.

The door clicked open, but no one was there. I nudged it open and entered.

"Hello?"

A frosted glass door to my right slid open. Steam swirled into the hall, curling up towards the wood beamed ceiling. Gabriella's face appeared in the mist, hair wet and sticking to her forehead. My stomach tightened.

"Hi, Alex," she smiled. "Sorry, I was just taking a shower. Go through and take a seat, I won't be long." Her face disappeared back into the fog and the door swished shut.

I made my way forward into the lounge. Once again, the fire was in full blaze, filling the room with its chestnut scent. I made my way over to the large window. It was damp with condensation. I wiped a palm across the surface and stared out. The winter sun had broken through gaps in the grey clouds and glinted off the rain soaked gravel, transforming them into diamonds. The damp grass on the roundabout shone as if it had been freshly painted. Everything looked spring cleaned, as if all the impurities had been washed away. Tabula rasa - a clean slate.

Like me.

I gave a deep sigh as the warm fingers of the crackling fire reached my back.

Turning back into the room, I descended into the seating area, my footsteps muffled by the lush carpet. A couple of pictures on the mantelpiece caught my attention. I picked one up. It showed a beautiful, newborn baby girl dressed in red pyjamas. A fine layer of black hair was already present on her soft head. She was reaching up, trying to grab the camera, mouth stretched into an excited grin. Her eyes were shimmering blue jewels. There was no mistaking who it was. I eased it down and picked up the other, which showed a man and woman sitting under a tree. Their lips were pressed together in a loving kiss. Even though their faces were side on I could tell that they were both incredibly good looking - especially the woman. Her long, dark hair cascaded down her back. Some draped over the man's arms, which were locked around her waist.

"They were my parents," said a voice from next to me.

I jumped. Gabriella was beside me, wearing nothing but a towel. Droplets of water trickled down her honey skin. The material hugged her curves. I swallowed and tried my hardest not to look at her.

She held out a hand.

"Sorry," I apologised, handing over the picture. "I didn't mean to pry. I was just curious."

"Don't worry about it," she smiled. With great care, she placed the picture back in the middle of the mantelpiece, inching it backwards and forwards until it was exactly where it had been.

"You said they *were* your parents?"

"They're dead," she said in a matter of fact tone.

"Oh…Ella, I'm so sorry. I…wait a second; you said that you moved from Italy with them."

Gabriella shrugged. "I lied."

"Oh…right. How long?"

"Ten years."

"That's awful, I'm sorry." I cleared my throat. "So uh, what happened if you don't mind me asking?"

Her gaze fell to the floor. For the longest moment she was as silent as the dead. Then she looked up, her eyes clouded. "It…" She took a deep breath, paused and shook her head. "I'm sorry; it's hard to talk about. Can we change the subject?" I could see her pain. It sat right below the surface, darkening her face like a shadow. I remembered the way she'd reacted when I'd told her that my dad was dead. The way she had seemed to understand. *Because she did. More than I ever could have known.*

"Of course. So what's next on the training?"

Gabriella padded back up the stairs towards the bedroom door.

"A change of order, I'm going to test for your gift."

I felt a surge of anticipation. "You mean which one of the five I have?"

Gabriella smiled. "I see you've been reading the handbook. Give me a couple of minutes." She closed the bedroom door behind her.

I watched the fire while I waited. The flames seemed alive as they danced in the hearth. They crackled and shifted occasionally, sending little flakes of ash floating into the air. At first each one seemed to disappear into nothing, but I found that if I really focused, I could track them all the way through their journey - from the log of wood, to the thick woollen twists of the rug. My senses really were so much keener since my Awakening.

The door swung open and Gabriella walked back into the lounge. She was wearing the same uniform that she'd worn when we'd intercepted Rahuman and his pack - except this time she'd let her hair spill free around her shoulders. I preferred it like that.

Gabriella pulled the electronic PDA she'd used in the car out of her jacket pocket. Heading for the couch, she sat down next to me, her knee touching mine.

"Okay, don't move."

I stared straight ahead, which happened to be right into her eyes. She pressed a few buttons on the contraption. A camera-style lens on the back projected out a blinding green light, which she aimed into my left eye.

"Hun, try not to squint."

I opened my eyes as wide as I could while the intense light painted the world green. The PDA unit beeped and Gabriella placed it in her lap.

"Okay it's over," she said.

I rubbed the spots out of my eye. "Is that it?"

"That's it. Biomotes are cutting edge technology mixed with Fae magic. They can do all sorts of things like make calls, perform tracking and scanning tasks, and create performance assessments. Right now, it's analysing your brain's energy outputs. It'll pinpoint the location where new mass is located. It's these newly formed parts that control our abilities. Once it identifies your mass, it'll tell us which one of the five gifts you have."

My heart was thumping with anticipation. *What if I'm a kinesist like Delagio?* The idea of being able to control inanimate objects seemed beyond awesome. *Or Charm?* I would never have to go through another awkward conversation again. I could even convince John to lay off me. *Or Teleportation?* I could visit anywhere in the world, whenever I wanted to. *Or maybe Pyromancy like Sophia.* I could-

The unit beeped for a second time. Gabriella picked it up and stared at the screen. She frowned. "This makes no sense."

"What is it? I asked. "What ability do I have?" I don't mind really. Any is fine.

"Well..." She drew the word out.

"Spill it Ella, the suspense is killing me!"

"Alex..."

"What?"

"You don't have one."

17

Disappointment swirled around my stomach like bad food.

"Oh."

"Maybe it was a scan error. Let's try again."

Hope replaced the disappointment. "You're probably right, I did squint a bit."

I stretched my eye open with my index finger and thumb, not moving a single muscle as the green light swept through once more.

Half a minute later the results were in.

"I don't understand," said Gabriella and I felt my shoulders sag.

We tried twice more. Each time the Biomote informed us that I didn't have a gift.

"Maybe it's broken?" I suggested, pointing at the unit resting in her lap.

"It's got Fae magic inside, no chance it can break...I'm sorry, Alex."

I gave a casual shrug in an attempt to hide my true feelings. "It doesn't matter; I still have super strength, speed and hearing. I'm not exactly hard up." As I spoke the words, I inadvertently cheered myself up. *I do still have all these incredible abilities. Who cares if I can't disappear into thin air or control someone's mind?*

"I've never met a Chosen who didn't have one of the five gifts. You fall outside all the boxes, Alex."

"Well I've never been one to do things the easy way."

We both broke into laughter. Gabriella slipped the unit back into her uniform pocket.

"I'll let Sage Faru know, he may have some more ideas. Right, well normally we would now be doing exercises to hone your gift, but doesn't look like that's an option now. Seems like we have some free time."

215

"What do you want to do?"

"Well, we could always just hang out. Since we didn't get around to that yesterday."

I frowned, not sure what she was talking about. Then it dawned on me that we'd agreed at school to spend the day together on Saturday. That had been before I'd been brought into the HASEA. Back when everything had been relatively normal. It seemed like months ago.

"Wow, I'd forgotten about that."

"Charming," she said, rolling her eyes.

"Ha, no I just mean with everything that's gone on. I'd love to hang out. What do you want to do?"

Gabriella paused for a moment. "I'm going to show you my favourite place in the base."

"There's a gun range?"

"Very funny, Mister Eden. And yes there is actually, but that's not where we're going."

"Well, now I'm intrigued. Lead the way."

I followed Gabriella out of her apartment. As we walked, I noticed three people coming in the other direction. Leading the way was a fox-like redhead, with an icy complexion and piercing silver eyes. She looked like the sort of girl who collected trouble. Behind her was a large, black man with long cornrows that fell to his shoulders. Next to him was a sallow looking man with yellow hair meticulously combed into a side parting. His eyes were dull grey. Thanks to the guide, I knew that both he and the girl were Vampires, and that the Draco Malfroy wannabe was hungry. He caught me staring and glared back, his narrow eyes closing further. I could have sworn I saw his lip curl up into a snarl. I shifted my gaze immediately. The group stopped just in front of us and the two girls shared the Chosen salute, followed by a quick hug.

"Ella, how are you keeping?" beamed the redhead. Her voice was rich and smoky, her accent Northern Irish.

"I'm good thanks Scarlett; it's great to see you." She smiled at the two men. "Hello, Tyler, Dakin."

The tall man replied and the Vampire grunted, but kept his steely eyes fixed on me.

216

"And this must be the famous Alexander Eden," said Scarlett, her shimmering eyes flicking to me. "It's nice to finally meet you in person."

"Nice to meet you too," I said and offered her my hand.

Scarlett lifted a slender eyebrow before offering her own. It was smooth and cool - like porcelain.

"This is Echo team," explained Gabriella. "We've been on several missions together; some of them pretty close calls.

"Nothing we couldn't handle," grinned the redhead.

"You're the ones watching my house?" I asked, glancing at the slick haired Vampire. He was still staring at me. I wasn't sure I liked the idea of this person anywhere near my home.

"Yep," answered Scarlett.

"Are the rest of Echo there now then?"

As soon as the words had left my mouth, I knew I'd put my foot in it. There was an awkward silence before Tyler glanced down at me. I could tell he was a Chosen like me.

"No, Trojan are watching the house. There are only three of us left in Echo now." He sighed. "A few months ago one of our team went rogue and joined the SOS. He set a trap and we were sprung by Devils. It's hard enough to survive one of the bastards. There were four. Six of the team were killed. We're all that's left." He folded his thick mahogany arms across his chest and fell silent again. Dakin glared even harder than before.

I felt my face grow hot. "Oh...I didn't realise, I'm sorry to hear that."

"Don't give it a second thought," smiled Scarlet. She looked back over to Gabriella. "You reckon we've been properly filtered now?"

Gabriella looked resolute. "I'm confident that Sage Faru has got his house in order."

"Let's hope so, for all our sakes." Scarlett shook her head. "All this fuss over one Chosen. You must be a pretty special guy," she winked, giving my arm a squeeze. For a split second out of the corner of my eye, I thought I saw Gabriella stiffen. "Anyway, we just got back from a mission. Some Harpy in Brighton decided to start kidnapping children in the early hours. About to kill one when we turned up." She lifted a hand and for the first time, I noticed a thick smear of red on the back. "It was worked up. Things got a bit messy. Still it was a nice change from staring at Alex's house. We're going to freshen up in Tyler's place." Nodding towards Dakin she added, "Maybe grab a little breakfast."

"I'm going to take Alex to the Sanctuary."

Scarlett gave her friend a look that I knew only she would be able to interpret.

"So, uh, you'll be at the joining feast later right?" said Gabriella, clearly changing the subject.

"I may be technically dead, but I'm still Irish. No way am I missing a party," Scarlett replied with a grin.

Everybody saluted before leaving, all except for Dakin, who just barged past me. *What's his problem?*

As if reading my mind, Gabriella jerked a thumb behind her. "Don't worry about Dakin, he's always been moody. That's just his way. Plus he's a little pissed about being on what he calls babysitting duty."

"Ahh...I see."

Gabriella led me downstairs and out the front doors. We made our way around the vast mansion and into the grounds. The area opened up into an expanse of garden. The blanket of green was lined either side with a phantasmagoria of flowers - which seemed to be thriving despite the time of year. We passed a large stone fountain that was home to a dozen golden Cherubs, spitting high arcs of water from their mouths.

The Sanctuary was positioned about five acres through the expansive grounds, hidden behind a row of tall conifers. It stood separated from the rest of the gardens by a large paddock style fence made from black iron. The entrance was being guarded by another agent. He stood with his arms behind his back, head upright as if attached to an invisible string, breath misting in the air. He nodded when we reached him.

"Good morning, Miss De Luca, Mister Eden. Is there anything I can help with?" he asked.

"No thank you, Agent Green, I just want to show Alex inside."

"Of course." He immediately stepped to the side and swung the large gate open.

As soon as we stepped through, I could sense the presence of something otherworldly. It seemed to radiate out towards us from within. Not menacing - but definitely not human.

The gate clicked shut behind us. What looked like oversized horse stables sat diagonally ahead. A large barn, built from redwood stood on the other side. I could hear the distinct sounds of animals shuffling about inside. Slightly smaller evergreens were scattered about, swaying in the icy breeze. Directly ahead was a very large lake. The surface rippled in lines of moving wrinkles. As we walked forward, I felt a sensation like a thousand cobwebs brushing over my skin. I didn't even need to ask to know we'd passed through some kind of invisible barrier.

Now everything was different.

The area was at least five times larger than it had been before. The grass had changed to a light shade of purple, with tiny pure green flowers sprouting in little patches. The trees were sweeping, spiralling masses of white bark. Golden leaves hung from their numerous branches, glowing with some kind of natural light. Bushes sprouting the most intricate flowers I'd ever seen were spread everywhere. The unassuming barn had become a giant silver arch with shimmering technicolour doors.

Above, odd-looking birds with two sets of sweeping wings looped about. The lake had evolved into a huge expanse of crystal blue water, complete with multiple levels and a grand waterfall, which crashed down from moss-covered rocks into the main pool. The whole place was bathed in light and soothing warmth from a hidden sun.

I was lost for words.

"It's amazing isn't it? Walk forward a bit, you'll see more," Gabriella said.

I stepped forward and instantly understood what she meant. Near the lake, for the first time, I noticed a pride of small lion-like animals frolicking about. Some rolled together in the grass or play-bit their siblings. Others turned their heads sideways and tugged at the reeds that grew around the lake edge. Their sleek brown bodies were topped with a set of matching feathered wings, which drooped over their undersized backs. Curled black stingers - sectioned like a scorpions, contradicted their cuteness like deadly question marks. As they played, they made funny sharp growls, which sounded like a blend of a mew and a hiccup.

Manticore. Wild beasts that roam the Bloodsand Desert of Pandemonia. I'd read about them in the handbook. I'd also read that despite their dangerous appearance, they were actually herbivores and only attacked when threatened.

The flash of a fish-like tail in the lake caught my attention. I watched in amazement as a merman flipped out of the water, somersaulted, and as graceful as a dolphin, cut back under the surface. More followed, and soon the lake was a circus, with merfolk flipping and spiralling out of their aquatic arena.

"They're such show-offs," laughed Gabriella. I smiled, but was distracted by something happening in the centre of the lake. The water had begun to churn and bubble. Waves rippled from the epicentre outwards in expanding rings that rolled all the way to the sides and lapped onto the grass. A hauntingly beautiful woman rose slowly out of the water like a sunken treasure. Seaweed clung to her naked skin as the water poured from her body. Once she was exposed up to her pelvis, she stopped.

And began to sing.

The sound was infinitely more beautiful than anything I'd ever heard. It was as if all of the world's best-kept secrets and hidden desires were wrapped up in each note. The melody made my head fizz and instantly it felt like my heart was overflowing with love and happiness. I wanted to go to this woman - to stay with her while she sang to me. Gabriella caught my hand and squeezed it.

"Take a few deep breaths and it'll pass," she said. I did as I was told and the sensations drifted away. The lady in the lake sung harder and then when I made no more reaction, she scowled in disappointment and slipped under the surface.

"That's a Siren right?" I said.

"Temptress of the sea in all her glory," Gabriella agreed with a nod. "Let's see what you can tell me about them."

I thought about what I'd read in the handbook. Each page appeared in my mind as if it were open in front of me. I mentally flicked to the right page and repeated the words aloud.

"Sirens use their hypnotic voices to lure unsuspecting males into the water to mate with them. But their unwilling lovers often drown, because they get lost in the moment and forget they can't breathe underwater."

"Exactly. And a Siren's song is..."

"A remembrance to all of their lost lovers."

Gabriella smiled. "You've been doing a lot of reading. I'm impressed Alex."

As we made our way around the lake, a colossal shadow bathed the area in darkness. I looked up just in time to see the mother of the Manticore cubs stamp down onto the ground. It was a fiercely majestic creature. Irises the shade of polished gold. Wings - unlike its offspring - in perfect proportion to its muscular body. Instead of dark brown, they were the plumage version of a rainbow - shimmering, swirling patterns of colour that shone in the winter sun. They gave the beast such an essence of regal beauty; any peacock would have hidden in shame. Its oil black tail whipped the air in sharp swipes. It padded over to the cubs and nudged them into a tight group, before looking back up at us.

Gabriella gave the creature a gentle smile and stepped around, giving the pride plenty of space. I copied. The Manticore snorted as we passed - a soft sound that could only be described as a friendly warning.

"So this is where you keep all the Fera that made it through the Veil," I said.

Gabriella nodded. "Most of them are acclimatised to Earth now. If we sent them back through the Veil, they wouldn't survive. So we keep them here, safely hidden and protected with magic."

We headed over towards the large stables, which now appeared to have been carved out of frosted glass that glinted different colours in the sunlight. Gabriella pointed towards one of the openings, near a paddock area.

"These are my favourite of all of them."

She made a light whistling sound.

I gasped as a real life Unicorn emerged from the stable into the paddock. The grand Equidae stood well over the height of a regular horse. Its coat was as pure and white as a snowdrift and a silky mane of hair swirled around its slender neck. Its intelligent turquoise eyes shone out at us like polished glass. But by far the most impressive feature of the beautiful creature was the long ivory horn, which extended from its forehead. A spiralling pattern that reminded me of seashells coiled around it, running all the way up to the sharp tip. The unicorn gave a little whinny and shuffled on its feet, before moving over towards where we stood on the other side of the fence.

"This is Isiodore, the stallion of the herd."

"He's so beautiful," I said and stretched a hand out to stroke him.

"Don't!" Gabriella cried.

Isiodore let out a high-pitched squeal and thrust his head forward, stabbing the horn directly towards me. I reacted just in time, diving out of the way - but not before the razor sharp tip caught my jumper sleeve, tearing through the thick material as if it were tissue paper.

"What the hell?" I shouted, checking my arm for damage. The Unicorn was pacing around his stable, stamping his hooves and letting out harsh snorts. His eyes had turned a dark blue and his lips coiled up into a snarl.

Gabriella pushed me further away from the opening. *"Dio dannazione!"* she swore, "Alex, you have to be more careful! I thought you'd read the handbook!"

"Not all of it! I protested. "Why did he attack me?"

"Unicorns are as fierce as they are intelligent. What do you think the huge spike on its head is for, idiot? Before you approach one, you have to gain its approval." She sighed. "Look, I'll show you. Stay there and watch."

Gabriella moved over to a nearby bush and delicately plucked a beautiful white orchid type flower from it. She held it in the centre of her outstretched palms and moved towards the unicorn, which was still thrashing about and snorting as if possessed.

"It's okay, Isiodore," she soothed as she edged closer to the opening. The Unicorn started to slow his movements and eventually came to a stop, although his teeth were still bared and lips coiled into the aggressive grimace.

"It's okay," Gabriella repeated. I watched as she sank to one knee with her head bowed and pushed her hands through a gap in the fence. The Unicorn regarded her for a second and then his snarl vanished. Like a departing mist, the dark blue seeped away from his eyes and was replaced by bright turquoise once more. He gave a soft whinny. Then I watched as he moved close and gently ate the flower from her hands.

Gabriella stood up, and put a hand over the top of the fence. Isiodore stepped forward and pressed the side of his face against her palm.

"Now you try," she said over her shoulder.

I emulated Gabriella, plucking a flower from the bush and knelt down, offering it out towards Isiodore.

"Keep your head down."

I lowered my head as much as it would go, so much my chin was in danger of penetrating my chest.

Isiodore gave a non-committal snort. I kept my head down. Then I felt a light tickle on my palms. I raised my head and drew in a breath as I saw the Unicorn eating the flower from my hands. His eyes were still turquoise as they met mine. He had forgiven me.

I stood up and moved towards the Unicorn. As with Gabriella, he pressed his head into my hand. His coat felt softer than the purest cashmere. I ran my fingers through the fine hairs on his muzzle.

I turned to Gabriella and gave her a smile. "I hope you don't mind sharing a favourite spot."

*

We spent most of the morning in the Sanctuary. I saw countless creatures that a week before I'd never have dreamed could exist. Some were cute, others creepy, but each one incredible and unique in its own right. Those that were small and safe enough to be handled, Gabriella carefully picked up to show me. I watched the way her eyes crinkled at the corners as she looked at them. Noticed how she always held them in exactly the right way and acted in the perfect manner so they didn't become distressed.

She really cares about them.

223

I'd heard that you could gauge if a person was good or not by the way they treated animals. If that was anything to go by, then Gabriella was hot on Mother Teresa's heels.

One of the last animals she showed me was a Welkin – a small fox/catlike creature with yellow fur and three bushy tails that it could move independently of one another. As she passed it to me to hold, our fingers touched. Neither of us moved. The charges started up, the noise as loud in my ears as a detuned television. My insides buzzed as if they were alive. My heartbeat trebled. When I dared to look up, Gabriella was staring at me. Our fingers stayed pressed together, mine over hers. Underneath, the confused Welkin wriggled about. I tried to speak, but I couldn't get hold of my voice. The world shifted on its axis and everything slid away.

All I could see was Gabriella.

She didn't move her gaze, just like that first day in English. Her irises started to expand. Her lips parted slightly.

Those lips. Perfect red lips that you could lose hours kissing...

"Are you guys re-enacting The Lion King or somethin'?"

I turned to see an amused looking Delagio leaning against the inside wall of the barn, a singular silver marble spinning around his hand like a moon in orbit. Instantly, Gabriella snapped her fingers away from mine. A tsunami of disappointment washed over me. My mind whirred in confusion. *Did we just have a moment?* My rational brain told me that the idea was ridiculous. *But why didn't she move her hand? And the way she looked at me...*

The Welkin gave a sharp bark. I looked down to see it writhing about; little paws waggling in the air. I set the animal down and it scurried over to the safety of its pack, sneaking the occasional wounded glance at us.

"Hi Del, what's up?" said Gabriella.

"Well, Alex here was s'posed to be with me for speed trainin' bout an hour ago. Scarlett said I'd find y'all here."

Gabriella glanced down at her watch. "*Mio Dio!* I'm really sorry Del, we lost track of time."

"Hey, no worries boss, I needed ta get some new toys from the Armoury anyways." He turned to me. "So fella, you ready to come test those stilts of yours?"

224

I tried not to let my shoulders sag. "Sure."

"Good stuff. I'll try not to get you killed." He winked.

"I'd appreciate that."

"Play nice, boys", Gabriella chuckled. "I'll see you later Alex - good luck."

Delagio and I headed out of the Sanctuary and onto a new path that headed to the far right of the mansion. The weather outside of the little paradise was miserable. Dark clouds threatened to spill more rain at a moment's notice.

Delagio draped his arm over my shoulder as we walked, his boots making an irritating clomping sound on the gravel.

He pointed to my shredded jumper. "What happened there?"

"Unicorn."

"Ahhhh. So you like her a lot huh?"

His change of track took me by complete surprise.

"I'm sorry?"

"You know what I'm talkin' about." He flicked his head in the direction we'd come from. "Lil miss sunshine of your life back there. I've seen the way you look at her."

Oh god, is it that obvious? I cringed internally. Externally, I shrugged. "Sorry Del, you've got it wrong. We're just friends."

"Agghh!" He threw up his hands in mock frustration. "You Brits drive me crazy! Where I come from, we like a girl, we tell them how it is - day or night. Y'all will deny it to your graves. That is unless you absorb enough liquor to do the drunken shuffle over and attempt to attach y'allself to their faces."

I snickered and then let out a defeated sigh. "Okay, maybe you're right. But it makes no difference; she doesn't see me that way."

Delagio made a noise like he was pondering. "I'm not so sure buddy. If there's one thing I know, its women." He paused to flash a salesman grin. "And I've noticed the way she acts around you."

"What do you mean?"

"Well look, you wouldn't be the first guy to have passed through and wanted to get to know her a little better if you catch my drift."

"Hey, it's not like that!" I bit.

"No, I know, I know," he appeased. "What I'm tryin' to say is that she never even gave them a second glance. But with you... look, she freaked out with worry after you escaped. She watched over you the entire time you were recoverin' after your mind merge. She tore through a dozen Hiveminds like they was pups when she realised you'd been taken by Rahuman. And that's not even mentionin' the rom-com scene I just walked in on."

I felt my mouth gape open. "That *was* a moment?"

"Looked like it to me." He shrugged. "But hell, what do I know right? I'm just a stupid hick!" We both laughed. It was hard not to like Delagio, even if he was a bit over the top. *He'd get on like a house on fire with Tim,* I thought.

I could tell that he looked set to ask me more questions about Gabriella. I racked my brain to think of something to deflect the conversation away from me.

"So, uh...what's the deal with Midnight and Sophia? They seem to get on pretty well."

Delagio clicked his tongue. "She reminds him of his daughter."

"Oh right. So he doesn't get to see his daughter much then?"

He paused. "Not any more. No."

His voice sounded sad. Plus his cryptic answer had an air of finality to it. I decided not to press any further.

We walked in silence for a minute or so. Delagio was once again spinning a marble around his hand and through his fingers. He stared at it for a while then looked up, eyes gleaming. "I almost forgot to ask! What gift did you get?"

"Um, none actually."

His eyebrows arched upwards. "No powers...*really?*"

I shrugged.

"Well that blows."

"Yep," I said sucking in some air and kicking a stone along the path.

"Don't sweat it man. If the Rahuman situation was anythin' to go by, you're still gonna be an absolute badass."

I smiled. "Thanks, Del."

A menacing cloud swallowed the pale sun completely and rain began to pour in thick rods. The addictive scent of damp soil rose from the ground.

"Ah damn it!" cursed Delagio. "I bet it's gonna ruin my hat."

"Shall we go back inside?" I asked hopefully.

"Sorry bud, I have more hats."

The path ended. Just beyond, a deep trench had been cut into the ground. We came to the ridge and Delagio jumped down into it. I followed, landing in a large puddle and soaking my trainers and jean bottoms in dirty water.

"Perfect," I muttered.

The trench was about three times my height, with about fifteen feet between each wall. It was like a huge scar in the land, snaking into the distance. The beginning of it stood right behind me. A metallic circle about the size of a dinner plate had been set into the compacted mud wall. A black line ran down the middle, suggesting it could open in some way. Next to it was a LED panel protected by a thin plastic cover.

Delagio stripped the cover off and rolled it into his pocket. Then he tapped his fingers on the screen. The circle beeped and the sides parted, revealing a pitch-black tunnel. I tried to peer in, but Delagio grabbed my arm, pulling me back.

"Probably not such a good idea."

I cast him a confused look and he breathed in deep. "In about thirty seconds, this hatch is going to release a whole bunch of Venenum.

I thought for a second. *No, haven't read about those.*

"Insect Fera," he continued when I didn't respond. "They look a bit like giant wasps. Your gonna want to run like you owe money. They ain't strong enough to kill ya, but trust me; their stings will make you wish you was dead. When you get to the end, there'll be somethin' you can use to take them out, but not before."

Without another word, he ran up the side of one of the walls and vaulted backwards off it, landing safely outside the trench. He pulled a Biomote out of his pocket and tapped the screen. Instantly, thick glass walls shot out of the ground, covering the sides all the way down the pathway. They kept growing higher and then curved together and joined at the top, trapping me inside a giant snow globe.

"I'd start running now if I were you," Delagio warned. His voice sounded muffled behind the thick glass. He'd barely finished his words before the first of the Venenum flew out of the hole. My breathing snagged in my chest. It was the size of a crow. Six spindly appendages hung from its black and red striped body. The back four looked like an insect's, but the front two were miniature black hands complete with spindly fingers. A sharp stinger curled out from its arched abdomen, tip pointing straight towards me. But the bit that really freaked me out was the face. It looked almost...human. Bulbous white eyes, with pulsing black pupils and a large, awkward mouth that stretched open to reveal sharp fangs. The Venenum noticed me and let out a high-pitched squeal and raced forward. Behind it dozens more flew out, the combined drone of their wings loud and eerie.

"You have got to be kidding me!"

I was racing at an incredible speed before I was even aware I was moving. The rain had turned the ground into a mud bath. Hidden roots and rocks snagged on my feet and it took all of my improved balance to keep upright. I surged forward, checking behind me. The swarm were still gaining, their high-pitched screams mixing with the steady beat of the rain.

Without warning a wall shot up straight in front of me. It was too wide to go around. I didn't have time to stop, so I vaulted as high as I could, using my momentum to run up the side. For a second I thought I'd made it. But in a stomach lurching moment, one trainer clipped the edge. I tumbled to the ground on the other side, grunting as I splashed into the mud and slid along the trench. The impact barely hurt at all. What did hurt was the dagger that sunk into the flesh between my shoulder blades. Pain exploded in my back, sweeping up my spine and smashing into my brain. A scream ripped from my throat. I turned to see that the leading Venenum had stung me. Each stab of pain felt like a sharp fingernail raking against an exposed nerve. I jerked out my foot and crushed the insect against the metal wall. There was a sickening pop and then a mess of black and green.

I darted back onto my feet as the others buzzed around the obstacle. I pushed myself harder - the pain still searing in my back - determined not to have a repeat experience. The path became a blur, as I jumped and twisted my way over the various

228

obstacles that shot out along the way. I glanced up through the glass, to see Delagio running alongside the trench, pressing the Biomote in his hand at certain points. With each tap of the pad, a wall or moving barrier appeared. *He's making the obstacles appear!* I gritted my teeth.

The path curved sharply around to the right. As I made the corner, I was horrified to see that the pathway was cut off. Only a shallow little crawlspace was available at the bottom of a huge wall. Behind me I could hear the swarm rushing closer. Their screams sounded demented now - presumably because I'd killed one of their own. I knew that if I tried to crawl, they'd catch me. So without even slowing, I dived. My body hit the ground and I slid along the damp mud at breakneck speed. The tunnel swallowed me, roots clawing at my arms and face as I swept through the darkness and broke through to the other side.

Bursting into the light, I barely had time to notice a metal table with a strange looking rifle laying on the top, before crashing straight into it. I collided with one of the metal legs. It buckled, causing the gun to roll onto the ground. It splashed into the wet mud and I scrambled for it as the swarm burst through the crawlspace. I rolled onto my back and with shaking hands, aimed and pulled the trigger. There was a pulsing sound and then...nothing.

They still rushed towards me.

My heart leapt into my mouth. I raised my arms up to protect my face. I waited for the incredible pain to hit. It didn't.

I dropped my hands to see that all of the Venenum had stopped. They hung in mid-air like they were contemplating something, their wings beating together, making that eerie noise that only insects can. Their bodies began to vibrate hard and their squeals rose in pitch until they reached a frequency that made my ears ring.

Then they all popped.

Their gore flew everywhere. I managed to cover my face just in time and felt it splash onto my arms.

"Gross," I muttered.

Around me, the glass barriers shrank back into the mud.

"Well done, buddy," said a voice from above. Delagio was staring down at me, grinning like the Cheshire Cat. He leaned

229

over and held out a hand. I took it grudgingly and he heaved me out of the obstacle course. I collapsed onto the wet grass, chest still heaving up and down as he studied the Biomote.

"Unbelievable," I wheezed to myself. I looked over at the mud slicked gun lying next to me. "I should use this thing on you."

He laughed - a rolling chuckle that made his shoulders shake.

"Sorry buddy, ah know these trials is harsh, but our job is a rough one. You have to make sure you're prepared for anythin'." He pulled a booster out of his pocket. "Here, this should stop the pain."

"Actually...it doesn't really hurt anymore."

Delagio raised his eyebrows. "Seriously? You mind if ah take a look?"

"Sure." I climbed to my feet and rolled up my gore-splattered jumper.

"Wow, ya can hardly see the mark!" said Delagio. "You're lucky; it must not have gotcha proper."

"Certainly felt like it got me," I said, dropping my top back down.

Delagio clapped me on the shoulder. "You did good, Alex. Real good. You're a fast one alright. The Biomote clocked you at fifty-two miles per hour. Most Chosen peak at about forty-five." He pointed a finger at his chest. "Yours truly got stung seven times."

I couldn't resist a wide smile. *Who cares if I don't have a gift, when I can run at over fifty miles an hour? That's one in itself.*

"How fast is Gabriella out of interest?"

Delagio grinned. "About sixty-five as an average."

"Sixty-five?"

"She's...different."

I frowned up at him. "What do you mean?"

Delagio waved a dismissive hand and pointed towards the mansion. "We should head back. Rachel will be waitin'. Though you should probably grab a quick shower and change first."

I looked down at the splodges of insect entrails that the rain had smeared across the ripped jumper. "I really can't be bothered to get ready all over again," I sighed.

230

But I was lying. If it meant another chance to see Gabriella, I was all for it.

18

To my disappointment, Gabriella wasn't about, so I ended up showering and changing in Delagio's room. The décor was GQ trendy - a sleek combo of black marble and wood. On the way out, I noticed an array of Stetsons hanging on a hat rack in the hallway. I tried one on and looked in the mirror. I hastily put it back again.

Think I'll leave the trend setting to Delagio.

Rachel was waiting for me at the foot of the main stairs. Her hair had been pulled into a tight ponytail, emphasising her Fae features - high, angular cheekbones and slender face. She re-adjusted the glasses on her nose as I reached her. I found myself wondering if she even needed them, or had simply grown used to wearing them as part of her disguise.

"Afternoon, Alex," she said.

"Hi Miss St- I mean Rachel."

She handed me a cereal bar. "I thought you might be hungry. This should help keep you going until the feast later."

"Thanks," I smiled.

We took an elevator at the far end of the hall. Rachel pressed a button depicting a sword.

Combat Arena, said Mrs Elevator.

As the cab hurtled along the Nexus, I discovered I didn't feel nauseous at all. My body had adapted.

"So how long have you been an Infiltrator for?" I asked through a mouthful of oats and berries.

Rachel smiled. "Put it this way, I brought in my first Chosen while Edison was still wrapping his brain around the light bulb."

I raised my eyebrows. "That's...wow. So, do you enjoy it?"

Her smile faded. "Enjoy is a strong word. It's an important and necessary part of what we do."

"It must be hard though, always having to pretend to be someone else."

Rachel gave a thoughtful nod. "It can be. But I never forget why I'm here."

The elevator drew to a close. I swallowed the last bite of the bar as the doors rolled open.

We stepped out into a large circular dojo. The walls were lined with thick white padding. A large tatami mat covered the entire floor, bowing ever so slightly under our weight. An array of hand-to-hand weapons rested in various racks around the perimeter, along with eight evenly placed Golems. They were marionettes without a puppet master - heads bowed and arms hanging by their sides.

Rachel walked to the edge of the dojo, slipped off the large heels she was wearing and nodded for me to do the same. Pulling a booster from her uniform pocket, she placed it neatly next to my trainers. I watched as she moved into the centre of the dojo, stretched her arms up to the ceiling and unfurled her wings. They burst through narrow slits in her uniform, making a rattling sound as she shook them out.

"Ah, that's so much better," she sighed. "I get horrendous back cramp when they are in retraction."

They were actually quite beautiful. At first I'd thought of them as insect wings, but on second inspection they looked like they'd been woven from the thinnest, purest silk. The damage they had received from the Rahuman battle was mending well. The tears were nothing more than raised lines now.

"Do you mind?" she asked, pointing upwards with a dainty finger.

"I uh, no...be my guest."

With a hop, Rachel spiralled into the air. For the next few minutes, she swooped and soared around the room, an expression of absolute serenity on her face. As I watched her, I fully understood the weight behind what I'd said in the elevator. How difficult it must be to constantly be someone else – over and over. I felt secretly glad that Gabriella's first infiltration looked to be her last.

Finally Rachel came to rest on a beam high above my head. "Sorry about that, I don't often get an opportunity to fly. It's restricted on this side of the Veil for obvious reasons."

"No, that's fine."

233

The Pixie drummed her fingers on the wood. "Right, this training is on your combat ability. We're here to unlock your innate fighting skills."

"I don't have to fight you do I?"

Rachel smiled. "No, don't worry. That's what these chaps are for." She clicked her fingers and two of the Golems reacted instantly, lifting their heads in eerie symmetry. Their blood stained eyes stared up at Rachel with dead emotion.

"Faru gave you control of them?"

"Yes. And he's about to give you something too."

"What do you mean?"

Rachel dropped backwards off the beam, somersaulting in the air and landing without a sound on the floor.

She closed her eyes. "Sage Faru, may I speak with you?"

There was a pause and then her whole body shuddered. She gave the HASEA salute. "Good afternoon, sir," she said to the empty space in front of her. "Yes, we are ready to begin. You can transfer your Farsight whenever you are ready." She gave another salute and then turned to me.

"Close your eyes, Alex."

I did as she asked.

I heard Rachel step forward and walk around me in a wide, slow circle. "Chosen can learn new skills in an extraordinarily short amount of time. However, traditional combat training can still take a couple of weeks to perfect. We are fortunate enough to have a Seelian's unique skills to reduce it to a fraction of the time. In a moment, Faru is going to loan you his Farsight ability. It will quickly condition your improved mind to sense danger better and develop instinctual reactions. In a real fight, skills like these will save your life. It's going to be a very strange sensation to begin with, but I'm here to guide you through it. Okay?"

I nodded.

It hit me. A torrent of colour rushed into my head, filling the darkness with a psychedelic rainbow of morphing shapes. My brain twitched uncomfortably as it attempted to process the swirling kaleidoscope.

"Whoa- wow- okay, I've got it. I uh- this is pretty intense Rachel!"

"It's okay Alex, I'm here. Just try to relax. It will pass."

234

I slowed my breathing and bit-by-bit the images settled. What remained was a plain of white-yellow light with a shimmering shadow person standing in the centre.

"Okay, I want you to focus on my voice. This may sound strange, but I need you to try and visualise how I sound, rather than how I look."

"I'll try."

Rachel continued to talk to me and I concentrated on every word. Slowly her form solidified. Vivid colours swirled in from the corners of my mind and applied themselves to her image until she became a superior representation of my science teacher. Her hair shone like freshly spun gold. Her eyes glinted like polished emeralds. In the centre of her chest, a purple orb of light radiated waves of energy outwards to the rest of her body. I made a gasping noise.

"I- I can see your-"

"Soul, yes. Good, that means you're getting the hang of this. I'd prefer it if you left it alone though, I've grown somewhat attached."

Rachel flew back up into the air, leaving a blue shadow trail in her wake, like plane contrails. They dissolved as she settled in what seemed to be mid-air. Focusing, I made out her perch, which had become a long beam of shimmering light.

"Golems will be much harder for you to see because they have barely any life-force."

"Isn't that a bit of a problem?"

"No, that's what we want. You're going to need to fully rely on your senses to beat them. I need to you to clear your mind and focus. Forget about fear, pain or anger. Give yourself completely to your instincts. You'll know when you're there."

I knew what she meant. I'd felt the sensation when the car had hit me and later on when I'd been running. *That switched that flicked. Like passing a barrier in my mind.*

"I think I know what you mean, I've done it before."

"Good. But I'm going to teach you how to do it all the time, without thought. First round is going to be basic hand to hand. Let's get started." She clapped her hands together.

A shuffling sound filled the arena. A second later an arc of silver light flashed towards me. There was a loud *thwack* and a glancing pain as something solid connected with my cheek. I spiralled sideways and crashed to the floor. The metallic tang of blood filled my mouth.

"Dammit! That hurt!" I yelled, spitting onto the mat. As I stared up, a flashing image of a Golem holding a crosier appeared in my mind before dissolving.

"Of course it hurts. Were you expecting love taps?"

"But I wasn't ready!"

"In a real fight you won't have time to prepare. It's that instinctual reaction we are going to unlock."

I slapped the ground in frustration. "Fine." I pulled myself to my feet.

"Again," she shouted.

A long trail of light sliced a path through the air. It came from above, bearing down like an executioners axe. Without thinking, I dived into a sideways roll. I heard the staff smack down onto the mat beside me. Before I could react another bar of light swung at me from the side. It connected with the back of my head. I stumbled forward and collapsed to my knees.

"Concentrate!"

"I'm trying!"

I climbed to my feet. *Come on Alex!* I scolded myself.

"Again."

This time, as a Golem swung its crosier at me, the switch flipped in my brain. Around me, everything intensified. The flashes of light became more solid, taking on the shapes of the staffs. The normally inaudible wisps of robes sliding against clay skin became wire brooms sweeping pavements. Its footsteps became booming drumbeats. Everything I needed to work out exactly where it was and what it was doing.

I opened my hands, palms facing outwards and the staff connected with a loud slap. Grabbing the crosier, I allowed myself to travel backwards, absorbing the intense blow. Using the energy from the Golem's heavy swing, I pivoted sharply on the spot and launched the staff with every ounce of strength I had. As I'd hoped, the Golem didn't let go of its cherished weapon - I could tell by the weight and the cushioned *whump* that echoed around the room as its body hit the far wall.

236

My hands stung, but before I could contemplate whether or not they were bleeding, I saw a staff come at me low, in a sweeping arc. I jumped up before it could connect and stamped down hard with both feet. I landed dead on and felt it buckle under my weight. The power brought the Golem surging forwards. I waited for a split second, until I felt the timing was just right, then linked my hands behind its smooth skull and pulled, adding to the momentum. I jerked up my knee and felt its face shatter at the impact point. I let go and heard the wreck of its body crash to the floor. For a moment I stood still, listening to my own ragged breathing. *The others aren't attacking. I think...I did it.*

The room was filled with a slow clap, which sounded like a cacophony of sound to my oversensitive ears. After a few seconds they readjusted so the sound was acceptable.

"Not bad Alex, not bad at all. You can open your eyes now."

My regular vision seemed odd after the Farsight. The first thing I did was look at my hands. I noticed with surprise that not only were they not bleeding, there was barely a mark on them. I scanned the rest of the room. A broken Golem lay at my feet. It was face down, hand still clutched around the now v-shaped crosier. Fragments of its demolished face were dotted around it, reminding me of a broken china doll. A shard near my foot was marked with XI.

I noticed the other Golem. It was propped upside down against the far wall. Its neck was twisted at an unnatural angle, left cheek crushed against the floor. Both eyes were shattered and red liquid pooled out of them like smashed eggs. Its right hand twitched, still searching for the staff that lay a few feet away from its mangled body. It had been given one task and it was still trying to carry it out. Its stony hand gave a final jerk and then fell lifeless to the mat.

Strangely, even though I knew they were just clay effigies created by Faru, I felt guilty. Rachel seemed to sense my unease. "Don't worry Alexander, they have no feelings. They may have some of Faru's life-force, but that doesn't mean they're alive." She slipped from the beam and floated over to the fallen Golems. Pushing her fingers into their mouths, she pulled out what looked like small flat stones. A few seconds later they dissolved into dust.

Rachel moved over to one of the weapon racks and slid out a samurai sword. She tossed it through the air. Without thinking, I caught it by the hilt and let the tip rest against floor. With a click of her fingers, two other Golems came to life.

"Next part, weapons training. Close your eyes."

*

We practiced for the next few hours. With the aid of Farsight I learned how to enter my instinctual combat state with barely a split second of thought. Rachel taught me how to handle the various weapons, using my new abilities. It unnerved me at how natural I felt wielding deadly blades and Bo staffs.

I dispatched the last Golem with a rising sword strike that removed its head. It rolled towards Rachel, who stopped it with her foot.

There was a series of clapping. I opened my eyes and turned to see Sage Faru, Gabriella and the rest of Orion by the entrance. I blushed at the sight of the unexpected audience.

Faru clicked his fingers and the remains of the defeated Golems disappeared into dust, leaving only the flat stones behind, which Rachel picked up. He walked over to me - his footsteps making no sound on the Tatami flooring - and placed a hand on my shoulder. A tickling sensation swept through my brain and I knew that the Farsight had gone.

"Congratulations Alexander, you have reached the end of your initiation training. I have been kept appraised of your progress. I must say I'm impressed. Despite the circumstances, you have managed to keep control and are progressing nicely. You will make an excellent addition to Orion."

I felt a rush of pride. "Thank you sir."

"However, there is still the matter of your final trial. It will take place now, here."

My heart stalled. I knew that I'd have to do it, but it had come about so quickly.

238

"In order to fully awaken the potential within us, we must first defeat the fear that keeps it prisoner." He called over his shoulder. "Bring him in."

Midnight disappeared into the elevator. When he re-entered, he was not alone. Agent Noble and two others agents emerged, tugging breathlessly at ropes. As they got further into the room, I saw that the ropes were attached to a large silver cage on wheels. Inside stood a hulking man wearing a tattered pair of shorts. His thick wrists were shackled in equally thick chains, which linked to a bolted loop on the cage floor. Long, knotted twists of hair hung around his shoulders like jungle vines. His body was a living canvass. Countless tattoos filled most of the free space from his chest downwards. There were black flames that licked up the sides of his arms, a screaming girl being consumed by a large dog over his stomach, a set of teeth marks on the side of his waist and an eerie moon shining behind a gothic castle on his right leg. But the tattoo that caught my attention was the crudely drawn eye placed over his heart. It seemed to stare at everything all at once - judging.

The man was a Soldier of Sorrow.

His real eyes looked dark and uncaring. He stared with little emotion around the room as Agent Noble leaned into the cage, using a large key to unshackle his hands. No sooner had this been done, that with the speed of a viper, he grabbed the agent's arm and snapped his wrist. The sound of bone breaking echoed around the room. I gasped in horror. Agent Noble let out a scream and fell to the floor. The other two scrambled to drag him away. Gabriella swore loudly and pulled out a gun attached to her belt. The caged man shrank away from it.

"Enough!" commanded Faru. "Gabriella, holster your weapon. Agent Jones, take Agent Noble to the Recovery Centre. Call Selene to assist. I will be along after Alexander has dealt with our unruly guest here." He stepped forward to the cage, wrapping his wrinkled hands around the steel poles without fear. The prisoner copied the movement, but made no attempt to attack the Sage.

"He was rude to me on the journey over," the man said in a matter of fact tone. His voice sounded deep and gruff.

239

"You are a despicable creature, Bargheist. I would like nothing better than to strike you down where you stand. A mangy beast put out of its misery. However, we honour our agreements. You have not forgotten the rules I trust?"

Bargheist nodded. A sure slow movement, which caused more of his thick black hair to tumble around his shoulders. "I fight the boy." He shifted his dark eyes to me and I recoiled. "It's a knockout battle only. If I kill him, you kill me. Otherwise, regardless of the outcome you will ensure my safeguarded deportation back to Pandemonia."

His words seemed to hang in the air as if they were real creatures capable of inflicting real damage. My legs went weak and I had to fight a strong urge to throw up. *Faru wants me to fight that? He's insane!*

Faru made an agreeing noise and stepped away from the cage. At the same time the sword slipped from my hand and the hilt smacked my foot. I jumped in shock, tripping and landing on my backside. Bargheist threw back his head and laughed. It was a sound that could have turned milk sour.

"QUIET!" bellowed Faru. Silence descended as if speakers had blown. "Alexander, please compose yourself."

I scrambled to my feet, grabbing at the sword with trembling fingers. "I can't fight him!" I croaked. "He's a psychopath. You all saw what he did to Agent Noble!"

Faru put up an appeasing hand. "I do not deny that he is a vile creature. One who made the choice to follow darkness." The Seelian paused. "He is also one of those who tried to kill you."

My jaw unhinged. I looked at the caged madman. "T-that's the Skinshifter? The one who chased me?"

"The very same."

I remembered back to the other night. The way those blood-filled eyes had glared at me from the woods as their owner pursued me unrelentingly. The evil flowing from them had made my skin crawl so much it'd been a miracle it stayed attached to my body. And now here he was, standing right in front of me – and I was supposed to fight him. My heart smashed against my ribcage.

Faru moved close to me. "You have a choice, Alexander. You can choose to go back to being the perpetual victim who was terrified to stand up for himself. The boy who hid in the shadows of life, afraid to stand up or speak out for fear of being crushed. Or you can choose to step out of the shadows, to believe in the potential you hold inside and become the man who stands tall against his opponents...and wins." He placed his hand on the back of my neck, a fleeting movement, but one that had a profound effect.

Thousands of images from my life flashed through my mind. They contained no moments of success or comfort. They were of times where I'd been doubled over, whilst bullies kicked and punched me. Of when I'd skulked home, bruised and alone. Times when I'd cried myself to sleep in desperation. Or when I'd watched John hug Mikey and I'd stood in the doorway, wishing I'd had a dad who hadn't gone and died on me. All of the moments when I'd felt worthless, like a stagehand standing in the shadows, watching the lead actors bow on stage as roses land at their feet. The images ceased, but the impact of them remained. I coiled my hand tight around the sword hilt.

"I'll fight."

19

E xcellent," smiled Faru, clasping his hands together. The team spread themselves around the edges of the dojo. The Sage made his way to the head of the room.

As Gabriella passed me she leaned in, so close that her breath played on my neck. "We'll have guns on Bargheist the whole time. If it looks for a second like he's going to do some permanent damage, I'm putting the mongrel down, okay?" She squeezed my arm, sending a few sparks flying through it.

True to her word, everyone pulled a gun from their belts - all except Faru. He remained hunched over on his cane, white eyes staring at Bargheist. I stood at the centre of a star of protection, vengeance ready to fire in from every point.

"Is the sword your weapon of choice Alexander?" asked the Seelian. I looked down at the ornate blade clutched in my white knuckled hands.

"Yes."

"Alright. Agent Green, if you would."

The remaining agent removed a set of keys from his blazer pocket with a shaking hand. He unlocked the front of the cage then darted behind it. Bargheist stepped down from the raised floor, taking a deep breath of relative freedom, like a prisoner in the exercise yard. The agent disappeared into the elevator, trailing the empty cage behind him at tremendous speed. The doors slid together. Midnight tapped on a Biomote and there was a loud beep as the doors locked.

Silence reigned.

"Show your true form Bargheist!" shouted Gabriella, smashing the stillness.

The man looked down at himself and sighed. "And I was just getting used to this new body. Oh well, *C'est la vie.*" Glaring at me, he crouched down onto his haunches. "You better know how to use that needle boy," he growled. Then I witnessed an event that no amounts of forewarning could ever prepare a person for.

The transition from man into hellhound.

Bargheist's jaw unhinged like a snake's. The skin surrounding his mouth became loose elastic, which slackened and dangled in rolls around his neck. His whole body shuddered. Then slowly his skin began to slide downwards like a sock being peeled from a foot. A pair of blood red eyes appeared in the cavernous hole that had once been Bargheist's mouth. A stomach lurching series of cracks and crunches emanated from inside. The skin continued to slither down the frame of the former man, gathering in a fleshy pile on the floor. A black muzzle pushed out of the yawning hole. The area around the skull had stretched to the point it looked ready to rip. The empty eye sockets were oval pits you could fit a fist through, the nose a bump of cartilage, between the shoulders. Then like a demonic birth, the head of a giant dog creature popped free from the slackened maw of the deflated man. Two black legs followed, topped by huge paws with scythe claws the size of a thumb. A third, back leg escaped the skin hole. The creature used his sharp grip on the mat flooring to drag himself from the husk. Finally, with a growl he burst free, leaving the shed carcass in a heap behind him like a discarded outfit.

Staring back at me was a hulking beast known as Bargheist. He was the size of a Great Dane.

How in the hell am I supposed to defeat this?

Then I realised with a surge of dread that he was *still growing.* His body jerked in weird directions, like he was being tugged by dozens of invisible strings. With each movement his form expanded. Bargheist yelped with every alteration. There was a final sweeping crunch as each vertebra in his spinal column popped into place.

I stepped back instinctively as I took in the Skinshifter's final form. Tangled fur hung from his muscular body in matted clumps. His head was long and narrow like a wolf's...but far larger. Bargheist rose up onto his back legs – casting a shadow over the entire dojo - and howled. The inhuman sound rushed through me, freezing my bones. The hellhound came crashing back down and the floor shuddered under the weight. I lost my

243

footing and had to dig the sword into the matting to keep me upright. He sank back onto his hind legs and stretched his front out; a coil ready to spring.

"Begin," shouted Faru.

Bargheist pounced.

I jumped to the right, dodging the attack. The Skinshifter flew past; his jaws making a deafening chomp as they bit nothing but air. The second time I wasn't so lucky. He leapt at me and a set of razor teeth sank into the soft flesh above my wrist. I screamed as white-hot pain seared up my arm. I tried to pull away, but Bargheist edged backwards, dragging me along the floor. Blood bloomed from the multiple punctures, pooling around his half buried teeth. From my awkward angle, I couldn't get enough of a swing, so I rotated the sword and brought the base down between Bargheist's eyes - hard.

The Skinshifter yelped, releasing my wounded arm. Bright spots of nausea flashed behind my eyes as I took in the multiple puncture wounds on either side. The beast was dazed. He staggered about, shaking his head from side to side. I ignored the pulsing throb in my arm and used my temporary advantage to attack. I ran forward and slashed wildly with the sword. Bargheist recovered just in time, darting away from the blow. I stumbled from the momentum, and the tip of the sword tore a large hole in the Tatami mat - exposing hardwood flooring underneath.

The attack left my back defenceless.

"Look out!" Gabriella shouted, but there wasn't enough time to do anything. Bargheist head-butted me in my lower back, causing the sword to helicopter out of my grip and sending me flying face first into the padded wall next to Delagio. I connected hard, pinballing off the cushion and spiralling to the floor.

Jumping up, I spun around at the same time Bargheist leapt at me. I put out my arms and caught his front legs with my hands. I tightened my grip, forcing him to remain on his back legs. Not able to slash at me, he gnashed his frothing teeth together, trying to bite my face. I had to dodge my head from side to side. From around me I could hear gasps and cries as each clamp of his teeth missed by inches. Bargheist's colossal

244

weight bearing down on me began to take its toll. My arms shook from the strain.

I can't hold him for much longer!

I knew I'd be in big trouble if I let go at the wrong moment. So I pivoted left, trying to duck out of the way and throw the hound off me. Bargheist mirrored the movement, hooking his claws into my shoulders. Each one was a razor blade slicing into my flesh. Grimacing through the pain, I tried to dodge the other way. Still the beast kept himself pinned to me, knowing I was tiring. From the outside, it must have looked like we were dancing - the most bizarre tango in history.

I couldn't stand any more. I dropped my right arm down and as the beast started to crush me under his weight, I sprung upwards, driving a fist into his throat. Bargheist roared and stumbled to the side, claws unsticking from my shoulders. Too disorientated to keep upright, his legs crumpled and he crashed to the floor. This was no victory won though - I knew I only had seconds. I sprinted over and grabbed the sword. After wiping the sweat from my eyes with the back of my good hand, I raised the blade and spread my feet into a defensive stance Rachel had taught me. Bargheist barked in anger and heaved his colossal frame back onto his feet. He shocked me by lowering his jaw and speaking.

"No more playing around!" he growled. Each word rumbled like a boulder falling down a cliff. I could feel sweat spreading between my fingers. My muscles popped with tension. Bargheist sprinted forwards, but at the last second darted away and spun in a rapid circle around me. I struck out with the sword, but the Skinshifter was too fast. I felt his teeth sink into the back of my ankle. I dropped to a knee, gasping in pain.

Bargheist repeated the tactic, looping in dizzying circles just out of my reach, waiting for me to attack and then darting in to bite my ankles. Every strike I made just sent strips of tatami mat flying around the dojo.

It felt as if a man o' war had attached itself around my legs. Bargheist was taking me down like a hyena takes down a gazelle. Trails of blood trickled from my heels and pooled around me. I glanced at Gabriella. Her face had gone pale with concern.

She knows I'm going to lose.

I knew it too. I felt helpless. Again and again Bargheist darted in and out, razor teeth ripping into my flesh. I flailed out with the blade, always missing and taking curved slices from the mat. The area around me was peppered with half circle grins, laughing at my failure.

I knew it wouldn't be long before they called an end to the fight. Forget that he'd bite through my Achilles tendons soon; if it carried on much longer I'd die from blood loss. *Then what? I can't go back to my old life after everything I've been through...I may never see Gabriella again.* The notion filled me with utter despair. I couldn't even contemplate it as an option. *Think Alex!*

The smallest detail gave me a glimmer of hope. As Bargheist sprinted around me for the umpteenth time, lining up another attack, he skidded slightly on a section of exposed wood. A series of memories flashed into my head. Of Monty - a neighbour's hyperactive puppy. Of our polished oak wood floorboards. Of his wide eyed fear as he skidded across the wood like a first time ice skater.

And fell down.

I darted up, ignoring the nauseating pain from my legs and sprinted away from Bargheist as best I could. I spun the sword and dragged it behind me. The blade made easy work of the matting, unzipping it as I sprinted. From behind, I could sense the beast taking up the chase. I charged directly towards Rachel's position. She moved out of my way, gun still trained on my pursuer. I waited until I could feel his hot breath on me, then veered left, grabbed an edge of the Tatami and yanked. It opened up like a weak seam.

As soon as Bargheist's padded feet hit the smooth wooden surface, they slipped from underneath his body and the Skinshifter crashed to the floor, legs splayed out in a starfish position. The hellhound yelped as he helplessly cascaded into a rack of Bo staffs. There was a loud *thump* followed by a clatter as the wooden poles collapsed around him.

I swung the sword back into position and ran along once more - carrying on where I'd left off. There was a sharp ripping sound as the matting came up. As Bargheist slowly started to revive himself, I carried on running around the dojo like a baseball player who'd hit a home run. With my free hand, I yanked the matting as hard as I could. As I hoped, a huge chunk rushed towards me.

Please work! I prayed.

I dropped the samurai sword and ran towards the centre of the room, dragging the matting behind me like a giant cape. I waited until I reached the hanging beam...and jumped. I flew through the air, stretching one hand out in front of me. It connected with the beam. I used it to propel myself forward, whilst I used the other to throw the matting through the gap. I hit the ground hard and rolled a few times. My wounded heels screamed with pain. I noticed the sword lying next to me. I snatched it up and dragged myself to my aching feet.

I looked up.

The matting was completely suspended, draped over the beam as if it were a huge towel rail. The ends dangled a few feet above my head.

The room shook. I snapped my head around to see Bargheist crash to the floor once again. Adrenaline surged through my body as I watched him. As I'd hoped, the Skinshifter was having a very difficult time with the new flooring. Every time he tried to sprint at me, his paws would slip on the polished wood and send him crashing to the ground. Wounded, and exhausted, I walked over to the thrashing beast. He tried to get up, but failing, instead tried to gnash at my leg. I skipped out of the way of the attack. Stabbing the blade into the floor, I jumped up onto his back. His fleece was rough and scratched against my skin. I seized his horse-sized head, gripping handfuls of tangled fur between my fingers. Using all of my strength, I smashed his skull into the floor.

CRACK!

The sound reverberated around the dojo like a thunderclap. I gritted my teeth together. Smashed his head down again.

CRACK!

The tremors ran up my damaged arm and caused fresh blood to seep from the puncture wounds.

CRACK, CRACK, CRACK!!

Again and again I drove his head downwards. The beast howled from the constant jarring impacts and his head started to loll from side to side. I released my grip and his muzzle hit the floor. I leaned over and unstuck the sword. Spinning it around, I poised it above Bargheist's head. I looked at Gabriella, who had an intense expression on her face.

She nodded.

I drove the blade hard into the Skinshifter's skull. It split the bone, sank through flesh and bust through the lower jaw, pinning Bargheist to the wood. He let out a piercing, strangled howl and collapsed to the floor, defeated. I rolled off his giant back, landing on my knees. I let out a long sigh and sank into as sitting position, resting my head between my knees. I was soaked with sweat and it felt as if my lungs were three sizes too small. Standing up was no longer an option.

A slow, steady clap filled the dojo. I blurrily looked up at Faru, who was standing in the centre of the carved up floor, wearing a satisfied smile. His blank eyes seemed to be twinkling in the light.

"Fantastic, Alexander. That battle demonstrated not only your strength and resilience, but also your resourcefulness. All characteristics a Guardian should poses. Congratulations my boy, you have passed the test."

I wanted to feel happy, but I was too drained. I was too drained to feel *anything*. Gabriella looked at me and then to her leader. He seemed to understand something unspoken, because he nodded. Gabriella sprinted to the booster by my trainers and then over to me. I dropped my head as a wave of tiredness flowed through my body.

I felt a pair of warm hands encircle me. The exhaustion was replaced by a sense of peace and comfort. My arm and legs stopped throbbing.

"It's okay Alex, you did it. I'll have you feeling better in a second," she whispered.

Her raven hair spilled onto my face and neck as she held me. I felt her gently roll up the jumper sleeve to find a spot to inject the booster. I let myself sink into her arms, breathing in her gorgeous scent.

"I already feel a bit better," I whispered.

Her body stiffened. "Oh my god!"

I snapped to attention, thinking Bargheist had freed himself.

"What?" I asked in confusion when I saw the Skinshifter's hulking mass still pinned to the floor.

"Everyone, you need to see this!"

I was panicking now. The rest of the team ran over.

"What is the matter?" asked Faru, who was last to reach us.

"Look at his wounds," Gabriella said.

I looked down and drew in a sharp breath.

They were fading.

The puncture wounds shrank in front of my eyes until they became nothing but pink dots. Then they disappeared completely. I glanced at my legs. The skin around the ankles slowly stitched itself back together, leaving thin pink trails of scar tissue. The raised flesh turned white and then dissolved. Underneath, the skin looked brand new - not a single trace of damage.

I looked up at the rest of the team. They were staring in amazement at the patches of fresh skin on my arm and legs. Faru stroked his long beard between his thumb and forefinger.

"Maybe he responds well to the booster?" suggested Delagio.

Gabriella held up the injector. The inside was still full of the dark blue liquid. "I haven't used it."

There were murmurs from the rest of the team. They looked at each other in confusion. Faru made a clicking noise with his tongue.

"What's happening?" I asked.

Gabriella ran a finger over the healed surface of my forearm. "I think we just found your ability."

20

L ater that evening, the Warren was a hive of activity. Agents and workers had been running around for most of the afternoon, transforming the mansion with decorations. Vivid green vines that resembled living tinsel had been wound up every single staircase. Ornate golden lamps sat on newly placed tables, burning with the same purple flames I'd seen in the temple. Large drapes of glimmering silver material hung over doorways that didn't need to be accessed and a red carpet had been rolled out through the front doors. Outside, every tree that lined the long driveway had delicate fairy lights entwined in their branches. Everywhere you looked, changes had been made to make the Warren shinier and more impressive. A warm glow had bloomed in my stomach as I'd taken it all in.

All of this is for me.

At the request of Sage Faru, the team and I had spent several hours after my defeat of Bargheist in a medical section of the base, where a very normal looking scientist in a white coat had performed all manner of tests on me. Finally, after tapping an alarming number of buttons on a Biomote and rescanning me, he had explained that my body had the capability of regenerating cells at a rate far superior to even those of a regular Chosen. He'd concluded with a slow stroke of his chin that I appeared to have the unique sixth ability of instant healing.

I'd tried to contain my excitement as we had made our way to the Temple to tell Faru the news. We had found the Sage sitting on the grand chair, deep in meditation - his two guards standing either side, heads bowed as if copying the action. Gabriella had told him the news regardless. He'd given a simple, slow nod. Then without the need for words, the notion that he would speak to me about it after the joining ceremony flashed into my head. It was followed by the suggestion that we take the opportunity to unwind until it was time to get ready.

Agents weaved their way past the team, barking orders through their wrist microphones and pressing their fingers against their earpieces.

Midnight frowned. "This ain't normal," he grunted, as Iralia tottered past him, carrying a bowl of floating candles.

"Maybe they're trying to lift the mood," suggested Delagio. "It's been tough on everyone lately."

"Don't they do this for all new Guardians?" I asked, savouring the smell of spices that wafted from the kitchen.

Rachel shook her head. "No, this is too grand. Something big is going on, and I want to find out what. You okay with that, Ella?"

Gabriella narrowed her eyes. "I'm curious too. Go find out."

Rachel peeled off from the rest of the team and disappeared behind one of the silver curtains. Midnight stopped near the base of the main stairs and scratched a huge finger against the nape of his neck. "As much as I love hangin' out with new kid here, I promised pint size she could practice some new spells she learned on me next time we had a moment."

Sophia's eyes brightened. "Can we, Ella? I want to make Midnight walk through a wall!"

Gabriella laughed. "I'm pretty sure he can do that anyway, but go on, have fun. Make sure you're not late for the feast though. And try not to turn him into a brick or something!"

"Thanks!" Sophia grinned and the two raced one another up the stairs. Midnight pretended to trip at the top, so that the little girl could win.

Gabriella turned to Delagio. "I suppose you probably have things you want to do too."

He patted the pouch at his side. "Well ah was kind of hopin' to get a couple of hours in at the target range."

Gabriella rolled her eyes. "Go on then."

Delagio tipped his hat. "Thanks, boss. See ya later Alex, try not to kill anything while ah'm gone."

I smiled and watched as he called an elevator and was swallowed into the depths of the Nexus.

"So what now?" I asked stepping to the side, so a man in a white apron could roll a glass keg of what looked like blood

251

between us. "I get the impression we're kind of in the way down here."

"We can go and check out your apartment if you like. It'll probably be ready by now."

"Sounds great. Lead the way."

I followed Gabriella up the stairs and along the balcony. We slipped through one of the silver drapes, which felt as light and soft to the touch as gossamer. As we passed the door that lead to Gabriella's apartment, I noticed the little plaque with her name on. *Even her name is beautiful.*

We headed a few doors down and then stopped. There was a backing plate with my name on it.

"Put your thumb on the scanner there," she said pointing to a little pad beside the door.

I did as she said. A wave of light ran down the pad and then there was a low click as the latch opened. Gabriella swung the door open and gestured inside.

The layout was similar to Gabriella's apartment, but the style was completely different. The walls were ocean blue - my favourite colour. The hallway was home to a bookshelf packed with novels. I glanced at a few of the titles. *Alice in Wonderland, The Enchanted Woods, The Dark Tower, Lord of the Rings, American Gods.* Copies of every book I had treasured growing up were all present and accounted for. What surprised me even more was that the shelves included books I'd wanted to read but hadn't managed to get around to.

In the lounge, a hulking plasma screen hung on the fireplace wall. Below, a cabinet was filled with a selection of video game consoles and games. A leather U-shaped sofa filled the sunken area. On the wall to the left of the opening, was a giant canvass of artwork done by Ryan Lloyd of Soulfire and signed by the man himself. On the other side was a perfect recreation of the peaceful beach from my mind journey with Faru. My mouth fell open in disbelief.

The kitchen was stocked with all of my favourite foods. The bathroom was a giant wet room, containing countless waterspouts and a Jacuzzi bath. The bedroom was stunning. A king-sized bed sat on top of a thick chocolate carpet and in the middle of an array of dark wood furniture. Another plasma television hung from a contrasting white wall. A selection of my favourite films stood on a unit below. Hanging from a wardrobe handle was an expensive looking suit bag.

I turned around to Gabriella. "I don't know what to say. It's...perfect. How did-"

"Faru," she said tapping a finger against her temple. "Okay, I'm going to head back to my apartment. Why don't you get you relax for a while, then get ready and come find me when you're done. The ceremony doesn't begin for another three hours, so no rush." She pointed a finger towards the suit bag hanging from the wardrobe. "Everything you need is in there."

*

My heart hammered against my chest as I unzipped the suit bag. Even though I was pretty sure I knew what was inside, I couldn't help but feel an overwhelming sense of anticipation. The rich scent of leather filled my nose as I pulled the sides of the bag away. Inside was my very own HASEA uniform.

The sense of acceptance I'd felt before came flooding back times ten. *This is me now. I belong here.*

I pulled on the black t-shirt, followed by the leather trousers. I smiled to myself as I put them on. *If these were by themselves, I'd look like some sort of nerdy rock star.* I removed the slim leather jacket and shrugged it on. It felt lightweight but strong. There was an indented space over the heart, where the HASEA badge would normally sit. I traced the outlines of it with a finger.

Next came the odd metal belt I'd seen the rest of the team wearing. As I lifted it out, I could hear a dull hum - as if it were conducting electricity. I noticed strange symbols etched on the inside. Shrugging, I wrapped it around my waist. The buckle was made of solid brushed metal and clicked into the other end like an airplane seatbelt. The last items at the bottom of the bag were a pair of boots that laced up to the shins, a pair of fingerless gloves and a duel sword scabbard, which slipped over both shoulders. Everything fitted perfectly.

I zipped up the jacket and walked over to the full-length mirror by the bed. I drew in a sharp breath. I looked like I'd been ripped from the pages of comic book. I looked like an actual superhero.

As I stared at my undeniably badass self in the mirror, I noticed a button on the side of the belt. Taking an instinctive look around, I pressed it.

My reflection disappeared.

"What the hell?" I cried out, stumbling backwards and knocking a shelf load of DVDs to the floor. I looked down and with a huge sigh of relief realised I was still there. I faced the mirror and pressed the button again. Two silvery waves rolled from the belt outward and my reflection re-appeared.

Like an excited child, I clicked the button a few more times and watched in amazement as I vanished and materialised in the space of a few seconds. *Okay, I'm definitely asking Gabriella about this one,* I thought as I headed out of the bedroom.

Not wanting to seem too keen, I wasted a bit of time playing on a PlayStation in the lounge. I couldn't concentrate properly and my avatar kept dying. Eventually I gave up and switched the system off.

The door of my apartment clicked shut behind me. I headed over towards Gabriella's room and pressed the bell, hopping from foot to foot as I waited for her to answer.

The door swung open and Gabriella was framed in the light, wearing what appeared to be a ceremonial version of the Guardian uniform. The black leather jacket was trimmed with golden stitching and ornate pads made from what looked like real gold sat on both shoulders. Her hair had been fixed into place using numerous hairpins and ran down her back. She looked me up and down and made an impressed face.

"Well don't you look dashing in uniform, Mister Eden?" she said with a cheeky smile.

I felt my face grow hot. "Yours is nice too," I said in an awkward voice.

"You mean this old thing?" she mock simpered. "It's something the Huntmasters have to wear whenever a new recruit joins the team. Come in." Gabriella opened the door further and ushered me inside. Music was playing softly from the lounge speakers. I recognised 'Destiny' by Zero 7. A bottle of champagne stood in a bucket of ice on the coffee table, along with two glasses. I sat down on the coach by the roaring fire. Gabriella picked up the bottle, which had a really worn label.

"I figured you could use a drink after everything that's happened. I thought it could be a sort of celebration."

"Sounds fantastic," I said. Pointing at the bottle I added, "That looks pretty old."

"That's because it is. It's a nineteen oh-seven shipwrecked Heidsieck," she explained, popping the cork. "It was meant to be shipped to the Russian imperial family in nineteen sixteen, but the boat sank off the coast of Finland. Divers found a case of two hundred back in ninety-seven. They were being sold for two hundred and seventy five thousand dollars a bottle in Moscow. Faru got a couple sent over for tonight." She gave a devilish grin. "So let's enjoy them."

My jaw unhinged. Gabriella laughed and poured two glasses, which frothed up to the rims. She handed me one. "A toast, to Alexander Eden - self-healer and soon to be Guardian of the Alliance."

We clinked our glasses together. I took a sip of the cool, crisp liquid and nodded with satisfaction. Gabriella sat down next to me and I felt the mild buzz under my skin. "So how are you feeling about tonight?"

"Apprehensive," I admitted. "But excited at the same time." I remembered about the belt. "Oh right, so I pressed this and had a pretty big shock."

Gabriella threw back her head and laughed. "Were you looking at your reflection any chance?"

I chuckled. "Maybe."

"It's a Kapre belt. They're recently extinct Umbra that used demonic magic to forge belts that made them invisible to humans and avoid standing out to other Pandemonians. When the Alliance first caught them, they copied the belt design and replaced the energy with Fae magic – its forbidden to mess with demonic magic. They're standard issue now, for times when a Guardian needs to get around without being spotted by a human or to blend in with other species. Humans can only see us if we talk to them directly. But for some reason if you activate it, you also lose your reflection."

255

I squeezed the belt buckle between my fingers. "Pretty useful. For a minute I thought I'd turned into a Vampire or something."

Gabriella smiled. Then something changed and she fell silent. There was a long pause, while we looked at one another. I could feel the sensations under my skin start to vibrate. After a minute she took a deep breath, her expression serious. "Alex, can I tell you something?"

I set my glass down on the table. "Of course. Anything."

For a long while Gabriella didn't say anything. Finally she sighed and squeezed my arm. "Do you remember what I said to you the day I arrived at Chapter Hill, when you asked me about myself?"

I cast my mind back to the first day, when we'd walked together through the corridors, whilst others watched in confused jealousy. "Yeah, you said it wasn't a question for then."

Gabriella set her glass down next to mine. "Well I think it's time I told you something about me."

I sat up straight. "Okay."

The look on her face told me what she was going to say was important. She took in several deep breaths as if trying to summon the courage to speak. When she did, the words burst out of her mouth.

"I'm a hybrid."

I blinked. "Sorry, what?"

"I'm half Umbra."

I stared at her. "You're joking right?"

Gabriella shook her head and then looked at me, biting her lower lip.

"But you're a Chosen. What... I mean, is that even possible?"

"It's a complicated story, but simply put my father was Chosen and my mother was Umbra."

"I didn't know Awakenings were hereditary."

"They're not usually...it's extremely rare."

I ran the palm of my hand down my face, curling the fingers around my lips. "What type of Umbra was your mother?" My voice came out muffled from behind my hand.

256

"A Succubus." Gabriella leaned over and put a hand on my knee. "But she was a *good* person, Alex. She loved me and my father."

I puffed air out of my lips. "Wow. I can honestly say I wasn't expecting that."

Gabriella stared down at her feet, rocking one of her heels on the thick rug - contemplating something. Then with a lightning speed, she unzipped her jacket and turned away from me, lifting her top up to reveal her bare back. Just below each shoulder blade were two thick patches of reddish skin, slightly mottled like scales and about the size of an outstretched hand.

"What-"

"Umbra skin," she said over her shoulder. "It's where my wings would be if I could grow them."

I stared at the strange patches of skin. Instinctually I stretched out a hand. I caught myself just in time and froze, hand hovering a few inches from her back.

"Can I..."

Gabriella turned slightly and her gaze caught mine. I swallowed hard.

"Okay."

I moved my shaking hand forward and touched the fingertips onto the scales. I was surprised at how soft they felt. They were warm and pulsed as if they had their very own heartbeats. I wasn't creeped out at all. They were part of Gabriella and that meant I loved them.

As our skin touched, the sensations became a fierce wave of electricity that rolled up my arm and collected at my fingertips. The scales seemed to react to each vibration, changing the speed of their pulsing as if it had become their new heartbeat. Gabriella shivered slightly and let out a soft sigh. I brushed my fingers around, tracing around the area where they met her human skin. For what could have been years, we stayed that way. Finally, Gabriella eased her t-shirt down and put her jacket back on. She edged around to face me again, her features strained.

"So, do I disgust you?"

The question knocked me for six. "Disgust me? Why on earth would you disgust me?"

She let her gaze drop. "Because I'm an abomination."

I'd never seen Gabriella so vulnerable. Ever since I'd met her, she'd been the one with the confidence. The one who knew where the pieces fit. It was humbling to see her like this – a real person with real insecurities.

"Hey." I lifted her chin up to face me. "Ella, listen to me. You are not an abomination. What you are is the most incredible person I've ever met. Don't let a twisted psychopath like Rahuman ever make you believe otherwise."

Her face broke into a smile so full of emotion it took my breath away. "You have no idea how relieved I am. I thought you were going to be repulsed."

I shook my head. "No, I think they are kind of...beautiful."

Gabriella curled her fingers around my hand and squeezed it. A fresh wave of sparks shot up my arm and made me shudder. I quickly dropped my hand and fumbled my glass from the table.

"So do you regress like them if you don't...you know...feed?" I asked taking a sip of champagne.

"No, no. This is how I've always looked. I don't need to drain. I'm basically Chosen, apart from having those patches and Umbra blood. That's why I don't use boosters. It also means I'm a bit faster and stronger than a lot of Chosen - and enhances my gift, but that's it." She fell silent.

I cleared my throat and pointed to the picture on the mantelpiece. "I'd love to hear more about your parents."

Gabriella shifted uncomfortably on her seat and sadness seemed to grow behind her eyes. "I want to, but I don't think I can yet. I- it's not something I've talked about for a really long time."

It was my turn to squeeze her hand. "That's fine; you don't have to tell me a single thing you don't want to."

We sat in silence for a while. I watched the flames flicker in the hearth and felt the warmth on my skin. We were so close on the couch that every breath I took was filled with her intoxicating scent. It mixed dizzyingly with the smell of freshly washed hair.

"I'm really glad we found you," Gabriella said suddenly. She brushed a hand against my cheek and the charges lingered after her touch. My heart pounded so hard it felt like it would burst

258

from my ribcage. Her fingers slipped around the back of my neck and she stroked the hairs, making them tingle.

"I-I uh...I'm glad too," I stammered. *Great, I can talk to any girl now, except the one who matters,* I groaned internally.

"You know I think you really are the kindest, sweetest person I've ever met," she whispered, letting her gaze lock with mine. Her pupils seemed to expand. She slid closer to me on the couch. My heart stalled as she closed the already tiny gap between us, and a cage of butterflies opened in my stomach. *Is this actually going to happen? Oh my god.*

"I do too. Uh - I mean I think you are," I replied awkwardly. *Oh my god. Oh my god. Oh my god.*

She giggled, her face lighting up. We were so close; I could see the reflection of the fire flickering in her eyes.

Then it felt like there was the smallest amount of pressure on the back of my neck from her hand - a tiny nudge forward. I was a mess inside. *Kiss her!!* one part of my mind screamed, but the other part yelled right back. *No, she doesn't want you! You're going to make an idiot of yourself!!*

For once, I ignored my degrading internal voice and decided to hell with it. I inched my head towards hers, which she raised a little, so they were level. My lips moved closer to hers - those incredible red lips that I'd spent nights thinking about. We were so close I could smell her sweet breath and feel it on my skin. She parted her mouth slightly. My heart was thumping so loud I was sure everyone in the Warren could hear it. Our lips were millimetres apart.

The doorbell rang.

Gabriella span away from me, sending her raven hair swishing over my face. "One second," she called and stood up.

No! I screamed in my head. *No, no no!*

But the moment was gone.

I snatched the glass from the table, draining it in one gulp. The rest of Orion poured into the lounge. They were all wearing uniforms like mine. Delagio was minus his hat - his thick black hair neatly combed over his head. A few stands dangled over his eyes in that way only cool people can manage.

I had never been so unhappy to see other people in all my life.

259

"Looking good dude," complimented Delagio.

Midnight gave a noncommittal grunt.

Sophia wrapped her arms around my waist. "I'm looking forward to having you in the team, Alex."

Instantly I felt a little better and couldn't help but smile. "I'm looking forward to it too."

Sophia unravelled herself and sat cross-legged on the carpet. Rachel settled herself onto the edge of the couch and let the Witch lean against her legs. She gave a little nod towards the champagne bottle. "Only two glasses? Looks like we weren't on the guest list."

Gabriella cleared her throat. "Rachel."

"Sorry. Anyway listen, I thought I'd wait until we were all together to tell you what I found out."

Gabriella plucked her glass from the table. "So what *did* you find out?" she said, taking a sip.

"Only that every leader from every single HASEA base is attending tonight's little celebration."

A chorus of confused replies rang around the room.

"But that's over fifty Sages!" exclaimed Delagio.

"Question is why?" said Midnight. "It certainly ain't for new kid here." He shrugged when I cast him a dirty look.

"Rumour has it there's going to be a meeting of some kind after the ceremony," said Rachel.

"About what?" replied Gabriella, glancing towards me.

"That I don't know."

Midnight slapped the wall, which made the whole apartment shudder. "I don't like being kept in the dark!" he growled. "I say we go to Faru and demand to know what the hell is going on."

"Calm down, Midnight. No one is doing anything of the sort," berated Gabriella. "You know that everything Faru does is for the good of the Alliance. If he doesn't want us to know yet, then there's a very good reason for it. If he wants to tell us - and I mean *if* - he'll do it when he's ready, with no pressure from us. Have I made myself clear?"

Everyone mumbled an agreement like scolded children - which technically one of them was.

"Glad you all agree. Right, well tonight is supposed to be a celebration so..." she disappeared into the kitchen and re-

260

appeared armed with the second bottle of Heidsieck and four more glasses, "...let's celebrate."

*

I followed the team downstairs carrying a warm, light-headed feeling courtesy of two and a half glasses of champagne.

The change around us was immediately noticeable. Whereas earlier, the base had been swarming with people, now it was pretty much deserted. Only Agent Green and another female agent I'd never seen before stood either side of the Feasting Hall doors. They nodded at us and swung them open.

I drew in a sharp breath. What I saw was worthy of a king's court. Walls decorated with numerous elegant shields and swords arched up into a domed ceiling, where dozens of crystal chandeliers dangled. On a raised stage at the far end, a group of musicians played a soft piece of classical music. Running almost the full length of the hall was the largest table I'd ever seen. There were easily over a hundred places. All of them - save the six closest to the entrance - were occupied. Some of the guests looked human, others far from it. Using the telltale signs from the guide, I identified Vampires, Succubi, Incubi, Skinshifters, Oni and all manner of Fae. Many wore uniforms just like mine. Others were dressed in ceremonial armour and capes. I spied Tyler and Dakin seated halfway down the table, but couldn't see Scarlett anywhere. Even more people stood around the edges of the room, including agents in their pressed black suits and doctors in their crinkled white coats. I even saw Iralia in the mix.

As we entered, everyone stood up and began to clap. I could feel my face glowing with embarrassment. I stood on the spot, not knowing what to do - no doubt sporting the mortified expression of a social recluse at a surprise birthday party.

"Stay here," whispered Gabriella, giving my side a reassuring squeeze as she and the rest of Orion took their positions at the table, clapping as they did.

The applause ebbed away, but everyone remained standing. I watched Faru dodder his way over to me, using his staff to prod his way forward. When he reached me, he settled the stick against the table and crossed his arms over his chest and extended his arms towards me. I returned the salute.

"Alexander Eden, you have more than proven your worthiness to become a Guardian of the HASEA. You have behaved with courage, bravery and selflessness, even though what you have already faced would be too much for many. I can only ask now that you take your final step and pledge allegiance to the HASEA. Will you do so?"

I looked around at the sea of faces watching me. At Gabriella.

"I will."

Faru nodded and gestured behind him. Two agents hurried over to where we stood. One carried a silver dish full of what could only be blood. The other balanced an emblem and dagger on top of a plush cushion.

"Please kneel," commanded Faru.

Once again his voice took on the acoustics it had in the temple. It boomed around the room, coming from everywhere and nowhere all at once. I lowered myself onto one knee.

"Extend your left arm."

Faru took the dagger, which had a hilt resembling a Dragon's mouth swallowing the blade. He dipped the tip into the liquid.

"I mark you now with the fortified blood of Leviathan, the last Dragon to stalk the Earth and slain by Saint George. Whilst you wear this, no matter where you are in the world, you walk with the full support of the HASEA."

He brought the blade down on my wrist and I had to bite my tongue as the coated steel seared my skin. Black steam curled up from the wound as he drew a cross on my wrist, followed by two semi circles either side. As soon as he had finished, the wound flashed red and then disappeared completely.

"This symbol will only appear when you need it," he answered before I could ask. He placed the dagger back on the cushion and picked up the emblem. Just like with the blade, he dipped the back part into the Dragon's blood. He grabbed his staff and used it to stable himself as he stooped down to my level.

"Whilst today you gain a new family, any that you have will be cared for as though they were one of us. You and they shall

262

never want for anything again, but in return, whenever you are needed you will stand and fight with your newfound brothers and sisters to your final breath. Do you agree?"

I had to swallow before I could answer. "I do."

The Seelian pressed the emblem into the space on my uniform. It sizzled and more black steam curled around the edges as it sealed itself into place.

"Dilecti Surgemus Socii Pollemus!" boomed Sage Faru. Everyone in the room repeated the words in a thunderous echo.

I knew without him saying what I had to say in return.

"Dilecti Surgemus Socii Pollemus" I replied in a voice that surprised even me.

"Now rise Alexander, as a Guardian of the Alliance."

I stood up.

PART III

EYE OF THE ABYSS

21

Every single person in the room saluted me. I returned the gesture, widening my arms at the end to incorporate the entire room. I caught Gabriella's eye and she gave a quick smile.

The two agents returned to the side of the room. Faru gave a nod and then another agent disappeared through a door in the middle of the room. He returned a few seconds later, carrying a long, blood red box with a silver trim. There were murmurs as people noticed what was in his arms. Gabriella's expression became one of shocked confusion. Dakin had a scowl so deep etched on his face that it looked like a permanent carving.

Faru raised his hands and the voices fell into a charged silence. The Sage took the box from the agent, who then slipped quietly back to his original position.

What on Earth is inside that can have this much effect on so many people? I wondered as Faru turned to face me.

"It is customary," he began, "for a new Guardian to be given a customary gift at this point." The murmurs began again, like a rising wave. "Alexander, my gift to you is one that I myself received long ago."

The voices grew even louder. People exchanged looks of disbelief.

Faru clicked the gilded, silver latches.

"I present to you the Crimson Twins."

He flipped open the lid at the same time that the room erupted into a storm of noise. Guardians gasped, and some even cheered. Others stood up to try and get a better look at the contents of the box. The whole of Orion had a universal expression of utter shock on their faces. Faru glanced towards the room and everyone fell silent once more.

I drew in a sharp breath as I stared at the savage beauty contained within the box.

The Crimson Twins were a pair of identical samurai swords. A meticulously carved black Dragon crouched on the base of each one. Both Dragons had two tails - made from a rich material - which snaked their way around the entire length of the hilt. Each guard was a circular wall of black flame that somehow seemed to shimmer in the dim light. The blades themselves were the colour of fresh blood. A complicated pattern of etched symbols had been carved along the length of each one. They were utterly stunning.

"Take one out if you like," he said.

I realised my palms were soaking with sweat. I had to wipe them dry on my trouser legs before I stepped forward and gingerly picked one of the swords out of the box. It felt perfect. Not too light that it felt flimsy and not too heavy that I would struggle to wield it properly. The material of the hilt felt smooth against my palms, but simultaneously had enough grip so that I felt confident it wouldn't fall out of my hands. The blade edge looked sharp enough to cut you in two if you stared for too long.

"The Crimson Twins were forged from the fangs of Ryujin, the long dead king of the Dragon Gods of Pandemonia. It is believed that they alone have the power to destroy any living creature on both sides of the Veil. Trust them with your life, for one day they may save it."

Faru gestured the box towards me and I lay the sword gently back inside. He flipped the lid closed and the agent rushed forward to collect it.

"I shall have them delivered to your quarters immediately."

"I-I don't know what to say," I stammered.

Faru gave a warm smile. "I believe the customary reply is thank you." The joke had the effect of dissolving the tense atmosphere in the room. Several Guardians laughed and I could feel myself starting to relax again.

"Thank you, Sage Faru."

The Seelian nodded and gestured a frail hand towards the empty seat. I walked over and stood behind the chair, now looking just like everyone else, except for the fact that I was at the head of the table. Faru ambled back to the other end of the hall. At the same time, the people who had been stood at the sides started to file out of the doors behind me. Iralia caught my eye and gave me a subtle wink as she passed. When they had all gone Faru took his place at the opposite head of the table and raised his arms.

"Now that the formal side of the joining ceremony has concluded, it is time for the feast. I don't know about the rest of you, but I am famished!"

*

I devoured the last mouthful of my main course - a slice of succulent meat from an animal called a Jackalope. It had a peppery taste that left a tingling sensation on the tongue. I washed it down with a sparkling glass of blue liquid that tasted even better than the Quinberry juice had. Wiping my mouth, I settled back into my chair and sighed.

"I think I might actually burst if I eat anything else."

Faru hadn't been lying when he had said it would be a feast. Every time I finished one of the flamboyant meals in front of me, the plate was whisked away and something else set down in its place. The food appeared to have been catered for each individual species. Vampires received some kind of circular reddish meat that resembled black pudding and a regular supply of blood in crystal glasses. The Luminar had a mixture of bizarre looking dishes, including what I guessed was a type of salad consisting of pink leaves that moved and numerous bright vegetables, including little orange orbs with knobbles. Skinshifters and Oni received hulking slabs of raw meat, which they tore into using their bare hands and teeth. Shortly after the first courses had been served, the chandeliers had been dimmed and the band had begun playing again. The whole table had descended into a comfortable buzz of conversation.

"Ah still can't get over the fact that Sage Faru gave you the *Crimson Twins*," said Delagio, pushing his empty plate as far away from him as he could.

"Yeah, why does new kid get special treatment?" added Midnight.

"I do have a name, Mister Steroids," I barked.

Midnight's lips drew together into a tight line.

Rachel rolled her eyes. "Will you two stop the alpha male dance please; you're putting me off my food."

"She's right, this is a celebration," agreed Gabriella. "Besides, I don't think it was special treatment at all. It was common sense. The Crimson Twins have been sat in Faru's quarters for years gathering dust. Why not pass them on to someone who can put them to use? It also means Alex only needs to carry those, a few Apotropes and a gun if he wants one. It makes sense."

The rest of the team nodded, sans Midnight.

"Well I still think that Faru should have given them to someone with more experience," he grunted, folding his arms.

"Jealousy don't suit you big guy," smiled Delagio, patting Midnight's shoulder.

A tinkling sound came from the far end of the table. The conversation slowed to a halt and the musicians stopped playing. Faru was standing once more, tapping the end of a spoon against his glass. He cleared his throat and spoke.

"Tonight it gives me great pleasure to welcome all the Sages to the Warren. They have come from the four corners of Earth to share in a truly momentous occasion. The Awakening of a new Chosen is a beacon of hope in an otherwise dark time."

There were shouts of 'hear hear' and glasses were raised.

"We want to show every Guardian that we are united in this fight. I know that the Alliance is suffering and that our allies in Pandemonia suffer even further, but we *must* have faith. The arrival of Alexander Eden is testament to the fact that all is not lost. We will continue to battle against the threat of the Soldiers of Sorrow and we will win!" His words rolled through the hall and there was a raucous response from the table. I couldn't help but join in; Faru definitely knew his way around a speech. He raised his glass. "So let us toast to the HASEA, and new beginnings." Sages and Guardians echoed his final words and drank. "Now if you would all like to proceed into the library, desserts and further drinks will be served there. I shall join you all shortly."

Everyone got up and began to filter through a large set of double doors halfway down the side of the hall. I tapped Gabriella's arm as we stood.

"Err...are there any bathrooms down here? Bit too much champagne."

She stifled a laugh. "Sure, just head out the way we came in, past the stairs on the right, turn left and follow the corridor all the way to the end. Be quick though, I'm sure people are going to want to chat to you."

I pushed through the main doors, which groaned their way open. The entrance hall was deathly quiet; my footsteps echoed as I walked across the marble.

After spending several bladder straining minutes navigating identical corridors and opening doors into sitting rooms and storage cupboards, I finally admitted to myself that I had no clue where the bathrooms were. So I threaded my way back and used the toilet in my apartment.

As I came back out onto the balcony I heard someone call Faru's name. Instinctively I crouched down and peered through the railings.

The Seelian was descending a set of glass steps that came right out of an opening in the heart of the giant painting. As he stepped off, they retracted like a tongue and the hole shrank until it disappeared completely. Then the paint swirled around and reformed as a solid portrait once more.

The man who had spoken was standing at the base of the main staircase. He had a Viking look about him - long blond hair and a thick beard platted at the end. He wore ceremonial plate armour and a flowing, red cape that ran down to his legs. I could tell immediately that he was a Bloodling Vampire. When he spoke again, I realised he was speaking in Norwegian.

"Sage Faru, I've been looking for you."

"Sage Asmund, I do apologise. How may I help?" Faru answered in the same language.

"Nice speech back there. But we all know it's got absolutely nothing to do with our presence here. One new Awakening does not warrant the gathering of every Sage on the planet. You and I go back a long way Faru, so I don't appreciate you keeping me in the dark on this. What's the real reason we were summoned?"

Faru nodded. "I am sorry for the deception Sage Asmund. With the number of SOS Rogues hiding in our bases, I could not afford to take any chances. Sage Etorre has provided me with some deeply unsettling news. As a result I have gathered everyone here so that we may discuss our next steps. You will be escorted to the Temple of the Divine Elements within the next hour."

The Seelian moved down the stairs and headed towards the Feasting Hall doors. Sage Asmund strode over to it and placed a large hand on the ornate handle. Before opening it, he turned to the other leader. "Does this have something to do with the boy?"

I felt my blood turn cold.

Faru nodded. "Yes, I believe it may."

Sage Asmund returned the nod and yanked the door open. Together they disappeared inside.

I sat on the balcony for a few more minutes, trying to return my breathing to normal and running through what I'd learned. Something so big was happening that Faru felt it necessary to gather every Sage from every Alliance base in the world to agree on a course of action. *And it could involve me.* All manner of scenarios ran through my head. Was it to do with my gift? Or maybe something to do with the swords? *Do they think that I'm an SOS or something?* The last thought filled me with a blind panic. *What if they kill me?* I shook the idea away. *What possible reason could they have for thinking that I'm SOS? They brought me in! But what's going on?* The solution was simple.

I have to find out.

I made my way back down the stairs and into the Feasting Hall. Two agents were standing either side of the entrance to the library. I recognised Agent Green.

"Mister Eden, we were about to come and look for you," he said.

"Sorry, I got lost trying to find the bathroom," I replied, forcing a laugh.

The agent smiled. "No problem sir, please head inside and enjoy yourself."

The library was like something out of a Dickens novel. A crackling fireplace stood in the centre of a world of books. Novels and tomes of all shapes and sizes were squeezed onto towering shelves. At the far end, an iron staircase corkscrewed up to a U-shaped balcony where the devotion to all things literature continued. Several comfy looking armchairs and a few worn looking leather sofas were dotted about. A mixture of Guardians and Sages were sitting on them, others stood in circles, chatting and laughing amongst themselves. Several waitresses moved between everyone, balancing flutes of champagne and other strange looking drinks on silver platters. Outside, the heavy rain had started again, which seemed to make the room feel even cosier. But I was far too tense to enjoy any of it.

Gabriella excused herself from the petite fairy she was talking to and rushed over. "Did you fall down the toilet or something? I've had to hold off like a million people who wanted to talk to you."

"Sorry I-"

"Doesn't matter. Come with me, there's someone I want you to meet." Leading me by the hand, Gabriella took me to where a tall, robed man who looked a little like an older version of Delagio stood speaking with a Chosen about my age. "Alex, this is Sage Etorre, leader of Castello."

The man smiled, causing crows feet to appear at the corners of his eyes. He extended a hand. "A pleasure to meet you Alexander," he said in Italian.

"You too sir. You're the leader of the base that Gabriella moved from?"

"I certainly am." Etorre lowered a hand to his waist. "I knew Gabriella when she was this big. I watched her grow from an awkward child into a strong, beautiful woman. She is a fantastic Guardian and we were all sorry to see her go." His gaze fell to Gabriella's hand, which was still holding mine. "Although I see it's unlikely we'll get her back now," he added with a grin.

She snatched her hand away and I noticed that without a doubt, her cheeks had flushed. Sage Etorre chuckled. Despite the churning feeling inside, it was impossible not to like him.

"Anyway, I was very impressed when I learned about you dispatching that vile traitor Rahuman. And without training no less."

I shifted uncomfortably. "Well, I got pretty lucky really."

"The way I heard it, you acted quickly and decisively in a deadly situation. I wish some of my Guardians shared those instincts." He patted my shoulder. "Anyway, I shan't keep you any longer. I'm sure you have plenty of other people you would rather speak to. I just wanted to take the opportunity to meet you." His face sobered for a second. "Look after each other." He turned his attention back to the Chosen he had been speaking to before.

Dozens of Sages came over and introduced themselves to me. I shook hands with them all and engaged in small talk in an array of languages, whilst keeping one eye fixed on the clock above the fireplace. I noticed that the number of people in the room was diminishing. Agents kept walking in and ushering the Sages through a door in the corner of the library.

I'm running out of time.

I made sure I sounded more and more confident with every person I spoke to. It had the desired effect of making Gabriella split off and leave me to my own devices. I finished talking to Sage Glid - a terrifying looking black Oni with red markings, who lead the Tokyo base.

Seizing the moment of solace, I moved over to where Rachel stood talking to Dakin. I'd almost reached them when I was intercepted by a gaunt woman wearing a long black dress. Her dark hair had been dragged back into a tight bun and her features were pointed and thin, reminding me of a bird. She extended a spindly hand, which I shook gently for fear of breaking it. When she spoke, her voice sounded stern, like a boarding school headmistress.

"Alexander Eden, my name is Sylvia. I am here on behalf of the Coven."

"Nice to meet you, Sylvia."

"Selene, the head of our Coven wishes to meet you in person. It is customary for all new Chosen. I trust this won't be a problem?"

"No, I would be happy to meet her." *Please not now.*

"Excellent, I shall arrange for you to be brought to her within the next few days."

I breathed an internal sigh of relief. "I look forward to it."

Sylvia gave a curt nod and then marched out of the room without another word. *What a strange woman.*

I reached Rachel and Dakin. The Vampire glared at me, top lip curled. He snatched a glass of blood from a passing tray, drained and slammed it back down without once looking away. His eyes flashed sliver. Then he barged past me and headed to the other side of the room.

"Seriously, what is that guy's problem with me?" I asked, jerking a thumb in the direction of the brooding Vampire.

Rachel shrugged. "To be honest I don't know. He's always been moody, but he seems to really dislike you. I think the Crimson Twin thing just rubbed it in for him. They are pretty sacred."

I sighed. "Whatever. Anyway listen, I need to ask you a favour, but you can't tell Gabriella."

Rachel frowned. "I'm not sure I like the sound of this. But go on."

I told her about the conversation I had overheard between Faru and Asmund. She listened intently. When I was finished she looked thoughtful and then tapped a finger in the air.

"I think we need Del."

Rachel dragged Delagio away from a group of female Guardians who were hanging off his every word. When we were sure no one could hear she made me repeat my story.

"No way buddy," he said when I'd finished. "You shouldn't have been eavesdroppin' in the first place, let alone plannin' to do it a second time! You heard what Ella said. Faru will tell us when he's ready."

I grabbed Delagio's arm. "Please, Del. How would you feel if something this big involving you was happening and you were being kept in the dark? I have to know!"

His face softened. "But why are you even tellin' me?" Something seemed to click. "You need my gift."

I shot Rachel a confused look. "Do we?"

"You do if you want to get close enough to spy on that meeting."

Delagio placed a hand in his pocket. "Ah don't know about this guys. We could get in serious trouble."

"I know. That's why I don't expect you to stay with me. If there is a way you can get me get me close enough, then that's all I ask. I'll do the rest by myself and if I get caught I'll say I was acting alone," I said.

Delagio's expression was pensive as he mulled over my request.

"Please."

He sighed. "Fine, I'll do it."

I let out a sigh of relief. "Thank you."

"But we have another problem. How're we gonna get outa here without raisin' any suspicions? After all, it's your party."

"I've got an idea, hold on." Rachel weaved over to where Sophia was sitting on the edge of a worn sofa, playing her handheld computer. As usual her tongue was sticking out at the side as she focused on the screen. Rachel bent down and whispered something in her ear. Sophia nodded. The Pixie stood up and threaded back over to us.

"Delagio, follow Alex out half a minute after he leaves."

"I don't under-" I started to say.

I was cut short by the sharp wail of pain followed by the stifled sobs of a child. I snapped my head around to see Sophia sitting on the floor clutching her foot.

Midnight was there in seconds. "What's wrong pint size?" he soothed.

"I did something to my ankle. It hurts so much," she wailed.

"Okay hun, don't worry. We'll go get you a booster." He went to lift her up, but she pushed him away.

"I want Alex to take me," she sniffed.

Midnight looked at me with the unmistakable expression of someone contemplating murder.

That is going to cost me.

I walked over, trying to avoid his skull-boring stare. Gabriella motioned to join me, but I shook my head.

"It's okay, I've got this. I'll take her to the training area in the gymnasium. We won't be long."

Gabriella smiled, resting a hand on Sophia's shoulder. "Okay."

I felt awful deceiving her, but I knew that this was one thing that we wouldn't agree on. I scooped the girl into my arms, noticing how she barely weighed anything. Looking around, I noticed that only Chosen remained in the room. All of the Sages had gone – including Faru. I hurried out of the doors. In the entrance hall, I pressed the elevator and waited.

"It's okay, you can put me down now," whispered Sophia. I placed her gently down on her feet. "Rachel told me to hide for a bit. Don't worry, I'll tell Midnight what happened later so he isn't mad at you."

"Thanks, Sophia."

She waved goodbye and vanished down a corridor. The elevator arrived at the same time as Delagio appeared on the balcony. He vaulted off and landed soundlessly next to me.

Inside the elevator, he pressed the button for the temple. We raced through the Nexus. As the cab began to slow, Delagio leaned over and slapped the emergency stop button, and we cranked to a halt. He lifted up a hatch in the ceiling and hitched himself up, until he was halfway out.

"What are you doing?" I asked his dangling legs.

"Checkin' how much further we need to go," came the muffled reply.

"I don't follow."

His legs disappeared as if some invisible beast had dragged him into the darkness.

"Del?"

His face reappeared in the hole.

"Over the decades the Nexus has been redesigned accordin' to changes in London's layout." He slipped deftly back down, his uniform covered in streaks of oil and dirt. "The old passages still exist; the elevators just don't run along em anymore."

"So where are we going?"

He jabbed a finger towards the ceiling. "But I need to get us in the right position first."

I watched as he moved into the centre of the lift. He held his hands out at his sides and shut his eyes. For a while nothing happened. Then the elevator cab started to groan and hiss. Slowly it rolled forward like a train pulling out of a station.

"Okay, we're good to go." He opened an eye and grinned at me. "You may want to hold on. This could get a lil' bumpy."

I grabbed a rail with both hands as Delagio gritted his teeth together. He took a deep breath and threw his hands upwards.

The elevator launched like a rocket.

I held my breath as we flew up the old tunnel. The elevator screamed and hissed as we were bumped from side to side. It was then that I realised with utter horror that we weren't on rails. The only thing keeping us airborne was Delagio.

After a few seconds he stretched one hand out towards the doors. They cranked apart and I could see the outside walls lurching back and forth as we pinballed up the old tunnel. Out of nowhere an old door appeared in a small recess. In a split second it was gone.

"Del! I think that was it!"

The kinesist coiled his hands into fists and the elevator screeched to a standstill. Carefully he lowered us back down until we were level to the door. He nodded a head towards the pouch attached to his side. "Take one of these. It start's vibratin' you've got one minute to get back before me and this puppy take a nose dive."

"Okay," I said, scooping a silver marble out of the bag. "Thanks, Del."

"Yeah, yeah. Just get going and for god's sake don't get caught!"

I winched the doors open further and leapt into the recess. Wrapping a hand around the handle, I gingerly pushed against the warped wood and entered.

It was pitch dark inside. In the distance, I could hear the unmistakable sound of voices. I ushered the door closed and lowering myself onto all fours, crawled forward.

What am I doing? I asked myself as I shuffled deeper into the gloom.

After a while, I noticed a glow coming from up ahead. The small amount of light was enough for me to work out that I was on a walkway high above the temple - the grand pillars reached the ceiling, which was only a few feet above my head. Reaching out, my hand pressed against the cool stone of a low wall. I used it to help hoist myself up and peered over the edge.

The Sages were standing in a large circle below. They were so far away they looked like ants, but their voices boomed around the area as if they had microphones fitted.

"How many settlements have fallen?" I recognised the speaker as Glid - the Tokyo leader.

"At least ten," replied Etorre.

"What of the Iron City?" Asmund asked.

278

"Gone," sighed Faru.

"What do you mean *gone*?"

"He means it has been wiped from the face of Pandemonia."

"Gods! Did anyone survive?"

"Those it didn't kill it turned into Depraved."

A rush of groans and gasps filled the room. I remembered what Faru had said about the poor, soulless creatures. I shuddered.

"How many follow it now?" asked Silvina, Fae Sage of Conduit - the New York base.

"Over a hundred at least."

"Including Prince Ashan," admitted Faru in a solemn tone.

A fresh round of horrified gasps swept around the room. A few of the Sages began to weep.

"Then that's it. The battle is lost," sniffed Silvina. "Pandemonia belongs to Hades."

"The hell it does," growled Glid. "I'd sooner forfeit my soul than let that cowardly bastard rule my home world!"

Faru made an agreeing sound. "Glid is right. This is not the end. We all know that someone else will rise in Prince Ashan's place. The Luminar will not lie down without a fight."

"There is also some good news. Some prisoners have broken out of the Colosseums and joined the fight," said Etorre.

There were murmurs of confusion. "They still live? How many?" asked Glid.

"At least two hundred."

There was a universal sigh. I leaned further over the wall desperate not to miss a thing. Each of their words mixed with the sound of my own pulse, which roared in my ears.

"Unfortunately, there is more bad news," sighed Etorre. "We think we know where it is headed."

As I heard the words, a chill swept through my body. I finally understood why they all sounded so fearful. *The Sorrow. They are talking about The Sorrow! It's tearing across Pandemonia, destroying everything in its path.*

"Where?" asked a Sage whose name I couldn't place.

I held my breath.

"Here."

279

My heart stalled. A deathly silence rolled into every crevice of the Temple, hanging in the air like a shadow.

"The path it has taken," explained Faru, "is a direct path to Fenodara. As you know, the water city is where the section of the Veil that connects to this base is situated. There are only a few settlements around it, and behind stretches a thousand miles of the Dark Sea. Simply put, there is nothing else it could be heading for."

Barely contained fear seemed to pour from everyone. Even from my place in the shadows - high above the crowd - I could *feel* it.

"You think it has something to do with the boy?" said Asmund. "That's what you told me earlier."

"I am not sure. Perhaps. Perhaps not. It appears to me that the timing of his Awakening and the sudden movement of The Sorrow seems a little to co-incidental."

"If this is true then we must be missing something - a connection of some kind," Glid pointed out.

"Maybe there's no connection at all," countered Silvina. "No doubt Hades has learned of his Awakening. Perhaps his accelerated use of The Sorrow is simply to destroy the major cities and claim victory over Pandemonia before a new wave of Chosen are born."

"You could well be correct, Silvina. However, I do not wish to take the chance. And that is the main reason I have asked you all here to the Warren tonight. For your consent."

A sharp pain in my knuckles made me realise that I'd been gripping the wall. I released them and used one to wipe away a cold sweat that had appeared on my forehead.

"Consent for what?" Asmund asked in a suspicious tone.

"I wish to seal the Veil."

The room erupted into a crescendo of panicked voices.

"But what about supplies?"

"You can't break the link!"

"What if Pandemonia needs your support?"

"You want to abandon Pandemonia?"

"Our kin are *dying* over there!"

"Please, please, everyone settle down," boomed Faru. Slowly the noise ebbed away, replaced once more by strained silence. "I am more than aware of the gravity of a decision like this. Nevertheless, I feel there is no other choice. The Sorrow cannot be killed. Not as far as anyone knows. The only option we have is to stop it in its tracks. I am not suggesting that we seal every piece of the Veil, just the Fenodara doorway at first. And not permanently. The spell would be reversible, but strong enough that The Sorrow would be forced to change its direction and head for a different section. At that point we release the former and seal the latter. And so on, effectively creating a perpetual barrier for its entry to Earth - *if* that is what it seeks."

I found myself nodding. I didn't know about the others, but it sounded like a *great* idea to me.

Etorre cleared his throat. "Sage Faru is not abandoning Pandemonia. There can be no question of his dedication to the cause. I know full well that if we ever grew strong enough to be a serious threat to Hades' forces, then he and his Guardians would be first in line to go through the Veil."

There were sounds of agreement from the rest of the leaders.

Faru took over. "Whilst the doorway is shut, we will strengthen links between the Warren and Castello. Extra supplies will come through their doorway and be distributed to Britain. I already have the support of our government on this. I just need yours."

"We have to protect Earth from The Sorrow. If this is the only way, then you have my full support," said Sage Asmund.

"Thank you, Sage Asmund. However, for an action of this magnitude to go ahead, the vote must be unanimous. All those in agreement, please raise your hand."

There was a long pause and then Faru spoke.

"Then it is agreed. We will seal the Veil."

At that moment my jacket started to vibrate- hard. I jumped at the sudden sensation and the marble twitched right out of my pocket.

Into midair.

I desperately swiped for it with a hand, but just ended up swatting it further away. I watched in absolute horror as it pinged against several of the columns and then landed on the temple floor below with a resounding crack.

I was already running by the time the yelling started.

22

I wrenched the door open and dived from the recess into the elevator, almost colliding with Delagio. His face was scrunched into a grimace and I stifled a gasp when I saw the blood seeping from his nose.

"About time!" he hissed through gritted teeth.

"Del, I'm sorry, but we need to go *now*!"

He threw both arms towards the floor and the elevator fell like a rollercoaster. My breathing was ragged. I slumped over one of the rails, trying to calm my racing heartbeat. After a minute of nerve-wracking descent, Delagio slowed the elevator down and there was a loud clunking sound as the cab settled itself onto the rail. I pressed the button for the main entrance and the metal box happily raced towards its destination unaffected by the death-defying detour.

"What happened?" he asked, wiping the blood from his nose with a handkerchief.

I told him everything I'd overheard and finished with what had happened to the silver marble.

"Goddamit" he barked.

"I'm so sorry. It was a complete accident!"

"I know, I know. It's just there are only a few kinesist's at the Warren and hardly any that use the weapons I do. The marble is a pretty big giveaway."

A cold dread ran through my veins. "Oh no, is Faru going to suspect you?"

Delagio fell silent for a moment, tapping a finger against the mirrored wall. "Not necessarily. Here's what we're gonna do. Go back to the library and tell Rachel to meet me outside. She'll know the spot. If Faru asks where we are, just point through the window by the fire, okay?"

I didn't understand the plan, but nodded anyway. "What shall I say about Sophia?"

"Say you took her back to her room." He slipped a phone from his pocket. "I'll text her to make sure she goes straight there now." He started tapping the keypad.

"Sophia has a mobile?"

Delagio raised an eyebrow. "It's the twenty first century dude. Who doesn't?"

"Fair point."

"Right, Faru will already be in the Nexus by now, takin' a different route. We've got about one minute from the moment we get there to do this. "You ready?"

"Yes. And I'm really sorry again, Del."

Still typing with one hand, he clapped my shoulder with the other. "Don't worry 'bout it. You were right to find out what's goin' on. This is a big deal." He looked up, his face suddenly drawn. "The Sorrow is the stuff of nightmares. I hope to heck that Faru isn't right about it headin' here."

The elevator stopped and we both rushed through the doors the instant they opened. Luckily the entrance hall was still deserted. Delagio slipped behind a curtained area to the left of the stairs.

I strolled as casually as I could through the Feasting Hall. A few waiters were milling about, collecting the last bits of cutlery from the table. None of them paid me any attention. I smiled at the agents as I passed between them back into the library. Through sheer luck, Gabriella was busy consoling Midnight, so didn't notice me slip right up to Rachel - who was leaning against a bookcase, sipping something purple from a champagne flute. I whispered Delagio's instructions to her. She nodded and shoved her glass into my hand. Within seconds she'd disappeared from the room.

I let out a long sigh of relief. Staring into the glass, I eyed the purple liquid. A large bubble swelled in the centre and burst, releasing an aroma that gave me a head rush.

Maybe not.

I set the glass down on a bookshelf and joined Gabriella, who was sitting on a sofa, arm wrapped around Midnight's colossal shoulders. The giant looked miserable, which had the effect of making me feel terrible. I decided to take a bit of a chance.

"Midnight, Sophia is asking for you," I said.

He jerked his head up. "Really? Where is she? Is she okay?"

"She's fine. I took her up to her room."

He stood up and swatted me on the arm with a bear paw. "Thanks."

When he had gone, I took his position on the sofa. A passing waitress lowered her tray and Gabriella picked off two flutes of Champagne, handing one to me. I wanted so badly to tell her what I'd find out, but I couldn't. I knew she'd be furious for me going behind her back. Not to mention spying on a private meeting between every Sage in the HASEA. After being a Guardian for a little over three hours.

"Is Midnight okay?" I asked instead, gesturing the glass in the general direction he'd gone in.

"He will be. He was just a little bit gutted that Sophia asked for you. He feels like it's his job to protect her."

"Why?"

Gabriella took a large sip of Champagne and sighed. "Sophia's mother was a hardcore drug addict. She used to sell her body to feed the habit. One of those clients happened to be an Incubus - that's how Sophia was conceived. Incubi don't stick around to raise their offspring, so it was down to the mother. Her only reason for keeping Sophia in the first place was so that she could claim benefits. That poor girl lived the first six years of her life in squalor. She was barely ever fed." Gabriella rubbed a finger on the side of the glass, as if removing a smudge. "Her Awakening happened as the result of her own mother kicking her down a flight of stairs."

My stomach lurched. "That's awful!"

"We didn't bother with an infiltration; just marched in and rescued her from that cess pit." Gabriella's eyes flashed with anger. "That woman was a sick bitch. When we brought Sophia in, she was covered in bruises and barely more than a skeleton with skin. It's a miracle that she turned out so sweet. Most of it was down to Midnight. He joined the Warren soon afterwards and became an instant father to Sophia. Helped her forget everything and become a normal person." Gabriella laughed. "Well as normal as a half-Witch, half-Chosen Guardian of Earth can be."

"So what happened to the mother?" I asked.

285

"Midnight happened."

A second later, Faru appeared in the library, followed by several other Sages, including Asmund and Etorre. He scanned the room, white eyes shimmering in the firelight. His eyebrows knitted together in a deep frown. I took in a deep breath as he doddered towards us.

Here we go.

I took a quick glance at the window and almost burst out laughing. Delagio and Rachel were sitting inside a wooden gazebo swathed in fairy lights, as the rain beat down around them.

Kissing.

In fact, kissing probably wasn't the right word for it. They were attached to one another as if their separation meant the end of all life. Gabriella followed my gaze and committed to the laugh I hadn't managed. "Honestly, it's any excuse for those two," she chuckled.

More than you know, I thought.

The Sages reached us. Faru went to speak, but Asmund barged past and stabbed a finger at us.

"Huntmaster, where is your kinesist?" he demanded.

Gabriella frowned and looked at Faru. "Why, what's he done wrong?"

"Please excuse Sage Asmund's abruptness my dear. There is no need for alarm. I simply wish to ask him a question, that is all."

Gabriella unwittingly acted out the last part of the plan for me, whilst attempting to keep a straight face. "He's out there Sage Faru, but you may want to give him a moment."

The leaders turned their heads to stare through the rain-covered window. Sage Asmund cleared his throat and shifted uncomfortably on the spot.

Ah," said Sage Etorre simply.

Faru pressed a finger to either temple. "I don't see...oh, right." A glimmer of a smile appeared on his face. "I believe that he could use some privacy."

"Shall I tell him you want to speak to him when he comes in?" asked Gabriella.

"No I don't believe that shall be necessary. Although, perhaps you could suggest that they be a little more discreet with their rendezvous next time," Faru said with a smile. He turned to the other Sages. "The hour is growing late; perhaps it is time we retired for the evening. Come, let us join the others and I shall have my Golems show you to your rooms."

"I think you're right," agreed Etorre. "Goodnight you two - don't stay up too late," he added with a wink.

We stood up to salute the leaders, who returned the gesture. They exited the library, with Asmund muttering something under his breath about 'unprofessional conduct.'

Gabriella and I spent the next few hours talking and drinking. I fired dozens of questions at her. At first they were mainly to help distract my thoughts from what I'd overheard in the temple, but after a while, I forgot everything and just enjoyed listening to her speak. She told me stories of her past missions - some dangerous, some downright hilarious. She explained how the base operated and how to conduct myself on a mission. Lastly, she taught me the rules of the treaty and explained that if I ever forgot I could find them at the back of the HASEA handbook – which reminded me of something I'd forgotten to ask, but decided to save until later. At one point I glanced out of the window and noticed that both Delagio and Rachel were gone. Neither of them had returned to the library. *Looks like the plan worked out better than expected,* I thought with an internal smile. Slowly the room started to empty of people, until we were the only two left – apart from the agents, who milled about, stoking the fire and talking quietly to each other.

"So how does it feel to be a protector of Earth?" Gabriella asked, nestling herself into the crook of the sofa.

"I'll let you know after I protect something," I said, draining the last dregs of yet another glass of champagne and setting it down on the side table.

"You heard Sage Etorre; you've got me to protect," she teased, poking a finger into my stomach.

"I get the impression you don't need much looking after."

Gabriella shook her head, sending hair spilling all over her face. She used a finger to hook it away before continuing.

287

"Everyone wants someone to protect them. Sophia has Midnight, Rachel has Delagio, Scarlett has…" She stifled a giggle then hiccupped. "Wow, I think I'm a bit drunk. That's strange; I'm normally fine with alcohol. Anyway what was I saying?"

"You were saying that everyone needs someone to protect them."

"Right, and you Mister Eden, are *my* protection. I look after you, and you look after me." She made an O shape with her index fingers and thumbs. "It's a perfect circle." Settling back against the sofa corner, she closed her eyes. "So, do you agree?" she half mumbled.

"Do I agree to what?"

"Do you agree to protect me?"

I looked at her curled up against the sofa, the shadows from the fire flickering on her soft skin. She looked so utterly angelic that my answer spilled from my lips before I had the chance to stop it.

"I would die to protect you."

My skin crawled from the epic cheesiness of my line. *Did I honestly just say that out loud?*

Gabriella opened her eyes and sat up slowly. She leaned forward and placed the softest kiss on the corner of my mouth. A tingling sensation reverberated all the way down my jaw. "That is the sweetest thing anyone has ever said to me."

I could feel my heartbeat accelerate as her face lingered close to mine. Then she slumped her head down onto my shoulder. "Oh no, the room is spinning. This isn't good. I think I need to go to bed."

"I'll take you up," I offered. I stood up and lifted her into my arms, like I'd done with Sophia. Gabriella rolled her head against my chest and her right arm dangled at the side. The agents pulled the doors open for me. I had to wait for them to ask two Golems to move, whose solid backs were now blocking the way forward. Outside, I noticed that all of them had returned to their guard posts, heads bowed in their silent prayer.

On the balcony, Agent Green swept the silver curtain out of my way. "You are welcome to stay in your apartment this evening if you'd like, Mister Eden. But if you'd prefer to return home, one of us would be happy to take you."

I thought about the way Dakin kept glaring at me. How he was one of the people supposedly protecting Mikey.

"Thanks, I think I'd better go home and make sure everything is okay. But I'd like to check something in the library first if you don't mind?"

Agent Green nodded. "Not a problem at all, Mister Eden. I'll have someone bring a car around to the front shortly."

I made my way along the corridor, still carrying Gabriella, who was now deep asleep in my arms. When I reached her room, I gently lifted her hand and placed the thumb against the scanner. The latch clicked open and I stepped into her apartment. The lights flickered on automatically.

I placed her down onto the bed and undid the laces of her boots. Slipping them off, I set them next to the wardrobe. In the kitchen I filled a glass with water and then placed it on the bedside table. Then I lifted the covers up and wrapped them around Gabriella. She moaned softly in her sleep and pulled them up to her chin. The aching feeling in my chest came back again. I brushed a stray strand of hair from her face.

"Goodnight Ella," I whispered and left the apartment.

The mansion hummed with silence. I rubbed a bit of sleep from my eye as I trudged down the stairs. Agent Green was standing by the front entrance. The other agent was nowhere to be seen. I presumed she would be the one driving me home. I signed five minutes. The agent nodded and said something into his wrist microphone.

After a staring contest with the Golem, it stepped out of my way. Inside the library, the fire had been left to its own devices and was beginning to dwindle. Specks of black soot had been coughed out onto the surrounding hearth. The only lighting came from the candles that had been placed around the room earlier. I picked one up and carried it with me as I walked. I knew that what I was looking for had to be in this library – I just didn't know where. I searched downstairs first, holding the flame close as I ran my fingers over the titles. There were novels by all of the top literary authors throughout the ages. Among others, I saw books by Lawrence, Austen, Nietzsche, Chekov and

Dickens. I stopped at the last one and pulled out an old looking copy of *Great Expectations*. I flipped open the cover and my eyes bulged. It was a first edition. Now holding it like gold dust, I guided it back onto the shelf and checked a few others. Nearly all of them were first editions. Some had even been signed by the authors themselves and dedicated to Mr Farris. I whistled under my breath. The collection must have been worth millions.

I jogged up the stairs and onto the balcony above. The books on that level had far more relevance to the HASEA. Some were occult books on Demons and Witches. Others were local legends and folklores, handwritten in regional dialects. I scanned diaries of panicked people claiming to have seen creatures skulking around their villages. I pulled out giant tomes, squeezed shut with buckles to prevent the pages bursting free.

I finally found what I was looking for in the far corner. I picked out the dog-eared copy of the HASEA handbook. It had a similar mottled cover to mine, but I could tell it was a far more recent version. I pulled open its string and thumbed through a few pages. Sketches still sat underneath each heading, but they were copied. Photographs had been added, as well as large blocks of printed text. I screwed my nose up - it felt too clinical, mine had a much more nostalgic feel to it.

But you might be able to tell me something mine can't. I flipped to the section right before the missing part of my copy and turned the page.

I froze.

The sketch at the top of the page broke my dreams. They came rushing back to me in a torrent of images. The hideous mask. The eerie graveyard. The derelict mansion. And that dark, suffocating fear.

The sketch was of the creature from my nightmares.

The one that found me.

The title at the top was thick, the words seeming to scream out at me from the page.

The Sorrow.

The candle slipped from my hands and snuffed out on the carpet. I cried out as I was plunged into darkness. Using my free hand to feel my way forward, I stumbled over stacks of books and bumped into tables as I frantically made my way back to the spiral staircase. I staggered down, using the same hand to stop myself from collapsing.

Something heavy barged into me.

Instinctively, I lashed out and my fist connected with something hard. The intruder stumbled backwards, hitting the wall.

Whump. A crackle of blue electricity bloomed in front of me. The burst of light mixed with two red dots and exposed the outline of a Golem.

"Wait, I'm a Guardian!" I shouted as it swung the crosier. The staff stopped inches from my neck. I could feel the hairs standing up on end.

"What's going on in here?" demanded a voice from the doorway. The main lights flickered on and Agent Green stared at me, wearing a look of utter confusion.

"Everything's fine," I said, trying to keep my voice calm, even though all I wanted to do was scream until I had no air left in my lungs. "I hurt myself. I think the Golem thought there was an attack."

"Are you okay now, Mister Eden?"

"I'm fine. I just need a few more minutes."

I barged past the agent before he could say anything else and sprinted through the hallway and up the stairs. I ran all the way to Gabriella's room. With a shaking finger, I stabbed the doorbell repeatedly. *Come on! Come on! Come on!*

The door swung open and a dishevelled looking Gabriella squinted out at me.

"What is it? What's wrong?" she asked.

I pushed the door open and barged into the apartment.

"The book," I blurted, "the book you gave me. It had pages missing from the back."

She looked uncomfortable. "So?"

I held up the copy in my hand. "This one doesn't. I need you to tell me why this *thing* is in my dreams." I opened the page and pointed to the sketch.

All the colour drained from Gabriella's face. *"What?"*

"I've been dreaming about this thing for weeks! But I haven't been able to remember them until now. Ella, why am I dreaming about The Sorrow?"

291

Her legs buckled and she slid down the wall.

"*No, no, no*, please god no. Not you too." She buried her face in her hands. "This can't be happening."

Her reaction made my blood run cold. I tried to pull her face towards me, but she refused. My hand came away damp with her tears.

"Gabriella, talk to me," I pleaded. "Why is The Sorrow in my dreams?"

It was no use; she had descended into convulsive sobs. Seeing her so upset made me feel like I was dying - her unhappiness was worse than any form of torture I could think of. Feeling useless, I could only rub her back while she wept. The normally pleasant charges had morphed into nasty little electric shocks, which made every part of my hand singe with pain. I didn't stop comforting her. I stayed in the same position for several minutes - my own heart thumping away in my chest - before trying again.

"Please tell me what's going on. Why is it in my dreams?" I whispered into her ear.

This time my words seemed to register. Gabriella lifted her head up and turned towards me. Her eyes were swollen and red. She swallowed hard before replying.

"Because it's tracking you."

23

Fear wrapped around my throat, choking me. "W-what do you mean it's tracking me?" I managed to croak.

Gabriella stared up at me, her eyes bloodshot. "That's how it tracks, using your dreams as a scent." She took a few sharp breaths before continuing. "If you're dreaming about it, then it's trying to find you."

A lump rose in my throat, which wouldn't go away, no matter how much I swallowed. "Oh god, in the last dream I had, it *found* me."

Gabriella pushed herself to her feet and seized my arms. "We have to go and speak to Sage Faru, he'll know what to do next." She was already at the door before she'd finished the sentence.

"We can't."

She whirled around. "What are you going on about? This is serious! We have to speak to him *now*."

I moved ahead of her and closed the door.

"I already know what he'll do next."

A deep frown appeared on her face. "And that is?"

"He's going to seal the Veil to stop The Sorrow reaching Earth. That's why the other Sages were here. To vote on it."

Gabriella shook her head in bewilderment. "Alex, how could you possibly know that?"

I took a deep breath. "Because I spied on their meeting."

Her voice was so shrill it hit my ears like a knife. *"You did what?"*

"I know. I shouldn't have. I'm so sorry Ella. It's just that I accidently overheard him speaking to Sage Asmund and he said that the meeting might have something to do with me. I had to find out, so I followed them and spied on the meeting. That's why I can't go and see him now; I'm too drunk and scared. If he gets inside my head, he'll know I was there for sure."

Gabriella drew her lips together. Her eyes were burning with such intense anger that I felt about an inch tall. "Tell me *everything,*" she demanded.

I told her, including how we'd almost been caught.

"You selfish *idiota!*" she screamed. "Do you have any idea the amount of trouble you could have caused? Everyone involved could have been banished from the Alliance!"

"I didn't realise, I'm so sorry-"

"Forget your apologies! You put everyone in a terrible position by asking them to do what you did! Not to mention that you went and did the exact opposite of what I *told* you to do! Like it or not Alex, I am the leader of Orion. So when I order you not to do something, you damn well listen!" She stormed past me into the lounge and I followed like a chastised puppy.

"Plus your little plan made Midnight believe that a girl he sees like a daughter was pulling away from him! God knows that man has been through enough in his life already."

"But, Rachel told her to do that, I didn't-"

"It doesn't matter!" she yelled, coiling her hands into fists. "It was you that started this mess!"

I held out my hands in an appeasing gesture. "Ella, please calm down,"

"Don't you *dare* tell me to calm down!" she screamed, swiping a vase of flowers off a side unit. It smashed against the far wall in an explosion of water and glass. Fresh tears were streaming down her face. "I thought we were meant to be friends. How can I trust you now, when you hide things from me?"

A sudden burst of anger surged through me. "Are you seriously talking about trust? After the number of times you lied to me?" I thrust out a finger towards the photograph on the mantelpiece. "You even lied about your dead parents!"

As soon as the words had spilled from my mouth, I knew I'd gone too far.

Gabriella slapped me across the face.

A sharp streak of pain swept across my cheek and I tasted blood in my mouth. I stared at her in utter disbelief. She looked down at her own hand as if it had acted without her permission.

"Gabriella, I-"

"Just go home," she said in a voice completely devoid of emotion.

"But-"

"Go home," she repeated.

Without another word I left the apartment.

*

I didn't sleep at all.

When my alarm finally buzzed, I couldn't even bring myself to pull the photograph out of the handbook - making it the first time I'd ever consciously not spoken to Dad's picture. The fear of The Sorrow tracking me mixed with the regret of the conversation I'd had with Gabriella. It settled into a feeling of malaise that hung over my head like a cloud.

I broke my promise of telling Mikey, because frankly I didn't have the energy to deal with the barrage of questions that would follow. He seemed to know that it wasn't the right time to ask, so we engaged in stilted small talk on the drive to school. He tried to cheer me up by telling me about a new girl - some hot redhead he'd met at the party he'd gone to, but I was barely listening. I gripped the steering wheel, trying to shake the images of my fight with Gabriella from my mind. Eventually Mikey got the message and switched on the CD player, sinking into his seat with a glum expression on his face.

The day dragged. The worst part of it was that Gabriella wasn't at school. I spent English throwing constant hopeful looks at the door, whilst Mr Hanley rattled on about the lack of self-belief the narrator had in 'Rebecca'. All the way through the lesson, I couldn't shake the nagging feeling that something was wrong.

Afterwards, I couldn't stop myself from ringing Gabriella. The phone rang until the voicemail kicked in. I hung up and slammed a hand into a nearby locker, creating a palm shaped dent in the metal.

Luckily no one was watching.

During my lunch break, I tried to track down Rachel. I asked the sinewy secretary at the front desk to help me locate my science teacher. After clicking the mouse a few times, she

295

informed me that Miss Steel was off sick. The feeling continued to gnaw at my stomach.

By the time the afternoon came around, my malaise had grown into an almost overwhelming sense of dread. I tried dialling Gabriella a dozen more times and each time it rang out. *Something's wrong.* I knew she was probably still furious at me - and rightly so - but to completely ignore me after what I'd told her? It was too extreme. I inwardly cursed myself for not taking the numbers of the rest of Orion.

Mrs Carter was late for History. Whilst the drone of conversation buzzed around me, I stared down at my phone, willing a call or a message to come through.

I sensed someone standing over me.

"Ella," I said, snapping my head up. Instead I saw an uncomfortable looking Grace standing by my table. *Of course it isn't Gabriella idiot; she doesn't even take History.* "Sorry," I apologised, putting my phone away in my pocket. "I thought you were someone else."

"Clearly," Grace said, fiddling with a pink ring on her thumb. "Anyway, I uh- I thought you were going to text me over the weekend."

I remembered the promise I'd made to text her after the night out. A knot of guilt twisted inside my stomach, adding to the growing amount of discomfort there.

"I'm really sorry, I had a pretty crazy weekend," I confessed truthfully.

"That's okay," she said with a sweet smile. "Listen, I wanted to ask you something, but I just need to know first, you're not like *with* Gabriella are you?"

The name cut through me like a hot knife. *God, please be okay.* "Um...Alex?"

"No!" I snapped.

Grace flinched from my harsh reply. Her smile crumbled.

"Fine, if you're going to be like that…"

"No, wait Grace, look I'm sorry. I'm having a bad day, that's all." In the friendliest tone I could manage, I said, "No, I'm not with her."

Some of the smile returned. "Okay great. Well then, I was wondering whether you'd given any thought about who you were going to take to the Christmas Ball."

With everything that had been going on, the normal world felt completely surreal, as if it no longer properly existed. Her words made no sense at all.

"Huh?"

"You know...the Christmas Ball that the Sixth Form is having?" Her voice was losing confidence by the second. I carried on staring blankly until the cogs in my stressed out brain finally turned.

"The Ball!"

"Wow, you are having a bad day aren't you?"

If only you knew. I gave a fake laugh. "To be honest I haven't given much thought to who I wanted to take."

Grace glanced at her friends, who were eagerly sneaking glances over their shoulders. "Oh right. Well I was wondering, you know, if you weren't going with anyone...then maybe..." she flicked her hazel eyes up, "you might want to take me?"

I let the information register and tried to think of a reply. If she'd asked me a few weeks before, I would have jumped at the chance. In fact it was more likely the universe would have imploded from the anomaly. But still, things had changed. If I went at all, there was only one person I wanted on my arm. *And I don't even know if that person ever wants to see me again, or even if she's okay,* I thought miserably.

I didn't want to be mean. After all, Grace was a really sweet person - even if she'd only chosen to speak to me after learning about my new car.

"It's really nice of you to ask, but I'm not even sure I'm going to be able to go. Can I get back to you?" I said, trying to look as conflicted as possible.

Grace exhaled in a deep whoosh. "Uh yeah okay. Well you've got my number so-" she half laughed and then turned and returned to her desk, where her friends leaned over in search of gossip.

I groaned and flopped my head onto my bag.

*

My phone rang.

I was lying on the bed, staring at the picture of my father. Gabriella's phone had refused to go beyond ringing tone all afternoon. After an internal battle, I'd left a deeply apologetic message and pleaded with her to call me. The dread gnawed at the pit of my stomach, each bite telling me that something was definitely wrong.

The number came up as unknown. My heart skipped about fifteen beats. I dived across the bed and scooped it up to my ear.

"Hello?" I breathed.

"Alex? It's Mum."

A surge of disappointment rushed through me. I collapsed down onto the bed.

She sounded panicked. "What's wrong?"

I paused. *Pretty much everything.* "Nothing Mum, I'm fine."

"Oh I'm relieved; you had me worried for a second. Is Mikey okay?"

"He's fine, Mum. Everything's fine."

"Good. Well things aren't so great here. I'm calling from the hospital."

I tensed up. "Is it Connie or Edgar?"

"No, no they're in top shape. It's John. He's come down with some kind of food poisoning. Nothing too serious, just lots of vomiting and uh...the other end, but the hospital want to keep him in for observation for a few days just to be sure. It means we won't be able to fly back tomorrow though."

I nodded. *So this is what Faru had in mind to keep them away.* It was wrong, but I couldn't resist a brief smile.

"Don't worry about it Mum. Tell John to rest up and come back when you're ready."

"I will honey. Use the emergency money if you need to. Depending on flights, we should be home by next Friday at the latest."

"No problems. I'll see you then."

"Alex, are you sure everything is okay there? I had an odd feeling."

"Honestly Mum, we're doing great," I lied.

"All right then. I'll speak to you soon. I love you, Alex."

"Love you too. Bye."

The phone clicked and she was gone.

*

I didn't allow myself to sleep that night for fear that The Sorrow would be in my dreams. I went into school Tuesday morning tired and bleary eyed. Mikey didn't even bother to ask; he knew he wouldn't get anything out of me. Maths dragged and I fled the room as soon as the bell rang, heading for science and praying that at least one of them would be there. I took my seat, nervously tapping a pen against the table. After a few minutes, people began to filter into the room.

Neither Gabriella nor Rachel came through the door.

About a quarter of the way through the lesson, a jaded looking Miss Cleveland came in and informed the class that Miss Steele was ill and that we would be watching a televised lecture on physics instead. The caretaker wheeled in a TV and activated the DVD player, before switching off the lights and shutting the door behind him. As expected, no one paid the slightest bit of attention to the TV. An absent teacher meant a licence to talk. Not having any desire to participate, I sank my head into my bag. I heard Elliot say something to me from behind and I just grunted a muffled response.

There was a click of the door, followed shortly by a thud next to my ear. I lifted my head up and I almost cried out for joy when I saw that it was Gabriella's bag that had made the noise. But it was replaced by dread when I noticed how dishevelled and drawn she looked. Her hair was tied back but several strands were loose, sticking out at various angles. There were dark bags under her eyes and her face looked pale. I knew without asking that my bad feeling had been justified.

"Ella, what's wrong? Are you okay?" I whispered as she slumped onto the seat.

She shook her head.

"What happened?"

"Not here." She pointed towards the door and stood back up. I clambered off my stool, almost knocking it over in the

299

process. People started making suggestive noises, but cut them short when they noticed how distraught she looked.

We walked to an alcove in the corridor. Gabriella's eyes were brimming with tears. She took a deep breath. "It's Sophia. She's really sick."

I didn't know how to correctly respond. My mouth flapped open and shut a few times before I could speak. "I don't understand."

"She's been bitten."

"Oh my god. By what?"

"A Bloodseeker."

My brain was spinning with questions. I tried to grab hold of them one by one. The first one was obvious.

"But she's a Chosen. I thought we were supposed to be immune to bites?"

"We can't be turned. But she's contracted Heptacemia."

Haven't read it. "What's that?"

"It's an extremely rare blood disease that we can catch from Vampire bites."

"Is it curable?"

"Normally. But because she's so young and only half Chosen, her immune system is too weak to fight the infection properly."

My mouth gaped open. "But she's going to get better, right?"

Gabriella's shoulders slumped. "We don't know. She's in so much pain. And she looks so frail." Her voice cracked. "Alex, I think she's going to die." Tears slipped down her face. I pulled her into my arms and smoothed her hair. I shut my eyes and thought about the poor little girl, with the sweet smile and rosy cheeks, writhing in pain as an infection slowly killed her. I forced the images from my head - it didn't bare thinking about.

Gabriella pulled away from me and wiped her eyes with the palms of her hands.

"Can't the Coven cast a spell or something?" I suggested.

"They're going to try. Rachel's gone through the Veil to collect some ingredients for it," she sniffed.

A sudden fear gripped my chest. "But what about The Sorrow, isn't that where it's heading?"

Gabriella gave a weak smile. "I told her everything. I think her actual words were 'The Sorrow can piss off, I'm going anyway'. As far as I can tell, Sage Faru hasn't sealed it yet. I guess he will once she's back."

"So what happened anyway? I've been so worried about you."

Gabriella ran a hand over her face. It was a harsh movement; she was clearly beyond tired and stressed.

"A few hours after you left, the Coven foresaw a Bloodling attack on a house a few miles from the Warren. I should have called you but I didn't - I'm sorry. To be honest I was still angry with you...and myself a bit for how I reacted."

"Don't worry about that now. Go on."

"Sophia sensed them. They were hiding in the attic waiting for the owners to return home from a night out." She shrugged. "It was easy, we arrested them no problem."

"So what went wrong?"

"As we were leaving, we were ambushed by the SOS, dozens of them. We were outnumbered and outmatched. We managed to escape, but Sophia got cornered by a Bloodseeker. Midnight pretty much tore the thing in half, but not before the bastard got his fangs into her." She paused, harshly tugging out a strand of hair that had slipped onto her face. "Alex, it was a setup."

"Wait…you mean there's a Rogue in the Warren?"

"It's the only explanation. They knew we were coming."

I blew air out through the side of my mouth. "That's the last thing we need."

We stood in silence for a moment.

"Can I come and see her?" I asked eventually.

"Of course. We can head in together later. Selene and the Coven have requested to see you today anyway. To be honest the only reason I'm here is to bring you in."

"Surely Faru could have just done that link thing with me like he did before, you didn't need to come here." As I said the words, it dawned on me that all my frantic call attempts could have been avoided. *The communication is two way – I could have linked with him.* I groaned internally.

Gabriella shifted her gaze down to her hands. "Okay, I needed to get out of there, in case...you know." She lifted her head up. Fresh tears welled up in her eyes. "Does that make me a bad person?"

"No, of course it doesn't...it makes you human."

She looked relieved. "Thanks. Listen, I also came here to apologise. It was wrong for me to act the way I did. I was terrified and overwhelmed by everything."

I shook my head. "No, it's me who should be apologising - what I said was completely out of order. And as for going behind your back, I promise I will *never* do anything like that again." I held out a hand and tried my best smile. "Friends again?"

Gabriella knocked my hand away and wrapped her arms around me. She pressed her cheek against mine and I felt the warm dampness of her tears on my skin. As I breathed in her wonderful scent, the knots in my stomach unravelled and all of the fear slipped away as if it had never existed.

*

I turned down the Soulfire song blaring from the car speakers and glanced at Gabriella.

"I've been thinking about what you said earlier. If there really is a Rogue in the Warren, why not force Bargheist to give up who it is?"

"That's yet another reason I think there *is* one. He was deported back to Pandemonia just before the ceremony started. The trap happened what - six hours later? I would say that's about the perfect amount of time for a message to be passed on and for an attack to be set up."

I indicated and overtook an old couple in a Beetle. "They knew you wouldn't be able to question him about anything."

"Exactly."

"Which also means that they must be close by."

Gabriella raised her eyebrows. "I don't follow."

"Think about it. If they were able to set up an organised attack like that within a relatively short window of time, there must be a base nearby."

"Alex, you're a genius! Of course they would need somewhere to meet safely. If we can find that base, we can take them all out."

302

"Yeah, but how do we do that?"

"That's the hard part."

We drove on in silence for a while. After a while of driving down the duel carriageway, under Gabriella's instruction, I pulled off onto a country style lane and followed signposts towards an area called the Warrens. The name sounded so innocent and normal. *Like hiding in plain sight.*

A thought occurred to me. "Do you think the attack was meant specifically for Orion?" I asked.

"I think so. It's common knowledge that Orion is the first response team for Chapter Hill. Echo and Trojan back us up if it's a big mission or handle specific jobs, like the occasional infiltration or protection – like they're doing with your house. The rest of the Guardians generally work further afield. Plus..." She cast an odd glance in my direction.

"What is it?"

"Well, there's been this feeling I can't shake. But I didn't want to worry you."

"You're worrying me now! Tell me."

"I think the trap was meant for you."

I stared over at her. A juddering under the wheels warned me that I was drifting off the road. I steadied the car. "Why do you think that?"

"Because you'd officially joined that evening. The SOS couldn't have known that we'd have an argument and that I'd choose not to bring you along on the mission. The attack is too much of a coincidence."

I gripped the wheel tight with both hands. "Why is everyone trying to kill me?"

Gabriella stared out of the window. "I don't know. But like I said before, if anyone tries it, they won't live very long."

The garage door cranked open and I eased the car down the slope, parking it in a space near the Nexus. In the elevator, Gabriella pushed a button of a cross with a snake wrapped around it.

Recovery Centre, said the voice.

We emerged into a sterile white corridor. Rows of black chairs had been placed outside uniform doors. The only way to

303

tell them apart was by the metallic numbers screwed onto the wood. I mentally counted down as we walked. The only break in the pattern was a door marked *refreshments*.

Sophia's room - number seven, was near the far end of the corridor. Delagio was outside; leaning backwards, foot resting on the wall. A marble weaved itself between his fingers in a constant loop. His eyes were closed. He opened them a fraction and nodded. It was a solemn gesture, which implied 'no change either way'.

I patted his arm as we walked past and creaked the door open.

The room was dimly lit. A single lamp sat on a corner unit, creating a large halo of light on the ceiling. Lying in a bed shaped like half a glass cylinder was Sophia. All manner of tubes and wires were connected to her. Each one trailed back to a cluster of blinking, whirring machines. I didn't have a clue what half of them were. The only one I recognised was a Cardiogram. A black line travelled from left to right on the screen, jerking into a lightning bolt in the middle. The bolt looked small.

It was hard to see Sophia properly, because of the shadow that Midnight's hulking frame cast over her. He was hunched over, dabbing her head with a damp cloth. He looked terrible. His face was pale from lack of sleep and his bloodshot eyes were ringed by dark bags. The tattooed scars were red and swollen, where he'd clearly been scratching. The smell of stale sweat made it clear he hadn't left the room to do anything, even wash.

He gave a weak smile as we entered. We made our way over to the bed and I had to stifle a gasp. I'd thought Midnight looked bad, but it was nothing compared to the state Sophia was in.

Her skin was completely grey. Even darker areas surrounded her protruding cheekbones and thin purple lines of infection - originating from two puncture wounds on her neck - spread out like a spider's web, mapping every part of the skin I could see. An oxygen mask covered most of her little face like some kind of clinical facehugger. Sophia had always been skinny, but now the poor thing looked in danger of simply disappearing. The only clue that she was even alive apart from the beeping monitor, were the occasional twitches and moans she made from the depths of her feverish sleep. Her sickness seemed to radiate from her, taking on its own menacing life form, which threatened to engulf the room.

We crowded around the bed, trying to find space amongst the tubes that sprouted from her like appendages. Looking at the sickly waif that had replaced the sweet Sophia made me want to cry. I bit my lip hard.

"She's trying her hardest to fight it," Midnight said as much to himself as any of us.

Gabriella gently placed the back of her hand against Sophia's forehead. Frowning, she pulled it away. "She's even hotter than before."

"One hundred and nine degrees," Midnight agreed.

My mouth gaped open. "How is that even possible?"

"Witches run hotter than normal humans," answered Gabriella. "Still that's too much - even for her."

"Isn't there anything we can do?" I said, feeling utterly helpless.

"There's nothin' anyone can do, not 'til Rachel gets back with the ingredients for the Coven's spell," Midnight explained, pulling the damp cloth from Sophia's head and dipping it in a bowl of water near his feet. He twisted out the excess before re-applying it to her forehead. "We have to hope she gets back in time before..." His voice wavered and he turned his face away.

Gabriella walked over and rested a hand on his shoulder. He patted it with his giant paw. "You're exhausted," she said. "I know there's no chance of convincing you to get some rest. So how about a coffee instead?"

He nodded.

"Alex?" she asked, heading for the door.

"I'm fine thanks."

She headed out of the door and said something to Delagio. I heard two sets of footsteps make their way down the corridor and I was left alone with Midnight.

I tried a few times to spark a conversation, but every time the words snagged in my throat. I couldn't think of the right thing to say. In the end it was Midnight who broke the silence.

"I won't let her die." His words were thick, his voice threatening to break at any moment.

"I know you won't. You really care about her don't you?"

305

Midnight nodded. A solitary tear sloped its way down his mountainous face. "She's the only reason I have to live."

He fell silent and stared down at the floor, fiddling with the locket that hung around his neck. The constant clicks of the latch opening and closing accompanied the whirrs and beeps of the machines. When he finally spoke again, his words seemed like they were coming from somewhere deep inside. The place where secrets and memories are buried.

"I haven't talked about them for a long time."

"Who?"

"My wife and daughter."

He needed to confide in somebody. I could tell by the expression of conflicted anguish on his face. I knew because I'd felt the same way so many times before, but always managed to force it away – until the day Gabriella had pulled it out of me. I knew I needed to choose my next words carefully.

"I'd love to hear about them."

Midnight raised his head and looked at me. A deep sadness stared out from behind his eyes. The brutal tough guy was well and truly gone. In his place sat a broken man, whose walls of protection had come tumbling down.

"You don't mind?" he asked, sounding unsure of himself.

"I'd be honoured."

Midnight told me his story.

24

The Dawn of Midnight

I was always a bit of a fighter. Constantly got into scraps at school. I dunno, maybe it was cos my dad was a drunken bastard - always hitting my mum - I guess I found violence natural. At first I always got beat up. I'd come home in tears, with a broken nose or a split lip, but over time I grew stronger. Their punches didn't hurt much anymore; my punches hurt them a lot.

At home, I'd wind my dad up so he'd hit me instead of Mum. She was so small and frail. Course, she tried to stop him, but I made her promise not to. Rather me than her. So he'd beat me and in turn I'd take out my anger on the kids at school. I guess I became a bully. By the time I turned fifteen, I'd already been expelled from three different schools. The son of a bitch finally died from alcohol poisonin' when I was sixteen. It felt strange, after so much physical and mental abuse, to suddenly be...free.

Mum and me built a new life together. I dropped out of school and worked a few dead end jobs over the years to help pay the rent. I thought things would be okay - but I was wrong. There was a darkness growin' inside of me. I could feel it bubbling away below the surface. I found it almost impossible to control my anger. It meant I couldn't hold a job down for long; the smallest thing would set me off. Once, at a pub I worked at, I threw my manager over the bar, all because he had a go at me for being late.

Lucky for me, my mum could see that I was headin' the same route as *him*. So as much as it killed her to see me go, she convinced me to join the Army. Best decision I ever made. It gave me a channel to focus my anger into. The structure kept me in line and I learned to respect authority. Plus, cos digs and food was free, I could afford to send most of my wages home. I progressed fast, made Sergeant in less than three years. The hardest part was that I only got to see Mum four or five times a year. The Gulf War was in full swing and I was constantly bein' dispatched out to that hellhole.

But Mum was doing good, had a nice little two-bed place just outside Brighton. She never dated again - she was too scarred for that - but she made quite a few good friends and even set up a book club. I was happy for her. But I wasn't happy for me. Somethin' was missing. I had no clue what it was until I was on summer leave and saw her walking along the beachfront. I don't know if you believe in love at first sight Alex, I never did until I laid eyes on her. Petit and perfect. Wavy golden hair and the most beautiful hazel eyes ever saw. Incredible.

She was singing to herself as she walked. She had the most beautiful voice, like an angel. For a moment all the darkness trapped inside me vanished - like her voice chased it away. It was replaced by a feeling so intense and wonderful I can't even begin to explain it. As she passed by, she stopped singing for a moment and gave the sweetest little smile. I literally went weak at the knees. I knew right then and there that this was the woman I wanted to spend the rest of my life with. She was way out of my league and I knew it. But I had to do *somethin'*. There was no way I could go back to my normal life - not now I'd seen her. It would have killed me.

I ran after her, panting and red as a friggin' beetroot. Somehow amongst my babblin', I managed to ask her out for a coffee. I'd been through all kinds of nightmares in Kuwait; shot at by rebels, driven through a field of landmines, had a gun to my head – you name it. But I'd never experienced fear like I did in that moment, waiting for her answer. But she just smiled and linked arms with me.

We were inseparable after that. Her name was Maria Quinn - an artist from Ireland. I called her Cass on account that she was always singing *songbird*, you know that one by Eva Cassidy? She called me…sorry you don't need to know this, it's only when I start talking about her… Anyway, I'd found my soulmate. When I was around her, the world seemed to take on a special glow. I couldn't get angry if I wanted to. All of the bad crap had been washed away. Cass made me feel special, like I was actually worth somethin'. She didn't care that I wasn't clever like she was

- that I was rough around the edges - she loved me for who I was.

I moved into her little studio apartment by the beach. I used to watch her paint - it was mesmerising. She seemed to be able to capture the natural beauty of things on the canvas.

The time came for her to meet my mum. I was so nervous I actually puked before we left the house. The only two women I'd ever loved were gonna meet for the first time. If they hated each other, my world would have fallen apart. They couldn't have got on any better. Mum loved Cass to pieces. I remember, I was making everyone a cup of tea when she came in to the kitchen and said, 'she's the one,' and walked back out. I started crying. I don't know why really, I think it's because at that moment, life couldn't have been more perfect.

But it couldn't last forever. I got orders that I had to leave for Kuwait the following week. It ripped me apart inside. I didn't know what to do. I couldn't bear to leave Cass behind. I told her I'd go AWOL, but she refused to let me. Said it didn't matter, that she would love me no matter where I was and that she'd be waiting whenever I came back.

The next day, Mum took me to her room and pulled a suitcase out of the wardrobe. Inside was a load of envelopes stuffed with money. She'd saved half of everything I'd ever given her from my wages. There was over fifteen grand in there. She insisted I take it to help build a new life for Cass and me. The look in her eye told me that nothin' I said or did would make her change her mind.

That same day I bought an engagement ring. I picked the prettiest one the store sold. Cost me three G's, but nothing was too good for her. The night before I was due to fly out, I took her to our favourite restaurant on the waterfront. I'd set up this big thing - total cheese, but I didn't care. I paid the owner to let me put a rented piano at the end, by our table. I hired a pianist and a singer to perform *songbird* at the end of our meal and dropped to one knee right there in the restaurant. My heart was in my mouth. I thought I was gonna pass out.

Cass started crying and I panicked. But when she looked up she was smiling and she said the word that right then was the most beautiful in the English language. The restaurant went wild, everyone clapping and cheering while we hugged and kissed. The ring was a perfect fit. Later we walked hand in hand along the beachfront, like the first day we had met. It was the first of two of the best days in my life.

The second came a year later, when my little girl was born. Cass and I'd been married six months. I was finishing my rotation in Kuwait and Cass was living with Mum, so that she could support her during the last stages of the pregnancy. I'd been back for three days when her water broke - during a game of Monopoly. While I was runnin' around frantic, she laughed and said it was her plan to stop me winning.

We rushed her to the hospital and the birth was smooth as silk. Only four hours in labour and no epidural needed. Already my angel was considerate. When I got to hold her, she wrapped these tiny little fingers around my thumb and stared at me with her big hazel eyes. For the second time in my life, it was love at first sight. I vowed to be the best damn father ever. Cass said we should name her Joy - after my mum. It was perfect, because it was also what she'd brought to our lives.

I put a deposit on a house down the road from Mum's and for eight years, everything was perfect. I managed to get myself an admin job in the Army. It was pretty boring, mainly paper-pushin', but it meant being around all my girls more, so I couldn't have cared less. I got to see my little baby grow up into a clever, beautiful young girl. She was an amazin' singer, obviously inherited from Cass, I couldn't hold a note if you paid me. Plus she loved to play around. Her favourite game was climbing on my shoulders and making me spin her around until she got dizzy. The sound of her laugh could have melted a heart made of ice. She... sorry, I just need a second.

Joy was everything her name suggests. Absolute light of my life. I spoiled her rotten. I'd always come home with little gifts. Cass used to nag me for it, but I couldn't help it. I adored her so much. Nothing made me happier than seeing her little face light up in excitement. But she never became spoiled, not like some of the little brats you see around. No, she was so caring and thoughtful. My life was perfect. The darkness had well and truly gone. When I was with my three girls, I felt like the luckiest man on the planet.

310

But happiness is a slippery thing. It lets you hold it for a while - me longer than most - and then it wriggles free and misery takes its place.

First it was Mum's breast cancer. Her doctor discovered the lump too late. It was stage four. She rejected the chemo; it would only have prolonged the inevitable anyway. She said she'd spent so long being weak and afraid, that she wanted to go out with some dignity. She faded fast. The disease had her in the hospital only a month later. I've always wondered if it's the knowin' that does you in. I mean if she'd never known, would she have lived longer?

Anyway...Joy was only eight at the time, so we left her with a close neighbour and stayed at the hospital. When the end came, we held Mum's hands as she faded away. Right before her final breath, she lifted our hands to her face and kissed them. Then she died.

The next few months were a total blur. I took compassionate leave from the Army and stumbled around in a daze. I'd pick up the phone and actually dial her number, before realisin' she wouldn't answer. Cass moved us into Mum's house, even though it was too small for us. She knew I needed to keep the memories of her alive.

Somehow, my two girls pulled me from the brink. Cass was patient and understanding, she put her own grief on hold to help me through mine. She was my rock. Even Joy seemed to understand what I was going through. She would just sit on my lap for hours and hug me while I cried. Eventually I was able to come to terms with it.

That was the first of two of the worst days of my life.

The second came three years later. I woke up on the thirteenth of August two thousand and four, with the crushing feeling that something awful was going to happen.

I'd agreed to go on a short logistical tour of Iraq to help out - all pretty safe. I was due to go home later that day. I couldn't eat my breakfast, I felt sick. I called as soon as I could to check my girls were okay. They were fine. I couldn't work out what was wrong. I stayed well behind neutral territory and even neglected some of my duties to keep me out of any possible firing line. I kept thinking, *if I die, who's gonna look after my girls?*

I spent the entire plane journey back in a state of constant panic. Every bit of turbulence would make me break out in a cold sweat. I called them four more times from the plane. Cass could sense my fear and became nervous herself. She asked me what she should do. I told her not to come and meet me at the airport like she'd planned, but to stay at home and lock the doors and windows.

I touched down at ten in the evening. The overwhelming sensation of dread was growing stronger to the point I was almost sick. I called from the airport. No one answered. I tried at least five more times. Nothing. I called from the car and still no one picked up.

My hands were shaking as I drove, the feeling was so intense, it was all I could do not to scream. I drove home at well over a ton in the pouring rain. Then my friggin' piece of crap car gave out a good ten minutes away. I jumped out and sprinted the rest. Made it home at ten to twelve. As soon as I got to the house I could tell something was wrong.

The door was open.

There was no way Cass would have left it like that after hearing how upset I was. The house was dark. I tried to switch the lights on, but they wouldn't work. It was real quiet. All I could hear was the dripping sound from my clothes. I called out. There was a scrambling sound from upstairs. Something heavy - moving fast. My insides went cold. I called out again but there was no answer.

I knew that whatever had been bothering me was happening, now...in my house. I ran upstairs and into the bedroom. Alex, it was unbearable.

M-my precious girls were heaped in a pile on the floor. There were cuts all over their bodies. Their wrists had been slashed and they were bleeding out right in front of my eyes. Cass had tried to cover Joy to protect her from whatever had attacked them, but it was pointless. There was so much blood. It was everywhere. On the floorboards, splashed on the walls. Even the ceiling. Some of it had been used to write the words *Chosen must die* on the mirror. I had no clue what it meant, and I didn't care. I only cared that my girls were dying.

I ran over to help them and that's when I saw it.

The thing stepped out from the shadows in the corner of the room. A Banshee. It had this rough, papery skin and these slick black eyes, like hardened oil. Long, lank hair that reached the floor and left a trail of slime as the thing moved. Its mouth was all twisted up and filled with thousands of these needle teeth. And the smell. Christ, the smell. Sickly sweet, like shit covered in syrup. But its hands were the worst part by far. The thing had these spindly fingers the length of an arm that curved into dagger nails at the ends.

They were stained with the blood of my family.

It gave me this teasing smile and then sucked their blood off its fingers with slow pops. I looked at the evil bitch and back at the mangled mess of my family - my life, and the darkness returned. It hadn't gone. It had hidden away, waiting until it was needed again. It was needed then. I felt rage like nothin' I've ever felt before. It was like white-hot, pure hatred.

The Banshee must 'ave sensed my fury, because it screamed. When a banshee screams, it's the worst noise you could imagine. It's the cries of a million tortured souls. Pray to god you never experience it. Only those it wants can hear the sound, so no one can help you. Its hair fanned out as if it'd been electrocuted. The sound brought me to my knees. I started to haemorrhage blood from everywhere.

For a minute I was frozen - bleeding to death. Then I saw my blood trickle into and mix with the blood of my girls.

The darkness took over. Somehow, I managed to summon enough strength to stagger over. Then I grabbed it and started smashing it with my fists for everything I was worth, screamin'. It lashed out, most hits missed, but one connected, carving most of the skin from this side of my face and blinding me in one eye. The pain didn't even register. I grabbed its throat and with a strength I didn't know I had, ripped out its larynx. Then screams became a gurgle and the slashing turned into pathetic taps, but I didn't stop. Because it couldn't scream any more, my attacks were stronger. I punched, bit and kicked until there was nothing left but lumps of meat and slime.

I was wrenched from my revenge by Cass's hand touching my arm. She crawled towards me, dragging Joy with her. I scooped them both into my arms. We all knew that it was too

313

late. They'd lost too much blood and the wounds were too severe. It was simply a matter of time. For some reason they were both calm. They looked up at me as I held them in my arms and Cass even managed a smile. I gripped them, sobbing uncontrollably.

At exactly midnight my whole world died in my arms.

The Alliance came to me a day later. They'd finally figured out who I was and what I was going to become. Apparently when they found me, I was still in the same position, rocking backwards and forwards with my girls in my arms. It took four of them to prise me away. I don't remember much about the few days after that. I do know that their deaths brought about my Awakening. I had it less than a week later. The sight in my left eye returned and the wounds healed a bit, but the poison in the Banshee's fingernails made it scar badly.

Sage Faru told me everything, probably the same things he told you. Gave me the whole spiel. Apparently they hadn't tracked me fast enough. The SOS has Witches working for them too. They found out about me first and sent a Banshee to wait for me. My family had been in the wrong place at the wrong time.

I didn't say a word the whole time. In fact I didn't say another word for the next three years. I blamed 'em for the death of my girls. All I could think was how the Alliance should have discovered me earlier - should have protected my family like Guardians are supposed to. I didn't need to tell Faru my thoughts; he saw it all in my mind. He didn't bother asking me to join the HASEA; he knew it was pointless. I didn't care about protecting the world. There was no one left in the world that I wanted to protect. All I cared about was being with all my girls again.

You know this strength that we have is great at saving our arses, but it's a curse if you want to die. I took six bottles of sleeping tablets – they only gave me chronic stomachache. I shot myself in the face - it just broke my jaw. I even jumped from the roof of a block of flats. Granted, it put me in the hospital for three weeks, but the point is I survived.

I couldn't die.

314

I was trapped in purgatory with my darkness. There was nothing left for me. Every time I looked in the mirror and saw the scars, I was reminded of my loss. So I tried to cover em with a tattoo. I thought it would help. It didn't. All it did was make other people more scared of me. I decided to use that to my advantage. I went back to my house for the last time and grabbed the only thing I cared about.

A few days later I used the same gun I shot myself with to rob a newsagents. The rush took away the pain long enough for me to feel somethin' again - if only for a few minutes. But then it was back again and stronger than ever. I did it again and again. I didn't even bother to wear a mask. I didn't care if I got caught or not. I didn't even spend the money. I left it in a backpack at the end of the crappy hostel I lived in.

It took longer than you'd think to get caught. But still, there's only so long a six foot nine bald guy with half his head covered in a tattoo can go unnoticed. I went down. Twenty years with a minimum of sixteen to be served. I didn't say a word through my sentencing.

My darkness consumed me. In the joint I put at least six guys in the med ward for lookin' at me the wrong way. I couldn't feel any remorse. It's like I sat on the sidelines watching myself. They kept addin' time onto my sentence and confined me to solitary. The whole time I kept thinking *I don't care, I deserve everything I get.*

You see I'd finally come to the understandin' that it was my fault that my girls had died. If I hadn't told them to stay at home, then...well things might have gone differently.

I served a whole year of my sentence before the HASEA came back to me again. Faru spoke to me in my mind one evening. I remember thinking I was having a seizure and then he appeared in my cell in front of me. He asked me to reconsider joinin'. I told him where to stick his offer, but then he said that he wanted to show me something. An image of a little girl appeared in my mind. My heart leapt into my mouth, apart from the eyes, the girl was the spit of my little Joy. He told me that the girl had lived a life as bad as mine. That she'd just had her Awakening and was scared. She needed someone to look after her.

He's a clever one old Faru. He knew exactly what he was doing by showing me Sophia - there was no way I would refuse. I agreed to join on a single condition. That he never referred to me as Michael Williams again. That man was dead. A new one had been born the moment my family died.

I told him my name was Midnight.

25

My throat had a huge lump in it. Midnight's eyes were damp with tears. He mopped them with back of one of his huge hands.

"I-I don't know what to say. What happened to you...no one should have to go through that," I said.

He sighed. "Sometimes I think about it and it's like I can't breathe. I just want to be with 'em again so much. But then I remember that I still have Sophia... and the memories of those eight fantastic years."

"Can I ask a personal question?"

He shrugged.

"Are you still only with the HASEA to protect Sophia?"

Midnight cast his gaze over to the little girl fighting for her life and then looked away again, closing his eyes in grief.

"Originally yeah. But then thought - what if one of those creatures or somethin' like it attacked another man's family? What if another dad came home to find his life in ruins? I wanted to help others avoid the pain I went through when lost my girls. My plan was to protect her and save everyone I could until the day one of those bastards finally kills me. But I failed. I failed to protect her, just like I failed my family." He put his head in his hands.

His words shook me to the core. I'd pegged this man down as a mindless thug, when he couldn't be further from it. I'd judged him before I got to know him. The very same thing that people had been doing to me all my life. I felt utterly ashamed of myself.

"You didn't fail anyone, Midnight. You did the best you could – and that's all you can ever do. I'll tell you another thing too, you're a *good* person and Sophia is lucky to have you to care for her."

Midnight looked up at me. He seemed to contemplate what I'd said for a moment. Then he leaned forward and shook my hand. "Thanks."

I pointed towards the locket wrapped around his neck. "Is that what you took from the house?"

He placed a hand around it, as if shielding it from my question. "Yeah, it was an anniversary gift I bought for Cass, 'cept I swapped my picture for hers after she...you know."

"May I see?"

Midnight seemed to contemplate the request for a moment. Then he lowered his neck and slid the locket over his head. I stretched over and he placed it in my hands.

The case was silver, polished to a shine. 'Michael & Maria' had been engraved on the back. I pressed a clasp on the side and the locket opened. Inside were two small photographs. One showed a very pretty woman with curly blonde hair. She wore a smile than seemed bordering on a laugh, which lit up her whole face. The girl in the other couldn't have been more than six when the photograph was taken. Even so, she looked so much like Sophia they could have been sisters. Right down to the rosy cheeks and sweet smile. Looking at the photographs, it was easy to see why Midnight had once been so happy.

"They were both beautiful," I said, closing the locket and handing it back to him.

"Thanks." He slipped the locket back over his neck and tucked it into his t-shirt.

"I have a picture of my dad that I carry around with me too."

Midnight held out a hand. "Only fair."

I rummaged through my bag and pulled out the handbook. I slipped the picture from the pages and handed it to him. He looked at it and nodded, before passing it back to me. "Looks a lot like you."

"You think?"

"Now yeah. Maybe not so much back when you were a massive nerd."

We both laughed. His was a deep rumble that rolled through his chest.

"So how did you get out of prison?" I asked.

"You kiddin? One call from the HASEA to the right people and I was out within a day, record as squeaky as an Eton schoolboy."

"Wow. I'll keep that in mind next time I'm planning on robbing some newsagents."

Midnight started to laugh again, but stopped dead when Sophia cried out in pain.

"It's okay pint size. I'm here," he said in a voice so soft I wouldn't have thought it possible. He busied himself once more with removing the cloth from her forehead and dipping it in the bowl of water.

Gabriella and Delagio returned, armed with mugs of coffee. Gabriella had to say Midnight's name three times before he tore his attention away from Sophia. She passed him a coffee and he downed it in a matter of seconds, even though there was steam curling from the top. She placed hers on a table near the door. Delagio took a long sip of his, set his cup down next to Gabriella's and returned to his position in the corridor.

The sombre reality of the situation returned with a ferocity. I leaned back into my chair as Gabriella stroked Sophia's cheek gently with the back of her hand. Time dissolved as we stayed locked in our positions. Midnight removing, rinsing and replacing the cloth. Gabriella stroking Sophia's cheek. Delagio standing vigil outside. Me sitting on my chair, feeling useless.

Then in a second everything changed.

Out of the corner of my eye, I saw that Gabriella looked on the brink of tears. I stood up and placed a comforting hand on her back. As soon as my palm connected, a giant wave of energy exploded in my chest and rushed down my arm. Gabriella arched her back and cried out. Instantly I felt drained. My knees buckled and I collapsed to the floor.

"Alex!" Gabriella gasped. From my position on the cold linoleum, I watched as Midnight jumped to his feet and Delagio burst into the room. Everything seemed to be happening in slow motion. Several sets of hands lifted me up and positioned me back on the chair. The room was spinning and I could barely focus.

"Are you okay, buddy?" Delagio asked, leaning over me.

319

I raised a hand. "I-I think so, just give me a minute." Slowly, everything seemed to return to normal.

"What just happened?" asked Gabriella.

I was about to reply when I saw Sophia's eyes flutter open. They searched around the room, not seeming to understand where she was. Stunned into silence, I could only point. Everyone turned to face the bed.

"Sophia!" Midnight dropped the rag clutched in his hands. It landed on the floor with a loud splat. He tried to speak, cleared his throat and tried again. "Hi sweetheart. How you feelin?"

Sophia gave a little nod of her head and tapped at the oxygen mask attached to her face. Midnight gently lifted her head and slipped off the mask. Her lips struggled into a tiny smile. "Better," she whispered.

"Guys, look at her skin!" exclaimed Delagio.

We all looked. The red lines of infection were retracting back into the bite wounds, as if they were threads of fishing line being reeled in. The purple puncture wounds turned pink and shrank, until they disappeared completely. Her skin changed from grey to white and then back to her normal tone. Last of all her cheeks bloomed, as if an artist had applied the finishing touches.

Midnight's mouth hung open in disbelief as the little girl dragged herself up into a sitting position on the bed. He stared from me, to Sophia, to Gabriella and back to me again. "I don't understand."

I stared down at my hands and then up at Gabriella. "I-I think I just healed Sophia."

Midnight barged his way past the medical equipment and scooped me up into a crushing bear hug. He spun me around in a circle and my feet sent both cups of coffee somersaulting off the table. He was laughing hysterically and tears of happiness flowed down his face. When he finally set me down, he did the same to Gabriella and Delagio. Sophia was laughing from the bed. If it weren't for the fact that she still looked too skinny, it would be impossible to tell she'd been ill at all.

Delagio clapped his shoulders. "Put me down ya big idiot," he laughed.

Letting him go, Midnight moved back over to Sophia. "You sure you feeling better darlin'?"

"Yup. I feel a bit tired, but that's it."

He pressed his forehead gently onto Sophia's crown and let out a long sigh as tears continued to slide down his face.

We stayed with Sophia for hours, fussing over her and revelling in her miraculous recovery. The atmosphere had changed so quickly from misery to joy.

"Right, I think ah should go let Faru know," said Delagio "He can send a message through to Rachel n' bring her home. Ah don't want her to be over there any longer than she needs to be."

"We should go too," agreed Gabriella.

I gave a tiny shake of my head and stared at her. *Me and Delagio together in a room with Faru after what we did? Bad idea.*

Gabriella seemed to understand my concern. "Actually, on second thoughts, Alex is due to meet Selene and the rest of the Coven soon. We'll head down there now and let them know that they don't need to worry about the spell. We can deal with how it happened later. The main thing is that Sophia is feeling better." She turned to face the bed. "You promise you're feeling better *mia bambina*?"

Sophia lifted three fingers. "Witches' honour."

The room broke out into relieved laughter.

"Okay, well I'm gonna go speak to the head honcho," said Delagio. "I'll see y'all later." He rotated his hand and the oxygen mask that Midnight had removed levitated from the bed and ruffled Sophia's hair with a blast of air.

"Hey!" she giggled.

He gave her a wink and disappeared from the room.

"You two will be okay here if we head off too won't you?" asked Gabriella.

Midnight wiped away a fresh set of tears. A grin spread from one ear to the other. "You kiddin? I got loadsa stories to bore her with. Get going."

Gabriella walked over and kissed Sophia on the forehead. We waved at each other. As I was leaving the room, Midnight called out my name. I turned back.

"I'll never forget what you did for us mate," he said.

"I...don't really know *what* I did."

"It don't matter. You still did it."

321

In the corridor, Gabriella threw her arms around me and planted dozens of kisses all over my face. Each one zinged my skin as if her lips were electric. I laughed and pretended to push her off me, even though I could have happily let her keep going all day.

"So I redeemed myself for the other night then?"

Gabriella held out her index finger and thumb in a C shape. "Maybe a little bit."

We reached the elevator and pressed the button. "Did you feel that in there?" I asked.

"How could I not? It was like you hit me with a Taser!" Reading the confused expression on my face she added, "Wait until we speak to Sage Faru. I'm sure he'll have some answers. He always does."

As we sped along the Nexus, I leaned against the side of the cab and tapped my fingers in a random beat on the rail.

"So why does Selene want to meet me?"

"It's standard for all new Guardians to meet their local Coven - especially Chosen. Witches get precognitive energy from us. The more of a team they meet, the stronger their premonitions will be.

"You've lost me."

"An attack premonition is like a jigsaw puzzle. When a Witch meets a new Guardian, that person - or piece - becomes available to them. The more pieces they have, the stronger their premonitions are and the clearer the overall pictures become. But if a Guardian that they hadn't met went on that mission, they'd appear as a sort of black spot in their mind that could cause them to miss things."

"Do you mean that if I'd met the Coven earlier then they may have foreseen the ambush?"

"Maybe. Normally their visions involve what happens if we don't intervene. But they may have sensed that there were more than just Blooding's in the area."

"Unless like you say there's a Rogue working in the base who knew I hadn't met the Coven yet, so planned an ambush knowing that the Witches would see me as a black spot-"

322

"And be blinded towards a separate attack directed at you. Yes, I hadn't thought of that! We have to let Faru know that too." She shot me a sarcastic look. "When you decide to grow a pair and speak to him that is."

The elevator shuddered to a stop and the doors rolled open. We stepped out into a rocky tunnel similar to the pathway to the temple. A pair of flaming torches hung either side on the rough walls. The light stretched our shadows into unnatural shapes that loomed over us. Gabriella lifted a torch from its holder and guided us forward. The narrow passage twisted around itself a few times. Our footsteps echoed around us. A musty scent like forgotten clothes drifted towards us from ahead.

Sophia wasn't lying about the odd smell.

In the darkness, something bumped against my leg. I let out a yell and shrank backwards against the wall.

"What's wrong?"

"There's something here!"

Gabriella aimed the torch behind me. Green eyes appeared in the light. A bundle of black fur hissed and sprinted away.

"Cat," I sighed, allowing my heart to recover.

"Familiar," Gabriella corrected.

"Ah." I thought for a second. "Hold on I got this one. They used to be cats, but now they belong to a Witch they can shift into loads of different animals right?"

"That's it."

"They act as a Witch's eyes and ears. So the Coven know we're coming now."

Gabriella made an impressed face. "You're getting good at this."

Eventually the tunnel came to an end. Gabriella placed the torch in another holder and we passed under a hulking archway. The room beyond looked surprisingly cosy. The rocky walls had been smoothed into a tear shape, joining together at the top, and a metal pentagram hung from the apex. The moon shone through a circular hole near the top – beautiful, but impossible considering we were underground and it was still daytime. Crooked shelves covered with dusty books and ornaments lined every wall. The light came from hundreds of flickering candles - some sat on dedicated shelves, their wax creeping over the edges like fingers - others were skewered on wall mounted and free standing candelabras. Worn chairs huddled in small groups and wonky wooden tables adorned with Crystal balls and Tarot cards lay randomly around the room, framed by long benches. Lush curtains covered purpose made holes that looked like they led to different areas. One out of place corner appeared to be dedicated to modern technology. A small television sat on a corner table and next to it, a digital telephone that stood upright in its cradle. All the wires were bound together by tape and disappeared through a little hole bored into the rock.

Dozens of familiars filled the room. They curled on chairs and rugs, washing themselves or napping, paws twitching in their dreams. One sat on the central table, facing us. It made a low moaning sound and shuddered. Its body shrank and its back sprouted feathers. It became a large raven, which in a flurry of wings, flew up to a shelf high above us. I waited for my brain to react in some way to what I had just witnessed - a burst of adrenaline, a moment of shock - but it didn't. It dawned on me that I'd finally accepted that these things could happen. That this world existed.

I'm used to it.

Suddenly a curtain was thrown back and half a dozen small children came sprinting through. "Ella!" they squealed as they fought to wrap their arms around her waist. She laughed and hugged them back. I noticed a small boy hanging in the background. He clung to a one-eared toy rabbit. It's not-so-white paws draped on the floor.

"Thomas, do you want to say hello?" asked Gabriella.

The boy nodded.

The others parted so that he could hug Gabriella. Afterwards he ran away, disappearing through the curtain.

I watched him go. "A male Witch?" I asked.

"Male Witches are Shaman. The Coven welcomes them, but they tend to prefer solitude. Thomas is a rare exception."

She turned to the group of girls, who were clutching onto her sleeves and wrapped around her legs.

"Everyone, this is my good friend Alex. Do you want to say hello?"

Instantly I was bombarded with hands, which tugged at my clothes and prodded my knees and legs. I raised my eyebrows at Gabriella, who laughed.

"Go back to your rooms children," said a stern voice.

I looked up to see Sylvia standing in the centre of the room. She wore an almost identical black dress to the one I'd seen her wearing the night of the feast and her hair had been pulled into the same tight bun. I got the impression she wasn't much of a trendsetter.

The children giggled and ran out of the room.

"Please excuse them. They haven't quite learned the correct manners yet."

"It's fine, Sylvia. We don't mind," said Gabriella. "We have some great news about Sophia. She has…recovered. The spell won't be necessary any longer."

The Witch gave a stiff nod and I imagined her pecking at grain on the ground. "I shall inform Selene. The rest of the Coven will convene shortly. In the meantime, may I interest you in some whiteroot tea?"

The question appeared to be aimed at me. "Oh, um no thank you, I think we're fine," I said.

"Very well," said Sylvia. With another curt nod, she slipped from the room.

Gabriella leaned in close. "Sylvia's the schoolmaster. She's a bit uptight. The rest are lovely," she whispered.

We waited in silence for a few minutes and then one by one, the Coven began to appear from behind various curtains. They came in all shapes and sizes. Several were tall and thin, others round like comic strip cooks and just as smiley. Some had blonde hair, others black or ginger. Their ages ranged from teenagers to unidentifiably old. Apart from the fact that they were all pretty pale and most had heterochromia, they looked very normal. None even remotely resembled the hideous hags depicted in books and stories. Not a pointed hat in sight.

There were twenty-six in total. They all arranged themselves into a semi-circle either side of the central curtain and bowed in a uniformed greeting. A moment later a wrinkled hand extended from behind the cloth and slowly brushed it to one side.

A grey haired woman stepped through. She looked as old as time itself. Her shoulders hunched around her narrow neck and a large crooked nose dominated most of her road-mapped face. She shuffled into the room, beady eyes watching each step, as gnarled fingers lifted her black dress off the floor.

"Alexander," she began in a voice like scrunched paper, "I Selene and the rest of the Coven would like to welcome you to Moon's Edge – our home."

"Thank you, it's a pleasure to meet everyone."

Selene's face cracked into a warm smile. "Right now we've got all that formal rubbish out of the way, we can relax."

I raised my eyebrows at Gabriella who gave a little smile.

Selene gestured towards the centre table. "Please, sit, sit." I headed over and sat down. Instead of joining me, Gabriella walked around the side and hugged the old Witch. "It's so good to see you again my dear," sighed Selene. "It always feels like years between your visits. The children do miss you so."

"I know, I promise I'll visit more. It's just been so hectic with Alex's Awakening."

Selene placed both hands on the sides of Gabriella's arms. "Sylvia told me that Sophia has made a sudden recovery. I thank the moon and stars."

"It was a miracle. We still don't understand quite how it happened. But we know it had something to do with Alex."

"Did it now?" The Witch turned to me. "Then that makes you my newest favourite person. Thank you."

"Err, my pleasure."

Turning back to Gabriella she said, "I pray that this will make that poor girl see sense and come and live here at Moon's Edge, away from all that horrible danger."

Gabriella gave a slow shrug. "You know she won't leave Midnight."

The Witch made a tutting noise. "Well then you tell that brute to make sure he keeps her out of harm's way in future or he'll have me to deal with."

Gabriella smiled. "I'll pass on the message." She joined me at the table, squeezing my shoulder as she sat.

"Well then, I suppose we had better get down to business," said Selene, settling herself down at the opposite side of the table. She leaned across and placed her arms on the table, palms upwards. "When I nod, I need you to put your hands in mine. Don't worry, it'll only burn a bit," she added, aiming an unsubtle wink at Gabriella.

Around the room, the Witches all joined hands and bowed their heads. Selene closed her eyes and began to mutter something under her breath. Her body rocked backwards and forwards. Occasionally her body would jerk in an odd direction as if an invisible force were pulling her. I watched her and waited for her signal. After a while, she gave a slow nod of her head.

I placed my hands in hers.

As soon as I touched her, an image of a giant face formed from the earth and trees seared into my mind. A burst of energy surged from Selene, sending Gabriella and me flying across the room. I smashed against a shelf, scattering jars of herbs and candles across the room. Gabriella hit the floor hard and slid along, ending up in a heap next to me, half covered in a rug. I looked back up at Selene. Her body had gone as stiff as a rod. Her eyes were wide open staring blindly at nothing.

One of the Witches called out Selene's name. The group gathered, trying to calm her. At the same time, the candles began to flicker as if a strong breeze had entered the room. The Pentagram screeched as it swayed from side to side. Selene started thrash about. One arm swatted the Tarot pack, sending a cloud of cards whirling around the room. Spittle flicked from her thin lips onto her chin. Panicked I looked at Gabriella. "What's happening? Is this a premonition?"

"No! I-I don't know! This isn't normal!"

The children, who had been peeking from behind the curtains, began to cry. The familiars were going crazy, hissing and swiping at the air, or morphing continuously like their shift switch was broken.

"She's having a fit. Lay her down for heaven's sake!" shouted Sylvia.

Two younger Witches tried to place their arms around the thrashing woman. Selene flung them away from her as if they were rag dolls. One collided with the far wall and fell unconscious. The other flew onto a table, smashing the crystal ball. Selene's jaw unhinged like a snake's. She wrenched back her head and a voice completely unlike hers boomed from her throat. The message was fractured, like a radio tuning in and out of frequency.

THE TWELFTH YEAR OF THE THIRD MILLENIUM MARKS THE AWAKENING OF THE SECOND TWIN. BOTH MARKED BY SORROW...BETRAYED BY THE MOON AND STARS. FACING THE ABYSS, HE SHALL SEE WHAT IS HIDDEN...WHEN THE NIGHT SKY IS ABLAZE WITH WINGS OF FIRE...THE FURY UNLEASHED SHALL END THE AGELESS WAR AND BEGIN THE RISING. WHEN YOUNG BECOMES OLD...STAND AGAINST HADES. ALL SHALL PLAY THEIR PART.

Selene's mouth snapped shut and she slumped over the table. The candles stopped flickering and the pentagram came to a rest. A mixture of confusion and fear filled the room. Some Witches went to help the injured ones and a few more gingerly approached their fallen leader. This time they were able to lift her up and place her down on the table. Sylvia rushed from the room and re-entered with a pillow, which she placed under the old woman's head. Around us, the familiars were pacing the room in cat form, sniffing the corners and letting out deep guttural moans.

I looked down and realised that at some point, Gabriella and I had locked our hands together. We unwound our fingers and rushed over to the table.

"Selene, its Gabriella. Can you hear me?"

For the longest moment, there was no sound at all. Everyone waited with baited breath. Then the old woman made a groaning noise and placed a hand over her eyes. "I'm getting too old for this nonsense," she sighed.

"Selene what *was* that?" I asked.

"I'm not entirely sure dear."

I ran my hands through my hair. "Why does all this stuff keep happening everywhere I go?"

Gabriella placed her hands on her hips and stared at me.

"Enough is enough. We're going to Faru."

26

We stood underneath the hulking picture. Gabriella knelt down and gestured for me to copy. We stayed that way in complete silence for a moment until I felt the familiar grip of electricity and a voice emanated from within the painting.

"Gabriella, Alexander. Is everything alright? You both appear troubled."

My friend spoke without moving her lips, but I could hear her words perfectly, like we were on a telepathic conference call. "We are, Sage Faru. Please may we have a minute of your time?"

"Of course."

With that we shuddered and were released from the grip. I stared in wonder as the picture began to swirl around like fresh paint on a canvass. At the bottom, where the end of Faru's beard had been, the hole appeared. It grew in size until it filled most of the painting and the glass steps emerged from the middle, coming to rest just in front of where we were kneeling. Gabriella stood up and hurried inside, pulling me with her. As soon as we were through, the steps retracted and the painting was sealed once more.

We made our way along the strangest corridor I'd ever seen. The floor underneath our feet looked like tropical ocean water - complete with lapping waves - but felt as solid as concrete. A run of silver trees like the ones I'd seen in the Sanctuary stood next to one another. They were so close together that you could barely see where one finished and the next began. Their branches arched over our heads, knitting together whilst their glowing leaves bathed the hallway in a warm golden light. At the far end of the hallway a set of ornate doors swung open by themselves.

Inside was an office-like room, but far more beautiful. The floor looked identical to frosted ice, but rippled like silvery water with every step we took. Behind the various bookcases and shelves, the walls were moving strips of light that rolled around each other and settled in different positions. They were solid one moment and transparent the next. Majestic plants the height of a bungalow - with leaves of the brightest yellow - stretched up from the floor, giving the room a bright, summerlike feeling. A spiralling silver staircase at the back of the room appeared to ascend into a patch of swirling blue clouds in the ceiling. A workbench stood in one corner. The half formed torso of a Golem sat on top, surrounded by numerous carving tools.

The Sage was standing in the middle of the room, behind a shimmering crystal desk, which appeared to be hovering a few feet from the ground. Amusingly, placed on the desk were painfully ordinary items, like a cordless telephone and stack of newspapers. He was looking through a large, rectangular book. Closing and setting it aside, he gestured towards the area in front of the desk.

"Please take a seat."

I looked around, confused by the distinct lack of chairs. I watched as Gabriella motioned to sit down. In an instance, a shimmering silver tube reached up from the floor and flattened out into a circular surface, like a pin. It collected Gabriella and moulded itself to her shape. I shrugged and did the same. I was caught by a warm, surprisingly comfortable seat.

Faru sat down. Placing his elbows on the desk, he leaned forward. "I am assuming that this has something to do with Sophia's sudden recovery."

Gabriella and I exchanged a glance.

"Among other things," I said.

We told the Sage everything, taking it in turns. About how I'd been dreaming of The Sorrow and how we suspected that there was a Rogue in the base. We reiterated about me somehow healing Sophia through Gabriella. We finished with the crazy events that had happened at Moon's Edge. We told him what the voice had said, reading from the back of my handbook, where I'd written it down word for word.

Once we'd finished, Faru didn't say anything for a long time. He simply sat stroking his beard between his finger and thumb, like a philosopher musing on the meaning of life.

"This is all beginning to make sense," he said finally. "It appears everything that has happened is connected."

I sat up. "Connected how?"

"First of all, you must promise to remain calm."

I glanced at Gabriella, who frowned. "Okay, I promise."

"I already knew The Sorrow was tracking you."

My stomach lurched. "Wait, you *knew*? How could you know?"

He tapped two fingers against his temple. "When I merged minds with you, I saw everything, including the nightmares."

"How could you keep this from him? It's his life!" Gabriella half-screamed, ignoring her usual manners around the Sage.

Faru raised a hand. "Please settle down, Gabriella. I can understand your distress, but let me reassure you, it was not my intention to permanently hide the truth from Alexander, but merely to avoid unnecessary panic until I had a clear solution to the problem and more details about why he was being targeted."

My heart was pounding. I wanted to ask if he'd sealed the Veil. Or why he hadn't told the other Sages he knew for sure. But I couldn't - he'd know I'd been the one spying. Looking at Gabriella, I could tell she was thinking the same thing. Her expression was a mixture of horror and disbelief.

"Hopefully I can further alleviate your concern. The moment Rachel returned through the Veil, I used Fae magic to seal it. The Sorrow cannot travel through whilst that seal remains in place."

I breathed a sigh of relief. *It's done.*

"But there are other doorways. Surely it could just come through those," Gabriella countered, playing the game, even though we both knew the answer.

"We shall use our allies in Pandemonia to keep track of The Sorrow's movements. As The Sorrow approaches each section of the Veil, we shall seal it and open the previous, effectively creating a moveable barrier. It will never reach Earth."

"That's a good plan," I said and meant it. *I really hope it works.*

"I believe Hades sent The Sorrow to find you as a failsafe in case the Soliders of Sorrow were unable to kill you first."

"But why?" demanded Gabriella. "Why target Alex?"

"Because of what you heard in Moon's Edge."

"What exactly did we hear?" I asked.

331

Faru leaned forward and steepled his fingers together. "I believe you heard the voice of one of the Elementals."

Gabriella's mouth fell open. "You mean like Lafelei and Phoeton?"

"Yes."

I looked at them both in turn. "Does someone want to fill me in?"

"The four Elementals are the closest beings to Gods in Pandemonia and are worshipped as such by the Luminar," explained Faru. "They are as old as the world itself and can see past, present and future simultaneously. They are mostly benevolent and seek only to exist in peace, rarely ever making contact with the world. Dragons however – the equivalent beings worshiped as divine by the Umbra - were malevolent. They were among the first to pass through the Veil, wreaking havoc on this side. Eventually the Elementals intervened, joining together to block Dragon's foresight, allowing them to be slain by Chosen. After that, the Elementals retreated back to where they came from. But sometimes they release their words into the ether, and on certain occasions those words are picked up by those who can reach into the cracks between existence."

"Do you mean like a prophecy?" frowned Gabriella.

"I suppose you could call it that, yes. Because their words transcend time, they can often speak of events that have not yet occurred."

I suddenly remembered the tapestries I'd seen in the temple. "Wait a second...when Selene touched me, I saw an image of a giant face made from trees and grass and stuff, like that picture in the temple."

Faru nodded. "Then that confirms it. The words are Lafelei's, the earth Elemental. Hades has somehow managed to hear the words before we did."

"But what has that got to do with Alex?" asked Gabriella gesturing towards me.

Faru took in a deep breath. "Actually it involves both of you, something that I had discovered recently and has now been confirmed by Lafelei's words."

I could feel my heart pounding against my chest. "Go on."

332

"Firstly you must understand that each soul is completely unique, like a fingerprint. The energy it gives off carries its own frequency signature. That is how I am able to single out and communicate with individual people when I need to. However, I noticed something when I compared the two of yours together."

"What did you notice?"

"They are identical.

I frowned. *That doesn't make any sense.* "I don't understand. How is that possible?"

"When were you born Alexander?"

"Seventh of August, nineteen ninety-four," I answered. "Why?"

"And you Gabriella?"

"The same day," she admitted.

"At what time?"

"Twelve noon exactly."

I almost fell out of my seat. "That's when I was born!"

"But what does that mean, Sage Faru?" asked Gabriella.

He clapped his hands together. "You are twins."

The words hit me like a sledgehammer, shattering my world. I felt the colour drain from my face. I stared at Gabriella, who wore the same expression of utter shock that I was probably wearing. *No, that's not fair. No! No!*

"Not actual twins of course. That would be impossible. But rather your *souls* are twins." Faru scratched the back of his neck uncomfortably. "Or in simpler terms...you are quite literally soulmates."

Relief washed over me. I had to restrain myself from leaping over the desk and kissing the Sage right on the lips. I looked over at Gabriella, who appeared shell-shocked. *We're soulmates!* I wanted to jump up and do a victory dance. Now it all made sense. Why I felt drawn to her. Why I felt so much calmer when she was near me. Why I could feel all those strange vibrations when she was touched me. Why I was able to- "Wait. Does that have something to do with the fact that I was able to heal Sophia?" I asked aloud.

Faru nodded. "I believe so yes. I think that when near each other, your souls somehow act as amplifiers to one another. So

333

by touching Gabriella whilst she had a hand on Sophia, you were able to project your gift temporarily. I cannot be certain, but I would expect that the same would work with Gabriella's gift."

"But what does it mean?" she asked. "Us being soulmates?"

Faru shook his head. "That I simply do not yet know. All I do know is that you both act like magnets to one another. It is my belief that you were always destined to meet one another, and that a series of infinitesimal events transpired to make that meeting possible. I have never seen anything quite like this before. Only time will tell what it truly means."

"So Lafelei's words, about the twins-" Gabriella started.

"Are relative to you, I'm certain. However, Hades does not know that you are soul twins. All he knows is that the second twin, the one he believes to be a threat, had his Awakening this year. And since there has only been one…" he trailed off.

"You mean me," I said. "But how can I be a threat to Hades? I'm not a threat to anyone!"

"Only time will tell Alexander. But regardless, I believe this is why you are being targeted. However, only the three of us know that you are soul twins. And to keep at least Gabriella safe from The Sorrow, we must keep it that way."

Gabriella stood up. "To hell with that. I don't want Alex going through this alone. If we are soulmates, then that means we fight side by side."

I was touched by her passionate words, but I stood up too, shaking my head. "No way. I'm not letting you get involved in this. You've done enough for me." I lowered my voice, so only she could hear. "The other night, you asked me if I was going to protect you. This is how I can do that. By keeping what we know a secret, so you don't get targeted too."

Gabriella tried to protest but I refused to listen to her arguments. I turned back to Faru. "We'll keep it a secret."

He nodded. "Good. Then I believe we should draw the meeting to an end here. I will speak with the Coven and attempt to decipher more of Lafelei's words. I shall of course inform you if I discover anything further. In the meantime, carry on as normal and please try not to worry. I will ensure that The Sorrow never gets anywhere near you."

334

"Thank you Sage Faru," I said and saluted him. Gabriella did the same and started to leave.

"Alexander, may I have a brief word in private?" asked Faru. I looked at Gabriella and made an 'I don't know' face. She headed through the doors.

Faru pulled something from his robes and threw it to me. I caught it and opened my hand. I felt a jolt of panic as I stared at the marble I'd dropped in the temple.

"Please give that back to Delagio," he said. "And the next time you decide to spy on one of my meetings, do try and be a little more discreet." He smiled and then waved me out.

*

For the next few days, nothing much happened. Still, after the chaotic events of the previous week, my anxiety levels had set themselves at high alert and seemed confused by the lack of threat around me. Every little noise would cause me to snap to attention and I felt constantly on edge. The next time I saw Gabriella at school, I told her about it and she laughed, explaining that it was common for new Chosen to feel that way and that it would eventually subside.

I'd decided to stay at home to keep an eye on Mikey. Even though I knew there were Guardians watching the house constantly, I felt better being around – especially as I still wasn't sure about Dakin. Gabriella understood. We spent all of our free time at school together. Sometimes Tim would be with me, so we'd be forced to talk about normal, everyday things. When he wasn't, she filled me in on the happenings around the base. I learned that Sophia was getting stronger by the day and the doctors expected her to make a complete recovery by the end of the week. I was surprised to learn that Midnight had been in talks with Faru to transfer her to the Coven, even though it made Sophia seriously pissed with him.

I'd made the decision to tell Mikey everything - I just hadn't found the right opportunity. Not to mention the fact that he spent ninety per cent of his evenings hidden away in his bedroom with his new girlfriend. He only ever surfaced to grab food and drink and then retreated back into his love nest. I still hadn't met her, because whenever she slept over, she'd be gone by the time I got up. I didn't really care. I hadn't seen him so besotted in a long time. *As long as he's happy.*

On the Wednesday evening, I drove home determined to tell him everything. He'd been there for me when I felt scared and alone. The least I could do was tell him the truth. I settled the Audi into the driveway and climbed out. Leaning against the door, I took a deep breath. *Okay Alex, just walk in there and tell him. If he's with his girlfriend then demand he talks to you privately. You can do this.*

I jiggled the lock open and stepped through the door.

"Mikey?" I called out.

"In here bro," he replied.

I dumped my bag onto the sideboard and headed towards the blare of the television coming from the lounge.

Mikey was curled up on the sofa with Scarlett.

My keys fell from my hand as I stared at the scene. I blinked slowly, telling myself that my on-edge brain was playing tricks on me. But when I opened my eyes they were still huddled there, watching the TV. They looked up together.

"Hey Alex, how's things?"

"Uh...good," I said, swallowing.

"This is, Scarlett," Mikey said, gesturing towards the Vampire.

"I know."

"Oh right, have you two met?"

"She's uh...Gabriella's friend."

Mikey's eyebrows shot up. "Really?" He turned to the redhead. "You never told me that! Great, we can double date."

"Gabriella and I aren't dating," I said.

He rolled his eyes. "Ok mate, whatever."

"Um, Scarlett, can I talk to you for a second in the kitchen?"

"Sure," she said, detangling herself from Mikey. My brother shot me a suspicious glance, which I pretended not to notice.

"What the hell are you doing?" I hissed when we were alone in the kitchen.

Scarlett hopped into a sitting position on the counter. "Watching a really bad film. You know, your brother has awful taste in movies."

"You know what I mean! Why are you *here?*"

She shrugged. "Protection."

"I know that. But why aren't you outside with the others?" I clapped a hand over my forehead. "Oh sweet lord, this is what Faru meant by special protection!" I pointed towards the lounge. "Does he know?"

She shook her head, a flicker of fire. "Not yet."

"You can't be around him! What about if you get…urges?"

She gave a devilish grin. "You little pervert!"

"Stop messing about, Scarlett!" I growled.

The Bloodling pointed to her eyes with a slender finger. "Look at the colour Alex, bright as a new coin. Do you really think I'm stupid enough to hang around a human hungry? Plus I've been taught how to control the urge well. I'd never harm him."

I stormed up and down the kitchen. "Great, Faru forced a Vampire to seduce my brother."

"Whoa, hold on - no." She used a chalky hand to stop me pacing. "It isn't like that at all. My mission was to become part of Mikey's life, that's it. To keep an eye on him – especially when he wasn't at home, in case someone tried to kidnap him to get to you. How I did that was my choice."

"But he thinks you're dating!"

"We sort of…are."

"Oh god!" I leaned over the work surface, placing my hands in my head. "This can't be happening."

"Alex, I…like him." The words seemed to struggle from her mouth, like she wasn't used to confessing.

"He's fifteen!" I barked, lifting my head up.

"So? I'm only sixteen! Well…technically."

"But you hardly know him!" I retorted. "You met him what, a week ago? You can't like someone that soon. It's ridiculous!"

"Was it ridiculous for you to like Gabriella so soon?"

I tried to respond, but had nothing to say. *Seriously, is it stamped on my forehead or something?*

Scarlett jumped of the counter and marched close to me. "Look, you want Mikey protected right? I'm protecting him. What happens between us beyond that is *none* of your business.

337

Christ, you think because I'm a Vampire I have to sacrifice my life? I may be dead, but I still have feelings!"

The sound of a throat clearing made me jerk my head around. Mikey was standing in the doorway. "Does someone want to tell me what the hell is going on?" he said.

Scarlett and I exchanged a glance.

"You better take a seat."

*

"I can't believe you're a *Vampire*," Mikey whispered, his back pressed against the kitchen cupboards. Scarlett let her fangs slide back into the thick membrane at the top of her gums. Even after I'd explained everything it had still taken a demonstration to convince him that we weren't winding him up. It was understandable - what sane person would believe it unless they saw it first hand?

"So I was just an assignment for you?"

I could see the hurt in his eyes. I imagined it was how I'd looked when I'd thought the same thing about Gabriella. It was the first time I'd ever seen him react emotionally to a girl in his life.

"At first," she admitted. "But then I started to like you."

"Why?"

"What?"

"Why do you like me?"

"Because you don't take anything too seriously and you're just happy to be alive - I love that about you. It reminds me of how I used to be…before everything went to shit."

Mikey looked at me and then back to Scarlett. "Wait…are you like...dead?" he asked.

"Sort of. Yes."

He pulled a face. "B-but we…oh god!" He ran to the sink and threw up.

"Perfect," said Scarlett.

The Bloodling moved away from us with the lithe speed of a wildcat. She wrenched opened the back door and I watched as she vaulted onto the roof. The cold chill rolled in behind her. I walked over and shut the door.

338

"I think you offended her," I said, keeping my voice low.

Mikey was still rinsing his mouth. He spat water into the sink. "Offended *her*?" He wiped his hands on the towel. "I was the idiot tricked into falling for a bloody Vampire!"

I raised my eyebrows. "Falling? Hold on…you really like her don't you?"

He shrugged, but his face gave the secret away.

"You do."

"Okay fine. I've never felt this way about a girl before. She's just so intelligent and fun and sexy and great at…" He balked and put up a finger.

I walked over and put my hand on his shoulder. "Listen, Mikey. Now you know what she is and what I'm a part of, you have a choice."

"Do I?"

I nodded. "I can get Gabriella to make you forget all of this. She can do that. You can carry on none the wiser. Scarlett will still protect you - but from a distance. Or…you can chose to accept everything, at least for now. Hopefully without puking," I added with a weak smile.

My heart hammered as I waited for his response. He clenched his jaw and let out a deep sigh.

"I need to talk to her first," he said pointing upwards.

"Come on," I said and opened the door. He followed me outside. In the unruly backyard, nature had regained control. Gardening had never been a family strong point. The one trait we all shared. A rusted lawnmower - promised restoration and use by John - lay abandoned by the dilapidated shed. The grass reached our shins and weeds strangled their way around most of the winter flowers, which lay dotted around, distributed by nature alone.

Moving over to the overgrown patio, I crouched down. "Hold on tight."

Mikey grabbed onto my shoulders and I sprang into the air, landing on the roof. Scarlett was sitting at the other end, watching the setting sun. As we neared, I could see that her eyes were damp and the corners of her mouth were turned down at the ends.

Mikey noticed too.

339

He sat down next to her and there was silence for a few moments. "Sun not a problem?" he said eventually, pointing towards the sinking orb.

"No," she replied. "Not for us *dead* ones anyway."

Mikey grimaced, but persevered. As their conversation continued, I made my way back down, wanting to give them privacy. I smiled as I saw him stretch his fingers towards hers and she took them, curling them into her own.

*

I was lying on my bed, reading the last part of the hand guide when I heard someone knock on my door.

"Come in."

The door nudged open and Mikey stepped in, a smile wide on his face. I set the book down on the table, using Dad's picture as a marker. He sat down on the edge of the bed and took a deep breath. I could hear Scarlett pottering around downstairs, clattering pans about and opening the fridge.

"So," he said.

"So."

"So my brother is a superhero whose job is to protect Earth from monsters from a parallel world."

I gave a slow shrug. "In a nutshell, yeah."

Mikey nodded. "You could probably use a brother to talk to about all that then."

I sat up. "You mean…"

"I've decided that I want to be part of your new life, yeah. Even if that does mean being afraid of the dark until I die," he added with a grin.

Inside of me, something released. A tension I wasn't aware of slipped away. I hadn't realised, but I'd desperately wanted to hear Mikey say those words. *Needed* him to. Before I knew what I was doing, I'd grabbed him into a hug.

"Thank you," I whispered.

He patted me on the back. "That's what brothers are for right?"

We let each other go and I settled back against the headboard. "And Scarlett?" I said, gesturing towards the door.

He raked a thumbnail along his eyebrow and made a noise with his throat. "Ha, that was a bit trickier. I think puking in reference to your girlfriend is a general no-no, even if they are a Vampire. But, she forgave me eventually. I think I'm going to try and get used to it. I mean my bird is a Vampire. How cool is that? And besides, it's not like she's *dead* dead. Although she is pretty cold. I mean this one time-"

I put up a hand. "Enough said."

He laughed. "Anyway, I want her as my protection. I want her around full stop. See where it goes." He pulled a face. "Wow, who'd of thought I'd give a crap about a girl this much? Anyway if it doesn't work out, I still have my solid big bro to look after me don't I?" He gave me a light punch on the arm and stood back up. "You know, Scarlett ate food I cooked her, even though it makes her feel ill. How sweet is that? Anyway, she's offered to cook for us both tonight. Apparently she's quite good. Used to be a kitchen maid or something when she was still human."

"Sounds great."

"Okay cool, I'll go and tell her you're in then." He motioned to leave.

"Mikey?"

He turned to face me.

"I'm really glad you know."

"Me too, bro."

He vanished from the room. A second later, his head reappeared in the doorway. "Oh, you know you're a badass and everything now?"

"Yeah?"

"I bet you're still crap at football!"

I jumped from the bed and he sprinted away down the hallway, laughing his head off. I lay back down, chuckling to myself. Picking up the guide, I carried on where I'd left off, reading a passage about Lamiae; rare Umbra that could send their ethereal forms through the Veil and possess humans.

My phone rang, vibrating against the desk. I set the book down in my lap and grabbed it. As soon as I saw Gabriella's name on the screen, butterflies filled my stomach.

"Hey, what's up?" I said pressing the receiver to my ear.

The sound of rushing wind and traffic filled the receiver. I could barely hear Gabriella's voice. "Are you at home?" she shouted over the roaring noise.

"Yeah, why?"

"I'm on my way to you now. Rachel just called me. The Coven has picked up an attack at a local bar, happening in a few hours."

I jumped up, spilling the book onto the floor. Adrenaline coursed through my body.

"This is it, Alex. Your first real mission."

27

The Black Tap was a bar for Pandemonians. Gabriella filled me in as we sped along the Nexus, heading for Balham. Apparently, illegal bars existed all over the world. Places where Pandemonians could drink and socialise in peace, away from the watchful eye of the HASEA. They were always moving about and were hard to track down. The Alliance usually chose to ignore their existence, unless any rules were broken.

Chosen were not welcome.

Gabriella assured me that as long as we kept calm, our adapted Kapre belts would make it difficult for any of the punters to identify us.

The doors of the elevator rolled open and we stepped out into a foul smelling alleyway. I turned to see a solid brick wall slide back into place. The only clue that it was an entrance to the Nexus was an almost imperceptible cross with two semi circles either side, carved onto a brick at the bottom. I guessed it was also the button to call the elevator.

The whole of Orion was in attendance, minus the recovering Sophia. We were all well armed. I wore the Crimson Twins low over my back, concealed underneath a specially designed trench coat. A gun was holstered to my Kapre belt, loaded with multipurpose stun rounds made from a cocktail of iron, silver and wood filings. Next to the gun hung a few pairs of handcuffs, lined with various Apatrope materials. A tiny receiver had been fitted in my ear, and an inconspicuous bracelet acted as the microphone. The others carried a mixture of stakes, guns and swords. The only exception was Delagio, who had a single silver dagger and a pouch full of various marbles.

The sky was overcast, the weather thick and oppressive. Thunder rumbled in the distance. It looked like there was going to be a storm.

Gabriella squeezed the side of her bracelet. I heard her voice deep inside my head, as if she were my own internal narrative. "Can everyone hear me?"

We all nodded.

"Okay. This should be pretty straightforward. Humans are going to enter a Pandemonian bar within the hour. They are going to get attacked. We stop that attack. Any harm to a human by a Pandemonian or hybrid constitutes a violation of the treaty, so agents will come in after we're done and shut the place down. I would prefer to avoid a mess if I can, so let's try for arrests. Unless they engage us directly, in which case anything goes. Trojan are on standby if we need them. Is everyone clear?"

Everyone agreed.

"Okay, activate your belts," commanded Gabriella. I watched as everyone in the team apart from Rachel pressed the button on the side of the buckle. A shimmer of light rolled up their body. Rather than disappear, a silvery hue surrounded them, like an aura. *Guess the invisibility part does only work on humans.*

I pressed the button.

The main street was crowded with people. Businessmen smooth-talking on mobile phones, harassed mothers trailing kids, and teenagers in hoodies all battled their way along the pavements. As we moved forward, each person stepped around us as if we were obstacles in their path, but didn't give it a second thought.

A multi-storey car park stood at the top of the road. We entered at the ground level and followed the ramp down several stories. At the bottom, only a few cars were dotted around. We ran forward and crouched behind a white van plagued with rust. Gabriella leaned around and pointed towards a door at the end marked with the words: **Maintenance, staff only**.

"According to Crows Nest, that's where The Black Tap is."

Crows Nest was the official name of the command centre I'd seen shortly before the Rahuman fight. I'd learned that it was where non-combat teams and Data Techs – the humans I'd seen in white coats - provided logistical support to hunter squads.

I looked to where Gabriella was pointing. The door looked so normal; it was hard to imagine what supposedly lay behind it.

"Okay, Midnight, you wait here and keep an eye out for the victims. If I call, you teleport in ready for a fight," Gabriella ordered.

"No worries."

"Del and Rachel, you go in first. Get a drink and find a seat. Use a Biomote to do a head count. Alex and I will follow after and cover the entrance. No one act until I give the order. Okay?"

Everybody nodded. Delagio stood up and offered out his hand to Rachel. "Ready honeybunch?" he said with a wink. She rolled her eyes and took his hand. Like a happy couple, they strolled up to the door. It opened and they disappeared inside.

We waited for what seemed like an eternity. Finally, Gabriella turned to me. "Okay, Alex. Are you ready for this?"

I breathed in deep. My nerves were tingling with anticipation. "I think so."

Midnight patted me on the back. "Don't worry mate. You'll do fine."

Gabriella encircled her arm around my waist. I draped mine around her shoulder and together we stepped out from the protection of the van. Each footstep we took towards the door made my heart beat a fraction faster. "What if someone recognises us?" I said in a low voice.

"They won't, as long as we stay calm and keep the belts switched on."

The sound of Gabriella's knock was loud and hollow. A few seconds later the door opened an inch and a pair of silver eyes stared at us. My stomach clenched. I tried to look as nonchalant as possible as Gabriella gave a slight nod. The gesture was mirrored and the door opened. The bouncer - a large Mexican looking Vampire with a sizeable white Mohawk - moved out of our way and we walked inside.

For a temporary bar, The Black Tap was impressive. Red lanterns cast a rich crimson glow over everything. The bar itself had been carved from black wood. A lush carpet stretched from corner to corner. To the right were several booths - with leather seats the colour of set cream. A magnificent mirror with a flamboyant gold frame filled an entire wall, the corners of which had been sculpted to resemble Dragon heads. On the furthest wall a fire crackled in a stone hearth, surrounded by sofas and

345

leather beanbags. In the middle stood a couple of pool tables, lined with black upholstery. Hidden speakers played chilled out music with a seductive bassline.

The bar was quite busy. Like at the feast, clusters of Pandemonians stood chatting and drinking odd substances from glasses. In one booth, an Oni was laughing at something a Vampire had said. His open mouth resembled a Venus flytrap waiting to snap.

Behind the bar was a barman and women. The woman was moving in little dipping motions. As we approached I realised that this was because she was hovering, silvery wings beating behind her. The barman - who had long, wavy hair - came over and smiled. I hated to admit it, but he was very good looking. It seemed to radiate from him. His eyes were like polished gold and he used them to stare at Gabriella with a look that could only have been lust.

"What can I get you, sweetness?" he said, ignoring me completely and speaking only to her. His voice was the vocal equivalent of stroking velvet. It took me only a few more seconds to understand what he was. *Incubus.*

Gabriella looked at me.

"I'll have a beer," I said.

"One Blackheart beer and a vodka on the rocks please."

The barman winked at her and set to work. Using a metal opener, he flicked the cap off my beer and slapped it, sending it flying expertly into the bin. He slammed the bottle down in front of me and then proceeded to flair with the vodka bottle. He spun the neck between his fingers, rolled it along his arm and flipped it up with his inside elbow, caught it and then spun it on the flat of his hand, all without his eyes never leaving Gabriella. I could feel the irritation growing in my stomach as I watched him show off. He flipped the bottle into the air once again. Before he could grab it, Gabriella snapped her hand out like a snake. When she lowered it, the bottle was still spinning on her middle finger, aimed at the bartender.

"Sorry, but I'm *really* thirsty," she said with a fake smile. "Could we save the theatrics for someone else?"

God, I love this girl.

The bartender's cheeks flushed red and his good looks seemed to diminish, as if they were connected to a dimmer switch. He continued making the drink in silence, only speaking again to ask for the money. His voice had lost its silky tones, sounding rough and grumpy instead. Once paid, we settled down in one of the booths near the entrance.

"Most Incubi are like machines – always trying it on," Gabriella said. "At least Succubi show a bit of class. They annoy the hell out of me." She made a disgusted face and took a long sip of her vodka. I looked down at my beer. The label depicted a Skinshifter standing over a fearful, bleeding man, and the word *Blackheart* was printed underneath in bold letters. I peered inside the bottle. The beer was the colour of Guinness. I took a swig and coughed as it seized my chest.

Gabriella laughed. "Strong isn't it? Made in Pandemonia. You'll get used to it."

In a corner table, Rachel and Delagio were canoodling as if the world around them didn't exist, so I was surprised when the kinesist's voice appeared in my ear. "Thirty-two souls includin' the bar staff. We may need Trojan for this one."

Gabriella pretended to rub her arm, letting her pinkie activate the bracelet. "Understood," she whispered. "Let's see how this plays out first."

"Okay, boss."

I leaned forward, rolling the bottle between my hands. "So what's the deal with those two anyway?"

Gabriella smiled. "They have a pretty volatile relationship. On and off." She took another sip of her vodka and crushed a bit of ice between her teeth. "Mainly off."

I glanced over again. Rachel was running her hand along the nape of Del's neck, smiling as he whispered something into her ear. Either they were on again, or just very good at their jobs. I couldn't tell.

"So what do we do now?"

"We wait for Midnight's call. If Sophia was here, she'd be able to use magic to sense the troublemaker. She's really skilled in the art of the ether for her age, most likely to do with her being a Chosen as well as a Witch. But since she's not we're going to have to play this one step by step. Although my money's on the silver fox to your three o'clock."

I glanced casually over towards the fireplace. A solitary Bloodling dressed in an expensive suit lounged on one of the sofas. He rolled a tumbler of blood between his fingers. It was mostly empty, but his eyes still seemed dull. His grey hair had been combed back over his head and he had a shadow of matching grizzle around his jaw. I put him in his early forties when he was turned – although god only knew how old he was now. I watched as he prodded a tongue gently at his own fangs. His demeanour was one of self-assured arrogance.

We waited - me taking slow sips of my beer, trying to get used to the harsh taste. As we sat, listening to the slow thump of bass that accompanied the chilled music, I let my thoughts wander.

"I was meaning to ask," I said after a while. "What's the deal with school, do I have to leave now or what?"

"Not if you don't want to. The Alliance encourages life outside of the job. You just need to be available when they need you."

"Good to know." I smiled. "You know, if you'd have told me a few weeks ago that I could leave that social hellhole, I'd have been out of there like a flash. But now...I'm kind of starting to enjoy it. People are nice to me, no more bullying..." I trailed off. Something I hadn't mentioned occurred to me and I felt disgusted with myself that I'd barely given it a thought. "What happened to TJ in the end?"

Gabriella set up straight in her chair and cleared her throat. "He's fine. When we got to him, he was on his way out, but a booster brought him back. They are pretty dangerous for humans in general, but we needed to take the chance. We got lucky. After he'd healed I made sure he didn't remember a thing."

"Where is he now?"

"I charmed him into changing to a different college. I think it will do him good to get away from Terry."

I stared down at my bottle. "I'm glad he's okay. What I did to him..."

"Was his fault, Alex. No one is denying that you went way over the top, but that was because of your Awakening. He came into that alleyway with a *baseball bat*. Don't forget that."

We fell into silence for a few minutes. I let everything that had happened so far wash over me. It seemed so much. I thought about how much of a contrast the world I'd become part of was to school, with its boring lessons, sports matches and winter balls. The last part snagged stuck in brain.

Gabriella took a slow sip of her drink and surveyed me over the glass.

"You look like you have something else on your mind."

I tore a piece of the label from the bottle and folded it into a little square. "Well there was something I'd been meaning to ask you." Inside my negative internal voice tried to stop me speaking, but I forced it away.

"You can ask me anything, you know that."

I cleared my throat, not moving my gaze from the square of paper resting between my finger and thumb. "Well, I don't know if you'd even be interested, but well…there's this sixth form ball next Friday. It's probably a bit stupid…but I…was wondering if-"

Midnight's voice filled my head, cutting me off midsentence. "Look sharp guys, three loud arse chicks coming your way. Think this is it."

"Okay, Midnight. Del, Rachel, you get that?"

"We got it boss."

"Good. First port of call is to get them the hell out before anything happens. Then we can leave without any drama and everyone's happy. If not, we wait for the attack to start and act before any damage is done."

"Waitin on your word, Huntmaster," said Midnight and the earpiece fell silent.

Gabriella placed her hand on mine for a split second. "Let's come back to that conversation later." She stood up and motioned for me to follow. We made our way over to the bar and ordered another round of drinks. I pretended to take a swig and then settled the bottle on the counter and waited for the new arrivals. Not long afterwards, the sound of giggling burst from the doorway and a group of three girls stumbled into the bar. They were all dressed up ready for a night out and clearly drunk.

"I can't believe it," a blonde one said.

"They wasn't messin' about," a short one with pink heels answered. "Proper secret this place!"

"It's wicked!" slurred a third with dyed black hair and a lip piercing.

Looking around I could see that every pair of eyes were on the girls. There were murmurs from the occupants of the booths and I saw the ones who couldn't pass for human shrink instantly from sight and disappear through a door hidden in the shadows at the back. The barwoman's wings retracted into her back with a feathering sound.

The girls staggered over to the bar. One put her hands in the air and shouted *'wooooo'* at the top of her lungs. I could feel the mood in the room growing hostile. The Incubus barman slid uneasily over to them and I noticed him glance over to the same man we were keeping an eye on. When he served them, he didn't try and use his charms. Not that it made any difference to the girls.

"Oh my god you're well fit!" cooed the blonde one.

"Have a drink with us," said the one with the lip ring.

The barman didn't answer, busying himself with preparing the drinks they'd ordered instead. Around me I could feel the room stir. More Pandemonians started to leave, shaking their heads in disgust. Only a dozen or so remained.

Gabriella edged her way over to the girls, armed with a winning smile.

"Hi girls", she beamed. They turned around and frowned as if trying to stare through fog. One by one they noticed her.

"Wow, you're so pretty!" said pink heels.

"Thanks. Looks like you're having a good night."

"It's been quality so far," said blondie.

"It would be better if hottie over here gave me his number. What do you say babe?" said lip piercing.

The barman cringed and glanced over at the Vampire again.

Gabriella carried on talking, her voice taking on a diplomatic tone. "Listen girls, I don't want to ruin your night or anything, but this bar is actually private. I think it might be better if you enjoyed your night somewhere else."

The girl's demeanour changed in a split second. Pink heels folded her arms and rested on her back foot, expression full of attitude. "Well the bouncer let us in so it can't be that private, *actually*." The other girls chimed in with 'yeah.'

"And who do you think you are, comin over here and tellin us to leave?" piped up lip ring. "Why don't *you* leave?"

Gabriella raised her hands in an appeasing way. "Girls I'm not trying to start an argument. I just think you should go and have fun somewhere else."

"Not a chance, bitch," said blondie.

Gabriella stiffened.

"I see what it is," slurred lip piercing. "You want to have all the guys in here to yourself!"

Pink heels leaned over. "And what are you wearin? Mate, the Matrix isn't real yeah?"

The girls all burst into a savage laughter. I felt a sudden temptation to march Gabriella out of the bar and leave the vile girls to their fate. But as grudging as I felt, I knew they had to be protected.

The atmosphere in the bar was now as oppressive as the weather had been outside. I could hear the patrons starting to grumble. A Bloodseeker crushed a glass in his hand.

Gabriella reached backwards for my hand. I knew what she was going to do. I closed mine around hers.

"Listen to me now," she commanded, her voice raising and taking on a sharp tone. *"I want you to turn around-"*

"Stop the music!" shouted the Vampire in the suit. The bartenders looked warily over at him and then one passed through a door. A second later the music cut off. The man unwound himself from the seat and poured his drink onto the fire, causing the flames to flare angrily.

I unbuttoned my coat and held it closed with one hand, ready to go for my weapons. Gabriella moved out of the Vampire's way. He walked over and stared at the girls one by one.

"Who are you?" lip piercing girl asked, making a sucking sound with her teeth.

"Who am I?" he growled, curling his fists into balls. "I'm Malachi, the god damn owner of this bar. Who the hell are you?' He emphasised each word, pointing a finger at each girl in turn. They shuddered.

"I think that maybe we should go," said pink heels to her friends.

"Now that's the best idea you've had all night," he said, his voice taking on a calm, acidic tone. "Unfortunately it's no longer that simple. You came into my bar through a fatal error by my doorman." He cast a menacing look at the bouncer, who shifted uncomfortably. "You inappropriately propositioned a member of my bar staff. Your very presence forced my...shyer customers away and your ugly behaviour offended others into leaving. And worst of all, you had the bare-faced cheek to insult another to her face!" He gestured towards Gabriella.

Well that backfired.

"You are so disgustingly human," he added with a hiss.

"So human?" said lip piercing, her voice growing smaller. "W-what do you mean?"

The Vampire didn't answer. Instead he took a step closer. The girls moved towards the door, but after a glance from his boss, the bouncer blocked it with his large frame.

"I've tried so hard to accept your species…after all I used to be one. But every single time I try, something happens that reminds me why I hate you all so much. I'll have to move locations. But it will be worth it to rid the world of three more vermin."

The girls screamed and scrambled for the exit. They clawed at the doorman, trying to escape, but he didn't even flinch at their efforts.

"Let them go," warned Gabriella.

Malachi turned around and stared at her. "Who do you think you are, talking down to me in my own bar?" His eyebrows swooped down over his eyes and he leaned forward, his nose turned up like he had smelled something sour. "What…are you anyway?"

Oh crap.

One of the girls let out a hysterical scream. Malachi gave a predatory smile and turned to address the bar. "Bloodseekers and Bloodlings listen up. You've got some drinks coming your way. On the house!"

Some of the Vampires laughed and rose to their feet.

Gabriella squeezed her bracelet. "Now!"

Everything happened at once. Malachi charged for the blonde girl just as we all cast off our jackets. I went to draw the Crimson Twins, hesitated and then opted for the stun gun instead. Gabriella ran for the owner and pulled him away - the points of his teeth millimetres from the girl's throat. She dragged him back by his neck and threw him over the bar. The Incubus had to dive out of the way as Malachi came flying past. He collided with the spirits shelf, smashing bottles and sending glass tinkling to the floor.

The barman's eyes went wide. "Chosen!" he yelled, pointing at me. There were roars of indignation as the camouflaging effect of the belts became redundant. A few more patrons scrambled through the back door and others stood up to join the fight. A gaunt looking Bloodling charged for me. I aimed the gun and squeezed the trigger. The bullet hit him in the chest, lifting him right off his feet and sending him careering through a table and chairs. He made a groaning sound and then passed out.

I watched as Gabriella rescued two of the girls behind her. She tried to help the remaining pierced lip girl, but the bouncer sent her spiralling to the floor with a backhand swat. He grabbed the screaming girl's hair and wrenched her head back. His fangs slid down.

There was no time to do anything.

Without warning, all of the oxygen drained from the room. My lungs felt constricted, like an elastic band had been wrapped around them - I literally couldn't catch my breath. Around me, those who needed air were gasping. The bouncer stopped his attack and looked around, confused. The pressure in the air grew stronger and both my ears popped. Then the space in front of the bouncer shimmered and became Midnight.

Whoa.

He slipped two wooden stakes from his pouch and drove them through the bouncer's kneecaps, pinning him to the door. The Vampire screamed in agony and the girl escaped his grip.

353

Midnight grabbed and flung her towards the others. Then he smashed his forehead into the bouncer's nose. There was a sickening crunch and the Vampire's head flopped into his chest.

Something hit me hard from behind - the impact knocking all the air from my lung - and I stumbled forward. I dropped the gun and it bounced underneath a table. I turned just in time to see a furious Bloodseeker before he drove a fist as solid as a brick into the side of my face. White hot pain seared across my temple and down into my jaw. I dodged the next punch and pivoted on the spot, smacking the Vampire on the back of the head with my elbow. He grunted and stumbled a few steps. I sprung forward and rugby tackled him to the ground. Pinning his arms down, I grit my teeth and repeatedly punched his face. When he looked woozy, I reached my hands over my shoulders and drew both swords. His eyes went wide when he saw them. I scissored them across his neck.

"I suggest you stay still."

I heard a yell and looked up. A female Skinshifter had flung Rachel over a table and was now shedding her skin. Before she could complete the transformation, Delagio sent her flying with a helicopter kick to the chest. The half emerging beast yelped as she glanced off a pillar. Delagio turned towards the pool tables and extended his hands. The pool balls shuddered and swept off the table towards him. They started spiralling around his body in rotating loops, faster and faster, until they were a blur. Then he thrust his hands out in the direction of the dazed shifter. The balls shot out like bullets from a machine gun, slamming into the creature with dull thuds. She howled and collapsed unconscious to the floor.

I sensed the Incubus before he reached me. I turned to see him charge, wielding a kitchen blade. My instincts took over and I swept out with one of the swords. A loud hiss, like burning oil filled the room. We both watched as the hand - still clutching the knife - separated from his arm. It spiralled through the air and landed on the table, tip of the blade burying itself in the wood. Despite the gruesomeness of it, I almost laughed - it was like something from a cheesy horror movie. The Incubus let out a bloodcurdling scream and sank to his knees. Black smoke rolled from the edge of the sword. I looked at the Incubus's

354

wound and saw that it had been somehow cauterised by the blade. Midnight moved over to him, looked at his handcuffs, shrugged and then put the barman into a sleeper hold until he passed out.

The rest of the team carried on fighting until they were the only ones left standing. I ordered the Bloodseeker to turn over and snapped a set of handcuffs on him. His skin sizzled where the oak lining bit into his skin. After a moment it took effect and he became subdued. Midnight dragged him over to the middle of the room, where all of our attackers lay in a row, cuffed and silent.

Gabriella leapt over the bar, landing in a crouch next to Malachi. I heard a click and she stood, hoisting the dazed Vampire up by his collar. His hands were cuffed behind his back. He groggily snapped his teeth at her, before his head fell forward to his chest. I stood up and breathed out hard.

The girls were whimpering, huddled together in the corner. Scared witless, but unharmed. I scanned the bar, surveying the damage. It was only then that I saw the bathroom door open and a familiar figure creep out and attempt to move through the shadows unnoticed.

Dakin.

What's a Guardian doing in an illegal bar?

He didn't seem to notice that I'd spotted him. He slipped silently through the doorway.

"Ella, come here," I said.

Gabriella set Malachi down next to the others and headed over.

"What's up?"

"You don't need me now do you?" I asked.

She raised an eyebrow. "Well no, but where are you going?"

I was already heading towards the back of the bar. "No time to explain. Trust me."

I slipped through the exit.

28

I shadowed Dakin as quietly as I could. The escape route led to a dusty corridor system. Emergency lights brightened the area into a sickly yellow hue. The walls may have been white once, but now were thick with grime.

I watched as Dakin rounded a corner and waited for a few seconds before following. I kept low to the ground, trailing him around and down a dizzying number of corners and passages. As I turned into yet another corridor, the acrid stench of urine and blood attacked my nose, making me gag. Ahead, a set of metal doors had been wrenched open - presumably by the escaping punters. They led to a ramp, which Dakin scrambled up. Keeping my footsteps as light as I could manage, I followed after him.

A Hivemind screamed at me.

I had to clamp a hand over my mouth to keep from crying out. I scrambled away and covered my face to protect myself from the inevitable attack. When it didn't come, I opened my eyes and realised that the creature was locked inside a giant cage set into the wall. It stared at me from behind the wire mesh. I noticed dozens more behind it, drool dripping from their teeth and forming puddles on the floor. Again they screeched at me, but stayed motionless, staring with slick black eyes, unable to attack without permission. I shuddered.

Hurrying past, I headed up the ramp and out into the muggy night. I found myself in an industrial area that I vaguely recognised.

We were back in Chapter Hill.

All around me were warehouses. Dakin jumped onto the roof of one up ahead. I waited a few seconds and then followed, praying he wouldn't see me.

Where the hell is he going?

All I knew was that I didn't trust him. Rachel and the others may have vouched for him, but the way he kept glaring at me, it was more than just dislike – it was hate.

356

He vaulted from roof to roof and I followed as stealthily as possible. After a while, my eyesight adjusted to the darkness and trailing Dakin became easier. I hid behind air vents and brickwork to keep from being spotted. But Dakin never even glanced in my direction. *He thinks he got away unnoticed.* Even so, I wished I could stop my heartbeat the way I'd held my breath, in case he heard its frantic drumming.

The Bloodling dropped down onto street level and slunk towards an unassuming warehouse near the back. Without warning, he checked over his shoulder. I dived behind an old skip. It felt like a hummingbird was beating its wings against my chest. A cold sweat broke out on my forehead as I waited for him to come and confront me.

Nothing happened.

I leaned out. Dakin was still looking warily in other directions for signs of pursuers. Then he curled up his fist and banged in a complicated rhythm on a metal door. A few seconds later it was opened and he disappeared inside.

I counted to thirty and then slipped from my hiding place, running low towards the warehouse. I pressed myself against the wall and was just about to leap onto the roof, when I noticed a small symbol painted in white on the metal by my foot.

The Eye of the Abyss.

Fear gripped my chest. Suddenly I wished I'd brought the rest of Orion with me. *Not this…I didn't expect this.*

I took a deep breath to calm my nerves. I knew I couldn't turn away now; I needed to find out exactly what Dakin was up to.

Vaulting up, I wrapped my hands over the warehouse roof edge and hoisted myself carefully onto it. I scanned around in the darkness and found what I was hoping for. Light shone out into the inky night from a section of skylight windows. I ran to them and lowered myself onto my stomach. The glass was filthy and I had to use my t-shirt to clear a little patch in the grime before I could peer through.

The window looked into a large room. The walls had been painted with dozens of the SOS symbols. They glistened in thick black - little tears of paint - seeping down from the main art. At one end were dozens of racks, filled with a multitude of vicious weapons. At the other end stood a plinth, which had been fashioned into a rudimentary stage. Standing in front of it was a large crowd, dressed in red, hooded cloaks. From my angle I could just about make out their faces. There were all manner of species. Some I'd seen before, including Vampires, Oni and Skinshifters, as well as some I hadn't but recognised from the pages of my handbook, like Imps and Goblins. But the one that looked the most terrifying dwarfed even the tallest Oni. It had oily black skin and a goat-like face. Two black horns protruded from its forehead and curved into twin spikes that arched above its head. I'd heard Tyler mention them once and read about the species recently in the handbook.

Devil.

I kept scanning the room, taking in each face to see if there was any I recognised. None of them looked familiar, which provided a small amount of comfort. I'd met most of the Guardians at the joining feast, which meant that the only Rogue appeared to be Dakin. That thought evaporated when the Devil stepped forward and for split second I saw a face I couldn't mistake. The birdlike features. The pale skin.

Sylvia.

I grit my teeth together in anger. This woman represented the Coven. She passed on our missions. If she was corrupt then the entire chain was corrupt. The bitch could make us walk into a trap any time she wanted.

A door opened and Dakin entered the room. He had changed into the same cloak as the other members. He merged with the crowd and I lost him amongst the sea of red.

All those in attendance were talking amongst themselves. Their noise blended into a single roar of sound and even with my improved hearing, I couldn't single any of them out. One by one, they stopped talking and turned to face the stage. I craned my neck to see what they were looking at. A man stood on the plinth, hand raised to silence the Soldiers of Sorrow.

The man was Sage Asmund.

I couldn't believe what I was seeing. Sage Asmund wasn't a disgruntled hybrid or Pandemonian or even a pissed off Witch. *He's the leader of an entire base!* I finally understood how much the HASEA was suffering. The corruption was everywhere, like a cancer that could not be stopped. A sick feeling rose in the pit of my stomach and it took all of my strength not to vomit.

Sage Asmund raised a second arm to join the first and complete silence descended on the room. "My fellow Soldiers of Sorrow," he announced. "Before we get to the reason I have called you all here tonight, Brother Dakin has brought it to my attention that he narrowly avoided detection whilst trying to recruit new brothers and sisters in the Black Tap. Yet again, the HASEA fiends swooped in, raining down their bigoted oppression of the superior races. And for what? Humans?"

There was a roar of indignation from the crowd.

"Well no more!" Asmund grew louder. "They think they can do what they want without repercussions. Where was the justice when their newest recruit - the one they put their misguided faith in - killed Brother Dakin's maker?"

There were more cries and fists pumped in to the air.

I froze. *Rahuman was Dakin's maker? No wonder he hates me!*

Around me there were more roars of anger. Bloodseekers hissed and shifters struggled to keep their human form intact.

"The HASEA is nothing more than a bunch of human lovers who have made weak Pandemonians and hybrids roll over like faithful dogs!" However, mark my words! Tomorrow evening that changes!" He paused. "Tomorrow The Sorrow comes."

The room hushed.

I leaned in further, pressing my nose against the glass. My heart hammered in my chest. I prayed no one looked up.

Sage Asmund pointed a finger at the crowd. "So far, none of you have managed to complete the simple task of killing one solitary little Chosen. But it is out of your hands now. Hades has spoken. The boy is to be left for The Sorrow."

There were murmurs of disapproval from the crowd. The Devil let out a guttural growl that drowned out everything, like a vocal tidal wave.

Asmund looked at the beast warily. "Do not let yourselves become angry brothers and sisters, you all still have so much you can give. This is what we have been waiting for. Why some have pretended to be faithful to the Alliance and others have remained hidden for so long. As I speak, The Sorrow lies in wait, unable to pass through the Veil. But its tracking is complete. The boy cannot run or hide. Tomorrow evening, we will attack the Warren and force that old fool Faru to unseal the Veil! The Sorrow will pass through and claim this Alexander Eden!"

There was a crescendo of roaring enthusiasm. I could feel my skin crawling. I'd thought I was safe. But these people were declaring all-out war. Just so that *thing* could come and kill me.

"The boy represents more than a simple threat to Hades. He represents *hope*. Hope of a new rising of Chosen. Hope of our defeat. Hope of an end to the Ageless War. When The Sorrow extinguishes his life, the hope of the HASEA dies with him. More will turn to us." He raised his hand into the air and coiled it into a fist. "Then we will crush those who remain!"

The room exploded into a roar of noise. He continued to shout above the snarls, growls and hisses. "Brothers and sisters, many of you may lose your lives tomorrow. But know that you fight for a cause greater than yourself. A right to be free of the Alliance! To sweep aside the human vermin. To prepare Earth for Hades' reign!" He thrust both fists into the air and the roar from the crowd was so heavy, it made the window vibrate. I shrank back from the glass. I didn't need to hear any more. My mind was racing. *I need to get back. I need to warn everyone.*

The SOS were coming to kill us.

*

"I'm going to rip his frigging head off!" hissed Scarlett. "I trusted that bastard with my life."

"Scarlett, calm down," said Tyler, wrapping an arm around her shoulder. "Sage Faru, how did no one know that Dakin's maker was Rahuman?"

The whole of Orion - minus Sophia - as well as Scarlett and Tyler were standing in Faru's office. After witnessing the SOS meeting, I'd sprinted all the way back through the maze of corridors to the Black Tap. The bar had been crawling with agents, loading the arrested into armoured vans. Gabriella and the rest of the team had still been there, and I'd breathlessly explained what I'd seen to a horrified reception. We'd headed straight back to the Warren and called an emergency meeting with Faru, where I'd repeated what I'd witnessed again.

The Seelian placed his hands down on the desk and shook his head slowly. "He made us believe that his maker had been a Bloodling long since dead. He had always been such an honourable Guardian; I had no reason to doubt his words."

"But what about the mind thing, surely you would have seen?" I said.

"No. I cannot see into the minds of Pandemonians, or hybrids. I can only establish communication links with them. That is all." His face seemed to crumble with distress. He bowed his head and took a deep breath. "Sage Asmund was a dear friend to me. I have known him for over a century. How could he do this to us? Dakin served this base for decades. Never once did I suspect he had ulterior motives." His hands coiled into fists on the desk. "And Sylvia. All of these years, supporting the Alliance and protecting the Earth from the threat of Hades. How could I have been so close yet failed to see it? Even Lafelei's words alluded to her betrayal."

"What do you mean?" I asked.

"Betrayed by the Moon and Stars."

The words sank in and it dawned on me. "Moon's edge. The name of the Coven. And Witches, they worship the stars don't they?"

The Sage nodded and lowered his voice until it was barely audible. "I thank the Elementals that you were able to discover the meeting, Alexander. If not, I truly believe it may have been the end of the Warren." He bowed his head. "I am so sorry for my failure. I should have known."

I looked around at the room. Everyone seemed beyond uncomfortable at seeing our leader so upset. I tried to think of something to say, but couldn't find the right words. Rachel found them instead.

"Don't blame yourself, Sage Faru. We all trusted the wrong people. Dakin was my friend. I can't believe he was part of something like this." She gestured towards Echo. "Scarlett and Tyler worked with him every day and had no idea. We all feel hurt, but there's no point in going over why he did it. Tomorrow night, this base is going to come under attack. We need to protect Alexander and everyone else from what's waiting beyond the Veil."

Her words were met with sounds of approval. Faru raised his head. "Rachel is right. We must not allow personal emotions to cloud the facts." His tone shifted. "We need to prepare ourselves for battle. I shall speak with the other Sages and request additional support. Tyler, on my orders I want you to take a group of Chosen and place Sylvia under arrest. Put her in the prisons." He took a deep breath. "I am disbanding Echo. When tomorrow comes, you fight with Orion. If Dakin does return for any reason - which I doubt he will – no one is to speak a word of this. Are we clear?"

Tyler nodded, saluted and left the room. Faru turned to face the redhead. "Scarlett, I am promoting you to second–in–command for Orion. However, for now your task is to take Alexander's brother as far away as you can, to one of the Outposts. Tell no one here which one you choose. And stay there with him until the battle is over."

Scarlett reacted as if his words were blows. "What? No way!" she shouted. "My teammate betrayed me; I want to be part of this fight too. I can drop Mikey somewhere safe and come back."

Faru stared at her with his white eyes, which seemed to be shimmering with a newfound intensity. "You are my ward Scarlett, and you will do as I command. I understand your passion and we all truly appreciate your dedication to the Alliance. However, if tomorrow's assault does not go to plan for the SOS, they may attempt to use Alexander's brother as insurance. We cannot bring him here, because that would only endanger him further. We must get him as far away from Chapter Hill as possible. And I need someone I can still trust to keep him protected."

I nodded in agreement. "He'll need you to protect him, Scarlett. And besides, if anyone was going to watch over him, I'd want it to be you."

The Bloodling folded her slender arms across her chest and clenched her jaw.

"You want him to be safe don't you?" I added.

Her shoulders slumped. "Of course I do. Okay, I'll do it."

"Thank you Scarlett, your commitment has not gone unnoticed," said Faru.

"Alex should go too."

I spun around to face Gabriella, who purposefully avoided my gaze. She cleared her throat. "The SOS are coming here to free The Sorrow. The Sorrow wants Alex. It's better if he isn't here in case…you know…they succeed."

Scarlett nodded. "She's right. He'll stand a better chance the further away he is."

Faru looked pensive. "Perhaps it is better if you were not here, Alexander."

"Are you kidding me?" I almost shouted. "Not a bloody chance. I'm not going to let everyone around here die for me, while I'm hiding hundreds of miles away." I tried to calm myself down. "Besides, The Sorrow found me. Running is only delaying the inevitable and puts people I care about at risk." I shook my head. "When I took the oath of a Guardian, I swore to stand by you all, even if that meant dying. So when the SOS attack tomorrow, I'm going to be standing right there next to you."

I stared at each person in the room. Most of them looked impressed, which hadn't been my intention. I didn't want to impress. I wanted them to understand how I felt. I'd spent so long feeling powerless and afraid, but I wasn't afraid anymore. I had friends and people to care for and protect. I had a cause to fight for, one I believed in. I looked at Gabriella, who returned the gaze. Our eyes stayed locked together like they had the first day at school.

She smiled.

Faru stood up straight. "Thank you, Alexander. Your selfless courage epitomises what it means to be a Guardian and a Chosen. You do your forbearers proud." He gestured towards us all. "I shall sound the sirens to gather everyone together so that we can begin preparations for tomorrow."

As he said the words, a sudden thought clicked into my head and my stomach burst with adrenaline. "Sage Faru, is there a way to prevent the sound of a Siren affecting non-Chosen?"

Faru raised his woollen eyebrows. "A simple Witch's spell could easily do so, yes."

"And what about the Fera, is there a way to get them to help us?"

"Most of them are remarkably intelligent. It would simply be a case of explaining the situation in a manner they could comprehend. Which I would likely be able to achieve," answered the Sage.

I clapped my hands together. "Okay, we're going to need loads of speaker wire. I think I've got an idea."

*

The clouds were the colour of burned flesh. Loud growls of thunder boomed in the distance. Streaks of lightning ignited the sky and crashed down to the ground in jagged forks on the horizon. The rain fell in thick sheets, hammering against the glass.

I turned away from the window and headed back to the fireplace. Gabriella was sitting on the sofa, dressed in a sleeveless top and jeans, her bare feet curled underneath her body and her hair spilling over the back cushions. She ran her fingers absently along the exposed skin of one of her arms.

It was several hours after our meeting with Faru. Sylvia had never managed to make it to the prison – a connected policeman had found her in a dumpster not far from where the meeting had taken place. Her throat had been slit.

Mikey was safe, hidden away somewhere several hundred miles north. The thought of my family so far away from the danger made me feel better. It no longer shocked me at how much I cared about them - even that idiot John...a bit.

Faru had assembled a Guardian meeting in the Feasting Hall. The room had been full to the point of bursting. There'd been waves of shock and anger as he delivered the news, followed by a resigned acceptance. Afterwards we had all gone to our apartments to eat and get some sleep so that we could rise early in the morning and begin to prepare. I'd sat in silence for a long time on my couch, before I'd heard someone knocking at my door and opened it to find Gabriella standing there.

I sat down next to her on the sofa, warming a hand by the fire. "I don't know if I'm ready for this," I said staring into the

364

flames. "I thought I was. But then it occurred to me...I'm going to have to actually kill people tomorrow aren't I?"

Gabriella sat up straight. "You already have killed, Alex. Rahuman, remember?"

"I know. But I did it without thinking...you know like survival instinct. At the bar, my instincts told me to go straight for the Crimson Twins but I fought them and chose the non-lethal option instead. It almost cost me. Tomorrow, I know that it's kill or be killed. I'm just...I don't know if I can."

"Alex, I know that it's hard. Killing somebody is not a decision any of us take lightly. But the Soldiers of Sorrow are the worst kind of evil. They are coming here with the sole purpose of killing as many of us as they can and serving you to The Sorrow on a platter. You need to understand, you're a Chosen Alex – a walking weapon. It's inside you. You have to stop fighting it and let it take over."

I turned around to face her. "That's what I'm frightened of." I pressed a hand against my stomach. "What's inside scares the living hell out of me. You saw what I did to TJ. I couldn't stop myself. Midnight told me about the darkness he felt inside. I-I think I have it too."

Gabriella paused for a second. "Alex, I already told you. When you hurt TJ, you were drunk and going through your Awakening. You weren't yourself. Look, I don't know how you feel inside. All I know is what I see. And what I see is a kind, strong, caring person who is willing to put his life on the line for what he believes in. We all have a darker side," she placed a hand on my arm, "but we all have good too."

I felt myself relax. I leaned back into the sofa and let out a deep whoosh of breath. "You're right...as always," I said sarcastically.

"Hey!" She laughed and swatted my arm.

"You know, as morbid as it sounds, this could be our last night alive," I said, looking into the crackling fire once more.

"So what shall we do?" Gabriella asked from behind me.

I turned around and stared right at her. "I want you to tell me about your parents. Everything."

Gabriella's face drew tight and she squirmed as if I'd asked her to imagine her deepest phobia. She looked away in some

365

subconscious attempt to avoid the question. I leaned over and gently pulled her around to face me. Stared into her eyes.

"Ella, I know that something bad must have happened. But you can't keep it inside forever. I think it's time you told someone."

I could see the anguish in her face. It seemed like she were caught in an internal struggle. Something seemed to give. She let out a long sigh.

"Okay."

29
Baptised in Blood

Most of what I know I've had to piece together from diaries my papa kept and what Sage Etorre told me. Papa's name was Antonio De Luca. He was born in a small village about thirty kilometres south of Roma. It was the sort of place where everybody knew everybody else. His family wasn't rich - my grandfather was a tailor by trade. He had two sisters, Milena and Angelica. The family were devout Catholics; before he could even walk, my father attended Mass. Antonio idolised my grandfather – his early diaries were full of extracts about him. He helped out at the tailors, working hard to make life easier for his father. He even expressed a desire to continue the family business, which he wrote made my grandfather really proud. It was a humble life I guess, but Papa seemed happy. That was until he turned eighteen and had his Awakening.

His diaries don't explain what could have caused it. All I know is how scared Papa was when he discovered he had all these extraordinary abilities. Back then, the HASEA wasn't quite so organised. They didn't approach him for some time. Not knowing what to do, he went to my grandfather for advice…it didn't go well. He thought his son was possessed by a demon and carted him off to see the local priest, who apparently performed all manner of frightening exorcisms on him. When it didn't work - which naturally it wouldn't as he was about as far from possessed as you can get - the priest proclaimed him to be the spawn of Satan. The whole family was shamed. In turn, Papa's own family shunned him. He was told to leave with little more than the clothes on his back and some parting money from my weeping grandmother.

Being deeply religious himself, Papa believed what the priest had said. He was convinced that he was evil. That it was only a matter of time before he seriously hurt someone…or worse. So

367

he headed to the nearest bar with the intention of drinking himself into oblivion. He was sat in the corner, drowning his sorrows when my mother walked in.

Mamma's name was Lorena. As I told you before, she was a Succubus. She'd come to the bar looking for men she could drain. But I need to explain something. Succubi aren't like Incubi; they don't exist just to breed. They drain life force not just to stay young and beautiful – that's a by-product. If they don't they decay and eventually die. If they want to live, they don't have a choice. But some are lazy and can't be bothered to spend more than one night feeding. They drain a single person until they are dead to get what they need. Those are the ones the Alliance has a problem with. Others 'hop' - taking the bare minimum from each person and moving on. Sex is the trade-off. All the victim remembers is a great one-night stand and a few days of flu afterwards. Not a bad deal really. Anyway, Lorena was the latter, not evil, just doing what she needed to in order to survive.

So she came into the bar and was working on several of the men. Succubi have a few talents, one of which is the ability to gather in the surface information of their victims. Then they use it to help them relate to the person. That's what Iralia did to you the day you first came to the base. Not that they really need the skill, because another is that they can charm others into falling in love with them. Naturally this helps when they want the person to go home with them.

So anyway, Lorena noticed Papa sitting away from the others and how much more powerful his life force was. She headed over to try her charms on him. Obviously they didn't work; Antonio was immune to her allure. Mamma had never before met a Chosen and was confused and intrigued by him. She wanted to know more, but couldn't use the shortcut, so decided to try the old fashioned way. But Papa refused to open up. He just sat there and drank, staring into his glass, whilst Mamma talked to him. At the end of the evening, he was very drunk. When Lorena offered to take him home he admitted he had no home to be taken to. Maybe it was the curiosity, or maybe she was starting to feel something, but Mamma did something she'd never done before. She invited him to stay at her place.

Apparently he made weak efforts to refuse, but she insisted. He took the sofa, and turned down all her advances. In the morning, when she came down, he'd gone. That evening, she found him in the same bar once again drowning his sorrows. And once again, she sat with him and talked while he drank and for the second time offered him a place to stay. As before, in the morning, when she came downstairs, there was no sign of him.

The pattern continued for at least a week. Every evening, he'd head back to the bar and start drinking. After my mother finished her shift at a local restaurant, she'd join Papa and sit with him whilst he drank. She told him little things about herself - all the truth, leaving out only the parts that were Succubus related. Little by little, he began to open up. He spoke about his family, about his past. Told her about what he thought was the evil inside of him. Finally told her the things he could do. He demonstrated by melting his glass with a hand. It was at this point that Mamma realised what Papa was. She knew she should fear him, but instead she felt something else. And he felt the same thing when he looked at her. No tricks or allure. They were falling for each other.

I found a passage at the back of one of Papas' diaries, which were words she'd said one of those nights. She told him: 'No one is evil by default. Everyone has choices. The choices you make are what define you. You can be whoever you want to be, whoever you are.'

That night, Papa didn't sleep on the couch. That evening when Mamma came to the bar after her shift, he was sober. He never said it, but it was obvious that he had found something to live for.

It had been two weeks since Lorena had fed. She refused to allow herself to drain Antonio. Aside from the fact that he would likely remember, she cared for him too much. Succubi need to feed on average at least once a week, or they start to degenerate. But something strange was happening to Mamma. Her looks weren't declining. If anything, she was becoming even more beautiful. She didn't know what it meant, but she didn't care - she was happy.

After a while, Papa moved in with Mamma. He got himself a job at the same bar he'd visited so many times. It was another month before the Alliance came to him. They caught up with him as he was walking home and told him what he really was. He had to believe them, they knew too much about what he was going through to be lying. He went with them to Castello, where they filled in the blanks.

They also told him what Lorena was.

As soon as they did, he left the base and went straight home. He confronted Mamma about it, demanding the truth. She broke down and told him. He was horrified and left her sobbing her heart out. I know this makes him seem like a horrible person Alex, but he was just really scared. Don't forget how he was raised. It was almost impossible for him not to apply religion to what he'd learned. But religion has so much wrong. It refers to most Umbra species as demons. And demons within that context are completely evil. And Succubi are supposedly demons by what mythology tells us. So he believed my mother was evil and had been sent by the Devil to help corrupt his soul.

Papa was followed by the Alliance and brought back in. Over the next few days, without my father around, my mother began to decay rapidly. At first she thought that it was because she'd subconsciously been draining him without either of them realising. But she attempted to drain a random person and it made no difference, it was like she was dying of sadness.

Papa was hurting too and despite his beliefs, he snuck over to Mamma's house and looked through the window. Apparently she was slumped against the lounge wall, looking at least sixty years old. Instead of being repulsed, he panicked. Broke the door down and went to her. Told her that he didn't care what she was. That someone had told him that no one is evil by default. Within hours she began to heal. By the morning she was back to the beautiful woman he knew and loved. He vowed that he'd never leave her again and she forgave him, because she knew both figuratively and literally that she couldn't live without him.

They joined the HASEA together and were honest about their relationship. There were no laws forbidding relationships between Pandemonians and Chosen, but it was frowned upon back then. However, they were in love and didn't care either way. The longer they spent together, the more human my mother became. She didn't need to feed any more, somehow Papa kept her healthy. So when she started being sick in the mornings, they both knew it was for another reason entirely.

A union between an Umbra and a Chosen was bad enough, but neither of my parents knew what the consequences of a resulting child would be. You already know that Witches and Shaman are the result of Pandemonians breeding with humans, but it was believed that a Chosen and a Pandemonian couldn't produce a child. In the history of the Alliance, not a single case was reported where it had happened - I guess it essentially goes against nature. I know this sounds really cheesy, but I was a miracle. Because my parents simply didn't know what would happen to me if the HASEA found out, they kept me hidden away for fear of me being taken away. Don't get me wrong; even though I was a 'secret', I was loved unconditionally. I had an amazing life and was spoiled by both Mamma and Papa.

Then it all went wrong.

I was seven years old when the SOS found out about my parent's relationship. The information made it all the way back to Hades. He was furious and took what he saw as one of his own joining with a Chosen as a personal insult against himself and the Umbra. So he gave The Sorrow its first mission on this side of the Veil.

Kill my parents.

For the week before the thing came, Papa began to have the worst nightmares. He'd wake in the middle of the night screaming. Hearing him sound so frightened made me cry. Then a few days later, the storms started. I remember it was the worst weather I'd ever seen. Skies the colour of blood. Thunder so loud you thought your eardrums would burst. Constant rain. The lighting was relentless and so destructive. I remember that Mamma had to keep comforting me, because I genuinely thought that the sky was going to collapse and kill us all.

The final night, we were huddled in the living room. The power had gone out. I was wrapped in a blanket which I carried everywhere with me. I loved it, because it smelled of my parents. I was sitting on the edge of the settee, stroking Papa's hair. He was resting on the couch, writing in one of his journals that he'd converted into his own version of a HASEA handbook – the one you now own. He'd barely been getting any sleep at all. More bad dreams he'd told me, but he never told me what about.

I remember Mamma was sitting on the floor holding Papa's free hand. None of us were talking, we were just happy in each other's company.

Papa heard it first. Or sensed it, I'll never know which. He jerked up, almost knocking me off the armrest. He looked down at my mother, who seemed confused for a moment and then...scared. The atmosphere frightened me. I asked what was wrong, but they wouldn't answer me. They ran into the hallway and I followed, dragging my blanket with me. I watched Papa open a metal vent above the stairway. He pulled out a bag and ran back into the lounge with it. I followed him back in. He placed it on the table and pulled out all sorts of things I'd never seen. I know now that they were Alliance weapons. Mamma pulled away a small rug, which exposed a trapdoor I'd never even known existed.

They were acting frantically and it was scaring me so much I could barely breathe. I started to cry. Papa stopped and looked at me. I'll never forget that face as long as I live. He looked so sad.

Mamma...sorry this is so hard. No...it's okay, I'm okay.

Mamma knelt down and hugged me so tight it hurt. Papa did the same. They both held me as if it were the last thing they would ever do. I was crying and hiccupping from being so scared and confused. Mamma shushed me and smoothed the back of my hair, the way she always did when I was upset.

I remember, she pointed at the trapdoor and said, 'Listen carefully *mia bambina*, you need to go down here and keep very, very quiet okay?'

I told them I didn't want to. I-I didn't want to be away from them.

Then Papa said 'please.' Maybe it was the way he said it, or because of the look he'd given me before, but I agreed. They both hugged me one more time.

Then they said their last words they would ever say to me. Mamma said, 'We love you with all our hearts.' And Papa said 'Always.'

They lowered me into the crawlspace and I pulled the blanket up to my face. There was a sort of rustling sound overhead and then darkness. The dirt below me was damp, from where the rain had found its way in through the cracks in the foundations of the house. I was sitting in a cold, filthy puddle. But I stayed completely still. Even though I was still only a human, I could tell something bad was coming. I could sense it.

I waited.

If God really existed and had any mercy, he would have made me deaf at that moment. It started with the screeching of some horrific creature from outside. It sounded like a horse's neigh mixed with nails on a blackboard. I know now that it was the sound of that poor, soulless Unicorn that that evil creature rides around on.

Then there were the heavy, slow footsteps. All I could think of was the giant from the Jack and the Beanstalk story Papa used to read to me. All sorts of thoughts ran through my head. Was the giant real? Had it come for us? Its footsteps were so powerful they made the mud jump up around me. I remember lumps of it flew up into my face and up my nose, making me choke. There were more frantic footsteps as my parents ran around the living room, doing god knows what. I had to resist the urge to call out to them.

The front door burst open and I heard Mamma shriek. The thunder was so loud, as if it had come right into the house. I could hear the rain beating down and the howl of the wind. Then there were the pounding footsteps of this *thing* coming closer.

I heard Papa's voice. He was shouting above the roar of noise. He said that he knew it would come. That he knew it wasn't just a dream. Mamma pleaded with it, saying they wanted nothing to do with the war and only wanted peace.

There was no answer to their words. I remember straining my ears above the noise to hear if the giant said anything. But there was only silence. Then I heard another sound like creaking hinges followed by another I didn't know then, but know all too well now. The sound of a sword being unsheathed.

The final words Mamma ever said were, "please don't."

Then there were gunshots. So…many…gunshots, as if a full-scale war were happening in our lounge. I screamed then - I couldn't help it. Luckily it was too loud for me to be heard. I stuffed the wet blanket into my mouth to stifle my screams.

The sound of gunfire was cut short by two sharp sounds. The first was followed by Mamma making a high-pitched squeal. The second, even more disturbing was a sound like Papa being sick. Then nothing but the wind and rain.

I stayed frozen for what seemed like forever, too scared to do anything. Then I felt dripping on my arms and forehead, more and more until it was all over me. At first I thought that the rain had seeped through into the lounge, but it was too warm. I was too petrified to move, so I stayed in the same position, wrapped in the blanket with this warm liquid pouring over me. After a minute or an hour - I couldn't tell - the heavy booming footsteps started again. Somehow I regained control of my body and managed to stand up. I nudged at the trapdoor and peered out.

I saw it. The Sorrow in full view. Not that I knew what it was then. It was standing in the hallway, so big that most of its head was hidden by the doorframe. It was facing away, breathing slowly. I could hear these harsh rasping sounds as it inhaled. It was wearing dark armour, covered in spikes and creepy symbols, and it carried this colossal sword. The sword was covered in blood. I froze again. It was like staring at the embodiment of a nightmare. The image seared itself into my brain. I see it every single night and probably will until the day I die.

The Sorrow spun around. It was unnaturally fast for its size. Somehow instinct kicked in and I ducked back into the hole. I waited for an eternity for the creature to open the trapdoor and pluck me out. But it didn't. I heard its footsteps start again, first in the hallway and then splashing in the rain outside. Then I heard that horrific baying noise and thundering hooves.

Then nothing.

I pulled myself out of the trapdoor. It was then that I noticed my parents. They were laying together, Papa holding Mamma against him just like the way they did when they slept. But this time...they both had red slash marks on their chests, which were pulsing out blood...so much blood. The whole floor looked like it had been painted red. I looked down and realised so was I. Only then did I understand what the warm liquid I'd felt was.

374

The t-thing that I remember most was Mamma's hand. It was palm down right next to the trapdoor. In her final moments, she'd tried to be as close to me as possible. Grief hit me. I-I actually remember the sensation; it felt like a rock crushing…crushing down on my chest. I-I couldn't breathe. I crawled over to them and tried to wake them up…b-but they wouldn't. They were gone. So I pulled Mamma's arms around me, closed my eyes…and willed myself to die.

30

Gabriella looked at me, eyes damp with tears.

"I... I miss them so much."

Her face crumbled and ten years of repressed grief broke free. She buried her head into my shoulder and sobbed uncontrollably. Sounds of pure anguish escaped from somewhere deep within her, each one like a claw tearing at my insides. I wrapped my arms around her quivering body, ignoring the painful tremors that ran up my arms. I wished I could somehow take her pain away. Gabriella's suffering felt far worse than any of the beatings I'd taken from Terry; more soul destroying than the thousands of acidic words that had dissolved my confidence over the years. What made it even worse was that I'd forced her to remember. *I caused this.*

Tears blurred my vision. I tried to blink them away, but there were too many. Instead, I closed my eyes and leaned over, resting my cheek on the top of her head. "It's okay Ella, I'm here," I soothed, rocking her gently back and forth as she wept. My words were hollow and I knew it. But no combination of words in the world could ever console the sort of ordeal Gabriella had experienced. All I could hope to do was help carry her through the pain, until she emerged on the other side.

Time seemed to grind to a halt. Minutes became hours that stretched forward towards infinity. At some point, Gabriella's sobs became deep sighs. Then they stopped altogether. She kept her head buried in my shoulder, as if trying to hide.

I sat up and waited.

Like a timid animal, Gabriella eventually emerged, lifting up and pressing the heels of her hands against her eyes. They were swollen and red. Without another word, she slipped from the couch and disappeared into the bathroom. When she returned, all physical signs of her breakdown had been wiped clean. But I could still see the grief behind her eyes.

Gabriella sat down close to me. "You know I've never told anyone that before."

I looked down. "I'm sorry. What happened to you...I had no idea. I feel so guilty for forcing you to talk about it."

Gabriella shook her head. "No, it's okay…really. I needed to, I just didn't realise. I can't explain how much better I feel now. It's like I've been purged."

"Still, it wasn't fair of me to make you relive all that purely for my sake. Although I am really glad you told me about them. They sounded like wonderful people."

She nodded. "They were."

"Sage Etorre was right. I bet if your parents could see you now they would be so proud of the person you've become."

Gabriella closed her eyes and fresh tears slipped down her cheeks.

"Oh Ella, I didn't mean to…"

She shook her head and took a deep breath. "They would have really liked you."

I felt a squeeze in my stomach at what was easily the best compliment anyone had ever given me. Gabriella brushed the back of her hand against my cheek, which vibrated where our skin connected. "It's such a strange sensation," she said, pulling her hand away and wiggling her fingers.

My mouth fell open. "You...you can feel that too?"

"Since the day I first met you."

"Why didn't you say something?"

She smiled. "Why didn't you?"

I had no answer.

Gabriella looked away from me into the fire. As she stared at the flames, something shifted in her expression - became conflicted.

"I need to tell you something else," she said in a voice barely above a whisper.

"Anything."

"If I tell you, promise me that you won't freak out."

I panicked internally. Gabriella had already told me she was half Succubus and that her parents had been murdered by The Sorrow - the same nightmare that was after me - and neither times had she looked as nervous as she did now. *What could possibly freak me out more than what she's already told me?*

"I won't," I promised.

She turned back to face me. Her expression looked so torn, I could feel the knots wrapping around my insides. "No it's too soon, oh god, I don't know-"

"Gabriella, tell me!"

"I think I'm in love with you."

The words burst from her mouth as if they had escaped without permission. For a few seconds they didn't register. Then like a delayed response, my body came alive with emotions. My heart skipped so many beats it seemed like it would never regain its rhythm. The knots transformed into a flurry of butterflies that beat a storm of wings against the walls of my stomach. Adrenaline surged through me, igniting every inch of my body and pushing all of my senses into overdrive.

Gabriella looked away. "I'm sorry. I know it's a lot to take in. I-I'm confused myself. Maybe it's the soulmate thing. I don't know...I can't help it."

This can't be real. I'm dreaming. But the look in her eyes told me it was real. I was sat in front of the most incredible girl ever to grace the Earth, and she was confessing her love for *me*.

Words were beyond my reach.

Gabriella stood up suddenly. "Look, don't worry, it was stupid. Forget I said anything. I'm going to go downstairs." She started moving towards the door.

Not this time.

I sprang off the sofa and marched after her, grabbing hold of her arm.

"Gabriella."

I pulled her around to face me and pressed my lips against hers. They felt a thousand times better than in my imagination. The charges rolled through my body - they were different this time, more exciting. Our mouths parted and tongues gently touched and explored. Gabriella's lips slid along mine as we kissed and a soft moan escaped her throat.

I pulled away and stared into her eyes. "I love you too. I did from the second I saw you."

Gabriella's face broke into a smile. She grabbed at the back of my neck and pulled me close. We kissed in short, breathless bursts. A wave of charges rolled down my spine making me shudder with pleasure. I ran my fingers up and down her bare arms, each one sending a fresh wave of electricity coursing through my fingers. My heart thundered in my chest.

With a sudden burst of control, I lifted Gabriella up. She wrapped her legs around my waist and placed her hands either side of my neck. Still kissing, we stumbled towards the sofa. I threw her down and slid on top of her. I slowly kissed the side of her neck as she let out sharp breaths, fingers raking through my hair. My lips buzzed every time they met her skin and she shook gently in response. She grabbed at my t-shirt, and I stopped so she could slide it off. I placed my hand in the small of her back and lifted her up into a sitting position. Gabriella crossed her arms and pulled her own top off. My breath caught in my throat as I saw her naked skin, covered only by a bra. *She's perfect.*

Gabriella wildly kissed me all over. My face, neck, collarbone, chest. Each kiss sent vibrations rushing through my body. I wrapped my arms around her and felt the warmth of her Umbra skin on my hands. I sank back down onto her and pushed my lips against hers. The charges made everything more intense. I couldn't believe I'd ever seen them as a bad thing. The more intense we got, the more pleasurable the electric connection got. *I had no idea that anything could feel this good.* Gabriella's sweet breath filled my mouth as our tongues wrapped around each other. Her breathing grew heavier and she pushed a hand against my chest, breaking away. She moved her mouth to my ear and whispered into it, her voice breathless.

"Alex I want you... now."

I didn't refuse.

*

I woke up to a red glow pouring through a crack in the curtains. For a split second I thought the base was on fire, before I realised it was only the sunrise.

Gabriella's naked body was wrapped around me, her head resting on my chest. Her raven hair flowed over it, spilling onto the sheets. I ran my fingers up and down her arm, letting the tips flow over her soft skin. She sighed in her sleep and nestled into me. At that moment, I was the happiest I'd ever been in my life.

379

In the tranquil silence of the morning, I let myself remember the night before and my stomach filled with butterflies all over again. It had been the most amazing experience of my life. At some point we'd ended up in the bedroom. Afterwards, I'd held Gabriella close and listened as she told me the rest of her story.

She'd still been wrapped in her mother's arms when the HASEA had found her. Gabriella had thought it was the 'giant' come back to finish her off. Instead a kind, female Guardian had picked her up and soothed her whilst another spoke on the phone. He'd told the person on the other end that they'd been too late. He had moved away from her and lowered his voice, but she'd still heard him say, 'One more thing, Sage Etorre. They had a child.'

I kissed Gabriella's cheek and gently slipped from underneath her. I pulled the duvet up and wrapped it around her body, tucking her in. Moving over to the window, I opened the glowing curtains and gasped.

The sky looked as though it were on fire. Streaks of scorched clouds stretched into the horizon. Directly above was a yawning hole of blackness as dark as death. I twisted the drapes in my hands. *This isn't a sunrise.*

"It's the Red Storm."

Gabriella's voice made me start. I turned away from the window. She was sitting up, covers drawn up to her collarbones. "The Sorrow's influence."

"What does it do?"

"It's a symbol used to invoke fear. The storm always arrives before The Sorrow does."

"But I thought Faru sealed the Veil?"

"He did. But unfortunately that doesn't stop its influence."

"Will it do anything?"

"Not without The Sorrow to control it. Except that now every Rogue within a hundred mile radius knows where to come."

I took a second look at the hellfire sky. It felt like I was watching Armageddon unfold. "It's not the end of the world. But you can see it from here."

"Sorry, what did you say?"

I shook my head. "It doesn't matter, just a saying I heard once."

Someone knocked at the door. I looked at Gabriella, who shrugged. Grabbing a dressing gown from the wardrobe, I padded into the lounge, tying the cord as I walked.

I opened the door to see Delagio leaning against the frame. He stepped back, surveying me through squinted eyes. Then he gave a broad smile.

"What? Why are you looking at me like that?"

"Oh nothin'," he grinned. "Ah was lookin' for a feisty brunette. Only there seems ta be one missin' from her apartment. Say, you haven't seen her have you?"

I could feel my face growing hot with embarrassment. Before I could answer, Gabriella's voice floated over my shoulder.

"I'm here. What's up, Delagio?"

I turned to see her appear next to me, wearing one of my t-shirts. Delagio's eyes widened as he saw her. Gabriella sighed and leaned against the door. "Yes it's exactly what it looks like. It's five in the morning, what's going on?"

The kinesist nodded his head approvingly, giving me a not too subtle wink. Then his face was all business. "I'm here for Alex."

"How come?" I asked.

"Support from the other bases is comin' soon. Faru wants to mind merge with you again. See if he can identify any more SOS that was at that meetin'. You know, make sure everyone fightin' with us is on our side."

"Give me a couple of minutes?"

"Ah'll be right out here." He let out a long sigh. "Looks like this is really happening." With that he pushed off the doorframe and settled against the opposite wall – marble spinning between his fingers.

"Promise me you'll stay here and wait for me to get back," I said once the door was closed.

"I promise."

*

The sheets were still warm as I slipped back into bed. Gabriella was lying on her side, breathing softly. She smelled of soap. I pulled her close to me and wrapped my arms around her.

"Everything go okay?" she said sleepily.

I sighed. "As well as it could have I suppose. Faru found seven more he recognised."

"Seven?"

"Apparently some were from Outposts."

Gabriella closed her eyes and sighed. "At least he knows now."

"But there are so many of them. The SOS are *everywhere* we look. How can we fight against something like that?"

Gabriella lifted onto her elbows. "Don't underestimate the strength of the Alliance Alex. You're right; the Soldiers of Sorrow are powerful. But collectively we're far more powerful than they are. For every Rogue, there are dozens of Guardians who would gladly die if it meant protecting Earth. That's why the SOS is forced to rely on insidious tricks and secrets to gain the upper hand. This attack could have devastated the Warren *if* we were unprepared. But thanks to you we're not. Trust me, Faru won't waste the advantage we've gained. Especially not with your idea. I promise you, we *will* survive this."

I pulled an impressed face. "Nice speech."

"Thanks, it came out better in rehearsal."

We both burst out laughing. As I watched her face light up, I prayed that it wouldn't be the last time we laughed together.

I held her gaze. "I hope you're right. I couldn't bare it if something happened to you."

She kissed the tip of my nose. "It won't. I'm not going anywhere and neither are you."

"So then, if we do somehow manage to make it through this mess in one piece, do you have any plans for the fourteenth of December?"

Gabriella smiled up at me. "That depends, what did you have in mind?"

"Well, there's this school ball that I thought we could go to."

"Finally!" she said with mock exasperation. "I genuinely thought I was going to end up asking *you*."

I raised my eyebrows. "You want to go to the ball?"

"Of course I do. I've lived in Alliance bases since I was a child. I've attended dozens of joining ceremonies, hallows-eve celebrations with the Coven and countless feasts, but I've never been to a proper ball like a normal teenager. I was really excited. I bought a dress and everything."

"You bought a dress?"

"A *hell* of a dress."

"Well in that case…" I took her hand and cleared my throat. "Miss Gabriella De Luca, would you do me the honour of being my date to the Christmas Ball?"

"I would love to, Mister Eden," she smiled.

"Well then it's decided. We both have to survive so that I get to see you in that dress." I paused to kiss her. "And then out of it," I added with a wink.

Gabriella pretended to be offended and elbowed me playfully in the arm. But then she pressed herself closer against me and we lost ourselves in each other.

*

The distant blare of the speaker siren woke me the second time. I stretched out for Gabriella, but was disappointed to find her side cold and empty. I squinted at the clock. It was half six in the evening. *Well I've definitely caught up on lost sleep.*

Wiping away the traces of sleep, I sat up and looked around. A note had been left on the bedside table, along with two guns and a pouch of ammo. I recognised the handwriting straight away.

You looked so peaceful sleeping; I didn't want to wake you. Had to go and discuss tactics with Faru. When you wake up, get dressed for battle and come to the Feasting Hall.

love you

xx

P.S. Swords can't shoot, so I thought these might come in handy.

I picked up my handbook. Opening it at the back, I placed the note next to Dad's photograph. Then I opened the wardrobe and unzipped the suit bag, pushed the book into the inside pocket.

It took me a long time to get ready. Almost as if my subconscious knew it could be for the last time.

I slowly wrapped the belt around my waist. The click of the buckle seemed to echo around the empty room. Sliding the two guns and bag off the side, I fastened them to my waist. I plucked the cross sheath from the bottom of the suit bag and slipped it over my jacket. The only thing I left behind were the gloves - I found it easier to handle the swords without them. Last of all, I headed into my apartment and over to the mantelpiece in the lounge. The red box stood over the cold fireplace. As I took it down, I noticed that my hands were trembling. Setting the box on the coffee table, I opened it and stared at the Crimson Twins. My fingers hovered over them, unable to move the last few inches.

I'd been riding on cloud nine and the grim reality of the situation had finally hit. A sinking sensation filled my stomach. *The Soldiers of Sorrow are coming here tonight. There's going to be a huge battle. People are going to die. Maybe even me - or Gabriella.*

I clenched my fists together and shook them out, trying to calm down. Holding my breath, I picked up the first blade, rotated it and slid it down into the sheath. It made a *shuunk* sound as it slotted into place. I repeated it with the other. Then I exhaled in a long whoosh. I was armed. Ready for battle.

That was the easy bit.

I dialled Mikey's number first. The phone rang several times before I heard the familiar smoky tone of Scarlett's voice.

"Alex. Is everything okay?"

"It's fine. How are things there?"

"Not too bad. Pretty boring. Mikey's climbing the walls."

"You haven't told him anything have you?"

"No."

"Thanks. Listen can…can I talk to him?"

Scarlett paused. "I understand. Hold on, I'll get him."

The phone went silent for a while. Then there was a rustle and the sound of a fed up and sleepy Mikey saying hello. I felt a stab of emotion in my stomach.

"Hi Mikey."

"Alex, this place is old and smells like arse. When can I come back?"

"Not for a couple of days bro. I just got to take care of a few things first."

He gave a long exaggerated sigh. "Okay, but be quick about it."

"I'll try."

I could feel tears pricking at the corners of my eyes. I waited for a moment before speaking again. "Mikey, I've got to go. But listen, I know we've had our differences in the past, but I think you and I have grown closer over the last few weeks and well...I love you. I just wanted to let you know."

The tone of his voice changed. "Alex, is everything okay? What's happening there?"

"I'm fine," I croaked, my throat tightening. "I've got to go."

"Okay," he said in a way that meant he wasn't at all convinced. "I love you too bro."

"Bye, Mikey."

I ended the call and wiped away the tears that had formed in my eyes. I accessed my contacts list and dialled Mum's mobile. I held my breath as I waited for it to connect. It cut straight to answer phone and I listened to Mum's chirpy voice asking me to leave a message. I held my breath as I waited for the tone, not quite sure what I wanted to say.

Beep.

"Hi Mum, hi John, it's Alex. Just wanted to say I hope you are both okay. John I hope you got over...well whatever it was you had. Anyway...I-I've missed you. Mikey and I both have. We can't wait to see you both again..." My voice cracked and I had to swallow a few times before I could continue. "So anyway give my love to Edgar and Connie and have a safe trip home. See you when you get back."

"I hope," I added under my breath as I hung up.

Lastly, I felt around inside my jacket pocket for the guide and took out the picture. My father looked back at me, the subtle smile eternally present. I pressed it against my forehead and closed my eyes. *Please watch over us, Dad. Help us get through tonight.* I kissed the picture and placing it back in the guide, returned both to my jacket pocket. I ran my hands over my face and took a few deep breaths to calm myself.

Then sucked it up and headed into the fray.

385

The Warren was buzzing with life. There were Guardians everywhere I looked. Vampires stood in groups, draining blood from surgical bags. Their eyes flashed and turned bright silver. Skinshifters had reverted back to their hound forms. They padded about on their thick paws as agents ran around after them, stuffing their shed skin into sacks. One used its muzzle to nudge past me and I couldn't help but shudder, reminded of Bargheist.

As I excused my way through the entrance hall, I bumped into Rachel coming from the other direction. Like me - and everyone else around - she was dressed in the full Alliance uniform. A staggering array of guns and knives hung from her Kapre belt. An odd looking metallic bow was attached to her back.

"Evening Alex." She nodded her head towards the main door. "Have you looked outside yet?"

"I did earlier."

She shuddered. "I can't even force myself to look at it."

"I know. It looks so creepy. On the bright side, it'll give the local weathermen something to talk about."

She smiled. "Was that a joke, Mister Eden?"

"I think it might have been."

A hulking Oni carrying a twin bladed axe clomped past us. His towering frame blocked out the light from the chandelier for a few seconds. He gave us a large needle pointed grin and passed through the open doors of the Feasting Hall.

The siren blared above our heads for the second time. Slowly, the area started to clear of people, as they filtered into the adjoining room.

"We should head in," Rachel said.

"What about Gabriella and everyone else?"

"They're already in there. Except for Sophia. Midnight made Sage Faru agree to remove her from duty until this is all over. She's locked in her room, sulking."

The news came as a small relief. If it had been my decision, she would have been right next to Mikey and Scarlett wherever they were. But out of the direct firing line was the next best thing.

386

Rachel and I joined the back of the crowd.

The Feasting Hall had been emptied of the table and chairs. Every inch of space was now taken up by Alliance members, of all race and creed. The windows to the courtyard were open, so that the Bloodseekers could listen whilst standing outside with their feral brethren, who sat like tame dogs. Their scaled skin had been marked with white paint, to show their allegiance.

The atmosphere was tense and thick. Everyone was facing forwards, watching and waiting for someone to speak. Both Sage Faru and Sage Etorre were standing on the stage where the band had played a matter of days ago. In a long row behind them - as silent and lifeless as forgotten marionettes - were all thirteen Golems. There was a lectern in front of them. It had a microphone attached but I suspected its use was just as much to keep Faru on two feet as anything else. He looked so frail that he appeared in danger of collapsing at any moment. As I stared, something Gabriella had said about the Golems jogged loose in my mind. *Each one contains some of his life force.* It suddenly dawned on me why he appeared so weak compared to the other Sages and why there were normally only a few Golems at one time.

The more there are, the weaker he gets. They must drain his soul.

Both Sages stood very still, staring into the mass of bodies. Rachel and I managed to squeeze our way towards the front, where we joined Midnight, Delagio, Tyler and Gabriella. I wrapped my hand around hers.

At last Faru spoke. His voice sounded cracked and frail, requiring the microphone to allow it to reach the corners of the gigantic room.

"Guardians, we stand united today against our sworn enemies. Many of you already know this and why. However, for those who have joined us from Castello and other bases, please allow me to explain. It has come to my attention that the Soldiers of Sorrow are planning a full scale attack on the Warren this evening." A wave of whispers and murmurs swept around the room. Faru raised his hands and the room hushed. "Their plan is to force me to unseal the Veil." He drew in a long breath, "Which I did to prevent The Sorrow from entering Earth."

There were cries of horror from around us. I tightened my grip on Gabriella's hand as Faru continued. "Most of you will have either met, or no doubt heard of Alexander Eden. A new, unique Chosen, who we hope is the first of a new wave of Awakenings. It is Hades' plan to have The Sorrow kill Alexander and anyone who stands in its way to set an example. We cannot and will not let that happen."

In contrast to Sage Asmund's speech, which had created hysteria amongst his crowd, Faru commanded a respectful silence. There were nods of fervent agreement. I felt a sense of overwhelming gratitude that these people – most who barely knew me - were willing to put their lives on the line for my protection. *This is what an Alliance truly means. Unity and standing beside one another no matter what.*

"You must place your upmost faith in those you fight alongside. Guardians I promise you, if we all work together, we *will* prevail." Faru coughed loudly, spluttering into the microphone. Steadying himself, he resumed his speech.

"However, with that in mind, there is a matter which must be dealt with. Agent Noble, if you would."

We all turned to see the agent near the back open the double doors. Waiting just outside were more agents, standing beside a wheeled cage. This one was far larger than the one that had held Bargheist. There was a murmur of confusion from the crowd. Faru turned to the Golems and nodded. In unison, they stamped their crosiers into life. One by one they descended the steps and marched into the crowd. There were cries of indignation as they barged past people. One moved roughly between Gabriella and me, forcing our hands apart. They found their intended targets and went to attack.

Chaos ensued.

One of the identified SOS - an Incubus named Zasri - was quick on the uptake. He pivoted on the spot, cracking the face of XI with a vicious backhand. The Golem reeled backwards, sending a number of people flying. The Rogue barged through the crowd and sprinted for the window. At the same time, VII launched itself through the air. It sailed over the heads of the crowd and came crashing down- knee first into the escapee's back. The force drove Zasri's head into the window ledge. Part of the stone crumbled as his jaw smashed against it. He sagged to the floor like a spilled sack of rice. The Golem placed the blazing end of the staff against the Incubus's neck, electrocuting him until his eyes rolled up into his head.

From around the room came frenzy of confused yells. Yesenia - a skeletal Bloodseeker - raised her bony hands in the air as the crosier was thrust into her neck. "LONG LIVE HADES!" she screeched before sinking to her knees. The third – a muscular Pixie named Sahel - managed to get to a blade in time. He brought it down between the eyes of III and the Golem collapsed into a pile of rubble. As the others closed in on him, a set of wings burst through the slits in his uniform. He vaulted into the air and tried to swoop over our heads and escape through the open doors.

I heard a whooshing sound and the Pixie's wings separated from his body. With a scream of agony, Sahel kamikazied out of the air and smashed into the open cage. I spun back to the stage, where Sage Etorre stood, one arm extended straight out in front of him. Inside his robe was a selection of curved blades. Two were missing.

The remaining two Rogues were brought down by the Golems. They jerked about like broken dolls as the electricity coursed through them, and one by one they sank into the cold arms of the clay giants. They were dragged past confused members and deposited in the cage. I noticed that Dakin was not among them. *He must not have come back.*

Agent Noble twisted the key in the lock and along with the others heaved the cage away. The doors closed with a resounding slam. The remaining Golems returned to their positions behind Faru. There was a cacophony of noise as people shouted, demanding explanations.

BANG!

The Golems smashed the base of their staffs against the stage floor in unison. The sound hit my stomach like an invisible fist. Instantly, everyone fell silent and stared at Faru. The Sage had his hands up - palms out - and carrying the same apologetic demeanour he'd used on me before.

"I am sorry you all had to witness that. Unfortunately, it transpires that these people were working against us. It saddens me to inform you that they were in fact members of the SOS."

There were gasps of surprise and horror at the news. I heard a few people shout *'no'*. One Luminar Guardian hid her face as she began to cry.

"I know this comes as a shock and no one is as saddened as I am to have learned this truth. These were people we believed to be our allies... our friends. These are dark times and some have chosen to follow the wrong path. We *must* however, put this behind us and continue."

The crowd began to settle and once again everyone was waiting for what Faru would say next.

"There will be a break in usual units. We will play to our strengths. All Luminar are required on the rooftops. Your accuracy with ranged weapons will give us an advantage if our enemies approach from the front - which is likely, as they are unaware that we are anticipating their impending attack. All those able to fly will give the Fae aerial support. I need Skinshifters in the woods around the base as well as Bloodseekers and your hives. Bloodlings will be stationed at the rear of the base and inside the Nexus. The elevators have been deactivated, but I have little doubt that the SOS will utilise the decommissioned routes to gain access. Regardless, your superior night vision will make you invaluable. The Golems, Sage Etorre and I will create a wall protecting the entrance to the Veil. Chosen, you will break yourselves into these aforementioned sections, fighting in your relevant squad groups. Guardians positioned in the Nexus will be under the overall command of Huntmaster Larik Godren. Those at the rear, Huntmaster Ivy Affron. Those at the front and roof, Huntmaster Gabriella De Luca."

I felt her straighten up beside me. She looked proud, with a hint of nervous.

"I trust that you will do everything in your power to make this base safe. The HASEA owes you its gratitude for your courage. *I* owe you gratitude." He nodded that he was done and moved away from the lectern with the aid of Sage Etorre. The other leader took his place at the podium.

"Please remain here. The Coven will arrive shortly to perform a spell and explain the rest of our strategy."

Without another word, the two Sages left the stage and exited through rear doors. The Golems followed like a pack of faithful dogs.

A solemn silence filled the room. The reality of the situation had dawned on everyone else, the way it had for me earlier. People knew that they might not make it through to the next day.

I felt Gabriella's hand take mine.

31

They came for us.

It was late evening and we'd been in position for several hours. As Faru had requested, everyone was strategically placed. Gabriella had co-ordinated the remaining Chosen teams; Orion was outside the front door – minus Rachel - using the low wall by the steps as partial cover. Metal blockades had been set up a few yards in front and dozens of Chosen kneeled behind them, guns out, locked into the distance. Several large speakers - screwed to tall poles - were dotted around us, their wires snaking the length of the mansion and disappearing into the grounds. Everyone and everything had taken on a red hue, tainted by the apocalyptic sky above.

I watched the black shapes of the shifters slinking around the trees that lined the base. Their red eyes shone like coals in the darkness. In the hallway behind us was yet another blockade, with a mixture of Pandemonians and Chosen crouched behind them. Up the stairs stood Faru and Etorre. The wall of Golems stood just behind them, blocking the entrance to the painting and the Veil beyond.

I was crouched next to Gabriella and Tyler. Midnight and Delagio were huddled a few feet away. Rachel stood on the roof high above our heads - one in a large row of Luminar - staring through the lens of her metal sniper bow.

It started with a piercing howl. The unmistakable sound of a Skinshifter. Not one of ours, because we'd all been told not to make a sound until the battle began, so we didn't give away our positions.

More howls followed and then a tremendous roar that rattled the windows of the mansion in their frames. A sea of red appeared on the horizon, as if the sky had bled down to the earth. They evolved into countless Rogues, dressed in their hooded crimson cloaks, which whipped around them in the wind.

So much for being discrete.

"Hold!" shouted Gabriella. No one moved a muscle. The cries of the SOS grew louder as they broke into a run.

"Hold!"

They were getting closer. I felt a stray bullet smack into the wall next to me. I breathed out hard. My hands were slick with sweat as I kept my gun held steady, aimed at the advancing mass.

"Now!"

There was a crackle of static as the speakers switched on. The Siren's melodic song flowed through. As if they had hit an invisible wall, the advancing SOS jerked to a halt and their eyes glazed over. Some dropped their weapons on the ground and began to stagger towards the speakers like zombies. Skinshifters - muzzles coated with red paint - staggered sideways and fell over.

"Luminar. Now!" shouted Gabriella.

Thuck thuck thuck.

A cloud of miniature arrows arched over our heads. I followed them as they darted down, piercing into their targets. The dazed Pandemonians made no sound as their bodies flew backwards from the force. Gravel splashed about as fallen SOS collapsed to the ground in heaps, tiny arrows sticking out of their chests like oversized acupuncture needles.

The Siren's mournful melody became a tribute to each person who sank to the ground and became still.

Something shoved its way through the collapsing masses. The shadowy face hidden inside the deep cowl reminded me of the Grim Reaper coming to collect. The Devil ran forward, lifting an arched blade above his head. He barely flinched as torrents of arrows bored into his flesh.

"He's going for the wires!" someone yelled.

"I've got him!" shouted Tyler and ran out from behind cover. He tried to engage the creature directly, but the Devil broke through him as if his bones were made from eggshells. As quick as the snap of fingers, Tyler was dead.

Before anyone else could react, the Devil severed the speaker wires, cutting the Siren's song short. He slipped around the corner of the mansion and disappeared from sight. I watched in horror as the surviving SOS instantly came back to their senses. The first part of my plan had barely had time to work before it had failed.

"Chosen. Now!" Gabriella yelled.

Everyone around me started to fire. I aimed one gun at a Bloodling and the other at an advancing Skinshifter.

I grit my teeth and pulled the triggers.

The stake hit home first, slugging into the centre of the Bloodling's chest. It disappeared in a screaming burst of ash and flames. The silver bullet a split second after. It grazed against the side of the shifter's hulking frame. It howled in fury but kept coming. Then without warning, its legs buckled and it collapsed to the floor. Next to me, Delagio flicked his wrists and a dozen silver marbles plucked themselves from its body and gravitated back towards his hand.

Midnight was standing upright, his body completely exposed from cover. He laughed maniacally as he pumped the triggers of his guns. In front of us, bodies flew backwards and sideways as the shots connected. I gasped as I watched a bullet hit him right in the arm, but he just laughed even harder.

"IS THAT ALL YOU GOT?" he bellowed and carried on emptying the rounds into the advancing attackers.

More and more SOS took the place of the fallen. There were infinitely more than had been at the meeting. Gabriella had been right about them knowing where to come - a constant stream appeared on the horizon. I couldn't fire fast enough. For every bullet, another two SOS would appear in the gloom. I stopped to slide a clip of iron rounds into my gun. I discarded the crucifix weapon - its ammo spent.

"Ella," I yelled above the torrent of gunfire, "I'm running out!"

After dispatching a Pixie with a headshot, she nodded. "Secondary attack now!"

There was a flurry of unfurling wings and then I watched as a flock of Guardians appeared in the sky and began dive-bombing the SOS. From the sides, a mass of Skinshifters raced into the action. Close behind came a stream of howling Hiveminds, followed by their Bloodseeker leaders.

Those of the SOS who could fly unleashed their own wings and pounced into the air, intercepting the flying Alliance. There where loud whacks as they collided. The burning sky was filled with the silhouettes of spiralling bodies. All I could hear were the sickening sounds of screaming, blades slicing and bones snapping. A Succubus collided with Rachel mid-air. They tumbled around in a ball, slashing and hacking at each other with teeth and nails. I winced as my science teacher received a vicious uppercut to the face. She whirled backwards, but used the movement to her advantage, unleashing an overhead kick that caught the Succubus on her jaw. The dazed Umbra fell to the ground, landing hard on her back. Instantly she was set upon by a pack of Hiveminds. I had to look away as the sounds of her tortured screams filled my ears.

"Third attack!" commanded Gabriella.

A dark shadow materialised overhead. I glanced up to see the Manticore from the Sanctuary soar over the mansion roof. It circled around the fighting Pandemonians, letting out a ferocious roar. In unison, the Guardians pushed up and away from their enemies, leaving them hovering on their own, confused. The beast drew near, snapping out its stinger in a rapid drumbeat. The SOS screamed as their bodies ballooned from the poison. One by one they fell out of the sky into the sea of chomping jaws below.

At the same time, a tremor of hooves drowned out every other sound. A herd of Unicorn appeared from the side of the building, led by Isiodore. He lowered his head and charged into the crowd, skewering a Rogue Skinshifter on the end of his horn. The others copied the action, turning the attacking SOS into macabre kebabs.

It was then that I felt something hit me twice - hard. I coughed and looked down. At first I couldn't see anything, but then two little blooms of red appeared on my chest, followed by thin trails of purple smoke.

Midnight tuned to look at me and his eyes went wide. "Alex is hit!" he bellowed and caught me as I fell backwards. He pulled me down behind the wall. Bits of dust flew up and over us as bullets connected with the brick.

Gabriella and Delagio stopped shooting and crowded around me. At the angle I was at, I could see through a hole in the wall. I saw other Chosen, lying still around the blockades, their bodies surrounded by pools of blood. The Unicorn were being attacked by droves of Hiveminds. They let out agonised screams as the creatures tore at their flesh.

This isn't good, was all I could think as the edges of my consciousness began to waver. My mind was growing sticky.

"Why isn't he healing?" shouted Midnight.

Gabriella pointed to my chest. "Look at the smoke. Damn it, the bullets are coated in Banshee poison! We need to get them out now!"

She ripped open my jacket and jerked up my t-shirt. Around the wounds, the veins had turned an ugly purple colour. She looked over at Delagio, who nodded. He knelt over me and placed his hands a few inches above the wounds. Confused, I frowned up at him as he gave an awkward smile.

"Sorry buddy. I hope this doesn't affect ah friendship."

Agony. Absolute, unparalleled agony.

I screamed until I thought my lungs would burst. Midnight used all of his superior strength to pin me down. Delagio's hands twitched as he coaxed out the bullets. Inside my body, I could feel them start to wiggle about like burning insects trying to eat themselves free from my flesh. The pain was white hot. I could taste it. For what seemed like an eternity, they worked their way closer to the surface.

Both bullets burst out of my skin with a loud pop and settled in Delagio's hands. As I watched him throw them away, I had to resist a strong urge to vomit.

Gabriella placed her hand on my face. "Come on, Alex. Concentrate."

"I-I…"

She took my hand in hers. I felt the charges roll under my skin, strong and powerful.

"I'm here to help. Now concentrate!"

I concentrated. I thought about my wounds and how my skin looked before. I squinted my eyes and focused with everything I had.

"It's working!" shouted Delagio.

I opened my eyes and stared as my skin started to knit itself back together. After a few seconds it was smooth. Apart from the bloodstain and the holes in my clothes there was no evidence I'd been shot.

"Okay, we need to get him inside," Gabriella said in an urgent tone. "Can you stand?"

"I'm fine," I assured her and together we half stood.

"I've got you covered," shouted Midnight, who was already leaning over the wall and shooting.

We ran inside and dived behind the next set of blockades. Peering out, I saw that the fight was dying down. There were a lot of dead Alliance, but the number of red-cloaked bodies far outweighed them. A blood drenched Isiodore stabbed at the fallen bodies to ensure they were dead.

We're going to win! I thought with a sudden rush of hope.

I tempted fate.

As soon as the notion had formed in my mind, a set of doors was wrenched open and the Devil stormed through, followed by scores of SOS. Including Dakin.

I stood up quickly and unsheathed the Crimson Twins. The others jumped to their feet and we threw ourselves into hand-to-hand combat. We were joined by half a dozen Golems, who charged down the steps and into the battle.

The Devil came straight for me. His hooded cloak was down and his animalistic face was slick with blood. He bared his teeth. "The Sorrow be damned, you're mine," he snarled and lashed out with his sword. I parried it and spun out of his reach. His robes swished around him as he swung again. This time the edge of the blade caught my skin. I winced as it cut through the leather, creating a thin red line.

He hissed as he dodged a counter lunge from me. I spun out of the way of another attack. He pounced at me, butting me with his horns. All the air rushed from my lungs as I was propelled backwards into a Golem. It caught me and set me back on my feet just in time for me to dive out of the way of a downward attack from the Devil. The blade connected with the top of the Golem's head, splitting it in two. I felt a twinge of guilt as it collapsed, crosier clattering to the floor.

I reacted fast, pivoting and bringing a blade down on the Umbra's back. A plume of black smoke billowed up from where I connected. He roared in pain and spun around, slashing wildly

397

with a claw. It threw him off balance and I swiped up and out with both blades, severing his horns. Two jets of black blood spewed from the wounds. Instinctively the beast raised his hands to stem the flow. I charged forward, sinking both swords into his chest and carried him with me. I didn't stop until his back slammed against the far wall, creating a huge crack. My swords pinned him there, rolls of thick smoke hissing from his wounds. I pressed my foot against his stomach and wrenched one of the blades free. He growled as the dark blood spilled from his cracked lips and took a final swipe with his sword. I had to duck for fear of losing my head. As I uncoiled, I drove the sword into his solar plexus. He let out a roar, which turned into a gurgle and his body started to dissolve. Soon there was nothing except a pile of what looked like compost and a scorched shadow on the wall. Panting, I turned around.

Midnight appeared in the doorway, dragging a struggling Imp and Vampire in his arms. The air was sucked out of the entrance hall as his form wavered and then disappeared - taking his two hostages along for the ride. Their screams sank into the void with him. When he reappeared in exactly the same spot, the enemies were rag dolls in his arms. He let them go, and they sank to the floor. Without stopping for a breath, he ripped a Bloodseeker away from Delagio by its neck. He tossed it aside, like an unwanted toy. The shocked Vampire flew through the front doors and smashed down on the gravel, sliding several yards in a shower of gravel.

"Midnight, look out!" yelled Gabriella.

Instinctively he jumped to the side just in time to avoid a dagger thrown by Dakin. It whirled past him and stuck into a banister. Gabriella ran at the Bloodling and unleashed a spinning kick to his head. He fell to one knee, but caught her leg as she tried to deliver a second. Her scream jolted my stomach as he began to crush her kneecap.

Midnight had his hands full with the Bloodseeker he'd thrown outside. The flesh had been flayed from one side of its face and it had come back with a grudge. I tried to reach her, but was sent sprawling by a Skinshifter. My swords spiralled out of my hands. As I wrestled with the giant dog, I watched in horror as Dakin used his other hand to strangle my soulmate.

"Help her!" I screamed at the top of my lungs.

I saw Sage Etorre run from his position at the top of the stairs and vault into the air. He landed hard on Dakin and the two went careering along the marble floor. Gabriella took the opportunity to limp away.

With Gabriella safe for the moment, I turned my attention back to the shifter that was trying its best to consume my face.

"Get off me!" I raged.

I used the crook of my elbow to get his muzzle into a headlock position. Using all of my strength against the bucking hellhound, I dragged us both towards the nearest Crimson Twin. The wrong end was closest to me. I ignored the searing pain as I closed my hand around the sharp edge and slid it towards me. Wrapping both hands around the hilt, I rotated the sword and forced the blade into the shifter's mouth. It clamped its jaw together and teeth screeched against blade. I pushed with all of my strength and felt it connect with something soft. I twisted the sword. The beast made a strange coughing sound and collapsed. I withdrew the blade, which sent a wet spray of blood across my face. The bitter metallic taste filled my mouth. I spat it out and shoved the creature off me.

I grabbed the Crimson Twins and scanned for Gabriella. She was hobbling her way towards me. I grabbed her hand and closed my eyes, feeling the electric waves rush through me. When I opened them again, she tested her leg and nodded. I looked down at my previously wounded hand. *Good as new.*

I hadn't seen what had happened between Dakin and Sage Etorre, but the Vampire was nowhere to be seen. Etorre was badly hurt. He stumbled his way back up the stairs, clutching his side. I wanted to go and help him, but I didn't get the chance.

Droves of SOS poured through every door in every direction. All of the Golems were now fully involved in the fight. I swore under my breath.

"Guardians, back to back!" yelled Gabriella, who had already re-entered the fray. Everyone on our side formed a circle in the middle of the entrance hall. The battle continued, but now we were on the losing side. Around us I watched as the Golems fell one by one, overwhelmed by sheer numbers. Their eyes winked out like dying embers. I went to bring my sword down on a

Bloodling, but the tip of a blade pressed against my throat. I turned to see a second Bloodling holding the weapon.

"Don't even think about it," he barked. He nodded towards the floor and I let the Crimson Twins drop. Around me, I could see that everyone else had been overpowered. We were outnumbered three to one. Outside I could still hear the battle raging on and I could only imagine that there was fighting in every part of the Warren. The mansion was alive with the sound of death. But right there, where it mattered, there was only about twelve of us left and three times as many SOS. I looked at all the bodies that littered the floor and my heart sank. At the top of the stairs I saw Faru leaning on his staff, watching the battle as if he were a judging a boxing match. All of his clay effigies were lying in twisted piles around us. A final member of the SOS stepped through the doorway. His red robe rippled around his body. A hulking war hammer rested across his shoulders.

Sage Asmund.

"Sage Faru," he bellowed. "Maybe now you see just how powerful we are. Unseal the Veil and we will leave your Guardians alive. Do not condemn so many to death for the sake of one."

I winced as the blade against my throat dug in harder, drawing blood. Next to me I heard Gabriella whisper to Midnight.

"Teleport. Save yourself."

"No," he replied. "I'm not leavin' you guys behind."

I watched as Faru placed his hands together. He pressed them to his lips and appeared to ponder the situation.

"Asmund - I believe you have forfeited the right to be referred to as a Sage - you know I simply cannot allow that to happen."

"Don't be a fool old man. He's one boy," Asmund shouted, walking forwards until he was at the base of the stairs. "Unseal the Veil, otherwise we will kill everyone where they stand - including the boy - and I shall serve your soul to The Sorrow as a replacement!'

Faru exhaled. It was a long and exaggerated. "I believe that puts us in somewhat of a quandary. I do however have an alternative proposition for you Asmund."

The Vampire leaned forward, resting his chin on the base of his hammer. "Oh, this should be interesting. Please tell me what it is."

"If you let everyone go now and withdraw the SOS, I will allow your followers to live."

Asmund threw back his head and laughed. It was a shrill noise, which defied his Viking-like appearance and made goosebumps shoot down my skin.

"Sorry old friend, I'm afraid that's not going to happen."

"Asmund, I beg you to reconsider."

"Not a chance."

Faru gave a sad, slow shake of his head. "Oh dear, I do so abhor violence. I had hoped it wouldn't come to this."

Confused, I glanced at Gabriella. She gave an almost imperceptible jerk of her head to the right. I strained to look and noticed a pile of Golems dissolving into dust.

Wait...

I glanced at Faru. He appeared to be growing younger by the second. Asmund worked out what was happening a beat too late.

Faru moved so fast he was practically a blur. In a flash he'd descended the stairs. He came to me first and slammed an open palm into the Bloodling's chest, launching him high into the air. Next a knee came into the back of the Succubus subduing Gabriella. Her sword was collected and Faru spun around, lopping off the Umbra's head. He drove the blade into the chest of the Pixie locking down Midnight. Then the blur moved around the circle, striking with his walking staff. He swept the legs of a Bloodseeker from underneath him and stamped the base down between the Vampire's eyes. He then used it to uppercut a Goblin. The whirling blur kept sweeping around the circle, stabbing, crushing and severing his way through the SOS. The sword that had been at my neck had only just clattered to the ground by the time Faru came full circle. He grabbed a Crimson Twin from the ground and threw it at the still airborne Bloodling. It sliced through the air, causing him to burst into flaming dust and came to a wobbling halt in the wall above the doors.

He left Asmund for last. The ex-Sage barely had time to lift his hammer before Faru reached him. He grabbed the Vampire in his hands and closed his eyes.

"Goodbye, old friend."

A blue energy appeared between his fingers, encasing the Vampire. He screamed as his body became a skeletal x-ray and then dissolved into nothing.

My mouth fell open in awe. Faru had dispatched everyone in the room in a matter of seconds.

The energy had gone from the Sage. He looked like a worn, old man again and his expression was one of grief. Using his staff, he shuffled his way back up the stairs and re-joined Sage Etorre.

"All able-bodied Guardians back outside," shouted Gabriella.

It was then - of the corner of my eye – that I saw Sophia appear on the balcony. Dread raked its cold fingers across my skin.

Dakin had his arm locked around her waist.

The Vampire's robe was ripped, his bloodied face twisted and barely recognisable. A knife was pressed against the little girl's throat.

"Midnight!" I croaked.

He turned to look and froze.

"Faru!" shouted Dakin, holding against the struggling Sophia. "Listen to me! If you don't open the Veil door, I will open her throat instead! By Hades I swear it!"

Gabriella gasped and placed a hand over her mouth. The Sage looked upwards, a helpless expression on his worn face.

Rachel rushed into the hallway. She was covered in blood and one of her wings was missing. She looked up and saw what was happening. "Dakin, no!"

"Shut up, bitch." Dakin pointed his free hand at Faru. "Listen to me you pathetic old man. Do as I say unless you want to be responsible for a little girl's death."

Faru gave a single nod of his head.

I felt a surge of panic, even though I knew he had no choice. I only prayed he had a plan up his sleeve.

"Tell your drones to stay where they are!" Dakin warned.

Faru looked at us each in turn. "Do not move. Any of you," he said, holding his gaze on Midnight the longest. I looked up at my friend. His expression had become oddly calm, his enormous chest expanding and contracting very slowly.

Faru turned his back and began to press the bottom of the giant portrait in various places. When he was done, he stood back and the picture began to shift, as it had done before. The staircase appeared and descended to his feet.

"Faru, what are you doing?" said Sage Etorre.

"I cannot allow anyone else to die," he said in an apologetic tone.

Midnight whispered down towards me. "Promise me you'll look after her."

My chest tightened. "Midnight, don't do anything stupid," I pleaded, but knew it was too late. Already the air in the room was thickening. "I promise," I whispered to empty space.

Midnight reappeared behind Dakin, reaching his arms around the Vampire in an attempt to grab him. But Dakin was too quick. He shoved Sophia forward and spun around, sinking the blade into Midnight's sternum.

Sophia screamed. A soul wrenching sound that I knew would stay with me for the rest of my life. Midnight blinked and stared down at the wound. Purple smoke rolled up from around the handle.

"Coated blade," hissed Dakin. "I told you not to try anything!" He yanked the blade back out and started for Sophia again.

Midnight sank to his knees. The thump echoed around the hallway. We all charged forwards. Rachel used her remaining wing to aid her jump. She made it to the edge of the balcony first, grabbed Dakin and before he could react, pulled him over the railings. He hit the ground hard, but her wing slowed her fall. As they thrashed about, I saw her pull out a wooden stake. The last look on Dakin's face was one of complete shock as she plunged it into his throat with a scream. She stood up as the fire burned.

We crowded around Midnight. Purple ooze was dripping from his lips.

403

Sophia was crying. "Help him please," she begged, staring at me.

"Gabriella, give me your hand!"

She linked her fingers with mine and I placed my free hand on his chest. The boom of energy rolled my arm and Midnight's body convulsed as if my hand were an electric pad.

Delagio placed his fingers at his friend's neck. "It's not working!" he yelled. "Try again!"

I placed my hand on Midnight's chest again and once more the rolling boom of electricity surged into his body.

"No, no, no!" shouted Delagio. "Why isn't this working?" He ripped open Midnight's shirt and we all saw why. The knife had entered directly into his heart. Where it had continued to beat, the poison had spread through his arteries into other parts of his body. His chest was a map of grim purple lines. The fingers of the infection had started to creep up the side of his neck. I tried to place my hand on the wound again, but Midnight caught my wrist. He shook his head.

"It's not gonna work, mate," he croaked.

"I have to try!" I said, tears forming in my eyes.

"No you don't. Listen, do me a favour guys - give me moment with Sophia."

I looked over at Gabriella. Tears were streaming down her face, but she nodded. Together we all stood up and walked away.

Sophia moved close, trying to wrap her arms around Midnight. They didn't even reach the ends of his waist. Even though we'd moved to the other end of the balcony, I could still hear every word and it broke my heart.

"Hey, pint size," he croaked. "Listen, I've got to go away now."

"No stay with me...please," she wept, nestling her head into his neck.

"I wish I could, sweetie. I really do. But sometimes things don't go that way."

"But what do I do?" she sobbed. "I don't know what to do."

"I want you to go and live with the Coven. They'll keep you safe."

"But I don't want to."

"I know, but you have to. Will you do that for me?"

"Okay," she sniffed.

"Good girl." His voice cracked. "Listen, you see Alex over there? He's a good guy. I trust him and I know he's going to make sure you're cared for. And you know that Ella and Del love you to bits too."

Sophia nodded and looked up at me. Gabriella had pressed her head against my shoulder. Together we nodded back at her and I tried to smile, but couldn't manage it.

"I've got to go and see my other girls now," he said with tears in his eyes.

"Does that mean you'll forget about me?"

"Are you kiddin' me, how could I forget about you? Tell you what; I'll make you a deal. Are you listenin?"

Sophia nodded and lay her head down on Midnight's shoulder. He pressed his cheek against hers.

"Okay. Well I want you to live your life and be happy. And I promise that when it's your time, we'll be waiting for you. Me, you, Cass and Joy. We'll all be one big family. How does that sound?"

"You promise?"

He raised three fingers. "Chosen's honour."

Sophia closed her little hand around his. He wrapped his arms around her as his eyes closed.

"I love you, kid," he whispered.

"I love you, Dad."

Midnight died with a smile on his face.

32

The harsh wind whipped at my face. We were sitting on little white chairs that had been set up in an expansive graveyard area behind the mansion. A podium was positioned at the front. As the day had progressed, people had come up to it, recounting fond memories of their friends and fellow Guardians who had died in battle. A sombre silence had drifted through the crowd, made more evident by the whistling of the cold wind. The Red Storm still hung overhead, a harsh reminder that as long as the Hades and The Sorrow lived, there could never be peace.

Faru stood at the back, hunched over his staff. His face was drawn with a deep unhappiness that looked like it would never shift. He wasn't the only one. There was an underscore of sniffles from around us and some were openly weeping. The sadness curled inside my stomach like a disease, threatening to eat me alive. Beyond that, I had a bad feeling I just couldn't shake. It had been with me the moment I'd woken in the morning and stayed with me right through the afternoon. The night before, I'd slept badly, once again dreaming of The Sorrow. This time however, it was a repeat of the first dream, moment for moment. I was confused by what it could mean.

Gabriella sat next to me, arms encircled around Sophia. Midnight's locket dangled from the girl's neck. She was staring numbly forward, clutching a piece of paper in her hand. Sophia had been inconsolable from the moment Midnight died; no one had been able to coax a single word from her. She refused to eat. As much as it hurt us to see her that way, we knew that only time would heal her wounds. Gabriella looked over at me and offered a weak smile.

The part came that I'd been dreading - the lowering of Midnight's casket.

Gabriella and Sophia stood up. Together they walked hand in hand over to the podium. Gabriella cleared her throat and leaned into the microphone.

"Midnight was a Chosen, Guardian and a teammate. But beyond that he was a friend. Most people would look at him and see a thug - someone to be feared. But those who knew him knew differently. We were fortunate enough to know the person inside. We knew Michael, the man who had been a wonderful husband and father until his family was cruelly taken away from him. The man who became a parent all over again, for Sophia. Midnight didn't deserve to die. But as they say, the good ones always go first. All I can hope is that if there is a god, he knows that that man's soul deserves an eternity of peace. Midnight, you will be missed." Tears flowed down her face. She moved away from the microphone and placed a chair down, so that Sophia could stand on it. Then she took the piece of paper from the little girl and read it, whilst Sophia stared down at the locket in her hands. "Sophia wanted me to read this for her," said Gabriella in an unsteady voice.

"I don't really remember my mother. I try not to. What I do remember is Midnight. He was my dad. And now he's gone and it hurts so much."

I had to swallow a lump in my throat. Next to me, Delagio had a hand covering his eyes. His body was shaking. Rachel's face was one of stone. She looked broken - like her emotions had been sucked away by the previous night's events.

"Dad, I don't know if you can hear me up there, but I wanted to play something for you. Hopefully you're with the rest of your family and you can all listen together. I miss you already." From somewhere around us, speakers crackled and Eva Cassidy's 'Songbird' began to play. The haunting melody and beautiful words filled the silence. I struggled against the tears. Sophia began to cry and Gabriella pulled her into her arms. I felt sick. *This shouldn't have happened.* At that moment I despised Hades more than I could ever have described.

As I sat there, listening to the music fade away, it suddenly dawned on me what it was that was bothering me so much about my dream. *I need to speak to Faru.*

By the time the ceremonies had finished, the afternoon was fading into twilight. Faru had concluded with a moving speech about remembering those who had fallen, but also not forgetting what we had prevented from happening. How we needed to

407

stand united and carry on. It was hard, but he was right. We'd lost so many – we'd lost Midnight. But Gabriella was still alive, as was Sophia, Delagio and Rachel. I was still alive. The Sorrow hadn't been allowed to pass through the Veil. There was at least that to hold onto.

As everyone walked back to the base, I joined Faru. The Sage was walking slowly, arms folded behind his back. There were no Golems around and he looked younger and healthier, but still he wore his melancholic expression like a mask.

"A terrible few days," he mused as I fell into step with him. "But we must remain strong." It seemed as if he were talking to himself as much as me.

"I know sir…we will. I'm sorry to burden you, but I thought you should know that I dreamt about The Sorrow again last night. The one where I'm in the graveyard."

He raised his eyebrows. "Interesting."

"Yeah, but it wasn't *quite* the same. It didn't feel like I was being tracked. More like I was dreaming it for another reason. I mean why that graveyard? And that derelict mansion - surely they must all mean something?"

He pondered the question for a moment. "That has actually been puzzling me too. The locations of your dreams have been very specific."

"So it might mean something?"

"Perhaps. Perhaps not. I will re-visit them. If I find anything of interest, I shall send someone to investigate. Would that be acceptable?"

"That would be great, thank you."

He gave a slow nod. "You are welcome. Now go and join the others. You will need each other to help stay strong."

I saluted him and ran off towards Rachel and Delagio, who were walking with their arms wrapped around each other - as if one would collapse without the other.

*

"Hold still," laughed Mum, wrapping the bowtie around itself. She kept glancing at the instructions lying on the table. "These things are impossible."

408

I was in the lounge, wearing the tuxedo I'd rented for the Christmas Ball. It was a week after the funeral and things finally seemed to be getting back to 'normal'.

The past week had been hard, but uneventful. The bodies of the Soldiers of Sorrow who had died in battle had been buried in a specially created lot, far away from the Guardian graveyard. Controversially, a stone column had been erected, with each of their names on, as a symbol of respect. Those who had survived were deported permanently to White Mercy prison Pandemonia - Faru had refused outright for there to be any more death. Sophia was taken to live with the Coven. She had still refused to speak, but at least had started to eat a few small meals. Gabriella and I had visited her every day. She would always be sat in the same position on her bed, staring into space, whilst she fiddled with the remaining ear of the bunny that Tommy had given her.

The Manticore had died in battle. Luckily the cubs were old enough to be able to survive without her. Her body had been taken to the Sanctuary, wrapped in strange multi-coloured bandages and placed near the cubs. They had sniffed their dead mother and seemed somehow to understand. They'd made heart wrenching mewing sounds and lain with the body around the clock. Somehow, a few days later all that had remained was a bundle of bandages.

All of the Unicorns had survived the battle, but one of the mares had lost her horn, which meant that she died later in the week. Isiodore had been badly injured, but was being treated and - I was relieved to find out - was expected to make a full recovery.

The Red Storm hadn't subsided, but it was starting to roll away from the base, which suggested that The Sorrow was acting on Faru's prediction of moving to another section of the Veil. I just prayed they could work out which one it would be in time to seal it. The Red Storm had made Chapter Hill famous. There was no way that the HASEA or the government could cover up something that blatant. Masses of meteorologists and other weather analysts had flocked from all over the world - armed with ten-year-old readings of an identical incident in Italy - to try and analyse the cause. Obviously, none had worked it out, so had come up with all kinds of bizarre theories, most of which involved global warming. Religious zealots had also come in droves, carrying signs with the words '*Armageddon is Upon Us*' and *'Death is Coming'* scribbled on them. They were closer to the truth.

Mikey had been brought to the Warren the first morning after the battle, so that Scarlett could attend the funeral. I'd been so relieved to see him that I'd pulled him into a crushing hug. Afterwards he'd walked around the base with his mouth stuck in a permanent O shape.

Mum and a thinner John had returned home that same evening, faces filled with confusion at the menacing sky hovering over their hometown. For the first few days after their return, everything had been okay. Mikey and I were getting on so well now that he was a part of my new world, it seemed to have the effect of drawing us all together. Even John had started to be nice - for a short while. Then he reverted back to dickhead mode.

Gabriella and I had started to officially date, which beyond being more than any guy could hope for, also had the added effect of giving me an excuse for being out all the time. However, it also meant I had to put up with the constant knowing winks from Mikey every time I slipped from the house - my holdall bag containing a spare uniform and the Crimson Twins. Mostly it was just being prepared. If there were any SOS left in the country, they were keeping their heads down. I figured that word had spread about the failed attack on the base - I just prayed it would stay that way. Mikey had suggested that it was a good time to tell Mum and John everything, but I'd decided to keep things quiet for now.

Finished with the bow, Mum stepped back to admire her handiwork. "Perfect," she smiled. "You look wonderful! Doesn't he look wonderful, John?"

John was sat in the armchair by the window. His face appeared from behind the newspaper he was reading. He gave a grunt, and then retreated back into the sports section.

Mum gave a weary sigh. "Well I think it's wonderful that you and Mikey have such lovely girlfriends, even if your brother's is always sneaking out at ungodly hours." She kissed the top of my forehead and left the room, leaving John and me on our own.

410

"Still can't understand why Gabriella's interested in *you*," he muttered under his breath, not intending me to hear, but I caught it all right. His hurtful words twisted into my stomach like a knife. I marched over and ripped the paper from his hands.

"What the hell are you doing?" he demanded, staring at me in disbelief.

"You know what John; I've had enough of you. What exactly is your problem with me?"

"I don't have a problem with you."

"Oh yes you do. So come on, let's sort this out once and for all."

He stood up and tried to move past me. "I don't have to listen to this crap."

I grabbed his arm and wrenched him around to face me. I had the material of his shirt twisted between my fingers. He looked down and back up at me in utter shock.

"Yes you do, John," I repeated. "Things are going to be different around here from now on. So why don't you stop being a cowardly bully for once in your life and tell me what I've done that was so bad you've made it your life's mission to make me feel worthless?"

"Get your hand off me," he hissed.

I held fast, narrowing my eyes. "Not until you give me an honest answer."

We stared at each other. He coiled his hands into fists. I gritted my teeth together. "Tell me!"

"Because you're a constant reminder of *him*," he barked, shoving my hand away.

I hadn't expected his answer and I could barely get my words out. "I- you- what? You mean my real dad?"

"Yes."

I shook my head. "You are kidding me right? You've got an alpha complex over my dead father?"

He looked away from my intense stare. "You don't understand."

"No I don't. Mum is married to *you* John. She has been for over fifteen years! How in the hell can you be jealous of a man she's barely spoken about for all that time? It's beyond pathetic!"

John stared past me out of the window. "She does talk about him. Every single night."

My mouth fell open. "What?"

Tears had formed in John's eyes. "All I hear when she sleeps is the sound of her sobbing her heart out and repeating his name over and over. Like not having him rips her apart from the inside. She's never mentioned it. Not once. I don't think she remembers. I've lived with that for *sixteen* years. So don't you dare tell me not to be jealous! Not when I'm reminded every single night that I can never be the man to her that he was."

I didn't know what to say. My mouth kept trying to form syllables, but I couldn't arrange them into words. It all made sense now. After a minute I managed to ask, "So why haven't you left her then?"

"Because your mother is everything to me."

He gingerly placed a hand on my arm, as if unsure that the movement would work. "I'm sorry Alex, I know you don't deserve the crap I give you. You're a good kid and I care about you...a lot. It's just that I get so frustrated sometimes...and you're the most obvious target."

My head was spinning. "John, I'm sorry. I had no idea..."

He shook his head. "There's nothin' to say. Alex, despite what you believe, I *do* care about you. I've just never been able to show it very well." He lowered his eyes until he was staring at the carpet. "Listen, I'll try and go easier on you from now on. But you have to promise me that you'll keep this between us."

I stared dumbly at him.

"Promise me."

I nodded my head.

"Good." He wiped his eyes and then clapped me on the shoulder. "Smile, you've going to a ball with a super-hot date." With that, he walked out of the lounge. "Elaine… hun, can you remember what the pin is for the box office films?"

The doorbell rang. I looked out of the window. Agent Green was standing on the doorway, hopping from foot to foot as if it would help him avoid the rain, which was falling in rods. A sleek stretch limo was purring just at the end of the driveway.

I shook away the million thoughts buzzing through my head and put on my game face. I found Mum and kissed her on the cheek. John gave me a nod from the kitchen doorway. Shouting goodbye to Mikey, I grabbed a small box from the sideboard and popped it in my inside jacket pocket. I felt the other side to make sure Dad's picture was there and then answered the door. Agent Green opened an umbrella and held it above my head. As the door closed I heard my mother shout 'be sensible'. I rolled my eyes and headed for the limo.

Fifteen minutes later we pulled up outside the Warren. Agent Green opened the door and handed me the umbrella. I took it and headed for the front door, the rain beating a drumline on the material above my head. Inside the entrance hall, I waited at the foot of the grand stairs. For some reason I was nervous; I could feel my heart thrumming away in my chest. Iralia walked around the corner. A long gash on the side of her face - a wound she'd received in the battle - was slowly healing.

"Why don't you look dashing? If you and Gabriella ever split, you know where to find me," she joked.

I laughed. Iralia gave a mischievous wink and headed up the stairs. "I'll let her know you're here."

A minute or so later, Gabriella appeared at the top of the stairs. My jaw almost hit the floor. She looked breathtaking. Her hair was piled onto her head - held in place with jewelled pins - and long earrings sparkled in the light. She was wearing a black silk dress, which gathered at the knees and then flared out at the bottom. The dress was cut low, exposing her slender neckline. A matching clutch bag lay nestled between her arm and side. I swallowed hard, marvelling at her as she glided down the steps.

"You look- you...wow," I stammered.

Gabriella laughed. "You look very handsome too." She pulled me towards her and we shared a gentle kiss. I always loved it that when I opened my eyes; the first thing I saw was the deep blue of hers. It was a sight I prayed I'd see every day for the rest of my life.

"I have something for you," I said, pulling open my jacket and removing the small box.

"Oh, you shouldn't have." She used the tone that I'd seen in lots of movies. Where the girl says 'you shouldn't have', but what they actually mean is, 'I'm glad you did.'

"Well, I needed to do something with all that money that keeps appearing in my bank account," I teased.

She opened the box, and gasped. The diamond studded pendant necklace winked at us from its lining. "Oh Alex, it's...beautiful." I looked up and saw that tears had formed in her eyes.

"You like it then?" I said, feeling myself grow a little embarrassed. "I went to loads of different shops. As soon as I saw this one, it just felt right, you know? But if you don't like it I can..."

"It's *perfect*," she smiled. Removing the necklace from its box, she gestured it towards me. "Could you?"

I took the pendant and stepped behind her. Slipped it around her neck and fastened the clasp at the back.

"Let's see then."

Gabriella twirled around and a felt a rush of emotion. It *was* perfect. Like it had been made just for her.

"It looks incredible," I said truthfully. Gabriella's face lit up and she squealed, ploughing me with kisses.

"Shall we go then?"

"Definitely."

* .

As we made our way into the hub, I noticed Tim standing with Lucy Healy - one of the girls who'd insulted me all those weeks ago in the lunch queue. They were having their photo taken by a professional photographer. Tim noticed us and waved us over. I could see Lucy shrinking the closer we got. Tim gave me a high five.

"Alex, wow it feels like forever since I've seen you. Looking good mate. And Gabriella, wow you look...wow." He received an unsubtle elbow in the ribs from his date.

"Oh yeah and you know Lucy right?' he said gesturing towards her.

"Yeah I do. Hi Lucy," I said.

"Hi Alex, you look...nice."

"Thanks."

"I love your dress," added Gabriella with a genuine smile.

"It's nothing compared to yours. It's so stunning," Lucy said with an awkward smile of her own. She turned to Tim. "Can we go in now? I need to get a drink."

"Oh right- err ok," Tim nodded, his mass of hair flopping about. "See you in there guys. Come find me in a bit Alex, we need to have a catch up."

"Sure thing."

The two walked off and entered into the main hall, where most of the party was taking place.

As soon as we opened the double doors, we were hit by Christmas. The whole room had been transformed into a winter wonderland. The usual wooden floor had been covered with a soft snow like substance. A machine mounted on the ceiling puffed out artificial snow in a gentle stream. The walls were covered in fairy lights, which flashed in a kaleidoscope of colours, and a huge Christmas tree had been erected in the corner. Little red and blue orbs hung on its branches and even more fairy lights looped their way around it, and a golden star was perched precariously on the top. A makeshift bar had been set up at the far end of the room. Three barmen dressed as elves were serving eggnog and mulled wine to students with ID. Next to it was a cooking booth. The chef- a man large and hairy enough to actually be Santa himself was serving fried chestnuts as well as the more common hotdogs and hamburgers. In a booth on the stage, DJ Clawz had his head buried in his decks. Music pumped out of speakers mounted on poles at each end of the raised platform.

The room was pretty full already, some of the partygoers dressed in seasonal outfits. Masses of female elves gyrated with Santas on the dance floor. Others – like us – had gone with the more formal approach and were wearing suits and dresses. Many of the girls had abandoned their dates, opting for the safety of their friends. Several glum looking guys were sat on chairs sipping cups of cola and stealth vodka. I saw Grace look at me from her group of friends. We held each other's gaze for a moment and then she looked away. I felt a flash of shame for never getting back to her.

415

Within a few seconds of entering the room, most of the girls had swarmed around Gabriella like glammed up piranhas. They all gushed over her hair, her dress and - I noticed with a swell of pride - her necklace. I wasn't on my own for long as Elliot, Richard and some of the other football lads made their way over to me. A torrent of words were launched in my direction.

"Mate you look dapper!"

"Where'd you get the suit?"

"Are you here *with* Gabriella?"

"So are you guys together?"

"Are you going out after the ball?"

I tried to answer the questions as best I could, but it just provoked more. I gave Gabriella a glance, who shrugged in a 'what can you do' way. I pointed towards the bar and did the motion of a glass to the lips. She nodded and gave a smile. I noticed some of the other girls cast looks at me. Then they span back and babbled even more at her, probably about whether or not we were seeing each other.

"I'm going to get a drink," I said.

We all headed over together. As I reached the bar and several of the guys were trying to talk to me at the same time, I realised something I'd never considered before.

Being popular is bloody hard work.

Later, Gabriella and I managed to steal away some time together. We were standing outside the side doors, where a little marquee tent doubling as the smoking area had been set up. We stood next to the heater, sipping mulled wine from little red cups - courtesy of some Charm used by Gabriella on the barmen. The rain was coming down in torrents. It pattered angrily against the fabric roof, threatening to rip it down.

I took a sip of the spicy alcohol and savoured the warm glow in my chest. I pointed with my cup towards the party, which was still going strong inside.

"What do you think?"

Gabriella's smiled. "I'm really enjoying it."

"Me too. I have to admit they've really pulled the stops out. I mean I thought it would be some white spray on the windows and a couple of balloons. I'm really impressed."

Gabriella looked away with a knowing smile.

"What?"

"Let's just say that a certain Mister Farris found out and arranged for a little extra effort to be made."

I burst out laughing. "Really?"

Gabriella shrugged her shoulders and took a sip of her wine. Then she turned and pressed her back against my chest. I wrapped my arms around her and together we swayed gently to the faint music coming from inside. At the same time a boom of thunder growled from overhead. I cast my eyes into the distance and saw several jagged burst of lighting descend from a blood red cloud.

"Alex, does it look like it's heading this way to you?" Gabriella asked.

I didn't answer. I was too distracted by Terry stepping outside. He was wearing a tatty looking suit, the collar of his shirt dirty and not covering his tie properly. Not noticing us, he fished a packet of tobacco and papers out of his pocket and tried to roll a cigarette. He couldn't manage it, because one hand was wrapped in plaster. He kept dropping the tobacco and swearing under his breath. Eventually someone else offered to do it for him. Terry took the cigarette with a nod and lit it up.

"Are you okay?" Gabriella asked me.

I thought about it and realised I felt...nothing. Not anger, not hatred, not even pity. Compared to what I'd been through over the last few weeks, compared to all the incredible people I'd met...and lost, Terry didn't even register any more. He was nothing but a distant, bad memory.

"I'm fine. Let's go back inside."

As we moved past Terry, he noticed me for the first time. His eyes widened and the cigarette tumbled from his fingers, falling close to my foot. I picked it up and handed it back to him.

"Err...thanks, Eden," he said keeping his gaze on the ground.

"No worries," I replied and we carried on inside.

The music had slowed a little. Gabriella took the opportunity to pull me onto the dance floor. We slow danced, her soft cheek pressed against mine. Other couples swirled around us, alcohol helping them to re-discover their confidence. Most of the faculty

417

were standing in a group near the entrance. They were all laughing at a joke Mr Hanley was telling in an animated manner.

Everything went off.

There were gasps of panic as we were plunged into darkness. The music screeched into silence.

"No one panic," I heard Mr Hanley shout. "Just stay where you are."

A few seconds later the backup generators kicked in and the emergency lights flickered on. They were barely able to fill the large space. Looming shadows appeared in every corner.

"Okay everyone, it's only a power cut. Nothing to be frightened of."

"I beg to differ," said a cold voice from the gloom.

We all turned to look at the source of the voice. A dark figure stood just inside the doorway. He was shrouded in darkness. He took a step forward and my stomach heaved.

It was a Soldier of Sorrow.

The Rogue's face was hidden underneath the large cowl of his red cloak. The rain had matted it to his skin, which made it look like he was covered in blood. There were nervous whispers at the new arrival. Gabriella gripped my arm so hard it hurt.

"This can't be happening."

Mr Hanley separated himself from the other teachers and moved towards the intruder before either of us could react.

"Now listen here, if this is some kind of joke?"

The Rogue removed a hand from the folds of his cloak. Clutched in his fist was a blade. Mr Hanley's eyes went wide. He raised his hands and backed away - but not far enough. The Rogue slid the sword through his chest as if her were no more than a lump of butter. A sickening gurgle escaped from Mr Hanley's throat. He staggered backwards and collided with a drinks table, which collapsed under his weight. He fell silent. There were screams and people started to run for the fire escape doors. They were chased back in by at least a dozen more SOS, all wielding deadly weapons. I couldn't believe what was happening.

The Rogue leader wiped the sword on his robe. "As you can see, we are deadly serious. Now, two of you know why we're here. Step forward or everyone suffers the same fate as this pathetic human."

There were whimpers from around us. Gabriella looked at me and together we stepped forward out of the crowd.

"Ah, there you are," he chuckled.

"These are innocent people, you bastard!" Gabriella shouted.

The man shook his head. "Tut tut. Such language."

"What do you want?" I demanded.

"You know what we want." He pointed the sword menacingly at us. "You."

There were gasps of confusion from my schoolmates. I heard Tim whisper from behind me. "Alex, what's going on?"

"Tim, not now," I answered. To the leader I said, "Fine, if you want us then we'll go with you. But leave everyone else out of it. They're not a part of this."

"I couldn't care less," the Rogue answered. "They stay where we can keep an eye on them."

"So now what?" I said.

"First things first, slide over any weapons you're carrying. And don't try and trick us. For every one we find, we'll kill another human."

The crowed whimpered in response.

I raised my hands out. "We're at a school ball. We don't have any weapons!"

Gabriella cleared her throat. "Err…actually…" She opened her clutch bag, pulled out three Apatrope daggers and slid them along the floor towards the Rogue. He stopped them with his boot.

I cast her a look.

"Like I said, a real girl is ready for any situation," she whispered.

"Check them!" the leader ordered.

A Succubus and Bloodling marched over and jostled us about as they checked for hidden weapons. The Bloodling found my picture and stared at it. I snatched it back and glared at him.

"They're clean," he announced.

The leader looked past us. "Get everyone else in the middle," he ordered. The Rogues fell in around the students, herding them into a tight huddle on the dance floor. The whimpering DJ was yanked down from the booth by a Pixie. Her silver hair shone in the light, jarring with her vicious nature. She tossed him into the rest of the group.

The leader pointed towards the other teachers. "You too."

Together they shuffled past the fallen Mr Hanley. Miss Cleveland wailed as she looked down at where his lifeless body was slumped. They gave us horrified glances as they passed.

The room fell quiet. I scanned around, searching for a way to gain the advantage, and I could tell that Gabriella was doing the same. *It's no good.* We were trapped, outnumbered and defenceless...the situation was hopeless.

The Rogue leader pushed back his cowl, completely exposing his face. He was bronze skinned. Dense stubble covered his chin and his eyebrows were thick caterpillars crawling above his dark eyes. I hadn't ever seen him before, but yet there was something familiar about him.

"Don't recognise me?" he asked.

"Should I?" I retorted.

"Well I wouldn't expect you to in this skin." He put on a mock high voice. "But I'd hoped you'd be able to see past how I look on the outside." His voice reverted and he grit his teeth together. "I remember *you* well. If memory serves correctly, the last time we met, you skewered my head to the floor."

A wave of shock washed over me. "Bargheist," I choked.

He gave an exaggerated bow. "The one and only."

"But how? You were deported!" gasped Gabriella.

He tapped a finger against his nose. "Oh but that would be telling, and I don't want to reveal the big secret."

The other Rogues laughed. It was a cruel noise that caused fresh sounds of fear from the crowd. I glanced at Gabriella. She seemed just as confused as me. Bargheist checked the clock hanging on the wall by the Christmas tree.

"Time to go. Grab someone for insurance."

A Pixie leaned in to grab Lucy, but Tim pushed his date behind him. "Take me instead," he said. His selfless bravery took me by complete surprise.

"Whatever," said the Rogue and yanked him to his feet. She pushed my friend towards us and was joined by two of her comrades.

420

Bargheist addressed his remaining followers. "As for the rest, if any of them so much as sneeze the wrong way, kill them." He turned and walked out of the door. I felt the sharp sting of a blade prod into my back. The same happened to Gabriella and Tim. Together, we were forced out of the room at knifepoint.

The doors closed with a resounding echo. The hallway beyond was desolate. The money-collecting desk was empty and the photo area was bare. The stand had toppled over, the camera reduced to shards of broken machinery scattered across the floor. The emergency light continued in the hub, giving the whole place an eerie vibe.

I looked over at Tim. His face was panic-stricken. I could barely imagine what must have been going through his mind. Gabriella's expression gave nothing away. Her lips were a tight line. I could tell that even though her face was blank, inwardly her mind was whirring. A sharp pain in my back reminded me to keep moving.

"Listen, if we don't make it through this..." I whispered.

"Alex, don't. We're both making it out of this alive."

I shut my mouth and fought against the dread, which grew with each step. I was furious at myself. I'd known something was wrong - I'd felt it after we won the battle. I'd missed something; deep down I knew it. And now, the whole of the school were in danger. *Damn it! I should have at least hidden some weapons here!*

"This way," growled Bargheist, turning down a corridor. We followed behind.

The shifter jerked to a sudden stop.

He stayed motionless, as if someone had removed his batteries. Then a welt of blood bloomed in the centre of his back. He dropped to his knees, exposing Rachel, sporting a blood soaked silver dagger. Without questioning how or why, we seized our chance. I spun around and down, sweeping the Bloodling's legs from under him. Before he had even hit the ground, I wrenched the sword from his grip and brought it down across his neck, severing his head. A swipe of blades told me that Gabriella had taken care of the other two Rogues.

"Y-you just killed them!" gasped Tim.

"We had no choice, they would have killed us," I replied. We turned back to face out saviour.

"Rachel, thank god," Gabriella breathed, giving her a relieved hug.

"Are we glad to see you," I added.

"Wait, isn't that… your *science teacher*?" gaped Tim.

I had to resist the urge to laugh. "I'll explain later," I promised.

"Rachel, what are you doing here?" asked Gabriella.

Rachel looked confused. "Didn't Faru tell you? He sent me to keep an eye out, just in case. Easy considering I technically work here. I've spent most the night circling this bloody school." She nodded down at the bodies. "Saw this lot arrive."

At least someone was prepared, I thought glumly.

"Listen, we can't stay here," she said sheathing her blade onto the fully armed Kapre belt that hung around her suit trousers. "I don't know what the hell is going on, but the place is crawling with SOS. I've called it in. The rest of the HASEA are on their way. I told them to meet us at the Gymnasium. Come on."

"Will someone tell me what in the name of god is going on?" moaned Tim.

"Sorry mate, explanations later, running first."

Rachel turned and sprinted down the corridor, with us hot on her heels. We broke out of the side door, into the torrent of rain. The booming of thunder was so loud I could hardly hear myself think. The rain was coming down in droves; it hit the ground with such force, it bounced. We splashed our way through, heading out of the main school section. Gabriella had to bunch up her dress so that she could run properly. Her hair had come undone and thick strands were plastered down the side of her face. My heart was thrumming in my chest as we headed around the main area and into the Gymnasium. We entered together, apart from Tim, who arrived over a minute later. I'd forgotten he couldn't run at our speeds. When he got inside, he almost collapsed.

"H-how, can you r-run that fast?" he wheezed.

Looking around, I noticed it was dark and gloomy. Only one emergency light was working. I turned to Rachel. "What now?"

She pointed to the main gym hall. "Let's wait in there."

We opened the door. The gym was filled with more shadows and darkness. Decrepit foam mats lay stacked at the far end and climbing ropes hung from the ceiling like old nooses. I could smell stale sweat; it seemed to pour out of the walls. The room was deathly silent.

It was at that moment that I noticed that Rachel was wearing the ring I'd seen her drop all those weeks ago. I saw the crest on the top. A pyramid of 3 stars sitting inside a crescent moon. It was the same symbol as the one on the front of the derelict mansion in my nightmares.

Moonstella.

The word written above the mausoleum, I hadn't been able to understand what it meant, because it didn't actually *mean* anything. It was a family name. The dread I'd felt began to leak to the surface. We'd got it wrong. Lafelei's words hadn't been referring to the Coven.

Betrayed by the moon and stars.

Moonstella.

My blood turned to ice.

Rachel drew her gun and pointed it at us.

33

Rachel, don't do this," I pleaded.

"It has to be this way. I'm sorry," she said in a hollow voice.

Gabriella shook her head in disbelief. "All this time?"

"All this time."

"Will someone *please* tell me what's happening?" squeaked Tim.

Gabriella answered in a tone of sadness mixed with anger. "People like Alex and I protect humans from evil creatures. We thought Rachel was one of us. Turns out she's an evil creature."

"But why?" I asked.

In a flash, Rachel's voice became full of rage. "Because of people like you. Chosen," she hissed. "During the Great Purge your kind slaughtered my entire family as if they were nothing more than dogs! Not just my parents. My grandparents, sisters, brothers, uncles, cousins. All of them dragged into the streets and burned alive. You think you know grief? I found everyone I have ever loved in a charred heap at the edge of our estate." A tear rolled down her cheek. "So mutilated, I couldn't even mark their graves properly, because I couldn't work out who was who!"

Gabriella took a step forward, which made Rachel swing the gun in her direction.

"Rachel, I'm so sorry. What those Chosen did to your family was unforgivable. But the Great Purge was a long time ago. Those people are long gone. We're not the same as them. Rachel, we are your friends. Please let us go."

The Pixie shook her head. "I'm sorry, but this is bigger than you both. It's taken me centuries to create a new persona and establish myself as a trusted Guardian of the HASEA. I've had to hide who I really am for so long; I almost let myself get caught up in it all." She grit her teeth. "God, I'm so sick of all the lies!"

"What are you trying to achieve?" I asked.

424

"Isn't it obvious? My entire lineage was wiped out without so much as a second thought. Cast into oblivion. Well I didn't forget! And I'm going to make damn well sure that no one ever forgets me! I'll be the person who brought down the Alliance."

"Rachel, there are thousands of Guardians all over the world," Gabriella pointed out. "How can you ever hope to bring down the Alliance on your own?"

Rachel looked surprised. "On my own? I don't think you quite understand." She lifted up her top lip with the barrel of her gun. The Eye of the Abyss had been tattooed on the soft underside.

My brain started spinning. "Wait, you're a member of the SOS?" I asked in a confused voice.

"Not just a member Alex. I'm a leader."

Gabriella and I exchanged a horrified glance. I felt sick to my stomach.

"I don't understand," choked Gabriella. "You're a Luminar. Hades hates them even more than humans. He barely tolerates them being members of the SOS, why would he allow one to become a leader?"

"Because I have something that he needs."

"What could you possibly have that Hades needs?"

"A hidden section of the Veil, sealed and under my control."

Gabriella's face went ashen. "How...where?"

"It's on her estate," I answered instead. "Inside a Mausoleum."

The Pixie turned to look at me, sweeping the gun with her. "How do you know that?"

"Call it an educated guess," I said.

Rachel stared at me for a second, flexing her fingers against the gun. "It was a family secret. My ancestors sealed a section of the Veil and hid it away. Only someone of my bloodline would be able to unseal it. The idea was to use the doorway if they ever needed to escape from danger." She pulled a grim face. "Only your kind got to them before they had a chance to use it."

There was a thump as something louder than rainfall fell onto the roof. Gabriella looked at me. Rachel didn't react; she was lost in the past.

425

"I waited until the first time I was sent to Pandemonia. I went straight to Hades; told him that I wanted to bring down the Alliance and that when he chose to invade Earth, I had a doorway he could use that was completely unknown to the Alliance. In exchange he made me the leader of my own group of Rogues, so that I'd have the support I needed to weaken the Alliance in preparation for that day."

"You're working directly for the Umbra King? Have you lost your bloody mind?" shouted Gabriella. "Hades is the worst kind of evil! You blame Chosen, but as we speak, he is killing thousands of your kind!"

Rachel pressed the gun against her forehead for a moment, as if trying to squeeze out a bad thought. "Don't you think I know that? It kills me to have to work for that twisted son of a bitch. But I can't allow myself to become concerned with any of that. I have to stick to my plan."

The traitor turned to me, continuing her speech as if a robot returning to her default programming. I could tell that this was a confession, her way of achieving absolution.

"Hades learned that one of the Elementals had spoken of a new Awakening, one that could bring about the Chosen to stand against him. So when he was delivered the news about Alex, he immediately ordered The Sorrow to start tracking him. He wanted to use my doorway to send it through to Earth straight away. But I knew the moment I unsealed the Veil, Faru would sense it, investigate and my cover would be blown. Everything I'd worked so hard to put in place would come undone because of one, single boy."

Rachel let the gun linger on me. "You'd be dead, The Sorrow would return to Pandemonia and I'd have to go into hiding or on the offensive. I didn't want that. But still, it was an opportunity for me to advance my own plans. What I needed was a way to distract Faru and keep my cover in place. After I found out about Faru's plans to seal the Warren's Veil, I came up with the idea of the fake siege."

"Fake siege?" I said incredulously. "I was there; that siege was real. Midnight *died* in that siege."

"The siege itself was real, but the *reason* for it was false. I also made sure that you found out about it."

Gabriella and I looked at each other, lost.

"Think about the attack at the Black Tap. Out of all the Coven, who exactly had the premonition?" said Rachel.

"It was Sylvia," replied Gabriella and then covered her mouth as if she'd sworn.

"Exactly, and Sylvia worked for me."

Something clicked in my brain. "The attack in the bar was a setup. You *wanted* me to follow Dakin."

Rachel smiled. "Exactly. Poor Dakin genuinely believed he was there to recruit new followers. He also believed the siege was real. I couldn't trust him with the full truth. You killed his maker Rahuman - he was too volatile. I just had to take the chance that someone would notice him leave the bar." She gestured towards me. "Which the perfect person did."

"But what about those girls? They were real and so was what almost happened to them," I countered.

"That was easy. All it took was a few attractive young Bloodlings to mention a secret bar they were supposedly heading to. Malachi despises humans - seems to have forgotten that he used to be one. Plus he's a supporter of the SOS. There was no doubt in my mind that if we sent the drunkest, loudest girls in the area into his bar, he'd do the rest."

For the first time I saw the real Rachel. A woman so consumed with revenge that she teetered on the edge of madness.

"But what about all of the other SOS who attacked me?" I asked. "Surely that's going against your plans?"

Rachel shrugged. "Hades wants you dead. He didn't care how it happened - The Sorrow was a failsafe. He gave orders for you to be killed, and Sage Asmund sent in his own followers - including Rahuman - to take you out. Others did their own thing so they could fall into favour with Hades. Like Sylvia, who faked another premonition without my knowledge and organised a group of Rogues to kill you, or Bargheist who acted without my say so and got himself caught." She smiled. "Which is why they had to go."

I thought about Sylvia. How she'd been found dumped in an alleyway with her throat opened. *It was Rachel.*

Gabriella had one hand closed around the pendant on her necklace. The other was wrapped around the nape of her neck. At first I thought it was a position of distress, but then I noticed that with incredibly subtle movements she was attempting to undo the clasp with her fingers. It suddenly dawned on me. *The necklace has diamonds on it!*

"But why let us know what was happening; why not just attack us unprepared?" I asked, in an effort to keep Rachel distracted. "If you'd done that, then the SOS might have won."

Rachel shook her head as if I should understand her twisted logic.

"I already told you, the siege was a fake. I didn't want the SOS to actually succeed in unsealing the Veil. But Dakin almost managed to get Faru to do it, which is why I had to stop him. In fact it was the perfect cover, he needed to be dealt with anyway as his hatred for Alex was making him a liability." She nodded her head as if that justified her act. "I'd managed to convince Hades that opening the doorway and unleashing The Sorrow inside a Guardian base would be seen as an outright declaration of war against Earth. One that he wasn't yet in a position to deal with. So he agreed for me to pretend to the rest of the SOS – apart from my own followers of course - that there would be a real siege on the base to force Faru to open his section of the Veil. All the while it was just misdirection to keep the HASEA and Faru distracted...whilst I opened mine."

"No…" breathed Gabriella.

Absolute horror filled me up. "The Sorrow is here?" I choked.

A dark grin appeared on Rachel's face. "Not just here Alex...*here*. And you have nothing to defend yourself with."

Loud bangs hit the roof. They were followed by the sound of dozens of feet scrambling about. Then I heard it.

The unmistakable scream of The Sorrow's demented Unicorn.

"Not long now," breathed Rachel.

I glanced at Gabriella. She was still struggling with the clasp.

"So you're going to offer me up to get into Hades good books? Is that it? Very original, Rachel." I said sarcastically.

Rachel banged the gun against her temple. "No, no no. You don't understand! Hades is merely a means to an end. *My* end. I just needed him to trust me. I told him that if he gave me command of The Sorrow whilst it was on Earth, then not only would I get it to murder the Chosen Lafelei spoke of, I'd offer it up the hybrid baby that it missed the first time around."

Gabriella's jaw tightened. I could see she was trying not to lose her composure. She had also managed to get the clasp undone.

"So what's the plan after we're dead?"

Rachel turned to me. "That's the beauty of it. I'm going to unleash The Sorrow on the Warren anyway. Then everyone will know it was me and that I was working directly for Hades." She leaned forward with a huge smile on her face. "I'm going to start the war."

"How could you?" shouted Gabriella. "People we care about died because of you! And you want to kill *more?* What about all the people who you're betraying? Faru, Sophia...Delagio?"

The corners of Rachel's mouth turned down. "I don't want any of you to suffer, but this is the only way to get my revenge. You think I don't care but I do." She stared at us. "I care about all of you, but this is the *only way.*"

I took a step forward and the gun was instantly aimed towards my head.

"You've got funny way of showing it!" I shouted.

"Stay back!" Rachel ordered.

The howling grew louder. I could hear footsteps closing in from somewhere nearby. Each one sounded like the beat of a death drum.

"Or what, Rachel? We already know you're going to have us killed. So go ahead!"

"I said *stay back*!"

With a movement so quick it was barely perceptible; Gabriella threw the necklace at Rachel. It sliced across the Pixie's cheek with a loud hiss.

"Bitch!" she screeched, clutching the side of her burning face. Sprinting forwards, we both dived for her at the same time. Connecting hard, we all slammed to the ground together.

Gabriella pinned Rachel down and I prised the gun from her grip, throwing it to the other side of the room.

"NO!" Rachel screamed like a demented beast. She bucked, catching Gabriella unprepared and throwing her off. The frenzied Pixie kicked upwards with her knee, landing a powerful blow to the side of my head. Dazed, I collapsed to the floor, and through blurry vision I watched as Rachel sprang into a predatory crouch. She slipped the blood soaked dagger from its sheath. Behind her, Gabriella was still scrambling to her feet.

"I'm not going to let a Chosen kill me like you did my family," she hissed.

"I'm not trying to kill you!" I insisted, but she wasn't listening. I recoiled as she raised the blade above her head. The glow of the storm outside caught the edge and for a moment it winked red, like the eye of some demonic creature.

Bang!

The deafening sound made my ears ring. It was followed by a sharp gasp. Rachel's face twisted into a contorted O of pain and shock, as a little puff of smoke slipped out of a hole in her arm. Gabriella was standing next to a surprised looking Tim, who was holding the smoking gun. He dropped it as if it were on fire and looked at me with wide eyes.

"I-I shot her," he stammered.

"You *shot* me!" Rachel hissed. "You little bastard!"

Before I had a chance to react, she threw the blade at my best friend.

The dagger whirled through the air, heading straight for his jugular. It stopped a fraction from his throat - suspended in mid-air as if hanging from invisible strings.

"I can't believe I ever loved you."

We all spun around to see Delagio appear in the doorway, his arm outstretched and wearing a sad expression. "All this time I thought you cared about us."

Rachel gave Delagio a pleading look. "Del, I love you. Please don't-"

Delagio closed his eyes and jerked his arm to the right. The blade sliced through the air and buried itself into Rachel's throat. Her eyes went wide and she closed her fingers around the handle. I winced as with a rough movement, she pulled the blade

430

out and stared at it. A jet of blood squirted from the wound. Rachel gave a simple nod of her head as if everything finally made sense, then crumbled to the floor and fell still.

Delagio was silent. He seemed stunned by his actions, like he couldn't work out whether he'd actually done it or not.

I was about to speak, but a sudden thump on the outside wall stopped me. It was followed by another and another. Dozens of thuds that made the whole gymnasium shake. A sound similar to hundreds of crickets started up, but far louder and harsher.

"Depraved," breathed Gabriella, "We need to go *now*."

Something crawled over the fire escape door and for a moment the windows were blocked out by mottled pink flesh. A stench of decay pervaded the room, making me gag.

"Go!"

Delagio lifted Tim off his feet and together we all sprinted out of the Gymnasium.

Straight into the path of The Sorrow.

34

Gabriella let out a bloodcurdling scream so haunting it made me shiver all the way to my soul.

My heart stalled from the sheer horror of what I was witnessing. The Sorrow was far, far worse than I'd been able to capture in my nightmares. The soul-eater towered over ten feet in height; arching horns that jutted from its head grazed the ceiling. Amour the shade of dried blood and marked with unknowable symbols encased the creature, and long, urchin-like spines poked out from in-between each joint. A gruesome iron mask covered its face. The edges were studded and deep vertical slits filled the mouth plate. There were no eyes behind the mask, just hollow pits of pure darkness. The decaying mask was kept in place only by a set of fraying straps that locked around The Sorrow's head.

When it saw us it lifted a gauntleted hand and pointed. Its joints squealed like a tortured animal. Then it reached the same arm behind its back and unsheathed a sword easily as big as Sophia. It smashed into the floor, spraying up splintered tiles. The Sorrow started to walk forwards, the blade edge squealing and sparking as it trailed behind.

Gabriella had curled into a ball on the floor, hands covering her eyes. The confident, strong woman had disappeared, replaced by the terrified little girl from all those years ago. Tim's face had gone chalk white; he looked in danger of having a heart attack.

"Help me get them back into the gym!" I screamed at Delagio.

Together we dragged the weeping Gabriella and dazed Tim away from the advancing creature, back into the Gymnasium. Setting Gabriella down, I pulled her trembling arms away from her face. Her eyes were squeezed shut and her teeth clenched together. She must have bitten her tongue, because blood dribbled from between her lips.

"Ella, snap out of it!" I shouted.

She didn't react.

I could hear the thunderous boom of footsteps as The Sorrow drew closer.

"Please snap out of it!"

She made no indication that she could hear me.

I leaned in close and pressed my mouth against her ear. "*Please* Gabriella; if you don't snap out of this, The Sorrow is going to kill us both…I need you."

Something seemed to register. Her eyelids fluttered open and it only took one look for me to know that Gabriella was back with me.

"Come on," I said dragging her to her feet.

Slap!

I turned to see Delagio backhand Tim across the face. A trickle of blood spilled down from his nose. He glanced up – looking in a fair amount of pain - but the slap had done the job of bringing him back to his senses.

Gabriella gathered up her dress and together we all sprinted for the fire exit. I ran straight at it, barging with all my strength. The door burst open, sending the creature on it flying. It landed on its back with an indignant squeal. My momentum sent me hurtling to the ground - soaking my suit - and it was Gabriella's turn to pick me up. As we sprinted away, I chanced a look around and saw with a wave of disgust that the entire gym was covered in Depraved. They all breathed in unison, making it seem as if the building itself had come alive. One by one, they turned and saw us, black eyes widening. They let out excited shrieks and dropped off the building, landing with wet splashes on the ground.

Delagio and I grabbed Tim and hoisted him between us. We all ran as fast as we could. The swarm of Depraved chased after us, scuttling along the walls and leaping like demented frogs.

"Oh my god, oh my god, oh my god, they're getting closer!" whimpered Tim.

We raced around the front of the school and I saw what could only have been a dream.

A line of Guardians fronted by Scarlett.

They were armed to the teeth and aiming towards us. For a split second I thought we'd been tricked again – that she was a traitor too - but then I felt a bullet whip past my head and turned to see a Depraved crumple and roll along the ground. It was clambered over by its kin as the wave surged after us.

We broke through the barrier. The night was filled with the thunder of gunshots and the anguished screams of the Depraved. We reached the front entrance of the school, where dozens of Alliance cars and bikes were scattered around. We set Tim down on his feet. There was a bag by one of the motorbikes; Delagio picked it up and flung it to me. I caught it one-handed and unzipped it. Inside were the Crimson Twins and a Kapre belt, loaded with guns.

"I'm so sorry about Rachel," I said, pulling the swords out of the bag and then throwing it to Gabriella. She wrapped the belt around her waist, cast the empty bag to the ground.

"Don't worry 'bout that now."

I pointed at Tim. "I need you to get him to safety."

Delagio nodded. "What are you gonna do?"

"I have the swords now. I'm going to lure The Sorrow away from here. I don't want any more innocent people to die because of me."

Delagio's eyes went wide. "Alex, that's suicide!"

"It's here because of me. I have to try."

Gabriella threw me a set of bike keys. "Not without me you're not."

I went to argue, but could tell from her face it would be pointless. Instead I handed her one of the Crimson Twins. She used its sharp blade to cut the bottom part of her dress away, so that it stopped above the knee. She dropped the material and slid the sword into a makeshift holder on the side of the bike. I ran to it and used the keys to start it. Gabriella hugged her arms around my waist. I was reminded briefly of when she'd driven me to the underground station. I'd felt so weak and confused.

Things had come so far since then.

I looked over at Tim. He was staring at me with a dazed expression. "If I make it out of this alive, we'll have a chat," I promised.

He gave a slow nod.

I turned to Delagio, who gave a solemn tip of his hat. "Good luck," he said. Then he piled Tim into a jeep, jumped into the driver's seat and roared off.

From somewhere amongst the roar of battle, I heard the shriek of The Sorrow's demented steed.

"Go!" shouted Gabriella.

I twisted the throttle and the bike squealed into action. Doubling back, I rode us to where the Chosen were locked in combat with the Depraved.

"Come on you ugly bastards!" I hollered. "We're the ones you want!"

Their heads snapped to our direction.

Scarlett looked up from the carcass of a fallen Depraved. "Alex what are you doing?" she yelled.

"Look after Mikey," I shouted back. Kicking the bike around, I accelerated through the main gates. The Depraved broke away from the fight, jumping into trees and over school buildings in a frantic attempt to catch us. Glancing over my shoulder, I saw the deformed Unicorn vault over the school wall. The Sorrow rode atop, the thick chains clutched between its gauntlets. I twisted the throttle down as far as it would go.

We swerved in and out of traffic. Angry drivers smashed their horns and rolled down their windows to shout abuse as we shot past. The shouts turned to screams when they saw what was following us. The Sorrow overtook its soulless followers, leaping over one car and landing on the roof of another. The metal caved in and the driver dived out of the door, rolling along the road in a mass of limbs. The panic was contagious, spreading from person to person. Cars collided with one another, people scrambled into restaurants and bars, trampling each other and knocking bouncers down as they went. The thump of nightclub bass was drowned out by the sounds of pure fear. The only consolation was that The Sorrow and the Depraved were so singular in their focus that they ignored everyone else.

"We need to take them somewhere unpopulated!" Gabriella shouted above the roar of the engine, hooves and screams.

"Okay!"

I veered off down a quieter street, heading away from town. Glancing in the mirror, I saw The Sorrow and Depraved still

435

closing in behind. There were only about ten car lengths between our bike and the nightmare that followed.

And it was gaining on us fast.

I felt Gabriella's arms slide from around my waist and turned to see her swivel around in the seat.

"Keep steady!" she shouted.

"What are you doing?"

She detached two guns from her belt, cocked and aimed them. "Trying to even the odds a little!"

The bike shuddered as she started to pull the gun triggers. There were squeals and the unmistakeable thuds of bodies collapsing. The gun blasts seemed endless; again and again the sound filled my ears followed by the feral screeches as the Depraved fell.

"Bend!" I shouted over my shoulder. I heard the clatter as Gabriella dropped one of the guns into a side well. She wrapped an arm backwards around me, knotting my shirt material in her fist. We hit the sharp turn low, power sliding in the slick road, so close to the ground we could have touched it. The turn opened up onto a crossroad. We rocketed out – tyres squealing – and missed a bus by a few inches. The driver had a look of pure shock as he swerved out of our way. I turned and watched as he ploughed into a group of Depraved, sucking them under his wheels and spitting parts of them out the back.

The Sorrow didn't stop. It snapped the rusted chains and forced the Unicorn to vault onto the roof and gallop its length. When it jumped off, the bus had lost a third of its height.

"Faster!" yelled Gabriella above the gunshots. "They're getting too close!"

I looked down and saw that the throttle handle was tight in my white knuckles. The speedometer was pointing towards a space beyond the numbers.

"We're at top speed!"

"Damn it!"

Gabriella carried on pumping the triggers and then I heard the guns click. She swore loudly and threw them away. Leaning down she retrieved one of the Crimson Twins from the side holster instead.

"Plan B," she shouted. "Slow down."

"Are you nuts?"

"Trust me."

I let the throttle slip a bit and the speedometer sunk downwards. The Depraved caught up with us and tore alongside the weaving bike, their pink jaws open and salivating.

One pounced for us. I jerked the bike to the right and Gabriella swiped downwards, severing its head with a single blow. The two parts bounced separately along the road for a few more yards. Another tried its luck and was similarly dispatched. A third somehow appeared in front of us. It dived directly at me. I swerved the bike and without thinking, ducked down and retrieved the second sword from the holster. I stuck it out to the side. The Crimson Twin unseamed the Depraved from the jaw downwards, sending its innards splashing over the road. Several other Depraved slipped in the gore left by their fallen kin.

But still they kept coming, and I could tell Gabriella was struggling to take them out fast enough. All the while the looming mass galloped ever closer, its hooves pounding their death knell on the tarmac.

I need to find somewhere to go!

I gunned down the road; scanning for anywhere I could lead them. Houses flashed past as I sped up again. A crack of thunder boomed over my head. I looked up to see a swirl of red clouds gathering overhead. Each bloom of lighting exposed more streaks behind the clouds, like veins under bloodstained skin.

Behind us the pack grew within touching distance.

I finally found what I was looking for. A construction site closed for the holidays slipped past us. Through the fence I could see covered cubes of bricks, abandoned diggers and large hills of dirt. Most importantly, there were no people.

"Hold on!"

I spun the bike in a tight 180-degree turn and drove straight through the pack. Gabriella sliced and hacked her way through the Depraved. At the far end, The Sorrow lifted its colossal sword with both hands, waiting to strike.

Hold it, hold it. Now!

I swerved the bike away as the blade guillotined down. It missed by inches, hitting nothing but air. We smashed through a chain link fence and into the construction site. I slowed the bike and we both jumped from it. Unmanned, it wobbled and upturned, sliding into a dirt mound with a burst of wet soil.

Gabriella and I stood next to each other, Crimson Twins raised in our rain-slicked hands. The Depraved reached the entrance first - but didn't enter. They slowed to a halt, watching us through their dark eyes and twittering in their unknowable language. They parted way from The Sorrow, who galloped through the entrance on his awful mount. Above, the thunder was deafening. A sudden bolt of lightning hit a JCB in a shower of sparks, leaving a large scorch mark on the yellow paint.

"What now?" Gabriella asked.

"We have the Crimson Twins. We have to try and kill this thing."

"Alex, listen. I mean seriously, if we don't make it through this-"

"I know," I whispered. "You too."

The Sorrow stopped a few yards away. It jumped down from the corrupted Unicorn, which snorted and stamped its hooves on the ground. Then the twisted steed retreated to where the Depraved were gathered like some demonic audience.

The Red Storm had settled right over our heads. A thick pool of darkness, surrounded by swirling red clouds, hovered directly above. A constant stream of lightning smashed down around us, each blast so loud it left ringing sounds in my ears. Small fires ignited where the bolts struck the ground. The dancing flames were black and grey - as if nature had forgotten to colour them in. Rather than extinguish, the torrential rain seemed to fuel the flames, making them grow fiercer.

Adrenaline coursed through my veins. My heart threatened to hammer through my chest. My tuxedo suit clung to my damp skin. Gabriella's dress was as slick as oil and her hair hung around her shoulders in wet ropes. I wrapped my other hand around the hilt of the sword, raising it up like a baseball bat. Gabriella copied.

In response the Sorrow raised its own gigantic blade. Every one of my senses went into overdrive. I could smell the dirt in the pools of rain, could make out every individual drip as it slid down The Sorrow's rusted armour. I could see the rise and fall of its colossal chest. For what seemed like an eternity, no one

438

moved. We stayed locked in our positions, like chess pieces in an abandoned game.

Then The Sorrow curled two fingers into a taunting 'come here' gesture. I felt Gabriella's body tighten.

"Wait!" I warned, but it was too late. With a scream of pure hatred, she charged.

"Gabriella, stop!" I screamed. But ten years of misery had made her blind and deaf to reason. She continued to charge forward, Crimson Twin arched above her head, ready to unleash a devastating blow. It was a bad move - one borne out of hatred rather than years of honed practice. Gabriella sliced the sword down in a streak of red, the blow deflected easily by one of The Sorrow's own. The force of the impact wrenched the blade from her hand.

I sprinted to help her. But I was too late.

The sound of Gabriella's flesh being pierced was the sound of my soul tearing apart.

Her body jolted to a halt. A second later the tip of The Sorrow's sword appeared through the middle of her back. Blood pooled at the apex of the blade and poured down to the ground in a steady stream. I watched in horror as the life drained from my soulmate into a red puddle at her feet. A noise that was barely human escaped my lips.

Gabriella slumped to her knees, sword still skewered through her body. Perching a sabatoned foot on her shoulder, The Sorrow yanked its blade free, sending her rolling backwards along the dirt. She came to rest just short of my feet and I fell down next to her. The world sieved away, and all that remained was Gabriella. I gathered her on my lap. A horrific wound stretched from her chest to her belly button, pumping out blood in thick waves. She coughed and more blood seeped from between her lips. Barely able to see through the tears, I placed my hand over the wound and closed my eyes, trying to heal her. I waited to feel the surge of electricity.

Nothing happened.

Come on! Work! Oh god, please work!

I concentrated harder, but still I felt nothing happen. I opened my eyes and looked at Gabriella. Her eyes were half open. She stared at me, with a look that burned into my soul.

It was a look of pure sadness.

Tears streamed down my cheeks and splashed onto her arms. She placed a hand on my face. I nuzzled into it.

"I can't heal you…it won't work," I sobbed.

"It's okay," she whispered in a voice so small it was barely there at all.

"Ella, please don't leave me alone."

Tears spilled down her cheeks. "You need to run, while you still can."

I shook my head. "No, I'm *not* leaving you. I won't."

She gave a weak smile. "Still a stubborn one, aren't you?"

"Would you have it any other way?" I sniffed.

She stroked a thumb against my tears, wiping them away. "Alex?"

I stared into her perfect blue eyes.

"I love you."

She pulled my face towards hers and pressed her lips against mine, in a final kiss.

Then she died.

A tormented scream ripped from my lungs. I cradled her limp body against my chest, trying to squeeze the life back into her. *No, oh god, please no.*

Her body grew cold. My soul felt like it had been shredded to pieces. I couldn't breathe. There was nothing, *nothing* to live for. My world plunged into darkness.

Gabriella was gone.

I want to die, please god let me die.

Through blurry vision, I saw the Crimson Twin lying a few feet from where I huddled with my dead soulmate. It was all I needed to end the pain. Faru had said that it could supposedly kill anything.

Then it can kill a Chosen.

I gathered the sword into my hand and rotated the blade, pushing the tip against my solar plexus. I barely felt the pain as it started to sink into my flesh.

I looked up. The Sorrow was standing about fifteen feet away, its head cocked in amused curiosity at the situation. The rage inside evolved into something I'd never felt before. It ran

440

into every part of me, coursing through my veins, joining with my blood.

It consumed me.

I slid the blade from my flesh. Carefully, I lay Gabriella's body on ground and stood up. I extended an arm, pointing the tip of the sword towards the vile creature.

"YOU FUCKING BASTARD!!" I screamed in a voice I didn't recognise. "YOU KILLED HER! I'M GOING TO RIP YOU APART!!"

The Sorrow's only response was to point back at me.

Without another thought, I charged.

The Sorrow swept its blade out in a horizontal arc. I ducked and brought my fist up, connecting with the mask. It clanged and shifted to the side. The Sorrow made a bizarre grunting sound and stumbled back. If there was pain I didn't feel it. I ran forward again and jumped into a spinning kick, connecting with its chest plate and driving it further back. I struck out it with the Crimson Twin and a piece of its armour fell to the ground. It dissolved into an acid-like substance, burning a deep hole in the dirt. The Sorrow jabbed the giant blade at me, I jumped to the side and brought my own sword down onto its. A deep crack appeared on the top and the force made the Sorrow stumble forward. I took another slash at its chest. More of its armour fell away; exposing what could only be described as a black void underneath. *'Darker than the depths of despair and coursing with evil...'*

The Sorrow struck out with a fist. The knuckles hit my cheekbone and I felt searing pain as the spinal needles punctured my skin. I didn't care. With a scream of rage I struck again and again at the soul eater. Every time I connected, sections of its armour fell away like dismembered limbs. More of the deep darkness was exposed - a living abyss. It curled and shimmered in rolling shadows.

The Sorrow carved its sword towards me. The tip ripped through my left shoulder and I felt it slice through my tendons. The arm sunk lifelessly to my side as unbearable agony filled me up. I tried to make it heal, but couldn't.

A burst of lightning struck nearby. I was temporarily blinded and only heard the heavy whoosh of the sword as it arched through the air. I jumped back and pain exploded in me once again as the blade carved away the flesh and muscle from the side of my thigh. Still half-blind, I roared in fury and drove upwards with the Crimson Twin. I felt it hit something and stick.

When the spots had cleared, I saw that the blade had sunk right into The Sorrow's chest. It disappeared into the gloom. I stared at the thing, and its hollow eyes seemed to glare back at me. Then it made a strange huffing noise – a sound that could only have been a laugh. It pulled the blade from its chest with a sharp tug. It rested its own sword against its body and took the Crimson Twin in both hands.

And snapped it in half.

At that moment all hope of defeating The Sorrow vanished. It was just too powerful. Lafelei's words were wrong. Gabriella, my soulmate, had died in vain. Now I was going to be killed...or worse. The rage retreated and my despair became absolute.

I gave up.

The Sorrow raised a gauntlet towards the flame-scorched sky. The thunder became a deafening cacophony of sound, as if hidden gods were yelling in fury. The clouds blazed as the supernatural lightning gathered overhead. Then the Sorrow thrust its arm in my direction and I only had a split second to witness the biggest single bolt of lightning in human history, before it smashed into my chest.

Everything went into slow motion. I felt myself being lifted up, as if gravity no longer existed. The ground rushed underneath me, and a cool wind ruffled my hair and suit. Through dimming eyesight, I watched The Sorrow shrink in size until it became a dot on the horizon.

Clang!

I was partially aware of distant pain as my back connected with something.

Clang!

It hit another something.

Clang! Clang! Clang!

More and more of the metallic objects struck my back. Finally one refused to give way and jolted me to a stop. I hit the ground like a rock.

Scaffolding poles lay scattered around me. I heard a loud groan above and then an entire construction of beams and ladders collapsed down around me, scraps of wood and metal punching against every part of my body. Then everything became still.

I noticed my suit jacket lying in a tattered heap a few feet away from me. The lightning had cooked it to a cinder. A burning butterfly escaped the pile of rags. It floated through the air, before dissolving into ash.

Dads photograph.

35

The Depraved appeared in the distance – hundreds of them, scuttling, jumping and crawling their way through the pouring rain. A sea of evil, surging towards me.

It had all ended so fast. I looked down at my twisted, broken body and a bitter laugh escaped my lips.

Some hero I turned out to be.

I was meant to protect the world; I couldn't even protect her. My eyes welled up as it dawned on me that I would never hold her again, never smell her sweet hair.

I could taste blood in my mouth. I tried to spit it out, but had no energy left. It just dribbled pathetically down my chin. More came up to take its place. *Not a good sign.* I knew I should get up, should fight to my last breath. I was just so worn out, and without her, what was the point anyway?

The stench of smoke and scorched metal filled my nostrils. An intense throbbing in my side drew my attention. I discovered with a flash of nausea that a scaffolding pole had speared through my ribs, pinning me to the ground. I wasn't healing anymore; I couldn't even summon the will to try.

This is it then, the end of the road.

I'm going to die here.

I closed my eyes, trying to let the images of her face occupy my mind. I wanted my last thoughts to be of her as I died. For some reason I couldn't make them stay shut. The curiosity in me needed to see how it all ended.

The creatures surrounded me. There was a crescendo of baying and twittering laughter as they studied me. Standing in the centre was The Sorrow. Even though the iron mask covered its face, I knew it was wearing a sick, triumphant smile.

It crouched down, pressing a metal knee against my chest. The weight crushed all of the air from my lungs. I had to use all of my remaining strength to gasp the next breath.

The Sorrow lifted an armour-clad arm up to its artificial face, the screech of the metal joints like rusty door hinges. There was a click as it unlocked the straps. The mask dislodged with a wet pop.

So this is how it's going to be.

The excited chattering rose into an ear-splitting roar. There was no escape. It started to pull the iron face away, wanting to show me what lay underneath. I let out a long, final sigh.

Now comes the end of everything.

I felt a sensation like an electric current rush through my body. Losing my soul didn't feel how I'd imagined. It felt...familiar.

Alex.

The softly spoken word filled my mind.

Sage Faru?

Yes Alexander it's me. Listen, you must close your eyes.

There's no point. It's over. The Sorrow won.

It is not over. Please close your eyes...there isn't much time.

The Sorrow loomed over me, the mask hinging away from its face as I closed my eyes.

It doesn't matter. Gabriella's gone. Faru, it killed her.

She's not gone.

A spark of hope ingnighted inside me. *What do you mean?*

I can still feel her soul link. It is very weak, but still there. If she were completely gone, then it would have been severed. Alexander, there may still be time.

But I already tried to heal her. It didn't work.

I believe your gift is rendered unusable when you are near The Sorrow. If you were able to defeat it...

The despair came back in spades. *I can't, it's too powerful! Even the Crimson Twins didn't work.*

Alexander, there will be a way. There has to be. Think!

I racked my brains, but couldn't grab hold of anything. A sensation of crawling spiders prickled across every inch of my skin, and I knew that The Sorrow's true face was exposed. I squeezed my eyes shut as tight as they would go. I knew if I opened them, that my soul would be taken. I could feel The Sorrow leaning closer. It would be a matter of seconds before it

445

prised my eyes open and everything was over. My lifeforce would be devoured and used to fuel its own retched soul.

Its own soul...

Faru, give me your Farsight!

Instantly, I felt the psychedelic rush hit my mind. The world became a swirl of colours; the scaffolding around me shimmered as if not completely there. The Sorrow changed, becoming a moving mirage of black and red. The holes where its armour had once been were darker than black. Unknowable creatures with crimson eyes scuttled about in the darkness. Where the soul eater's face should have been was a swirling vortex of purple and black.

As soon as I saw it, my jaw locked open. Something deep within my chest began to unfurl and move towards my throat. My body grew cold. My mind began to waver. I could barely collect any thoughts. A blue beam of light pushed out of my mouth and floated towards the vortex. The Sorrow rose up, drawing my soul with it.

I had no time left. In seconds, I would become a Depraved, just like all the others that had stood against The Sorrow. Another hideous, mindless slave.

I scanned for what I prayed would be there - stared into the depths of the darkness, where the horrific red-eyed creatures crawled.

I saw it.

Deeper black than even the shadows around it – so dark it was as if it were formed from the absence of light itself. A pulsing orb of pure blackness at the heart of darkness.

The eye of the abyss.

I prayed to any god that was listening and heaved myself upwards. My broken bones screamed and cracked as I lifted my working arm.

I plunged my hand into The Sorrow's chest.

Unimaginable pain - burning and freezing and crushing and bursting all at the same time, raced up my arm. My fingers closed around the soul. It felt slippery, like raw meat coated in oil. The Sorrow let out a ear-stabbing shriek as I tugged backwards with every remaining ounce of strength. Its soul ripped free into my first and I tugged it from the darkness. Little wet strings of black

446

ichor covered my hand all the way down to the wrist. The orb beat like a giant heart in my palm.

I drove The Sorrow's own soul into the vortex.

The soul eater produced a scream so loud and high-pitched I thought my eardrums would burst. A bright light appeared in the centre of the vortex and grew, overpowering the exposed patches of darkness with pure white, brilliance. The creatures inside the shadows squealed and vanished. The light shone through the cracks in the armour like sunbeams through a curtain, growing until it was so bright it seemed to draw all the other swirling colours into it. The giant sword clattered to the ground and dissolved into a black puddle.

The Sorrow threw back its head and exploded in a shower of pure light. I shielded my eyes with a broken hand, but not before I saw thousands of souls shoot up in a fountain of pulsing energy. Something shot into my mouth, snapping my head backwards with incredible force, and I knew beyond a doubt it was my soul returning to its rightful place. When the light had dimmed enough for me to look again, I saw the freed souls snaking their way into the sky. As soon as they hit the clouds, the Red Storm was consumed by light. The clouds dissolved and the rain stopped falling. Something tickled my arm. I looked down to see the black substance coiling its way up my wrist and onto my forearm. It spiralled and looped into various shapes and then set like dry ink. It had turned itself into some kind of strange tattoo.

I was too exhausted to care.

Ignoring the excruciating pain in every inch of my body, I heaved myself onto my feet and limped as fast as I could to where Gabriella's body lay. As I grew near, I could feel my bones start to piece their way back together.

My heart broke all over again to see her lifeless, rain-soaked body. The water had washed her blood into a shimmering pink halo. However, with Faru's Farsight, I noticed something else. In the centre of her chest - so small and faint it was barely even there - was her soul.

I knelt down to her and lifted her limp body towards me. I stared into her closed eyes and prayed for something to work. For a moment nothing did. I felt despair dragging away hope

447

once again. Then I felt the charges start. They were no more than a tingle at first, but they grew quickly, gathering power. My body began to shudder; and in my arms Gabriella's body did the same. Behind her shining skin, I could see the little blue orb unfurl like a waking animal. It slid slowly up to her throat. I felt my own chest becoming warm. With my free hand, I ripped open what remained of my charred shirt and stared down in shock. A blue orb of light glowed in the centre.

An overwhelming need to cough seized my chest. I coughed a little, but the feeling didn't pass. I hacked again with as much force as I could manage. My jaw unhinged and the blue light poured from my mouth. It surged towards Gabriella. Her own mouth fell open and tiny snake of light rolled out. Mine connected with hers and instantly Gabriella's body arched upwards. Her soul grew brighter and more powerful - it changed from a washed out grey, going through every shade until it became a deep, electric blue. Her wound knitted itself back together; leaving nothing but a long, pink line.

The souls released each other and snapped back into our separate bodies. My head was thrown backwards, popping my neck with a loud crack. Gabriella's eyes flew open and she gasped for air.

"Ella," I wept, as tears of happiness flowed down my cheeks. *She's alive. She's alive.* I wrapped my arms around her. Gabriella pressed into me so tightly it felt like we were going to merge into one person. I could feel from her own shaking body that she was crying too.

Over her shoulder, I saw that without The Sorrow, all of the Depraved had died. Somehow in death, they appeared more human. Each one wore an expression of utter serenity. The Sorrow's steed was lying on its side - eyeballs rolling wildly in their sockets. A single orb of energy descended from the sky and settled nearby. The Unicorn looked at it and made a soft whinnying sound of remembrance. Its eyes changed from red to turquoise and the madness was replaced by tranquillity. It looked at me for a moment and then lay its head down and fell silent.

I closed my eyes and held Gabriella close.

Sage Faru, it's over.

I know. We are almost there. Hold on, Alexander.

There was no shudder before his answer. He hadn't left me.

Scores of cars and bikes appeared in front of us. They screeched to a stop a few yards away from where Gabriella and I sat holding each other. Sage Faru was inside the lead car; he stepped down and nodded at me, a smile appearing on his old face.

"Come on," I whispered into my soulmate's ear. "Let's go home."

I picked her up in my arms and carried her towards the waiting convoy.

EPILOGUE

Gabriella's hands pressed gently over my eyes.

"No peeking!" she laughed as she maneuvered me through the mansion grounds.

"You better not walk me into a tree!"

I could hear the sound of band music not too far away. It sounded familiar. Then I heard the sounds of a large crowd talking and laughing. My curiosity peaked. "Come on," I chuckled, "tell me what's going on!"

"Not yet, almost there…okay you can open them now."

Gabriella removed her hands and I drew in breath. We were standing inside a marquee tent the size of a football pitch. Someone had stolen Narnia. Snow, Christmas trees and towering ice sculptures were everywhere I looked. Fridges carved from frosted ice were lined with beers and wine. Waitresses dressed in white walked around with cakes and mince pies on platters. Silver banners with CHRISTMAS BALL II written on them lined the sides. A canopy of white balloons floated above our heads. The tent was filled with pretty much every sixth former from Chapter Hill School. But out of everything, what really blew my mind was the fact that Soulfire were playing on stage. Loads of people were gathered on a dance floor below, jumping around to the music.

"What is all this?" I asked in confusion.

"A second attempt at the Christmas Ball," smiled Gabriella, "because we never got to enjoy ours."

"This is incredible…how did you manage it?"

"I asked Sage Faru. He's a pretty powerful guy you know."

I laughed. "I'm convinced."

Mikey weaved towards us from the crowd, his hand linked with Scarlett's. The other clutched a beer. He gave me a hug, almost spilling the contents down the new shirt Gabriella had bought me.

"Alex, this party is *sick*! I can't believe Soulfire are actually here!"

Scarlett rolled her eyes. "Fifth beer."

"Don't tell Mum!" Mikey said with an unsubtle wink.

"I won't," I promised, trying to keep a straight face.

At that moment, the song ended and the marquee was filled with clapping and cheers. A waitress glided over to me, a multitude of drinks balanced on her silver dish. She plucked a beer from the top and handed it to me.

"For you, Mister Eden," she said and moved back off again.

I took a large swig and put my arm around Gabriella, kissing the top of her head. "Thank you so much."

"You deserve nothing less," she said kissing me on the lips.

I saw Tim in the centre of the dance floor. He was doing his best to ignore Lucy, who was nagging him about something. When he noticed me, he raised a beer and gave a knowing smile. I gestured mine towards him.

Ryan Lloyd tapped the microphone and cleared his throat. The room fell silent. "Hey everybody," he said in his Californian accent. "It's great to be here in London." The statement was met with a chorus of cheers, including one from me. "Okay, so this next song is dedicated to Gabriella and Alex."

A cheer went up and I felt my face flush. Gabriella squeezed my side.

"It's a new one called 'Changes.' Hope you enjoy it." He nodded to the band and started to tap his foot against the stage. The drummer rapped his sticks together and then they broke into the song. The riff was incredible. Gabriella took my hand and led me onto the dance floor.

*

A few hours later, the party was winding down. In a state of complete awe, I'd met the band and even had a drink with them all. They were really friendly and offered both me and Gabriella backstage passes to their next tour, which I hastily accepted.

Needing a few minutes to myself, I slipped away from the tent and headed further into the grounds. Silver fairy lights had been hung in the trees, and small bonfires set up with seats

451

around them. Couples were sitting in the chairs, wrapped in thick blankets, sipping drinks, smoking cigarettes and chatting.

"Best party ever, man!" someone called from one of the seats.

I raised a hand in the direction of the voice and kept walking, letting my mind wander.

Faru had realised that Lafelei's words related to the mysterious family crest in my dreams before I had. He'd managed to track down Rachel's old estate. As well as the unsealed Veil, he'd discovered records of her true lineage. Her real name had been Raquen Moonstella. Faru had understood then that Rachel was a traitor and that she'd allowed The Sorrow access to Earth. He sent every Guardian still remaining at the base to Chapter Hill School.

Rachel's Rogues had all been killed in the ensuing battle. Everyone apart from Mr Hanley had been unharmed. Afterwards, the HASEA had brought in every member with the gift of Charm and together, made everyone forget the experience had ever happened. As far as people were concerned, the school ball had had ended early because of Mr Hanley's tragic 'heart attack.' It made me feel sad that someone completely innocent had been caught in the crossfire. The only consolation was that Mrs Hanley had suddenly received a letter, informing her of a private life insurance policy that her husband had taken out, along with a substantial cheque. It wouldn't help her with the pain, but at least she would be able to live comfortably for the rest of her life.

It had taken over a week, but with the aid of the government, most of the people who had witnessed The Sorrow and the Depraved were tracked down and charmed into forgetting. Still, every now and then a story would pop up in the back of the tabloids about someone claiming to have witnessed a Horseman of the Apocalypse.

I continued beyond where the lights ended. Navigating in darkness was becoming much easier to manage. I made my way towards the Sanctuary. At the gates, a small light had been set up. Agent Noble was stationed there, his arm still in a sling. He shifted as he saw me emerge from the darkness.

"I'm sorry sir, I'm afraid that this area is off limits- oh excuse me Mister Eden, I didn't realise it was you."

"Agent Noble, right?"

"Yes sir.

I held out a hand. "Call me Alex."

The man nodded and shook my hand. "Simon," he said.

"How's the arm?"

"Getting better slowly thanks. They offered to let me use a tiny bit of booster, but I don't think regular humans should take that stuff. Besides, I'm milking it at home. I haven't washed up for two weeks."

We both laughed. "Listen Simon, do you mind if I have a few moments inside? I just need some time away from it all," I said.

"Of course, Mister E-Alex."

Simon opened the gate and stepped aside. I made my way into the Sanctuary, feeling the invisible cobwebs stroke my skin as I passed through the barrier. Two huge moons materialised high above my head, surrounded by thousands of winking stars. They cast their pale gaze over the area, bathing everything in a milky glow.

First I went to see Isiodore. He was leaning over the fence and staring at me with his shining, aquamarine eyes. I plucked a flower from the bush and offered it to him. He gently ate it from my palm and lowered his head. Part of his horn had been chipped away in the battle. I scratched the area around it and he made noises of contentment.

I left the Unicorn and headed over to the lake. The group of Manticore cubs were sleeping in a large group a few feet from the water. They were twice the size they'd been when I'd last seen them and their wings were starting to take on an iridescent shine. After watching them for a while, I gave a low whistle and after a few seconds the Merfolk began to splash about in the water. I looked up at the sky. Everything felt so peaceful. The dark feelings inside me had vanished - all I felt now was happiness and hope for the future.

My arm began to tingle. I pulled back my shirt and stared at the curious tattoo. In the time since I'd defeated The Sorrow, it had climbed its way up most of my forearm. I placed my hand onto it. Like Gabriella's Umbra skin, it pulsed as if it had its own heartbeat. My mind wandered back to Lafelei's words. There was no denying it, the first part of the Elemental's fragmented prophecy had come true. We had been betrayed by Rachel - the moon and stars. With the aid of Farsight, I'd seen what was hidden from sight. And both Gabriella and I had both been marked by sorrow. Or more specifically *The* Sorrow. Her psychologically, me physically. Then there were the rest of the words, which seemed to imply that I was supposed to stand against Hades.

Am I supposed to save Pandemonia?

The question hung in my mind like a cloud. It wasn't one I could even hope to answer now. *How can I possibly stop a Demon King?*

"Good evening, Alexander."

I jumped. I'd been so lost in my thoughts I hadn't heard anyone approach.

"I'm sorry. I appear to have a knack for startling you," Faru chuckled.

I turned to see the Sage standing beside me. He was carrying a rectangular book under his arm. The same one he'd been looking at in his quarters.

"No its fine, sir," I said. "I was just taking a moment."

Faru nodded. "I often come here myself. There is something soothing about it. I feel closer to my world."

"Have you ever thought about going home?"

Faru clasped his hands behind his back. "Often. Alas, I have too many responsibilities here. Besides, Pandemonia as it stands is not a place for an old Seelian like me."

The centre of the lake began to bubble. The Siren rose out of the water and started to sing a haunting melody. Faru clicked his fingers. The Siren stared at the leader with pleading eyes. He shook his head. The Siren sighed and slipped back underneath the surface.

"Thank you for tonight, Sage Faru. It's been fantastic."

"You are most welcome," he replied. "However, I must confess that it was Gabriella who did most of the organising. That girl is very fond of you, you know."

I smiled. "I'm fond of her too."

Faru chuckled. "Ah young love, such a wonderful thing. Anyhow, I'm glad I found you. I have been meaning to speak with you."

"Oh?"

The Sage took in a deep breath. "I have had a chance to fully go through Raquen's belongings. We discovered some hidden journals, both at the estate and in her apartment at the Warren. It appears that she was a very troubled individual." A sad expression crossed his face. "Raquen was still a fairly young Pixie when the Chosen came. It seems she was out playing and came back to find all of her kin dead. I can barely imagine the grief she went through."

"No wonder she hated us," I said.

Faru nodded. "Indeed. The Chosen never discovered the hidden doorway on the estate. After the attack, Raquen took all the valuables her family had stored in the mansion. She sold them to pay for her family to be buried in a graveyard at the back, and then killed those she hired. Lastly, she cast a spell that would deter anyone from ever purchasing the estate...and left."

The Seelian put out a hand. A tiny fairy settled on it for a moment, before spinning back into the air and flying off into the distance.

"There are no journals of Raquen's whereabouts for over a century after that. By the time she started writing again, the Chosen Alliance had just become the HASEA. She joined the Warren. This was when I was still a Guardian. She acted so sweet and friendly; you would never have dreamed that she was plotting revenge all that time. I assume that is why she was so competent at being an Infiltrator - she had disguised who she really was for most of her life. The rest you already know."

I stared out at the lake, letting the information sink in. "It's so sad," I said after a moment. "I mean I can't condone what she did, it was reprehensible. But I think I can understand. I mean if Gabriella had been born two hundred years ago, then what's to say her parents wouldn't have been condemned to death for their relationship by Chosen rather than Hades? Gabriella could have ended up being just like..." I shook my head. "What I'm trying to say is I think I know why she did what she did. I hope she rests in peace."

Faru nodded. "I am impressed with your attitude, Alexander. You have come such a long way since we first met."

We both stared out at the water.

"Sage Faru, I've been meaning to ask you something," I said after a while. It's about something my mother said to me soon after this all started."

The Sage shifted on the spot. "Of course," he replied in a slightly strained tone.

"When I came home after my Awakening, she went all strange for a moment, like she was in a different place. Then she whispered, 'I thought you'd been taken too'. I mean to start with, I figured she was worried that I'd died. But it was the expression on her face and the way she said it." I turned to the Sage. "Sir, is there something I should know?"

Faru said nothing for a long while. Then he let out a long sigh. "That is actually the other thing I wished to speak with you about. It is a burden I have struggled with for several years. You see, I made a promise. However, I feel that in certain circumstances, promises must be broken." Without another word, he held out the rectangular book. As soon as I took it, I realised it wasn't a book after all - it was a photo album. Lifting it towards the moonlight, I turned the page and my heart snagged in my chest.

Staring out at from the centre of the page was a photograph of Mum and Dad.

And Faru.

Fingers shaking, I turned the page. There was one of Faru holding a baby in his arms. It was swaddled in the same blanket as the one in the burned photograph. The baby was me.

I stared up at him. "What is this?" I demanded.

Faru looked at me with his shining white eyes. They were full of sadness. "Alexander, your mother Elaine knew about everything. Chosen, Guardians, the Warren, all of it.'

It felt like the world was crushing down on me. "How…how could she know?"

Faru placed a soothing hand on my arm. "Because your father was a Chosen."

The words hit me like a freight train. I could hardly comprehend what he was saying. "W-what? How could he be?"

"It is extremely rare for a Chosen to be hereditary, but it can happen, like in Gabriella's case." He drew in a sharp breath as if trying to steady himself for something. I looked at him, trying to prepare myself for what he was going to say.

"Alexander, your father may still be alive."

The album slipped from hand. It hit the ground and opened on a photograph of Dad and Mum hugging.

"How...no that can't be right. He was killed in a hit and run!"

Faru shook his head. "No he wasn't Alexander. Some time ago, Hades demanded for Chosen to be kidnapped and brought through the Veil, so that they could be placed into Colosseums - large battle arenas - where they would fight all manner of opponents to the death in front of large audiences. Rogues working in the bases helped organise it. You father was one of those taken. They rarely lasted long in those horrible places. I myself believed him to be dead...we thought they all were. However, recently I received news that a large number of Chosen escaped several of the Colosseums and joined the resistance, which means that many still live. Whether or not he was among the escapees I simply do not know. Chosen are very resilient and your father more so than most. I do not wish to raise your hopes unnecessarily, but there is a slight possibility that he is still alive over there somewhere."

I stared at Faru, unbelieving. I couldn't speak. I didn't know what to say. *Dad could be alive!*

"After he disappeared, it broke your mother's heart. We tried our hardest to find him, but it was turmoil over there. Our search came back fruitless. Your mother was so hurt; the not knowing was killing her. She said it would be better if she knew he was dead, at least that way she could try and move on, for your sake. One day Elaine came to me and begged for me to make her forget. To let her think that he had died so that she could move on with her life and focus on raising you." I could see deep pain in Faru's shimmering eyes. It hurt him to talk about it. "Your father was a dear friend of mine. I cared for both him and Elaine deeply. I honoured her request."

I thought back to all the times Mum's face had clouded over when I'd asked about Dad. I'd always assumed she was avoiding the question. But she wasn't. *She'd been charmed into forgetting.* That

457

was how she was able to move on so quickly - her emotions had been paved over. I suddenly remembered what John had said during our argument. *All I hear when she sleeps is the sound of her sobbing her heart out and repeating his name over and over.*

"She can't forget Dad," I said in a matter of fact voice.

Faru nodded. "It would seem that over the years, her enduring love for him is breaking down the Charm. It may be that one day everything comes back to her."

"So all the photographs...all the evidence of my father?"

"Elaine made us take everything. It is safe here in the base. You can have it all of course."

Silence descended. I watched the gentle ripples of the water's surface as hidden creatures swam about below.

"Thank you for telling me, Sage Faru."

The Seelian placed a hand on my back. "It is a relief to finally be able to, Alexander. However, I must ask, now that you know what will you do?"

I didn't need to even think about my answer.

"I'm going to find my father and bring him home."

I turned and walked back towards the party, leaving Faru staring across the lake, the moonlight shining down around him.

Alex and Gabriella's journey continues in The Corruption.

Thank you for taking the time to read The Awakening, I hope you enjoyed it. If you did, please consider leaving a review on Amazon or Goodreads. Reviews are what help us authors gain new readers and in turn allow us to continue writing new books.

Thank you again.

Stuart Meczes

To access exclusive and exciting content not available anywhere else, join the Guardian community at Stuart's official website: www.stuartmeczes.com

For the latest news, follow the author through his official channels:

Instagram: writeupyourstreet

Twitter: @Smeczes

Facebook: www.facebook.com/haseachronicles

About the Author

Stuart was born in the smoky outskirts of London but now lives in the little ol' city of Worcester. After years spent running the rat race, in 2008 he knew it was time to start working on the novel he'd been threatening to write since he was 16. Several scrapped storylines and one degree at the University of Birmingham later, *The Awakening* landed. Stuart was more shocked than anyone when it became a sleeper hit and set him on an entirely different and far more exciting path through life than he ever expected.

Nowadays Stuart spends most of his time in in Worcester, continuing to pen new science fiction and fantasy stories, all whilst avoiding the addictive siren call of daytime television.

In addition to the on-going HASEA Chronicles series, Stuart has written a children's book, *Tommy and the Simbots: The Golden Wing.*

Also keep an eye out for *The Grit Saga: London Burning* — book I in a brand new dystopian series, set in a grim and unforgiving future.

Coming winter 2020.

Printed in Great Britain
by Amazon